THE
GIRL
WHO
FOUGHT
NAPOLEON

ALSO BY LINDA LAFFERTY

THE GIRL WHO FOUGHT NAPOLEON

A Novel of the Russian Empire

LINDA LAFFERTY

Published by Lake Union Publishing, Seattle

www.apub.com

Amazon, the Amazon logo, and Lake Union Publishing are trademarks of Amazon.com, Inc., or its affiliates.

ISBN-13: 9781503937260
ISBN-10: 1503937267

Cover design by Shasti O'Leary-Soudant

Printed in the United States of America

To my beloved mother, Elizabeth Vissering Lafferty,
who was fascinated by St. Petersburg, Napoleon,
and European history.
And to my father, Frederick Reid Lafferty, Jr., who
loved my mother with all his heart.

Author's Note

This is a work of fiction. While it is based on historical events, liberties have been taken for creative license.

Prologue

Yelabuga, Russia
February 1864

He will have questions. I must have answers.

A wind is howling, hurling crystals of ice against the window. The pleasant tinkling sound has grown fierce, the driving snow threatening to shatter the glass. But I do not close the shutters. I want to see him the moment he arrives. How he walks. If he touches his hat with his fingertips, muffles his face against the cold.

I have waited years for this reunion. I do not want to miss a second of his presence here in Yelabuga. Such a remote place in Russia for such an honored visitor.

How long has it been since I have had a guest in this house? Not since my father's death.

Living alone suits me. No visitors.

Except for this one. Yes, I will admit him—and only him.

How can he travel from Moscow in such a wolf of a storm? I look out the window at the pelting snow, listening for the bells of his sleigh.

Babushka, one of many stray cats who have settled in with me, meows plaintively, begging for a caress. "Not now, my princess," I tell her. "I must prepare for his visit. Indulge me, won't you?"

I hear the scratching at the door to the hall—an old dog, Sasha, too old now to survive in the outdoor kennel with the rest of the hounds. My maid scolds him, pulling him away from the door.

I drag my fingertips over the once finely polished wood of my mother's china cabinet. A layer of silky cat hair coats everything. Wrinkled strands of tobacco mingle with the animal fur and motes of dust rise as I wipe my sleeve over the furniture.

It is hopeless. I have never been known for housekeeping!

But never mind that! This guest deserves above all others my story. I must remember faithfully, no matter how hard it is to recall such distant memories.

Nadezhda, make yourself remember!

Yes, I remember. I can tell the story. But I think there are two stories to tell.

Feodor Kuzmich is dying.

He lies on a sweat-soaked straw mattress, a coarse blanket clutched in his skeletal fingers. A bowl of milk stands curdled by his bedside, the only nourishment he had taken in the last two weeks. The old starets, a holy mystic, is determined to die here in his cabin in the northern wilds of Siberia.

The life he has lived is written clearly in the lines and creases of his face. He is nearly deaf, but his eyesight is still keen. A tall candle burns near the window, melting a clear circle through the ice on the glass, and Feodor Kuzmich gazes out at the hollow belly of winter enveloping his cabin. The icy fingers of bare birch trees scratch at his window as the wind blows across the Siberian plains.

He can see the pine trees bowed low under their heavy load of snow, more featureless mounds of white than living trees as the Siberian storm envelops the frozen plains and the tiny cabin.

His glassy eyes are fixed on the window, but his mind roams far and free, remembering St. Petersburg and the emperor who once reigned, so many years ago.

He smiles in delirium as he stares out into the storm. He remembers a soldier, slim and youthful . . . with such a delicate face.

Where is that soldier now?

Part 1
Two Young Lives

Chapter 1

Pirjatin, the Ukraine
1783

I was named Nadezhda after my mother, who was born Nadezhda Aleksandrovicheva in the Ukrainian village of Pirjatin, a three-day ride east from Kiev. She was a willful girl of rare beauty: raven haired, bone-white skin and blue eyes, her voice low and seductive, except when she lost her temper.

She was pursued by men from Pirjatin to Kiev, but none was heroic enough for my headstrong mother—until she met Andrej Vasilevich Durov, a dashing dark-haired captain with the Russian Hussars. She fell madly—and recklessly—in love.

My wealthy grandfather, a proud Ukrainian, threatened to disown her when she began keeping company with Captain Durov. Though my father was a man of gentle disposition and impeccable manners, he was a Russian. No failing could be more vile in the eyes of my grandfather.

"My daughter marry a Muscovite! They who disdainfully call our Ukraine 'Little Russia'! As if they were petting a dog's head. An insult! How could you offend me with such behavior?"

"But he is of Polish family! His Russian blood is diluted!" argued my besotted mother. "And I mean to marry him, Papa!"

Of course my grandfather forbade the marriage and any further visits from Andrej Vasilevich Durov. My grandfather prided himself on his obstinacy, regarding it as a mark of character. There would be no compromise.

But he should have known his daughter had inherited the same stubbornness, her head as impenetrable as Ukrainian oak. One night in the teeth of a howling storm, Nadezhda Aleksandrovicheva crept across the bedroom, careful not to awaken her sleeping sister in the bed next to her. Cloak and hood in hand, she tiptoed into the drawing room and out into the garden. She unlatched the gate and flung herself into Captain Durov's arms.

And so she left her father's home and the Ukraine forever.

A carriage drawn by four horses led them away into the stormy autumn night. As the rain splattered against the coach, they embraced under the warmth of bearskin furs, swearing their love. They were married in the first village they came to and then traveled on to Kiev to join my father's Hussar squadron.

Nadezhda Aleksandrovicheva soon discovered the true life of a cavalry wife. In peacetime, the families traveled along with the officers, bumping along rutted roads throughout the vast Russian Empire. Quarters were requisitioned from village to village, each night a different home. My mother, who had never known discomfort or travel, was given a handmaid to attend her, but the life of a Hussar captain's wife was never easy.

For two years my mother wrote to her father, begging forgiveness. She received no reply.

If only I could have a son to recapture my father's heart! A boy as dashing on a horse as my own Andrej Durov. He will be half Ukrainian—how could Father not love him?

And imagining this baby boy as her savior, she fell in love with her own dream. The boy that she would bear would be as handsome as Cupid, adoring and devoted to his mother.

Two years later she fought through a difficult birth in a Siberian log house near the cavalry encampment, attended only by a wizened old midwife. The woman insisted on letting blood to ease the spasms of childbirth that left my mother in agony.

Amid her hysterical screams, I was born.

"Let me see my darling boy!" my mother cried, still delirious from the loss of blood. "Give me my child, my son!"

But instead of the son she had dreamed of, she was given me, her most grievous disappointment. A baby girl with thick wavy hair, bawling at the top of my lungs. My mother pushed me from her lap and turned her face to the wall.

This was the start of our life together. Perhaps I sensed her animosity, for I refused to suckle at her breast. Instead I bit her nipple, causing her to screech in pain.

From then on, I was fed on the milk of peasant women as the cavalry marched through village after village. Every day a scout would ride ahead to find a nursing mother who could give me her teat for the night.

My mother suffered from lack of sleep, for I was a fitful baby. Perhaps the constant change of milk—cow's milk during the day, a stranger's breast at night—was the source of my colic. Despite the dust and jolting of the horse-drawn carriage I would sleep during the day, but come sunset I pierced the night with my screams.

One day when I was only a few months old, my mother suffered a fit of rage. At daybreak the cavalry had broken camp and set off on orders toward Kherson, a port in Crimea on the Black Sea. Because of my crying, my mother had not slept in many nights. She took me from the cradle into her arms, hoping for peace at last in the coach, but that day I awoke and began to bawl.

"Stop howling, you miserable brat!" she screamed, thrusting me into her maid's arms. "How your birth has cursed me!"

I bawled in red-faced rage, hour upon hour into the heat of the summer day, with the dust filtering through the curtains. Flies skipped over our skin, clinging to my tear-stained face. Clapping her hands over her ears, my mother could not escape my screams of fury. Finally, at the hottest hour of the day, my mother could endure my cries no longer.

She snatched me from the maid's arms and threw me out the carriage window!

The Hussars gasped in horror.

My father's orderly, Astakhov, spun his horse around, seeing me lying as still as a wooden doll in the road. Shouting up the ranks to my father, Astakhov vaulted off his horse to rescue me before my skull was crushed by horses' hooves or the rolling wheels of the wagons. He snatched me up from the dusty track, cradling me against the thick braid of his uniform. Tears spilled from his eyes, leaving streaks of mud down his dusty face. He examined my bloody face and bleeding nose as I stared back at him dazed and silent.

"You!" called my mother from the coach. "Give her to me!"

Astakhov began walking toward my mother's carriage to surrender me, though his boots dragged reluctantly. He clutched me tighter to his breast.

A cloud of dust enveloped us.

"Wait! Give me the baby!" My father's voice cut through the drama. Astakhov passed me up to his captain, blood still streaming from my mouth and nose, staining his uniform.

Astakhov told me later that my father cradled me in one arm, his other hand on the reins. He raised his eyes to the heavens to thank God that I was still alive, then rode to the carriage and screamed at my mother, "Give thanks to God that you are not a murderess! I will care for her myself."

And so began my life in the cavalry.

Chapter 2

Winter Palace, St. Petersburg
January 1789

A blazing fire in the nursery hearth warmed the cheeks of the twelve-year-old boy, rousing him from his sleep. He opened his eyes, hearing the Christmas bells toll in the winter air.

The heat from the towering white ceramic stove had warmed the pane of glass nearest his bed, the retreating frost edging the window frame with a crystalline lacework. Alexander was unaccustomed to such luxurious warmth, as his grandmother always insisted that the windows of the nursery be flung open at night to expose him and his younger brother, Constantine, to the harsh elements of the military life that awaited them.

Alexander sat up, making the straw mattress rustle.

"*Ah! Vous êtes réveillé, monsieur.*" Alexander's manservant Boris Petrov slept on a cot near the door, but he was always awake long before the young prince. French was the language of the Russian Court and aristocracy and Alexander spoke it with more command than Russian.

"*Joyeux Noël,*" said Boris, beaming at the young Alexander. "It is January 7—"

"Presents!"

Boris nodded but continued with his daily litany. "There will be no lessons today with Colonel La Harpe. You and Constantine will take a light breakfast, and your father and mother will be in attendance this morning at ten o'clock. The royal family will then join the empress in Nicholas Hall to view your presents. The empress has requested that you wear your formal attire for Christmas luncheon and for the public appearances. There will be four Christmas trees to visit. You will help distribute gifts to the cavalry at the horse ring directly following luncheon. If there is time, you may ride your pony this afternoon."

"Thank you, Boris," said Alexander. He squinted, looking at the gray light of dawn filtering through the clouds of St. Petersburg. The morning fog clung low along the banks of the Neva River, but Alexander could just make out the weathervane of the Admiralty building down Nevsky Prospekt, the snowy street.

"Will Prince Alexander Golitsen and Paul Stroganov be permitted to play with me today?"

"Not today, Tsarevitch. Tomorrow, perhaps," said the servant.

Alexander shook his head. Where he stood now by the hissing stove, he could not hear the servant's reply properly. His left ear was slightly deaf from standing hours on end beside the imperial cannons.

The young grand duke adored artillery, particularly cannons.

"Not today, Tsarevitch. You must attend to Christmas ceremonies."

Alexander frowned. He would far rather play with his friends than ride that stubborn pony.

"With your permission, I will select something suitable to wear, Master Alexander," said Boris. "I think your newest blue military uniform and the red sash would be appropriate."

"Yes, please," said the boy, rubbing the sleep from his eyes. "And wake up Constantine. My, he is a lazy bones!"

Constantine, two years younger than Alexander, pulled the covers over his head. The warmth of the nursery was too delicious not to stay abed and he was deep in dreams. "Leave me alone, Boris," came the muffled groan.

"But it is Christmas Day, Master Constantine!"

Constantine flung back the heavy wool blankets and leapt from bed. "Why so it is!" he shouted. "Let's open my presents!"

Boris smiled, amused at the young prince. He poured water from a porcelain jug into a washing bowl. Steam rose in a great cloud.

"Hot water!" cried both young dukes.

"Our good empress has declared you shall bathe in hot water to start your Christmas Day."

Alexander sighed happily.

He splashed his face with the hot water. Accepting a linen towel from Boris, he looked out at the frozen yards of the vast Winter Palace, shrouded with thick blankets of snow. The snow clung to the gilded moldings adorning the palace's windows and columns.

Despite the fire in the stoves, he shivered.

The prospect of his father's visit unnerved him. He thought of the wolves that his Swiss tutor La Harpe taught him had once roamed the city, eating the corpses of the serfs who died transforming the Finnish swamp into St. Petersburg. His father, Grand Duke Paul, reminded him of one of those hungry wolves. He skulked around the perimeter of St. Petersburg in his estate of St. Michael's or in the summer palace in Gatchina, watching hungrily for the death of his own mother, Catherine the Great, so that he might ascend the throne.

"Your comb, Master Alexander." Boris interrupted his reverie. Alexander looked in the mirror, parting his blond hair. The winter sun hunted the red glints he had inherited from his German Holstein grandfather.

"Will my father be joining us for all Christmas Day?" he asked, as Boris helped him into his uniform jacket.

"I believe the grand duke and grand duchess are only here for Christmas luncheon, then he must return to Gatchina."

"It will be pleasant for you to see your mother," said Boris, buttoning his charge's jacket. "She dotes on you, Duke Alexander."

Alexander sighed but said nothing.

"And your baby sister, Ekaterina. Such a beautiful child. She dotes on you."

Alexander's face broke into a smile at the thought of seeing Katia. Her high spirits and mischievous nature enchanted him. She represented the heart of the family he had never known.

Alexander and Constantine had no sooner been born to Catherine's son Paul and Maria Feodorovna than they were whisked away to the Winter Palace and sequestered in Empress Catherine's personal apartments. The two boys were raised and educated under the watchful eye of the empress herself.

Empress Catherine disdained her son, who had neither her looks nor her wisdom. Paul resembled a mad bulldog with his bulging eyes and wild expression. There were rumors that he had inherited the mental instability and cruel nature of his demented father, Peter III. Like Alexander, Paul had been whisked away from his mother as an infant, not to see her again until he was six years old, and so Paul grew up hating his mother, sensing her disappointment in him.

Alexander tried to please his grandmother, of course, but he also desperately wanted to curry favor with his father. But that favor was hard to find: Paul had heard the rumors that his mother meant to skip a generation and crown her grandson Alexander as tsar. And, indeed, those rumors were true. Catherine had no intention of ever letting her son inherit the Russian throne but instead groomed Alexander for that eventual future. Should any misfortune befall Alexander, his younger brother Constantine was prepared to take his place.

This was a burden that weighed heavily in the heart of a lonely twelve-year-old boy. Being under the same roof with his father and grandmother was a stormy proposition.

Entering the long portrait-lined marble hall, Alexander saw his parents and his grandmother waiting at the end of the corridor. Behind them, closer to the Christmas tree, were Alexander and Constantine's younger sisters—Alexandra and Elena—who stood quietly at attention but cast anxious looks, longing to open their Christmas presents. Alexandra, the elder, was six. She was dressed in white lace with navy blue ribbons, her hair held back a satin band. The little girl made a pouty face at her older brother, for all this ceremony was delaying her pleasure.

Ekaterina was held by a lady-in-waiting. Still a baby, she was nevertheless mesmerized by her eldest brother. She gave a shriek of joy, holding her chubby hand toward him.

Alexander's father was dressed in a green military uniform with a red sash crossing his chest; his mother, in an emerald-green velvet gown embroidered in seed pearls and silver. Her blonde hair was pinned up gracefully, emphasizing her beauty, even though she had given birth to six children.

He kissed his grandmother's cheeks and bowed.

"Merry Christmas!" said his mother, Maria Feodorovna, extending her white-gloved hand. Alexander bowed to kiss it.

"You look splendid, Alexander!" she said. She looked as if she longed to embrace him—every atom of her flesh trembled to take her eldest son in her arms and cover his face with kisses.

"Merry Christmas!" said Paul. Son and father clasped hands with a crisp, agitated motion. Then they moved a half a pace apart as if on cue, a practiced dance.

"You have not been to Gatchina in months," said Paul. "We shall expect you to pay us a visit soon, if the empress grants permission. I should like to show you the new maneuvers with the horse soldiers."

"And me, Papa?" said Constantine, emerging from behind his brother. "I want to shout orders and drill the soldiers."

"Oh!" said the grand duchess, seeing the fair-haired boy. She placed her hand to her heart. "*Oh*, Constantine! My dear son—"

Her husband turned to her, raising an eyebrow. He shot a look at his own mother, whose face stiffened at the show of affection.

Maria Feodorovna regained her composure.

"A very merry Christmas . . . Duke Constantine," the grand duchess said, gazing sadly at the marble floor.

But the young boy was looking past her to the tree and the floor spread with presents in intricately painted wraps and satin bows. The fir tree's boughs sagged with Christmas bounty, red ribbons holding gifts, sweets, and wooden soldiers, painted in brilliant colors.

"Constantine," said Catherine. "Your mother, the Duchess Maria Feodorovna, has addressed you."

Constantine's head snapped back, looking at his grandmother. Then the little boy turned to his mother, making a curt bow.

"Duchess Maria Feodorovna, madame. I wish the same to you. A very merry Christmas."

Maria Feodorovna flinched as if the little boy had slapped her. Tender words between mother and son would never be uttered in vast halls of Empress Catherine's Winter Palace.

The grand duchess watched silently as her son tore open his Christmas presents.

Chapter 3

On the Cavalry March
June 1785

Astakhov became my tutor from the day my mother hurled me from the carriage window. The flank Hussar was always at my father's side either in quarters or during a march, but now I was his chief duty. He was assigned my care and education, even my swaddling and feedings.

As a baby I rocked along in open wagons, gazing up at the sky and the green shimmering leaves of the birches as they swished over my head. As I grew older, Astakhov would lift me from my cradle, swing me in front of him on the pommel of his saddle, and point out the faults of other soldiers' riding and the virtues of horses that rode rhythmically in formation. The motion of the horse at a walk lulled me to sleep. I would awake in a cradle mounted in a flat wagon, nestled against the sweet-smelling bags of grain.

Astakhov would bring me to the squadron's stables, setting me up on horses' bare backs. He gave me his unloaded pistol as a toy, wrapping my baby hands around the butt even before I had the strength to lift it. He brandished his gleaming sword, slicing the air with the blade while I clapped my hands in joy.

At night my bed was near the campfire. The crackling of the burning wood accompanied the music of the balalaika, the instrument of the Russian heart. Vodka-soaked soldiers' voices singing ancient ballads mingled with the smoke, rising into the starry sky. This was my lullaby.

Astakhov would wait until I fell asleep to bring me into the tents or temporary quarters. If I caught sight of my mother I would howl, clinging to his neck.

As I grew older Astakhov taught me drill commands and maneuvers. I ran through the fields at a mock gallop on an imaginary horse, executing charges against an invisible enemy. I tossed hay with a miniature pitchfork Astakhov whittled for me, and I grained the horses when we could procure oats, wheat, rye. Sometimes we fed them roasted buckwheat.

"Grain can sustain a horse but it makes him hot and difficult to ride. Oats are as good as gold," said my tutor. "But a Russian horse must learn to live on whatever Mother Earth offers, especially in war. Kasha sustains our soldiers—it can sustain horseflesh as well. Roof thatch and birch bark will do when there is nothing else. But grains—every kernel is precious in nourishing a warhorse."

I thought of grains as coins of gold, the currency of life. I was eager to feed the squadron's mounts. I loved the silky slide of oats between my fingers, the dry rustle they made in the bucket as they spilled against the side.

My father smiled when he saw me in the stables, taking my lessons with Astakhov. It was Astakhov who taught me to read and write, using a rough slate and a stub of chalk. As I grew older, I was eager to decipher the cavalry manuals and learn more about horsemanship and battles.

"She knows military maneuvers as well as I," Astakhov told my father.

"Dry fare for a little girl," said my father. "But if she reads, good."

"*Horosho*, Nadya," Papa said, chucking me under the chin with his crooked finger.

My mother was not amused, however, when I returned to our quarters for visits. I galloped down the hall and into the parlor, swinging a stick saber. "Charge!" I screamed, attacking the invisible Turks and other Ottoman infidels who disguised themselves brilliantly as sofa and chairs.

"Stop that this instant, Nadezhda!" said my mother. She pulled me by the ear to my room, making me stand in the corner until my father returned home at supper time.

"Her wild antics weaken my heart," she told my father. "I simply cannot abide her unruly nature."

Send her away. Pick her or me. I could feel her unspoken demand on my father.

By the time I was two she was pregnant again, and—desperate to produce a son—she continued to have baby daughters every two years or so, until my brother Vasily's birth in 1799. My sisters were more obliging and feminine than I. They gave great comfort to my mother, who could not tolerate me as an infant—even less so when I grew into a wild young girl.

One afternoon during a bivouac, I lay on my blanket near the picket lines, the horses' swishing tails lacerating the air. My father ordered naps for me whenever possible, for I was a still a young child.

That particular afternoon, I felt sick to my stomach and my head throbbed. Astakhov came to wake me but instead looked sternly at my face.

"What is it, Astakhov?" I asked. "Why do you look at me this way?"

His hand swept over my forehead, he looked into my eyes.

"Open your mouth, Nadya."

I found my jaw slow to unhinge. His hand, smelling of leather and horses, lifted my chin gently.

"That is a good girl. Open as wide as you can, *dorogaya*."

I loved him when he called me sweetheart.

He examined my mouth and found ulcerations. He called gruffly to a Cossack near him.

"Call Captain Durov to come, immediately!"

He smoothed his rough hand over my forehead and temples.

"Can you see me?" he asked. "Can you hear me, Nadezhda?"

"Yes, I hear. But you are—smoky," I said.

"She cannot focus her eyes," he muttered to someone near us.

"I am so sore," I said. "My stomach aches. My head . . ."

Within minutes my father appeared, dismounting and handing the reins to the Cossack.

"What is it, Corporal?"

He whispered a word I had never heard before. I would never forget after.

"Smallpox."

My father sucked in his breath. "She must be quarantined immediately. Requisition a house. No, two. One for my wife and other children. One for Nadya and . . ."

He opened his hands, supplicating the heavens. He could not assign our one maid to take care of both houses. She had to remain with my younger siblings and mother.

Astakhov answered. "I will take her into quarantine and remain by her side, Captain Durov. I will make all the arrangements. If Nadezhda has smallpox, surely others in the regiment do as well."

At that time we were in the new Lithuanian lands near Vilna, seized for the Russian Empire by Catherine the Great. The Lithuanians despised the Russians, their oppressors. To requisition a house—in this case, two—meant not only that the families who lived in them were thrown out, but also that the one that served as quarantine would have to be burned when we left.

A cavalry must march. Although an extra day's bivouac was ordered to make quarantine arrangements for me and four soldiers also stricken with the disease, my father would have to leave us to our destiny come the following sunrise.

I remember little of the wooden house where I was sequestered, except for a traditional Lithuanian adornment. Over the top of the gable were two white flying horses, a blessing to all who lived under its roof.

The old withered grandmother, the matriarch of the requisitioned house, spat at Astakhov, cursing him in poor Russian flecked with Polish and Lithuanian.

"You filthy Russian pigs bring disease into the house. Can you not leave us to starve alone under this roof? You have taken everything we have, killed our men, raped our women!"

The babushka rushed for him to scratch his eyes, but her grandson stopped her, dragging her away.

"Grandmother, they will kill us. Please, Grandmother!"

The woman continued to scream. "Russian pigs!"

Astakhov raised his hand, signaling a soldier. "Show her Nadezhda."

I was in the shadows and the old woman was nearsighted. When she realized that there was a little girl being brought into the house, she stopped her tirade, wiping the spittle from her lips. I could hear her rasping breath as she approached me, looking at the red pox that covered my face. Her hand shook as she held it inches above my face, in a sweeping caress. I felt that hovering power as if she had pressed my face with kisses.

The babushka pointed to a small room—the only other room—in the house. There were the warm embers of a fire there, a folding cavalry bed, and a coverlet. She spread the blanket over my body, tucking the corners under my thin shoulder blades. The old woman did not take her eyes off mine, never focusing on the pox. Then she shuffled out the door.

A little while later she returned, bringing me a bucket of fresh water from the stream. She dipped a rag into the pail and began bathing my feverish forehead. Her touch was as light as a fairy's, gentle as the loving mother I never had.

From then on, she did not try to attack Astakhov, though she gave all the soldiers the evil eye. She kept the fire burning, sitting on a low stool, poking embers with a stick. She ordered her grandson and his wife to put their children to work gathering wood. She watched the soldiers boil the village chickens, feeding their sick men and me, while she licked her lips at the good smell of food she would not eat.

A strong smoke permeated the tiny bedroom where I lay on the canvas bed. Astakhov administered cool, wet cloths to my forehead, begging me to cling to life.

"Ah! When you are well again, we shall ride together, Nadezhda."

I tried to open my eyes to focus on his face.

"One day I shall buy you a horse, *dorogaya*, my dearest. One of the Cossack breeds from the high mountains in the east. Sure-footed and swift, you will see. But first you must get better, little one."

He tried to force spoonfuls of chicken broth between my ulcerated lips, but I gagged. I could not drink enough water. No matter how much I tried, I was consumed by thirst. I tossed with fever and delirium, my skin on fire. All the time, Astakhov stayed at my side. He told me stories of the cavalry and brave horses who charged into battle.

I heard the moans and retching of the four sick men stretched on pallets throughout the house. I smelled the sour pails of potato vodka that the cavalry had left us, the only medicine we had to combat our pain.

Rough-spun sheets partitioned the stricken. The coarse cloth would flutter when my door was opened, giving me a glimpse of the makeshift infirmary. A small stove heated our little room, though Astakhov insisted on opening the windows to let the sickness leave.

One night, I heard one of the sick soldiers cry out, calling for his wife and children who remained behind in Moscow.

"Marina! Marina, come to me!"

"It is all right, Corporal. You are here amongst your comrades."

"No! Marina, bring me my pipe. Bring the babe—let me. Let me. Let me hold her."

"You are hallucinating, Corporal. Bring more blankets," ordered another man's voice. "And a wet cloth for his head. Vodka! Bring—"

"Marina! For our Savior's sake! Bring me the child!"

"Shhh! Corporal, you wake the house and other sick patients."

"Get away! You stink of death and fire! Let my woman bathe me! Take me to the River Don, to my father's house. I will kneel and ask his blessing, I—"

"Shhh! Shhh!"

Near dawn I heard no further calls.

"What has happened to the corporal?" I asked the babushka who hovered over me. In the weak light of sunrise I saw her eyes watching me. Astakhov lay on his pallet, sleeping.

The old woman answered in her pidgin Polish-Russian but I did not understand the word she used.

"What? I do not understand. What has happened to the soldier who was screaming?"

She searched for another word that I might understand.

"*On spi*," she said. "He is asleep. Asleep forever."

I turned and looked out the window at the falling snow.

"The soldier who tends you. He tells you stories of horses, little one?" she whispered.

"Astakhov?" I said, turning slowly to look at her.

"Shhh! You wake him. I hate the Russians. Ah! But the stories . . ."

"You understood the stories?"

"The word *loshad*. The Russian word for horse. I watch his face and understand. Horse," she repeated. "Our word: *arklys*!"

Astakhov roused from his cot, hearing the woman's voice in the room. He sniffed the air and listened to the ebbing silence. Somehow he knew instantly what had happened. His eyes flicked at the closed door. He must have wanted to rush out to see his comrade who had died. Instead he moved to my bed to comfort me.

"Little Nadezhda," he said with tears making his eyes bright. "Have I ever told you about the best horse in the cavalry? A Circassian mare, given to General Kutuzov, the greatest commander in the Russian army. The swiftest, boldest horse in cavalry. Ah, but such a mare!"

"No," I said, shivering in my bed. "I want a stallion." The old woman drew up the blanket under my chin.

"Ah, then you are in for a treat. When you are well, I shall see that you have a horse as miraculous as that Circassian. Let me just check on the others in the house. I will return and tell you all about the marvels of the mountain breed. A most extraordinary horse, indeed!"

He nodded to the Lithuanian woman. "You will watch over her?" he said.

"*Da,*" she said, looking down at me. "*Da.*"

He closed the door silently behind him.

I began to rub my pustules with my mittened hands.

"No, no, little one. You mustn't scratch them," said the woman. I looked up at her, barely able to focus through my blurring tears. She lifted me up from the pillow, giving me a sip of water from a clay cup.

"I, too, know stories of horses. Magic horses," she said. It was then I realized that the old woman could speak Russian better than she let on.

"And Lithuanian tales of spirits. Our respect for the magic of water that harbors the spirits of the drowned." I started and drew back from the cup she held out for me to drink. "No, little one. Do not be afraid of the spirits. Live amongst them peacefully and rejoice. They surround us, always."

I grew so feverish, I could not see her face, nor that of Astakhov when he returned from paying his respects to the dead man. I heard only voices and fluttering blankets.

Astakhov stood over me, tears sliding down his face. "The pustules . . ." he said. "They are growing closer and closer together."

I heard her voice speak again in very bad Russian. She was addressing Astakhov.

"Do not . . . make water in your eyes, Corporal. If she goes, she goes with the goddess Saulė, pulled by the horse gods."

"I cannot bear to lose her," he said, his voice thick. "How would I tell the captain, her father. He loves her like a . . . son."

My eyelids fluttered as I sank down deeper into the abyss. *A son!* I clawed the air trying to resurface.

"Ah! That is the matter!" said the Lithuanian woman. "He loves her as a son. Not as the daughter she is? Where is her mother?"

"Her mother cannot risk contagion. She has three young children."

The old woman made a snorting sound, like a rooting pig. I felt her dry hand on my forehead, smoothing back my wet hair.

"Stay with us, little Nadezhda," she whispered in my ear. "Stay and watch the twin horse spirits carry the goddess Saulė's chariot across the sky from horizon to horizon. See their white coats and bright manes. She will reward them with golden hay when they reach their destination."

The pustules had grown dimpled in the center. Astakhov measured the distance between each with the width of his little fingernail. He knew if they grew and spread into one another, I would surely die. The old woman shook her head and left us.

She returned with a whitened skull in her hands.

"*Arklys*," she said. "Horse. Magic."

Astakhov shook his head, staring at the horse skull. "Madness," he muttered.

The babushka placed the skull beside my bed. "*Arklys* help little Nadezhda."

The old woman closed the shutters. She smothered the fire with dried herbs and a wet blanket, letting the fire smolder, and creating a dense smoke. She knelt and prayed in front of the smoking heap. She spoke a strange language I could not understand.

Astakhov did not protest. We were in her home, condemning it with my disease. Who was he to refuse her help, her incantations to cure me?

She spoke again in Russian. Her prayers were to the twin gods of horses, to intervene with the great goddess.

"We are all twins by nature. We are evil and good. We are man and woman. You must follow the one who truly captures your heart."

In my delirium I dreamt of the twin horses, galloping across the heavens. I became one, tossing my golden mane into the stars as I reared. I caught a glimpse of the goddess behind me, giving me free rein.

And smiling.

Chapter 4

Sarapul, Russia
August 1790

I recovered from smallpox, though two of the soldiers in the Lithuanian house did not.

Soon, my mother was pregnant again and my father realized he could not continue in the cavalry as a family man. When I was seven years old, he retired from the cavalry and was given a job as a civil servant in Sarapul, along the Kama River, west of the Ural Mountains. It was a harsh place to live, the gateway to Siberia. The town survived on the yellow sturgeon that were abundant in the river—in the local Chuvash language, *Sara* meant "money" and *pul* meant "fish." But the winters were long and hard, so cold and severe that the townspeople would mix their ground wheat with acorns or the bark of fir trees to make their flour last till spring.

And with that move there was an abrupt end to my freedom and my tutelage with the cavalry orderly Astakhov. We rolled away in a wagon, leaving behind the cavalry life. Astakhov stood outside the army camp, waving his hand and weeping like a child until our wagon had disappeared from sight.

I would never forget him, or my childhood cavalry days.

My mother was determined to introduce me to domestic life. She made me crochet lace. Can you imagine? I made a tangled mess of the yarn, cursing the crochet hooks. I hated my stiff dresses and endless house chores, and spurned all attempts my mother made to teach me etiquette and the gentle manners of a lady.

My mother, exasperated, locked me in the house, forbidding me to set foot outside. She would tame my wild spirit, she declared.

"Nadezhda! Who will ever marry you? You are swarthy, astonishingly ugly—you look like a goblin. The least you can learn is sewing and housekeeping, to make a man a good wife."

For a young girl brought up on the back of a cavalry horse, there could have been no greater torture. I yearned for the warm smell of horse, the spicy fir trees, and fresh air of the cavalry march.

My mother kept me out of the sun, trying to pale my weather-beaten skin. Smallpox had left my complexion scarred, the skin thickened with scar tissue. She told me over and over that I was ugly, that I did not even look like a girl. That I must work at making myself more appealing. Becoming a lady, performing domestic duties skillfully would win me a husband.

Simultaneously she bemoaned her station in life as a woman. She suspected my father of philandering.

"A woman must be born, live, and die in slavery. Eternal bondage!" my mother wailed. "Because I grow old, he abandons me for firmer flesh!"

She threw her looking glass at the wall, shattering it. "There is no creature more unhappy, more worthless, or more contemptible."

I watched her rage, snapping like a wild dog at her fetters. She convinced me that, indeed, a woman is destined to a life of repression, a hopeless destiny.

It was at that moment that I resolved, even if it cost me my life, to escape the curse that seemed to be the fate of all women.

Then Alcides came into my life.

Chapter 5

Winter Palace, St. Petersburg
January 1790

Grand Duke Paul and his son Alexander left the Winter Palace in a troika covered in bearskins, the January wind so cold it snatched their breath away, leaving them gasping. They traveled for two days, stopping in the empress's transit palaces, which were built a day's travel apart so the royal family would never lack proper accommodations while traveling to and fro between residences.

On the third day, the final stage of the trip stretched into the late afternoon. Winter night comes early in Russia, and by four in the afternoon it was already dark. His father put his arm around Alexander's shoulders, pulling him deeper under the furs to protect his skin and tender lungs.

"It is brutally cold," Paul said. "You do not want chilblains. And you will need your lungs strong for war, my son."

Alexander popped his head up from the coverings. He pressed his mittens to his face to block the wind.

"Oh, but Father! I want to see everything. I want to see the torches of Gatchina! Our home, yes, Father?"

His father gave him a rare smile, pulling his son close.

Gatchina was Paul's world and his joy. The grand duke despised the Winter Palace, where his father, Peter III, had been murdered by the Imperial Guards of his own wife, Empress Catherine. Haunted by that bitter memory, the Winter Palace reminded Paul of a lonely childhood with a mother who ignored him, then later came to despise him.

Now the grand duke squeezed his son to his breast, kissing the top of his head. "*Horosho*, Alexander. Good. Gatchina is our sanctuary. Do not forget you are my son, no matter what happens in the future."

Alexander felt the warmth of his father's body, impregnated with the scents of cologne, leather, and cognac. The tsarevitch breathed in both manly warmth and piney cold of the forests, an intoxicating infusion, the aroma of Russia.

"What does *sanctuary* mean, Father?"

Paul heaved a great breath into the winter night, enveloping him and his son in a heavy mist.

"A place where you won't be murdered in your nightshirt, son."

Chapter 6

When I was twelve, my father rode into our gated compound one evening on a black Circassian stallion. The young horse snorted and leapt, the muscle in his neck shining in the flickering lights of the stable master's torch.

"This wretched beast!" shouted my father.

I ran to my papa, embracing him. "Is he mine, Papa?" I said, stretching my hand out toward the stallion.

"No, Nadya. You stay away from this one. He is a brute. He could slice your head open with his hoofs. He bit me as I put on the bridle, the bastard!"

"Why did you buy him then?" asked my mother, coming out of the house. Her voice was shrill and agitated. A maid wrapped a shawl around her shoulders. My mother would not walk a step further from the front door. She hated horses.

"This beautiful stallion? He is a gift. A gift from Astakhov, my old orderly. He is stationed now in the Caucasus Mountains. No horse is more hardy or able on rocky terrain."

"Astakhov!" I said. "Then surely he is a gift for me."

My father squeezed me tight in his arms.

"Astakhov sends his loving regards to you, Nadezhda. He loves you as his own daughter. But this horse is untamable. I am not sure he is such a fine present after all."

I stared at the stallion, extending my hand. He backed away, snorting. His nostrils quivered as he drew in my scent.

"Nadezhda! Enough of that!" called out my mother. "Come into the house this minute!"

Since our cavalry days, my mother would not allow me to even walk down to my father's stables. I turned my back on her, approaching the horse.

"What is his name, Father?" I said. The horse took a step toward me, still sucking in my scent.

"Alcides," he said. "The birth name of Heracles."

"Alcides the all-powerful," I whispered, the horse's warm breath on my outstretched hand. "The strongest of all mortals!"

"Nadezhda! At once!" cried my mother.

My father watched me drop my hand and turn away. He nodded for the stableman to take Alcides but stood for a long time rubbing his chin before he followed us in.

I think he knew already I was in love with this new horse.

I waited until I heard my parents' bedroom door shut before I crept from my room to the kitchen. I had only a candlestick with a brass handle crooked around my finger. As quietly as I could, I rummaged for a loaf of white bread. I cut a few ragged slices and reached into the cupboard for the sugar bowl and sprinkled the bread until it glistened with sweetness in the candlelight.

Sheltering the guttering flame from the drafts, I slipped silently into the night.

The moon cast shadows on the gardens. The birch trees loomed like white giants, their black shadows stretched before me. I could hear the snorting of the horses, the restless commotion as they sensed the new horse stabled among them.

Alcides kicked the stall partition that separated him from my father's gray gelding.

"Easy!" I said to him. "Easy, Alcides!"

The stallion leapt back at the sound of my voice and the flame of the candle. He snorted from the corner of his stall.

"Come here, boy," I said, putting the candle down carefully on the stone floor. I stretched out my hand with the sugar-coated bread.

"Here! Look what I brought you, my friend."

The gelding in the stall next to him stuck his nose through the bars. He was greedy and smelled the sweetness of the treat. He made a low nicker, his lips probing.

Alcides was less sure. He flattened his ears at the searching lips of the gelding, though I kept the bread just out of his reach.

"Come, now, Alcides. My mother would beat me for stealing our sugar. Come, you take a risk for me now."

I do not know how long I stood there, though I had to tighten my wrap in the drafty cold of the stables. My teeth chattered and I stamped my feet to keep warm. But eventually Alcides took a few steps toward me, his hooves rustling the straw.

He took the sugared bread from my outstretched palm, nibbling it as gently as a rabbit. At last he took the whole slice in his teeth, shaking it up and down.

"No! You will spill off all the sugar!" I protested. I reached up and pressed the slice into his mouth. He did not draw back.

After that first night, Alcides would nicker and paw the ground when he heard my approaching steps, knowing it was me who brought his evening snack.

And the maid complained there was never enough sugar to make the weekly cakes. Lucky for me she blamed it on the house spirit—for every Russian household had one—the mischievous *domovoy*.

"It is his doing!" she proclaimed.

I said a silent prayer for our Russian superstitions and left little pancakes on the windowsill for our *domovoy* as a thank-you.

Chapter 7

Gatchina
August 1789

When he reached the age of twelve, Alexander was permitted to spend more time with his parents at Gatchina, a luxurious fortress, its massive limestone facade stately, if not elegant. Flanked by two lakes, the White and the Silver, Gatchina was isolated in the depths of a thick forest, sixty versts from St. Petersburg and a half-day ride from the summer palaces of Tsarkoe Selo, the imperial village where the St. Petersburg Court spent the months of June through August.

The vast southern facade of the palace, its central block adorned with pilasters, open galleries, and two towers, loomed in a semicircle over the parade ground. Here Paul drilled his twenty-four hundred horse soldiers obsessively, cultivating the Prussian precision of a military cavalry.

Alexander reveled in the military colors and pageantry of maneuvers. Soon, his father began to teach him how to command the troops, how to issue the orders for the complex and precise formations. The young boy didn't care about horsemanship, but orchestrating the movement of thousands of horse soldiers was another matter. While other

Russian children were content with toy soldiers, Alexander had his own live cavalry with which to play.

Paul frowned at his son.

"Your heels should be down," muttered the grand duke, who sat astride a large-boned warhorse. "And you sit too far back in the saddle, like an old man. There should be a plumb line from the tip of your nose to your knee to your heel."

The young boy shifted discreetly in the saddle, so as not to signal his father's criticism to the hundreds of horsemen he commanded in Gatchina's vast drill yard. Glancing up, he saw the heavy curtain move in the window of the duchess's apartments. His mother was watching.

She wishes to know what kind of commander I will be.

Grand Duke Paul looked his son up and down with disapproval.

"Does the empress not insist on daily equitation classes? Your riding must improve. One day you will be expected to lead men into war—"

"I do practice daily equitation. But I am commanding now, Father, not riding—"

"You are on a horse. And do not dare interrupt me! I am your father. Do not forget that. You will not usurp my position. Not at this moment and not ever!"

Alexander straightened in the saddle.

Does he know that Grandmama wants me to take the throne after her death?

"Watch me!" said Paul, his horse prancing. "Company! To the right, face!"

Alexander swallowed hard. He saw his mother's curtains draw closed.

At ten o'clock in the morning, the pale pink of a winter sunrise competed with the oil lanterns and convex gold sconces of the Winter Palace. Frederic-Cesar La Harpe paced slowly across the parquet floor of the study, hands clasped behind his back as he lectured.

"The noble savage is Rousseau's antidote to modern society and social class," said the Swiss tutor. "Our modern world—especially that of the aristocrat and nobility—removes man further and further from nature and simplicity, thus from inherent goodness. In doing so we forfeit our natural instincts, removing us from what is naturally good and right."

As La Harpe lectured, Alexander leaned on his elbows, his head resting in his hands. Had his father been in the room, the grand duke would have knocked his son's arms from the table in rage. No Romanov should sit with his head propped in his hands like an insolent serf, he would say.

But Monsieur La Harpe recognized his student's pose as total concentration. Alexander listened raptly, drinking in the philosophers—Hobbes, Locke, Rousseau. These ideas of freethinking, of the rights of man—even commoners—were radical, even dangerous. Yet his grandmother, Catherine the Great, had selected La Harpe herself.

"*Tabula rasa*," said Alexander. "The innocence at birth before corruption by society or government."

"The term *tabula rasa* was John Locke's, not Rousseau's," answered La Harpe. "But the precept is the same in Rousseau's philosophy. Before civilization can stain a soul, it stands as a blank slate, neither good nor bad. There is no innate desire to steal, lie, or murder, Mr. Locke would argue. Only when society, culture, or adverse circumstances make their ugly cuts into tender wood does the sapling bend or die. Each scar results in vices that erode a man's character and the way the trunk will bend, either toward or away from the light."

La Harpe looked at the sunrise, stillborn on the horizon. *It barely makes an effort to rise. Even the sun can't face a Russian winter.*

"Monsieur La Harpe," Alexander asked, toying with his quill. "I have heard it said that you organized the French cantons of Switzerland to revolt against Bern. That your ideas are radical." Alexander did not meet his tutor's eyes but sought out another sharpened quill from his writing box. He tested the point against his fingertip. "Is this true, Monsieur?"

"Yes," said La Harpe, his back stiffening. "The Empress Catherine knows as much. I am dedicated to the liberation of Bern."

"So you foment revolution?" La Harpe noticed a mischievous smile tugging at Alexander's lips.

"Only when it is just, Tsarevitch. As in the American revolution against the English. Thomas Jefferson borrowed John Locke's words: life, liberty, and the pursuit of happiness."

"Ah! I so admire this Thomas Jefferson."

"Perhaps you shall meet him some day as tsar," said La Harpe. "But the point is when there is a long history of abuses it is not only the right of a people to revolt, but in fact their obligation."

"And the Russian people?" asked Alexander. "Do they not have a right to revolution, Monsieur? Or the Poles?"

La Harpe's eyes shot to the gilt-framed door.

"Tsarevitch, I merely teach the doctrines of our most progressive thinkers, according to the express wishes of our gracious empress, Catherine," the tutor answered in a loud voice. "She has charged me with giving you an enlightened and liberal education. I follow her orders explicitly."

Alexander caught his lower lip between his teeth.

"I have heard that my grandmother expressed the keen desire to liberate the serfs when she first came to power."

La Harpe did not answer. He fingered his wide lapels.

"But the aristocracy persuaded her to refrain," continued Alexander.

"The empress did succeed in liberating many serfs," said La Harpe, sniffing. "That was no small feat."

"But many more were enslaved as spoils of war in Lithuania and Poland. The nobility say Russia would collapse without the serfs." Alexander looked intently at his teacher. "Do you think that is true, Monsieur La Harpe? What would Locke or Rousseau say of that?"

La Harpe leaned toward his student, whispering, "I think that the great philosophers would say that the question would be answered entirely differently if posed directly to the serfs. Or the Poles."

"When I am emperor," said Alexander, his sapphire eyes glittering, "I will liberate the serfs as my grandmother intended. And I shall study the matter of the Polish people—that much I promise you."

La Harpe drew a deep breath. *What more could I hope for in a student? To change the course of the most vast empire on Earth?*

He released his breath and a shadow crossed his face.

He is almost tabula rasa now. With my tutelage, there are the first chalk marks of respect, the etching of human kindness. But what hands will seize the chalk after me?

Two German princesses of Baden, Louise, age thirteen, and Frederika, age eleven, arrived at the final rest stop exhausted, their gowns powdered with fine dust. The coach had traveled with few stops between Karlsruhe and St. Petersburg. While Frederika chattered incessantly about Russia's golden palaces and the barbarous tales of Cossacks, Louise remained silent. She gazed out the coach window at the scarfed heads of the serfs, men and women carrying loads of grass and fagots for their fires, strapped on their backs.

"Are these old people slaves?" Louise asked her chaperone.

Frau Weiss sniffed. "Never use that word in Russia. They are serfs. They belong to wealthy landowners and royalty who care for their needs."

Louise looked out at an old woman who dared to raise her eyes to meet Louise's own. For one second their gazes met. Then the serf dipped her head in humility.

"That grandmother is too old to be carrying sticks on her back!" said Louise. "Where is the wealthy landowner to lighten her load?"

Frau Weiss said, "Beware of what you say. The footman may understand German. Never mention the serfs again in Russia."

Inside the rest stop, their chaperone ordered the valet to brush their garments and bring a washing bowl and pitcher so that the two little girls could wash their faces and hands before arriving at the Winter Palace.

"You must kiss the feet of the great Empress Catherine," said Frau Weiss. "Do not lift your heads until she gives you permission to rise."

"Yes, *madame*," said Louise.

"Must I rub my nose on the rug?" asked little Frederika. "Will it be very dirty from men's boots? Will it be quite smelly?"

Frau Weiss smoothed back the little girl's hair, not addressing her. It was too easy to become tangled up in little Frederika's imagination.

"Do not look the young grand duke in the eye. It would be considered exceedingly forward," said Frau Weiss, wetting a wooden comb and running it through Louise's ash-blonde hair.

How could the empress and the young grand duke not fall in love with this charming girl? Her almond-shaped blue eyes, the melodious voice, her height and carriage. And her intelligence and sensitive nature.

Frau Weiss said a silent prayer that this Russian grand duke would be kind to her precious charge.

"And me, Frau Weiss?" said Frederika, tugging at her guardian's sleeve. "Should I keep my eyes lowered as well?"

"Of course," said Frau Weiss.

"I shan't look at him at all," said Frederika, feisty as always. "I shall pretend he is not there. Poof!"

Frau Weiss laughed. Empress Catherine had expressly ordered both young princesses be sent. *But this little girl! What a nuisance.*

"Everything I tell your older sister applies to you, Frederika." She signaled to the servant that the basin and pitcher should be removed.

"All right," she said, her fan tapping at the coach door. The footman nodded.

The horses, refreshed with their draft of water, pulled the carriage forward at an energetic trot.

When the girls were admitted to the great hall of the Winter Palace, they did as they had been schooled. They fell at the feet of the empress, studiously ignoring the handsome blond young grand duke.

"Oh!" said the empress. "Look at this glorious cap of blonde hair! Like an angel. Do rise, princesses."

The two girls rose and curtsied in unison.

"*Très charmante!*" exclaimed Empress Catherine, nodding her head. "Now, little one . . . Mademoiselle Frederika, you may return to your governess." She turned to a lady-in-waiting, "But first take the young princess to see the musical peacock."

"Music? Does it sing?"

"After a fashion. It is a precious treasure, quite unique in the world. It is made of solid gold. Go along with the mademoiselle and she will show it to you as it sings on the hour. You must hurry."

Frederika took the hand of the Russian lady and hurried from the room to visit the strange mechanical fowl.

"Princess Louise, let me look at you."

Louise smiled becomingly as she had been coached to do.

"Such large blue eyes! And so tall for a thirteen-year-old!" Empress Catherine exclaimed. "Turn around. Oh, look. Such a fine figure and carriage. A Baden princess indeed!"

Alexander wasn't sure how to approach this German princess but did so to please his grandmother.

And Louise also did as she was told, not looking at the boy who seemed, at very least, indifferent.

"Such an exquisite creature, this German princess," said the empress to Alexander in private. "Did you notice the cloud of ash-blonde hair, her perfect profile like a Greek cameo?"

"She is pretty," admitted Alexander.

His grandmother fixed her steely eyes on her favorite grandchild. "It is time to grow up, Alexander. You are fifteen years old now. I cannot impress upon you how important it is to me—to Russia!—that you marry well. And I approve of this princess. She is from my homeland."

Alexander raised his head and straightened his spine.

"Yes, Empress," he said.

"All right. As long as we understand one another," said Catherine, nodding. "Now run along and visit with our guests. Make sure they feel welcomed."

As the months went by the young Alexander did manage to fall in love with the German princess. After a fashion.

Louise wrote her mother: "Alone in my room, he kissed me lightly as he had done in church in Easter ceremony. But those kisses in church were supervised by the Empress Catherine. These were our secret. He kissed me ever so lightly just touching my lips. Not at all like Papa does when he scratches me with his beard."

Alexander confessed to one of his tutors, General Protassov, that while he had passionate urges toward some of the women he had met at the court—especially the Polish princess Maria Naryshkina—they were not the same as the feelings he had for the young German princess Louise. His sentiments toward her were something altogether different: a deference, a tender friendship. He felt a sense of calm with her, more agreeable than the fiery passions evoked by other young women. He thought of Princess Louise as more worthy of love than anyone he had ever met.

When the empress read the general's report, she gasped in joy.

"Worthy indeed! I shall write her parents at once. Princess Louise must begin Russian lessons immediately, and her conversion to the Russian Orthodox Church must be completed before she can be married to my grandson. Many months of tutelage I would judge. She seems quite bright."

Empress Catherine's hips hurt. Because of her enormous girth, standing for hours was pure torture. But custom required that she stand throughout the lengthy Orthodox ceremony—and her delight at witnessing the wedding of her favorite grandson brought her such sublime happiness that she could almost ignore the pain. She tipped her chin up in a majestic gesture so that the tears—tears of joy not pain—did not spill down her cheeks.

Grand Duke Alexander, age fifteen, wore a silver caftan with diamond buttons, the ribbon of the Order of St. Andrew across his chest. The fourteen-year-old Princess Louise, renamed Elizabeth by the empress, wore a matching gown of silver and brilliant brocade, interwoven with diamonds and pearls.

Grand Duke Constantine held a crown over his brother's head while Prince Alexander Andreyevich Bezborodko, Catherine's foreign affairs minister, held another crown over Elizabeth.

Cannons boomed from the Admiralty less than a verst down Nevsky Prospekt from the Winter Palace. A similar volley thundered across the Neva at the Fortress of St. Peter and St. Paul. Church bells pealed endlessly.

"The marriage of Cupid and Psyche!" exclaimed the empress. "Has there ever been a more handsome couple?"

The ambassadors and dignitaries of Europe agreed: the young imperial couple was the most attractive the world had ever seen.

Chapter 8

Sarapul, Russia
June 1796

My father's philandering caused my mother's rage to burn like venom in her throat. She couldn't ignore it any longer.

Behind the closed doors of their bedroom, she screamed, "I have heard about the village girl! I know of your treachery!"

"Do not listen to gossips, Nadezhda," my father said. "The old wives relish spreading—"

"I curse you and I curse the day we fell in love! The day I threw away my noble Ukrainian name to marry a villainous Russian. My father was right!"

"Nadezhda! I swear the girl means nothing to me."

My mother opened the door suddenly and saw me staring at them both. She beat her breast with her fist.

"I give you my love, my honor, my life. And look!" she said, pointing at me. "Look what I have in return! An ugly monkey of a girl child, a cursed brat. And a traitorous husband who looks for love in the gutters of Sarapul."

She fell to the floor weeping. My father turned on his heel and left. I remained paralyzed, watching my mother's shoulders heave.

That was the night I decided to ride Alcides.

I had neither bridle nor saddle, only the halter and lead rope that tied him to a picket. He had taken to following me like a dog, knowing I had pockets full of sugared bread. I wore only my nightgown, for I no longer had clothes meant for outdoor activities. My mother had given them all away.

I led Alcides out the gate, closing it as silently as I could. I knotted the rope on the halter under the horse's chin and climbed onto the split-rail fence beside the road. In the moonlight I saw a trace of white that encircled Alcides's eye as he swung his big head around, looking at me perched on the fence.

"Just stand," I said. "Stand, Alcides."

I vaulted onto his back. He took a couple of panicked sidesteps away from the fence, startled by my weight. I clung tight to his mane and squeezed my legs around his barrel. Again he swung his head around, but this time nibbling at my toes.

I laughed. I gave him a gentle nudge with my heel and we trotted off into the darkness.

Those first few months I fell off quite a bit, especially at a trot. The walk is simple and his canter was rhythmic. But trotting shook me loose time and again and I tumbled off into the grass. Still, I was young and resilient. Alcides would wait beside me until I remounted him, never running away.

How I loved the smell of the river during the warm nights of summer, the wet stones cooling in the darkness! The crickets' chirps enveloped us, the wind shaking the moonlight high up in the birch trees. Ah! The intoxicating scent of freedom! All this revived me from the humiliation I suffered from my mother. Oh, to be out from under her roof! I cared not a lick for my bumps and bruises, nor for any dangers—real or imagined—of the night.

By day, I was a prisoner in the house. But at night, I was a free-roaming spirit. Like most Russian children, I had grown up with tales of ghosts, corpses, wood goblins, and even water nymphs who would tickle their victims to death. And of course the child-eating witch Baba Yaga, who lived in a house atop long rooster legs. Those orange, taloned legs would run down even the swiftest and most cunning child, pluck him up, and feed him to Baba Yaga. That is, if Baba Yaga did not catch him herself, flying in her mortar, rowing the wind with her pestle.

But I was not afraid of the night. I was part of its blackness, hidden from my mother. I could fly on the back of my horse away from her like a spirit of the netherworld.

Freedom!

Each night Alcides and I ventured farther and farther from home, traveling across the plains of Sarapul and along the Kama River. Finally, a year after I had first lit upon Alcides's back, I rode up Startsev Mountain. The call of the nightingale met us as we climbed the stony path, and my hair was swept by the low-hanging branches of oak, maple, and elm.

That night I had a fall. A hard fall indeed.

I can't remember what happened . . . I don't remember much about that night.

I returned home with a rip through the sleeve of my nightgown and mud and bloodstains I could not wash out. My maid Ludmilla was my mother's spy. When she saw the condition of my nightclothes, she suspected the worst. She reported to my mother that though I was only fourteen years old, I must be having a clandestine affair.

"We will watch her tonight," said my mother. "She must take after the filthy ways of her father. I will not let her further dishonor our family."

But when my mother watched me, she saw that I headed not directly for the gate, but to the stables. The stableman was a notoriously heavy drinker at night. His weekly pail of vodka was too often emptied by the very next morning.

My mother saw me emerge from the stable with the wild Circassian stallion and gasped.

"Rouse Karl!" said my mother, as I fumbled with the gate lock.

The maid ran and shook the snoring stableman awake and he came running, as best as a drunkard can run.

"Where do you think you are going, miss?" Karl asked, approaching me. He took the lead rope from my hand and led Alcides back to the barn.

There was nothing to do but return to the house and my mother's outrage.

When my father heard that I had been riding Alcides, he did not punish me. Instead he vanished for a few days, returning with a package wrapped in tanned leather and tied up with horse-hair rope.

"For my little cavalry girl," he said.

Never had I been so in love with my papa. He was proud of me! He wiped the tears from his eyes. "My Nadezhda, who rides a horse I can barely manage. You must be part Cossack."

"What is it, Father?" I asked, running my fingers over the smooth leather wrapping.

"Open it."

My fingers flew over the knots, untying the twine. I could not believe what lay within.

Indigo-colored trousers. A tall fur hat in the Turkoman style. And a blood-red tunic—a Cossack *chekmen*—with a leather belt, fringed with brass fittings and a small engraved box. Polished brass bullets were nestled in the small pockets of the *gaziry* set diagonally across each breast. Real bullets!

My father's eyes were moist.

"It is the uniform of the Cossacks of the Caucasus Mountains—to match Alcides's breeding. You will ride with me today on Alcides. Side by side. No one needs to know you are a girl, Nadezhda," he said, patting me on the knee.

Never had I been so happy. Never.

My father rode his chestnut mare beside us. She was a Prussian warhorse and, though much taller than my Alcides, could not outrun him on a straightaway. My father challenged me over and over to race on the dirt road, where we galloped wildly past hay wagons, vegetable carts, and even an aristocrat's carriage one morning.

Alcides and I left him behind to eat our churning dust, crossing the chosen finish line seconds ahead. I heard him erupt in laughter and shouts of "Hurrah! Hurrah, Nadezhda!"

I smiled, rubbing the chafed calves of my leg where the boots pinched my tender flesh, gripped against the saddle.

"I am used to riding bareback, Father," I said, rubbing my legs. "And in a nightgown."

My father laughed, pulling up his mare who pranced under him.

"That is why you have the natural seat you do," he said, nodding. "You have no formal training, which shows. But your instincts and way with the horse are striking."

A cloud of dust rose from the road about a half verst from us. I saw horses in the distance, with riders dressed the same as I, but in sky-blue tunics and britches, rather than my red. They rode in a ragged formation—hardly a formation at all.

"Cossacks!" I said.

"There is a Cossack regiment stationed here to suppress the Tatars' incessant thievery and murder," said my father, reining his horse in the opposite direction. "The Tatars are taking a toll on the region."

"But isn't this the Tartars' homeland?" I asked.

"It is Russia. All land belongs to the Romanovs! The commander of Imperial Guards has sent the Cossacks here to patrol."

"Are we returning home?" I asked.

My father turned to me, giving me a look from head to toe. "Yes, of course. The Cossacks may have something to say about your Cossack *chekmen*, little miss. I would rather they not discover you are a girl."

"Oh, but Papa!" I said. "I should love to meet them!"

"That savage lot? Ah, Nadezhda," he sighed. "You truly have no fear. If only you were a son, you would be the staff I would lean on in my old age."

I withered inside at his words, my heart shrinking like a drop of water on a griddle. I looked over my shoulder at the galloping regiment as it disappeared into the horizon.

Chapter 9

Sarapul, Russia
June 1801

Life with my mother was a relentless march of tedium and regret, tangled crotchet lace, crooked hems, and tongue-lashings. My father spent less and less time at home. My mother would not let me ride Alcides unless he was with me. She threatened to burn my Cossack uniform and throw away my riding boots.

"I shall send you to the Ukraine where you will learn to be a lady!" she threatened. "You will live with my family and my grandmother will teach you some manners!"

A flurry of letters arranging my transport arrived. The maids packed my trunk. The Cossack riding outfit was not included. It hung on a peg on the wall, lifeless and discarded.

Though I welcomed the chance to leave my mother and live in the Ukraine—I had grown up with letters from a loving grandmother I didn't know—my heart ached to leave my father. By this time, he had almost disappeared completely from our house. I yearned to see him before I left.

"I shall at least have a chance to say my farewell to Papa," I said.

"Your father is too busy with his mistress," my mother spat back. "You will find a new life in the Ukraine. You will learn and follow the old traditions."

"But Father will return to say good-bye, won't he?"

My mother's lips tightened into a brittle line across her mouth. She said nothing.

"I know he will! He will!"

My mother shook her head. "Go and say farewell to your horse instead. He is more faithful than your Papa."

I stood frozen at her words. *Good-bye to Alcides?*

"But—what do you mean? Alcides will come with me, tied to the wagon, yes?"

"You are traveling by carriage as a lady should. Alcides will remain here."

"No!" I ran from the house, slamming the door behind me. The stableman found me later, crying into Alcides's neck. He dragged me back to the house and into my bedroom crammed with the packed trunks.

I flung myself on the bed and cried.

My mother was determined to change my life. To ruin my life.

And I was still too young to fight her.

Chapter 10

Winter Palace, St. Petersburg
May 1794

Alexander and Elizabeth ate silently. The convex sconces mirrored the flickering tapers, the candlelight reflecting bright on the gold-leafed room.

"I must be going," said Alexander, dabbing his lips with the linen napkin. He rose to his feet as the servant pulled back the chair.

"Will you not stay at home tonight, Alexander?" Grand Duchess Elizabeth asked. "Please?"

Alexander regarded his wife, who seemed so small and wounded in her chair.

"No. I shall see you tomorrow for dinner," he said, moving to where she sat and kissing her on her cheeks.

Elizabeth's eyes filled with tears.

"My dear," said Alexander. "Whatever is the matter? I honor you—"

"By having dinner with me? When I know full well where you go. To see Maria Naryshkina—"

"Yes," said Alexander, drawing up to his full height. "Of course, you know full well. There is no secret here."

Elizabeth could not trust herself to look in her husband's eyes. She studied the porcelain saucer and its tiny, elegant rosebuds.

"Elizabeth," he whispered into her ear. "Do not torture yourself. We were married too young. I knew her before I met you. These affairs happen. You are beautiful, wise—"

"Perhaps you should have married my little sister Frederika. She was witty and full of mischief. I feel I bore you."

Alexander thought of the little Frederika, squealing with joy as she ran round and round the squawking mechanical peacock as it tolled the noon hour. But then his mind strayed, thinking of the night's pleasures: a flash of Maria Naryshkina's black hair across her white breast, a pink nipple peeking out between the strands.

"Alexander! Are you listening?"

"You are hardly boring, my dear. You possess a quick mind and wisdom that I treasure. I regard you in high esteem—"

Elizabeth's face crumpled. "Wisdom and intelligence do not bring you to my bedchamber."

Alexander glanced up at the two servants standing motionless against the wall.

"You are dismissed," he said.

The servants bowed, exiting the door.

"Elizabeth, listen to me. I love you."

"I beg you, call me Louise as you did when we first met. I hate my Russian name now, for it brings no joy to us!"

"Really, Elizabeth!"

"Won't you do this small favor for me? How I hate Russia now without your love."

"Stop, Elizabeth. The servants will hear."

"I don't care. I hate Russia and I wish I had never married you!"

Alexander walked close to his wife, whispering in her ear.

"I shall make a compromise. I shall from now on call you Elise. A marriage of Elizabeth and Louise. Quite perfect for you. Yes, Elise. Do you like it?" He smiled, lifting her chin with his finger.

"Elise. It suits you."

Elizabeth pivoted her head away from him.

"Elise," he said. "You must find contentment in your life, dear one."

"I cannot without you, Alexander. You are my life."

Alexander took his wife's hand.

"My life . . . and *your* life can be shared with others."

"What are you saying, Alexander?"

He squeezed her hand. A mischievous smile flashed across his face.

"You may take a lover," he said, magnanimously. "I shall not object."

Elizabeth's mouth opened aghast. She withdrew her hand from his. "Alexander!"

"Oh, come now, Eliz—Elise! You know my principles of equality and freedom. They must apply to marriage as well! I cannot bear to see you suffer, my dear. You are my eternal friend."

"I don't *want* to be your friend! I want to be your wife!"

"And you shall be my wife forever until we die. But there can be others who share our beds."

"What a filthy idea, Alexander!" Elizabeth grimaced in revulsion. "I am not your grandmother Tsarina Catherine, with her many lovers."

Alexander drew back as if he had been dowsed with scalding water. *How dare she insult my grandmother . . . and me! When I, grand duke of Russia, give her permission to love another!*

"Good-bye, Elizabeth," said Alexander, turning on his boot heel without giving her another glance.

Grand Duke Alexander did not neglect his duties and the protocol of Catherine II's court. The next day after the argument with his young wife, he proposed an outing, a walk along the Neva River together, to demonstrate his devotion to his marriage, and to quell any rumors that might have reached his grandmother's ears.

The Neva was the heart of St. Petersburg, flowing in front of the Winter Palace. As great ships sailed into the Russian capital, the flags of every nation flapped in the sea wind. The granite embankments were bordered by sumptuous residences, as ornate as French lace. Swans floated along the canals that flowed from the Neva, winding their way through St. Petersburg.

As Alexander and Elizabeth walked, sharing a most uncomfortable silence, a green carriage with red trim drew next to them. The gilded moldings and smartly dressed drivers, their plumed hats waving, caught the eye of the fifteen-year-old grand duchess.

The coach, maneuvering around two slower wagons loaded with white cabbages, came to a partial stop. Inside, Elizabeth saw two young men—one extraordinarily handsome—with dark curly hair.

"Ah! Those must be the Polish hostages, the Czartoryskis," said Alexander.

"Hostages?" said Elizabeth.

"Peace is never simple. The Czartoryskis are an ancient Lithuanian family and wield great power—Adam Czartoryski could be the next king of Poland and lead a revolt."

"Against Russia?"

Alexander nodded. "Empress Catherine thought it wise to have the two Czartoryski brothers—Adam and Constantine—here at her court. That way she can quell any thoughts of rebellion among the Poles. In exchange she may return Czartoryski properties that Russia confiscated. Perhaps."

Elizabeth studied the lush curling sideburns of the elder of the two passengers, black hair contrasting with his ivory skin. As if he felt her eyes, he shifted his gaze toward the grand duchess.

Their eyes met. Adam Czartoryski, the older of the two brothers, did not avert his gaze but stared directly at the young woman.

"Oh!" she gasped, instinctively pulling out her fan and spreading it before her face.

Her husband noticed the motion and recognized the spark in Czartoryski's eye. It was the same fiery look he had exchanged himself with Princess Maria Naryshkina at court.

Alexander smiled at the new arrival to St. Petersburg.

Adam Czartoryski entered the hall of the Romanesque Tauride Palace, his riding boots clicking smartly on the marble floors. A servant took his gloves and cloak.

Alexander raised his hand. "Prince Czartoryski! Keep the gloves and coat. I'd like to take a stroll around the gardens."

Prince Czartoryski bowed. "Yes, of course, Your Excellency."

Alexander made a gesture of opening his arm behind his guest, guiding him toward the door. Together they walked past the white columns supporting the portico and down into the English-style garden, replete with canals and well-ordered rows of imported trees and shrubs.

"I feel the need of a long walk today, Prince," said Alexander, his blue eyes blinking in the bright sunshine. "We'll walk around the little harbor."

The grand duke led the way, his long legs stretching in contentment to be out of the palace and away from ivory hills of paperwork.

"It is brisk but just look at the St. Petersburg blue skies! We are in for a grand day!" The grand duke's cheeks colored in the cool air. "I know of course, Prince, that you and your brother were brought here as political hostages by my grandmother the Empress Catherine, on her order," said Alexander, his hands clasped behind his back. "In the strictest confidence—for I have heard you are an honorable man—I wanted to offer my condolences."

Adam Czartoryski hesitated, not sure how to take these words. *The grand duke of Russia apologizing to a Pole!* He took care with his reaction.

"I thank you, Your Excellency. But I must say that the empress and my treatment at court have thus far been nothing but delightful."

"Yes, yes," said Alexander, waving away his companion's remarks. "But I am certain you would far prefer to be in your native country, would you not? Rather than being here as a perpetual hostage!"

"Your Excellency." Adam Czartoryski stopped walking, forcing Alexander to stop as well. The Polish prince looked into the grand duke's eyes. "There is nothing more dear to my heart than Poland. There never will be. I will forever be dedicated to my mother country and stop at nothing for her independence."

"Bravo, Prince! You know your soul!" said Alexander, his face animated with joy. "So few men do! Let me be clear. I despise despotism. All men have the right to liberty."

Is he sincere? Or is this a test, a trap?

Alexander nodded. "Yes. You are wary. But you see, I was taught by Monsieur La Harpe, a Swiss revolutionary. I take as my models the works of Rousseau, Voltaire, Hobbes, and Locke. Thomas Jefferson is my hero. I know well the Declaration of Independence. And the French Constitution. I admire both."

Czartoryski's dark eyes blazed in astonishment and then joy. But he remained guarded, as such words could be construed as treason—even from the grand duke.

"I could never talk to Russians about these things." Alexander beamed at his new confidant. "But I pity Poland, Adam Czartoryski.

Yes, pity! The country that gave birth to such a great hero as Thaddeus Kosciuszko! That glorious general fought alongside the American patriots to win independence from Britain. Now he rots here in a St. Petersburg prison—for what? For defending his own Polish homeland from Russian tyranny!"

"The American Revolution has given hope to many nations," offered the prince, still struggling to comprehend what he was hearing. A Romanov condemning his own country's imprisonment of a Polish revolutionary!

"As has the French Revolution after a mangled and hideous birth," answered Alexander. "Still the dignity of the human soul and rights to liberty have resulted in its aftermath. Monsieur La Harpe schooled me in all the French philosophers and democratic ideals."

Czartoryski looked up at a patch of blue sky through the branches of the trees.

Can I have found a kindred spirit in this most unlikely of incarnations? The grandson of Catherine, our great oppressor? The future heir to the throne of Russia dares to say such things!

"I hope that you do not think this some trap for you, Prince Czartoryski," said Alexander, noticing his companion's reticence. "I assure you I am most sincere."

Czartoryski stopped walking. He allowed himself to scrutinize the grand duke, Polish dark eyes looking into Russian blue ones.

"I swear to you upon all that is holy that my repugnance for tyranny is sincere," said Alexander. "I could never share these opinions with my countrymen, except for my dearest friends. Nor speak of democracy. You cannot comprehend how I have longed for a friend such as yourself."

"You cannot know how your words astonish me," said Czartoryski, feeling the lifelong wall of hatred for all that was Russian crumbling. Or if not the entire wall—for that could never happen to a proud Pole—at least a fissure large enough for Alexander Pavlovich Romanov to extend his hand of friendship.

"What Russia has done to Poland is despicable," said Alexander. "Someday the Poles shall have their freedom if I become tsar of Russia."

"In that case," said the Polish prince, the last stumbling block to friendship kicked away, "I think we will become fast friends, Grand Duke."

The two clasped hands, forming a bond that would last a lifetime.

Adam Czartoryski would learn that his new friend had an open heart and a conscience that would not endure guilt and the suffering of humanity, be it the Poles, the serfs, or even his wife.

These were Grand Duke Alexander's good qualities. Prince Czartoryski would also learn the bad.

As the years passed, Alexander found friends who shared his liberal consciousness. He invited Adam Czartoryski, Paul Stroganov, Victor Kochubey, and Prince Alexander Golitsen to join him in what they came to call the Committee of Friends. At the Winter Palace and the Tauride Palace, they drank champagne and cognac and dined on oysters and caviar at midnight. They talked late into the night. Together they pondered the question of liberating the serfs and making Russia a more democratic nation.

The heat of the great ceramic stove chased away the cold of the northern night. Prince Czartoryski lurched to his feet, a glass of champagne in his fist, his black curls plastered flat against his forehead, his black eyes shining. "You, Alexander, will lead this empire into enlightenment! What Empress Catherine has initiated will be your legacy in the future."

He tipped up the crystal flute, finishing the champagne. Then he dashed the crystal glass to the floor.

"Here, here!" chimed in the rest.

The crash and tinkle of broken glass filled the room.

A servant in a starched jacket scurried to sweep up the shards.

Alexander looked at his friends, his eyes swimming with tears. He was warmed at Prince Czartoryski's words and by the ceramic stove—and far too much champagne, vodka, and cognac.

"And what of my father's reign?" asked Alexander, the liquor capturing his tongue. He smiled at his indiscretion.

Adam Czartoryski's eyes narrowed. He knew Paul Romanov would do his homeland no favors.

"We have understood that our empress intends the throne to be yours, not your father's, after her death," he said.

Alexander glanced at the door. He leaned forward in his chair to whisper.

"She has told me that she intends for me to be the next tsar, yes. But I think the empress believes she is immortal! She has not signed the manifesto she proposes, at least to my knowledge."

Adam Czartoryski exchanged looks with his comrades. His pale skin grew red, aggravated by liquor and temper.

"But I am not disheartened, comrades," said Alexander, wagging a finger unsteadily. "My friends! Perhaps . . . just perhaps the Imperial Court is not the place for me."

"What do you mean, Alexander?"

"Why should I be obliged to be in society with people I would not have as servants? Sycophants, all of them. The Russian Court! I have a need to find peace and refuge from such machinations!"

"But Alexander!" protested Paul Stroganov, realizing the grand duke was quite serious. "We need you! You know the reforms that must be made."

Alexander smiled sadly at his friend, remembering when they were children playing St. George and the dragon in the gilded rooms of the Winter Palace.

"I've been contemplating my future and the future of Russia. The Imperial Court is far too brilliant for my character. I am a colorless bird upstaged by strutting peacocks. I long for a more simple life."

He rocked his head from side to side. The cognac burned his throat and dulled his inhibitions. "I will not usurp my father's position as emperor. I'm not the strong man he is. Let the Romanovs roar!"

"But Alexander—" said Prince Golitsen. He lowered his voice to whisper. "Your father will destroy Russia if he gains the scepter! The people hate him. There are already rumors of assassination plans should he become emperor."

Alexander waved his hand, silencing his old friends. "I have sworn to renounce the throne, one way or another! I would rather live a quiet life on the Rhine with my family than take the scepter of Russia."

Every arm that had been reaching for a bottle, every glass that was moved toward waiting lips, froze. There was complete silence in the room except for the hissing in the ceramic stove.

"What do you say to that, Committee of Friends?" said Alexander, swallowing another gulp of cognac.

Adam Czartoryski broke the spell.

"We are grateful Empress Catherine has groomed Grand Duke Alexander to take the reins upon her death," he said. "Destiny is not ours to see but may the will of the wise empress prevail. You shall be tsar, my friend. And a bright future of brotherhood shall dawn."

Paul Stroganov clapped his friend on his back.

"After all, Alexander," said Stroganov. "It is not merely your welfare but that of all Russia's that our great empress seeks to protect."

Alexander grunted into his snifter. Adam Czartoryski shook his head.

"You will come around, old friend. You cannot foresee the future. Alexander, you will not forsake your Mother Russia."

"Or Poland," muttered Alexander, smiling crookedly. The grand duke swayed unsteadily on his feet. "That's what you mean, isn't it, my friend?"

Adam Czartoryski raised his glass of champagne.

"To our next tsar, Alexander I. *Vashe zdorovye!*"

"To your health!" chorused the room of young men.

The Committee of Friends went back to drinking until dawn.

Chapter 11

Winter Palace, St. Petersburg
September 1796

The Swedish ambassador and Grand Duke Paul stood at the windows of the Winter Palace, overlooking the vast parade yard. A shaft of autumn light grazed their profiles, spilling a golden pool just beyond them on the marble floor.

"No one could have chosen a better day for a royal wedding," said the Swedish ambassador, sipping his champagne. "Early September is glorious on the Baltic. The empires of Sweden and Russia share so much."

Grand Duke Paul grunted a reply that the ambassador didn't understand.

"I beg your pardon, Grand Duke?"

Paul turned toward the Swede, his bulldog face puckered and eyes bulging. "Will your boy king try to force my daughter to become a Lutheran? That is what I said. Now answer me."

The ambassador coughed, taking a moment to compose himself.

"Monsieur Platon Zubov, your imperial emissary, made all arrangements when he was in Stockholm. Of course the Empress Catherine has had ample opportunity to inspect every condition."

"Princess Alexandra will remain devoutly within the Holy Orthodox Church of our Mother Russia. And this emissary Zubov—he is a complete nincompoop."

"I— I am sure that our good King Gustavus will be generously fair and just—"

"You liar! All you ambassadors dance around the truth. I am her father. And I will tell you now, no daughter of mine will become a Lutheran! She was raised in the Holy Orthodox Church and will not give up her soul for a Swede. You tell that to your little boy king!"

With that, Paul threw his champagne glass to the marble floor and strode back into the palace.

The Swedish ambassador was left blinking at the retreating host.

These Russians! Always shattering their glasses!

Empress Catherine swept into the gilded ballroom of the Winter Palace, her gown and throat bedecked in glittering diamonds. She had spent many hundreds of thousands of rubles on this lavish wedding, for it spoke of Russian pride and future alliances that were vital to her empire.

It was seven o'clock and the bridegroom had not yet made an appearance.

The empress had worked hard to forge this marriage, this coalition with Sweden. The two nations were ancient enemies. Sweden's Charles XII, a brilliant and ruthless warrior in the beginning of the eighteenth century, had repeatedly attacked Russia, defeating them soundly in pitched battles. Peter the Great had invaded Sweden's territory on the Russian mainland, capturing the swamplands at the mouth of the Neva River on the Gulf of Finland and establishing the northern capital of St.

Petersburg. The animosity burned between the two countries, always threatening to burst into flames with the slightest gust of provocation.

The wedding of Catherine's thirteen-year-old granddaughter Alexandra to young King Gustavus would at last form an alliance. To host such an event in St. Petersburg, the brilliant city that Russia—Peter the Great—had created from a Swedish swamp was the perfect culmination of their combined history, at least in the empress's eyes.

But he, the Swedish king—the bridegroom!—is not here. What unspeakable rudeness! Where could he be?

No one but his closest advisors knew that the young Swedish king had barricaded himself in his apartments. He was refusing to marry the empress's granddaughter because she was sworn to remain Russian Orthodox.

In the meantime, flutes of champagne were replenished and the meal was postponed, hour by hour. One by one the courtiers felt the effects of the wine and lack of food. They began to speak too loudly, bump into one another, and erupt in giggles or indignation. The evening was stalled and the guests were simply drunk.

Grand Duke Alexander was among them.

"How ravishing Maria Naryshkina looks today!" said the grand duke to Adam Czartoryski.

The grand duke exchanged sultry looks with the Polish princess, glances brazen enough to make Czartoryski blush.

Czartoryski looked up to see Grand Duchess Elizabeth gazing down from the dais. Her grief-stricken face made him swallow in sorrow.

Why does Grand Duke Alexander torment her? In public no less.

Czartoryski nodded to Grand Duchess Elizabeth. She bit her lip and quickly looked away.

"I think the Grand Duchess Elizabeth has no equal," said Czartoryski, sipping his champagne. "She is exquisite in all respects."

"If only she would not present such a sad face at court," said Alexander. "Look at her. She knows full well of my affairs, even of the children I have fathered."

"I wonder if that isn't difficult for her, Your Excellency," said Czartoryski.

Alexander had shifted his gaze away from his wife to his mistress. He frowned. Maria Naryshkina was laughing, clearly enjoying her conversation with a dashing cavalry officer.

"I suppose the grand duchess must get lonely," Czartoryski ventured. "After all—"

"I cannot confine myself to one woman! Ridiculous expectations! You think her father and his father before him did not have lovers? Besides, I have told her that we are on equal footing."

"Your Excellency?" inquired Czartoryski.

"Ours is an emancipated marriage, Adam! Equality and freedom—I extend those principles to my wife. She knows this. Elise should take a lover. I would not object. I have stated so in writing! The grand duchess is a heavy weight around my neck. I am only nineteen. I will taste love from other women in my life!"

With this, the grand duke left his companion and made his way across the reception hall to his Polish mistress, who was laughing all too merrily in his opinion.

Adam Czartoryski saw the Grand Duchess Elizabeth lift her chin, watching her husband.

Never has there been a more beautiful consort in all Europe. Not just beautiful but sensitive. How I wish—

The grand duchess, who had not been drinking, shifted her gaze to the Polish prince who stared so ardently at her.

Adam Czartoryski nodded solemnly. The grand duchess inclined her chin and looked away.

But she glanced over her shoulder a minute later. The prince was still gazing at her, unable to look elsewhere.

The fact that the bridegroom refused to appear at the wedding was an acute insult to the empress. She found herself choking on bile, spewing rage.

By ten o'clock that night, no one had been able to persuade the Swedish king to make an appearance. The empress sat on her throne, enduring the humiliation in front of all the aristocracy of both Sweden and Russia. Women whispered cautiously behind fluttering fans while men grunted bellicose comments to one another. Swedes no longer mingled with the Russians, but congregated in small groups. Slowly those groups migrated toward each other until all the Swedes were gathered near the gilded doors, ready to make a hasty exit.

The empress at last rose from her throne to address her court. She opened her mouth but only unintelligible sounds tumbled out. Her face twisted as she staggered forward, collapsing on the marble floor.

For two months, Empress Catherine suffered, her condition gradually worsening, though she tried to carry out her imperial duties. The disaster of the botched marriage was never far from her mind.

"How could you have ab-ab-abdicated your responsibility!" stuttered the empress to her young lover, Platon Zubov.

"Lie back against the pillows, my Empress," pleaded Zubov.

Catherine waved her hands furiously. Her lips twisted, white and trembling. "My granddaughter's right—to practice her—her religion, you fool! Fool!"

Zubov opened his hands to her, his shoulders rising.

"But Empress!" he implored. "There were so many conditions in the contract—her dowry, the property holdings, the number of Russian staff who would stay on with her after the marriage, the—"

"But the Orthodox Church! E-e-rasing her R-russian heritage!" she groaned, lying back against the pillows.

Zubov did not know how to answer. Catherine had done everything in her power to curtail the Orthodox Church's influence. She had liberated hundreds of thousands of serfs belonging to the church, seized the priests' lands, and introduced the Enlightenment to Russia.

But now, suddenly, religion mattered—and Zubov's mistake had brought on an attack of apoplexy in front of the entire Russian Court. And before all the dignitaries of Sweden, their archenemy. Instead of making peace between the two rivals, he had humiliated his empress and the entire Romanov family.

Catherine struggled up from her bed.

"Allow me to call one of your ladies-in-waiting, Empress!"

"No! Leave me in peace. I must answer the call of nature. I shall do it—alone, by God!"

"Of course, my Empress."

Catherine disappeared into her dressing rooms. Zubov stared at the depression in the feather mattress left by the weight of her body.

His fingers traced the hollowed outline, still warm from her heat.

When Catherine did not return thirty minutes later, Zubov grew concerned. He asked the two ladies-in-waiting just outside the door to check on the empress.

The women found her lying on the ground in front of the toilet, facedown on the cold stone floor.

Catherine the Great, the most powerful and dynamic of all the Romanovs since Peter the Great, died two days later.

Chapter 12

St. Petersburg
November 1796

Only hours after Catherine the Great's death, Grand Duke Paul was notified in Gatchina. He mounted his horse, galloping toward the Winter Palace to claim his throne as emperor of the Russian Empire.

He was not unaccompanied. He led his Prussian-style cavalry and foot soldiers into the capital—*his* capital. Overnight the grandiose Winter Palace—full of exquisite art, music, and enlightened culture—became a fortress with sentry boxes manned every few yards of the perimeter.

The inhabitants of St. Petersburg watched in horror as their beloved palace, the jewel of Russia, was transformed into a military barracks, where chandeliers burned bright throughout the night as Tsar Paul wrote imperial edicts, bitterly erasing the mark of his mother, Catherine the Great.

"Bring me her personal papers!" he roared. One by one he burned all that he could, vowing to destroy the empress's mark on Russia. He reinstituted the traditional laws of succession, specifically primogeniture—the crown would pass always and only to the tsar's oldest son. He proclaimed there would be no more "reign of women."

Paul had long detested his mother's love of fashions, debauchery, and immorality. St. Petersburg under his hand would become more like Berlin, the Prussian capital—austere, disciplined.

Meals would be only for sustenance. Nobles must eat a frugal dinner at one o'clock. No tailcoats, no round hats, no folded-down boots. Hair must be cut round, powdered. No foreign books or music scores were permitted. Study in universities outside Russia was forbidden. Children could not venture into the streets without parental accompaniment. Ribbons would not be tolerated or any garment deemed frivolous. Side-whiskers were banned, as was the waltz.

Paul's spite had no limits, especially when it came to his son Alexander. He seethed with jealousy at his mother's intentions to pass him over and give the throne to young Alexander. He immediately demoted Alexander to a junior officer in the imperial cavalry.

And so began the reign of Paul Romanov.

Chapter 13

Winter Palace, St. Petersburg
April 1798

Grand Duchess Elizabeth picked up the quill, after brushing away her tears, and continued her letter to her mother in Baden.

> Most of the public detests him. People even say the peasants talk about him with disgust.
> He has said it is all the same to him if he is loved or hated, as long as he is feared. And he is. He is feared and hated, at least by everyone in St. Petersburg.

A French lady-in-waiting, Countess Golovine, knocked discreetly.

"Grand Duchess, the grand duke would like to enter and speak to you, if you are not ill disposed."

"Please send the grand duke in," said Elizabeth. She pressed her fingertips to her eyes, drying her tears. The morning sun glanced off the gold samovar, making a bright coin of light in the far corner of the room. The lady-in-waiting stood at a respectful distance by the door.

"Elise, I am sorry to disturb you."

"I was only composing a letter to my mother. What is it, Alexander?"

"I would like you to accompany me to the military review tomorrow. We will appear on the balcony together—"

"Oh, Alexander! I am so tired of military reviews. I am tired of curfews and simple meals and plain dresses, no ribbons or pearls. How I miss the balls and gowns—the gay music of Germany and France. Books! Your grandmother's literary salons and graceful society. All Russia misses Catherine!"

Alexander darted a look at the lady-in-waiting. He frowned.

"You are excused," he said curtly to the French woman.

"Yes, Your Majesty," said the woman curtseying deeply. The tumble of boiling water in the samovar punctuated the imposed silence.

When the door closed, Alexander said, "Elise, you must be careful what you say. She could repeat your words. My father would punish us most severely."

"The Countess Golovine? No, she, like everyone else in St. Petersburg, detests your father. He has stripped all that is beautiful and alive from this heavenly capital! Replacing it with what? A garrison with not a trace of the grandeur your grandmother instilled."

Alexander opened his hand, caressing his wife's cheek.

"It is all right, Elise. We will survive . . . and so will Russia."

Elizabeth clasped her husband's hand, kissing it.

"Will we?" she asked.

Chapter 14

Alexander Palace, Tsarkoe Selo
July 1798

Tsarkoe Selo, the emperor's village of summer palaces, was a two-day journey north from St. Petersburg. The entire court moved with the tsar, enjoying the festive months of nearly endless sunlight. The darkness had hardly time to settle into dim starlight when the fresh morning dawned.

"It will be a sultry day, I wager," said Igor Ivanovich, cranking open the white canvas awnings as the maids opened the windows to let in the morning air.

His companion Dimitri Petrov worked the lever on the adjoining awning, shading the duke's reception room. He sniffed the air and turned to his friend.

"You should visit the bathhouse, Igor Ivanovich! You stink of cabbage and pork trotters."

Igor lowered his nose to his own armpit and smiled.

"I'll keep the smell. It reminds me of who I am. A humble serf from the country sent to serve his emperor. A true Russian. And I like pork."

"Mercy! Here comes the grand duchess! Now she is an early riser."

"No one disturbs her sleep. If you know what I mean."

"How will Russia ever have an heir?" whispered Igor. "Such a beauty, too."

The two servants bowed low, studying the pebbles of the pathways, as Grand Duchess Elizabeth passed by on her morning walk with her lady-in-waiting Countess Golovine.

The morning heat had begun to seep through the lush leaves and grasses of the garden, infusing the paths with a heady perfume. Elizabeth could detect a delicate scent of rot—decaying petals not yet raked by the palace gardeners?

When she walked with her lady-in-waiting, all others were ordered to vacate the gardens, thus the consternation of Igor Ivanovich and Dimitri Petrov. Of course the order did not extend to the emperor himself or to his officers.

And certainly not to Alexander's best friend, Adam Czartoryski.

When Elizabeth came around the sharp bend of the hedgerows, she almost ran into the Polish nobleman.

"I beg your pardon, Grand Duchess," said Czartoryski, reaching out to catch her arms and steady the young woman.

"Monsieur! I beg you!" admonished Countess Golovine at the sight of Czartoryski's hands on her mistress.

"Oh, forgive me!" said Czartoryski, blushing beet red. "I—I ask a thousand pardons, of course. Are you sure you are quite all right?"

"Of course, I am perfectly fine, Prince Czartoryski," said Elizabeth, collecting herself. She laughed. "I'm really not the delicate violet the Romanovs make me out to be!"

"So clumsy of me, all the same, Your Highness," said Czartoryski. "I was deep in thought. I should have heard your steps."

"Deep in thought?" said Elizabeth.

"The smell of the jasmine in the gardens. My memories of Paris, Your Highness. I was there right after the revolution, with my mother. What swift changes, reforms. And now Napoleon brings changes again! It makes one's head spin."

"You were in Paris?" said Elizabeth, brightening. "Were you really? Would you be so kind as to describe it to me, monsieur? I think I shall never see the grand city now given this nasty business with the Corsican."

Adam Czartoryski drew in a quick breath.

"I should love to describe Paris to you, Grand Duchess! If you will permit me."

Elizabeth turned to her companion.

"*Comtesse Golovine, s'il vous plaît.* If you would escort us from five—no, ten paces behind. I should like to continue my conversation with Prince Czartoryski."

"Of course, madame."

The young couple walked ahead, Czartoryski's hands gesturing in delighted animation.

The lady-in-waiting saw her mistress's face in profile as she turned to listen to the stories of Paris. The grand duchess's eyes crinkled in merriment, a smile gracing her delicate mouth, so often downcast in sorrow.

Countess Golovine, who loved her German-born mistress with all her heart, rejoiced in the floral scent of Tsarkoe Selo. She could detect no rot whatsoever.

Grand Duke Alexander invited—*required*—Adam Czartoryski, his best friend, to spend the summer wherever Alexander and Elizabeth were in residence: Alexander Palace or Catherine's Palace or even Stony Island in the Neva.

Most evenings Alexander disappeared to be "at home," as he called it, with his Polish mistress. The grand duchess took her evening meal at the palace and was delighted when Czartoryski accepted an invitation to join her table that very same evening, after their walk in the garden.

"Tell me more about Paris," she implored her guest. "What would I see if I could travel there?"

The Polish prince bowed his head.

"A city of lively people, thirsty for change, for liberty. For enlightenment! The main streets are lined with enormous palaces gleaming with the magical green patina of copper roofs. Ah, the majesty of that city! Classical, Roman, Gothic, Renaissance—layer upon layer of history."

"Not like St. Petersburg, then," said the grand duchess.

"No, though St. Petersburg is majestic."

"Oh, really, Monsieur Czartoryski. You do not have to flatter St. Petersburg for my sake. It was a swamp before Peter the Great. As beautiful as it is now, it hasn't the history of the rest of Europe!"

Czartoryski smiled. "Well, then. Paris. Fine carriages carry ladies and gentleman across the many bridges—themselves exquisite monuments. The avenues and boulevards are flanked by the most exquisite *palais*, with mansard roofs, their copper trim colored with a green patina. Boats line the Seine and fishermen stand along the banks. And intoxicating aromas fill the air, such cookery! The French are great appreciators of beauty and taste, much like the Italians. The poorest meal composed of the simplest ingredients is made savory by the culinary sorcery of the Parisians."

"If you could take me there," ventured Elizabeth, taking a sip of wine, "where would you choose to walk?"

Czartoryski blushed. He wet his lips, considering such an unimaginable delight.

"Ah, what a pleasure to contemplate. The winding roads of Paris are a hopeless tangle where a wanderer can stumble into colorful markets, street hawkers, cemeteries, or even circuses. But the streets that line the Seine, flanking the Notre Dame, rising with Gothic splendor—that is where we would walk. In the shade of the great plane trees."

Elizabeth closed her eyes, imagining.

"We'd walk along the Seine on a summer evening and smell the sweetness of lilies or blue-flowered rosemary from the gardens. Below us water laps against the banks. We'd taste the scent of spun sugar and crepes from the vendors in the river breeze. Young men and women laugh as they walk near us, bursting into song, patriotic hymns of their new-found liberty."

Elizabeth drew in a deep breath.

"We would go in plain clothing," said Czartoryski. "We'd speak French just as we are doing now. No one would know us. We would walk in secret, a part of the republic."

Elizabeth looked into her companion's eyes.

No one would know us. If only this fantasy were true!

"We'd watch the swallows dart and swoop over the Seine as the last of the light faded. Along the embankment we'd see the silhouettes of lovers embracing in the moonlight."

Czartoryski watched the grand duchess's blue eyes shine in the candlelight. Something he said had brought tears to her eyes.

"Forgive me, Grand Duchess," he said, his languid smile disappearing. "I have upset you."

"Oh, no," said Elizabeth, dabbing her eyes. "I think I might be coming down with a bit of a cold."

Prince Czartoryski said quietly, "Grand Duchess. Please excuse the servants. I must speak to you in private."

Elizabeth made a gesture with her hand. The three servants who stood against the walls bowed and retired to the antechamber.

Czartoryski moved his chair close to his hostess's. He quietly took her hand, holding it as gently as if it were an injured dove.

"Let me tell you more about Paris, my dear grand duchess. Privately. There is so much more I want to express."

Countess Golovine dismissed the servants. She alone peeked into the grand duchess's bedchamber.

Two lovers, dark and fair, were entwined in embroidered linen. The woman's white neck turned as gracefully as a swan to kiss her lover, his curly dark hair matted with perspiration from lovemaking.

The woman laid her head on her lover's chest.

"I can hear your heart beating," she said. "Adam, it is racing!"

"It beats with passion. With joy," he said, looking down at her. "I love you and have always loved you, Elise. Since the morning I arrived and saw you walking along the Neva with Alexander—"

The grand duchess raised her white finger to his mouth. She touched his lips with her fingertips.

"Adam, we both love my husband," she said.

Czartoryski drew a deep breath.

"Yes, we both love your husband. Alexander is my best friend."

This time it was the grand duchess's turn to sigh. "He is my best friend too. There lies the problem."

Czartoryski stroked her cheek. Lifting her gently from his chest, he rolled her gently into the feather mattress. Then he smothered her mouth with kisses.

"Elise, my love," he whispered. "There is not room for our mutual best friend in this bed. Surrender to me, to us."

There was no more talk of friends that night.

Chapter 15

Winter Palace, St. Petersburg
May 1799

On the twenty-ninth of May, Grand Duchess Elizabeth delivered a baby girl. She was named Grand Duchess Maria Alexandrovna.

Alexander was delighted. His Elise was in full bloom in her maternity, joyful at last. Alexander craved peace and equilibrium above all. With the arrival of the baby into the Romanov dynasty, his father and mother would be at least temporarily appeased, although with Paul's decree of primogeniture, Alexander knew that a son must be produced.

Still, Alexander, who was deeply in love with his Polish mistress, smiled down at the infant he held in his arms.

"Do you love her?" whispered Elizabeth.

"Of course I love her. I love *you*," Alexander answered. "I love the joy that fills your spirit, that blossoms on your face."

Elizabeth felt the milk begin to flow in her breasts. She turned away blushing.

Countess Golovine did not approve of the enduring liaison between the grand duchess and Adam Czartoryski.

A night's visit, a month's dalliance . . . Bien sûr! *But this* . . . *this continues, almost a year now! It will never do, not for a grand duchess who must provide a legitimate heir!*

Countess Golovine had become very attached to Elizabeth since her arrival at the Russian Court and harbored a jealousy of the Czartoryski affair. She found it astonishing that Grand Duke Alexander doted on his newborn daughter. Could he not guess it was not his? Of course, anyone could see!

And this Polish prince, Alexander's best friend!

Still, she held her tongue. For royal dalliances, *affaires du cœur,* Countess Golovine knew how to be discreet. *Tant pis* for the grand duke who left his young wife alone every night in bed.

And in the end, it was not Countess Golovine who destroyed the peace Alexander so craved. It was Count Tolstoy who whispered the truth to Alexander's mother.

The empress had never cared for her daughter-in-law who was so adored by Catherine the Great. Grand Duchess Elizabeth was the niece of Emperor Paul's first wife. Moreover, Elizabeth's sister, Frederika, had married King Gustav of Sweden, the young king who had refused to marry thirteen-year-old Alexandra, causing the great consternation that contributed to Catherine II's stroke.

The gossip that a Polish prince was the father of her granddaughter sent the empress into a rage. But she controlled herself just enough to wreak careful destruction.

When the infant grand duchess Maria Alexandrovna was three months old, the empress requested that the child be brought to her apartments. Alone, unaccompanied by Grand Duchess Elizabeth, she insisted. The ladies-in-waiting dressed the infant in her best satin and swaddled her in a fine white lamb's-wool blanket and brought her to her grandmother's chambers.

Then the empress carried the infant girl to the emperor's study.

In the antechambers she smiled at the emperor's staff, including Count Rostopchin and Count Koutaissov.

"Isn't she a delightful child?" said the empress, pulling down the blanket so the military men could see the little grand duchess.

"But such curious coloring," said the empress. "Such dark eyes and hair."

A quarter of an hour later, the empress emerged, hurrying out of the study, carrying the bawling child. Count Koutaissov was summoned to the emperor's study. When he reemerged, he muttered to Rostopchin, "What made this wretched woman come to upset the emperor with her atrocious insinuations!"

When Count Rostopchin entered the room, he found the Tsar in a black rage.

"Go, sir, and write an order to immediately send Adam Czartoryski to the regiments in Siberia!"

"Your Majesty?"

"The empress has given me reason to doubt the paternity of my own grandchild! Count Tolstoy knows as much about it as anyone—at least we have a faithful servant in him!"

"Forgive me, Your Majesty. Please give your order consideration. If you send Czartoryski to Siberia, it will reflect on the virtue of the grand duchess, who is as virtuous as she is innocent. There is no proof of this accusation—"

"Have you seen the black eyes and jet-black hair of the infant girl?"

"Yes, she is indeed a beauty, Your Majesty."

"How do two blond, blue-eyed parents produce such a child? Hmm?"

"Your Majesty, did Peter the Great not have dark hair and eyes?" said Count Rostopchin. "Your Majesty, I beg you, as your advisor, think carefully upon this order. Adam Czartoryski is the grand duke's best friend and advisor. The grand duke is wildly content with his newborn daughter. Surely he would be the first to notice if the paternity was in question. You will cast aspersions upon Grand Duke Alexander if you post Czartoryski in Siberia. Tongues will wag."

Paul fumed, pacing the Persian carpets.

"What would you advise me to do, then? I never want to see that Pole's face again in this court!"

"We need an ambassador at the Sardinian Court. The king's secretary has written several times remarking of our diplomatic absence."

"Fine! Send Czartoryski away . . . Immediately!"

When Alexander learned of Czartoryski's assignment to Sardinia, he rushed to his wife's apartments in Pavlovsk Palace. Before the door shut behind him, Elizabeth saw the consternation on his face.

"Alexander! Whatever is the matter?"

"Adam Czartoryski is to be sent away!"

"Sent away?" said Elizabeth, her lips turning white. "Where? Whatever for?"

"An ugly rumor has filled my father's ears. He doubts my paternity of little Maria."

Husband and wife exchanged looks.

"He's being sent as ambassador to Sardinia." He took her hand in his. "Rostopchin declares my father insane with fury."

The two sat across from each other.

"Perhaps it is best Adam is sent away," said Alexander. "At least until my father has calmed down."

"Yes," said Elizabeth, squeezing her husband's hand. "If his fury persists, Adam might be killed."

"I will tell him to leave at once," said Alexander, releasing his wife's hand. "Before it is too late."

"I must see Elise before I leave!"

"No! Your life is in jeopardy. You must leave. Now."

"I must see her. She is the mother of my child. She is the love of my life!"

Alexander gripped his friend's shoulders.

"Look at me, Adam. No, look at me!" Alexander grasped Czartoryski's shoulders tighter, shaking him. "If my father learns you are still here, worse yet, that you visited Elise, you will be seized by the Imperial Guards and shot."

"I must see her! I must see my daughter—"

"I will not let Elise witness your death, Adam. She has suffered enough." Alexander's voice rose, the last words pinching high in his throat. "I will convey all to her. All. I promise that, my friend. Just leave before it is too late for all of us."

Part 2
Leaving Youth Behind

Chapter 16

Sarapul, Russia
September 1806

The night before my saint's day—St. Sophia, September 17—I prepared
myself. My trunks were already packed for the journey to the Ukraine
and my mother meant to send me off within two days' time.

The Cossacks had returned and I knew my chance had come. I
couldn't wait any longer, living in this hell my mother had created for
me. I took my saber off the wall, the one that Astakhov had given to
me as a plaything, though it was quite real.

"I will wear you in honor," I said, kissing the flat of the blade, which
I then returned to its scabbard.

The next day my mother gave me a gold chain. My father, who
came as soon as dawn's pink tinged the horizon, presented me with
three hundred rubles. My little brother Vasily gave me a watch.

I spent the day with my girlfriends: Raya, who fidgeted constantly
with her fat yellow braid; Olga, haughty and full of herself for no reason
except that she was a distant cousin of a wealthy prince; and Veronika,
who hardly said a word but listened intently, her pretty white brow
puckered.

Olga and Raya gossiped about the Cossack regiment stationed fifty versts from town to the west. Some days the men came in for supplies, ogling the girls of the town.

"Ah, but they are not like the southern Cossack tribe that rode through town a year ago," Veronika said. "Those men were dusky, dressed in red. They shaved their heads, leaving one long lock hanging on their forehead."

"Those Cossacks are Zaporozhian! The ones stationed here are Don Cossacks, from the Don River in the Ukraine."

Raya, who tended to stutter when she got excited, said, "The devils shave their head so that if they are k-k-killed and go s-s-straight to hell, the Lord can pluck them from the fiery furnace by their f-f-f-orelock, to save their barbaric s-s-s-souls."

"Why do you call them barbaric?" I asked.

"Because they are," said Olga, sniffing with indignation. "None of the Cossack tribes follow the Orthodox Church. They are heathens, Nadezhda! And they are known for pillage and raping innocent women. On horseback!"

Something about what she said made me recall a dream I had a few nights earlier. I touched my fingers to my lips, trying to recall.

"Nadya! Are you even listening?" said Olga, shaking me. "You look as if you are sleepwalking!"

The dream flew from my mind. I slapped at her hands. "We Russians are known for such treachery too! I have heard that in Lithuania, the Russian armies raped those girls and their mothers. They stole. Even the Imperial Guards!"

"No!" said Olga, pulling back her head like a viper ready to strike. "How dare you insult—"

"And as far as pillage, my father said, it is because the Cossacks are not paid enough to eat or given forage for their horses. They are promised the spoils of battle, that is all they have as payment."

My three friends stared at me.

"How dare you say such a thing about our country . . . our tsar!" sputtered Olga. "They must have provided for the Cossacks, for all their soldiers."

"I do not criticize the Tsar. But neither he nor his commanders nor any Russian in history has paid the Cossacks anything but a few token kopeks. The Cossacks depend on the spoils of war to feed their families."

My girlfriends had no answer to this. They knew I had been raised in the cavalry ranks.

"There is one Cossack more dashing than the others," ventured Veronika quietly. "Blond, with a fair complexion. He wears a blue tunic. His eyes are green as the summer grass."

"He has the most striking bearing," said Raya. "He w-w-walks like a centaur, noble in his bearing."

"You must be mistaken. The Cossacks are all Mongols," sniffed Olga. "Nobility! They are heathen barbarians. Stay away from them or they'll burn your soul!"

I stared at her, unable to speak. I had dreamt of a Cossack. Tall with green eyes. I was riding Alcides on Startsev Mountain . . .

I was tired of my girlfriends' company, their tedious gossip. The conversation was laced with ignorance. But how could they know anything beyond their noses? They had never left the town of Sarapul.

I kept thinking of my saber and Alcides awaiting me.

I kissed my friends good-bye and returned to my room.

I can't wait to be rid of this constant chatter! To hear the wind in the trees, the snort of my horse.

I could not wait to be rid of them, free of society and its rules for women.

I cut wide strips of linen to bind my breasts. Never being a particularly buxom girl, I could flatten my chest with little trouble.

I could bring little with me so I had chosen carefully. In my chest were five fine embroidered handkerchiefs my Ukrainian grandmother had made me, a dowry present.

Marriage! I will never marry, ever. What would marriage do but to bind me further into female slavery.

I folded the dainty handkerchiefs carefully and put them into my small bundle.

That night I knew I was saying a significant farewell to my parents—although they had no idea what I was about to do. At eleven o'clock in the evening I went upstairs to my mother.

This may be the last time I ever see her.

I kissed her hands and clasped them to my heart—something I had never done before. She was so surprised at my display of affection she kissed me on the forehead.

"Go with God," she said.

Does she have a premonition I am leaving forever?

I clutched her blessing to my heart and crossed the garden to my rooms. I was relegated to the ground floor of the garden house now—for our family had grown. My father, who had permanently tumbled from grace in my mother's eyes, had his apartment on the second floor of the garden house. When he was home.

What I could not fit into saddlebags was stuffed into a cloth satchel that could be rolled across the back of the saddle or slung across my back. I pulled the saber from its scabbard, studying it.

Would I actually kill a man with this blade?

When I heard footsteps outside, I started, nearly slicing my finger. I put the sword back into its scabbard and opened the door.

"Papa!"

"What is wrong with you, daughter? You look pale."

"I am fine, Father. Quite fine indeed."

"It is getting cold and damp. Why do you not have the servants heat your rooms?"

Then he paused and gave me a stern look.

"Why do you not order Efim to run Alcides on a lunge? There's no getting near him. You haven't ridden him for a long time, and you won't permit anyone else to do it. He's so restive. He rears up even in his stall. You must exercise him, Nadezhda. This is not good horsemanship."

I looked into my papa's eyes. This was my last good-bye.

"I will ride Alcides tomorrow. I promise, Papa."

"You seem melancholy, my friend. Good night, go to bed," said Papa. He kissed my forehead. His eyes were soft and loving. He pulled me to his chest with warm arms, pressing me to his heart.

I began to tremble. I stepped back from his embrace so he couldn't feel me shaking. I grabbed his hands and kissed them.

"See! Your lips are like river ice! You are chilled through," he said.

I laughed, kissing his hands again.

"Then let me freeze your fingers with my kisses, dear Papa!"

He snatched his hand away, pulling me back to his chest in a hug.

"*Spokoynoy nochi*," he said softly. Good night.

He left and I listened to his boots strike each wooden step as he climbed to his apartments.

I knelt to the ground, my tears falling where his boots had rested just moments before.

How he will grieve when he realizes I am gone!

Later, when all was quiet in the little house, I took out my scissors, opened its jaws, and captured a long lock of my hair between the sharp blades. I took a deep breath. There would be no turning back now. Hair spilt in swirls to the floor.

I brushed the bits of hair from my shoulder and donned the Cossack uniform. I stared at myself in the mirror. I looked like a young man with light-brown hair, a somewhat swarthy complexion, and hazel eyes.

No one would recognize me as a woman.

I stretched my arms out to the icon above my hearth, the Mother of God, though I had never been particularly religious. "Bless me," I asked. Then I closed the door of my family home, wondering if I would ever see it again.

The moon was full, illuminating the forests and filling the lakes with liquid silver.

Efim the stable boy met me at the edge of the forest on the road to Startsev Mountain. He had been easy to bribe. A serf had little chance of ever earning money. He had taken the coins eagerly. Now he stood, waiting, my beloved horse beside him. Alcides snorted, seeing me approach on foot.

"He is restless," said Efim. "He reared twice as I stood here waiting for you. You might get hurt."

"Then help me mount him quickly. I will gallop the vinegar out of him on the hill road. He will settle down quickly enough."

I dug in my cloth satchel. "Here's the rest of the money I promised you. Now help me strap the bag behind the saddle."

He bowed and took the money. Then, as he tied the knots fastening the bag, he asked, "Is there . . . is there a message I should give your parents?"

"Help me up, Efim."

"But what shall I say?"

"Nothing, Efim. No message."

I reined Alcides around and took off at a gallop. Away from home.

Chapter 17

Mikhailovsky Castle, St. Petersburg
November 1801

Alexander reined his stallion to a halt at the green-watered moat surrounding Mikhailovsky Castle. He drew in a breath. He found the new castle, a medieval fortress, unsettling. The Moika and the Fontanka rivers flanked the castle, with two man-made canals connecting the rivers to form the perimeter moat.

Impenetrable. Like my father.

Everything about the emperor's new residence reflected his father's fears of assassination or coup d'état. The original whimsical wooden structure that Peter the Great's daughter Tsarina Elizabeth had treasured was razed to build Paul's fortress. The new Mikhailovsky Castle was built around an octagonal courtyard where Emperor Paul could amass a small army in case of attack.

Alexander spurred his stallion across the drawbridge. The horse's hooves echoed on the wooden planks, making him prance nervously. Each hoof strike made him leap higher, his eyes ringed white. The grand duke sat deep in the saddle, holding his breath as they clattered off the drawbridge and into the castle courtyard.

"Grand Duke, greetings," called out Count Nikita Panin. Alexander remembered Panin from lively dinners where he had championed Russia's alliance with England. Now the count had risen to become the emperor's vice-chancellor of foreign affairs, despite his unabashed love for the English.

As Alexander swung down from his horse, a stable boy caught hold of the reins.

"Your horse shows good spirit," said Panin jocularly. "I expect he has never seen a drawbridge before."

"You witnessed that, General Panin? I thought the brute would throw me into the water!"

"You handled him well," said Panin. Alexander noticed the approving gleam in the general's eyes. The grand duke's breast swelled with pride. So rarely did anyone admire Alexander's horsemanship, especially on his father's turf.

"The emperor expects you in his apartments," said Panin.

"Thank you," said Alexander, giving the hem of his uniform jacket a discreet tug. He brushed his sleeves and aligned his jacket cuffs.

"I shall accompany you," said the general. "Shall we go?"

Alexander nodded curtly. His attention was focused on the bronze equestrian statue of Peter the Great. The original inscription, "Petro Primo Catherina Secunda," "Peter I Catherine II," was gone. A new marble pedestal read "Like Great Grandfather, the Great Grandson."

As if Papa could ever scratch out his mother's mark on Russia and replace it with his own!

Alexander felt the general's eyes studying him, as palpable as a thin veil tossed over his skin.

At last, Panin said, "Please, Grand Duke. This way. The emperor awaits."

"Ah! You have arrived," said a voice from the top of the spiral stairs. "Come in, Alexander. Come in."

"What do you think of my new castle, Alexander?" said the emperor as his son entered the private apartments. "I have only just occupied my rooms this month."

Alexander glanced about his father's apartment, quite small in comparison with any other royal suite. The gold moldings contrasted with the stark white of the walls. A door that overlooked the Romanov private chapel of St. Michael's stood ajar, offering a glimpse of the golden iconostasis and, above that, a fresco of St. Michael hovering on the vaulted ceiling.

"Is it not splendid?" said the emperor. "Look at the chapel. We shall worship there on Sundays together in privacy." Then he waved a hand toward the window. "And look how the waters sparkle from the moat—much more light than the Winter Palace, that bloated corpse."

Alexander smiled.

He is in a good humor, grace be to God! If only it could last.

"You have created an elegant palace," he said. "Encased by a formidable fortress. I do not know that I have ever crossed a true drawbridge. My stallion was quite nervous."

Paul puckered his forehead, scowling at his son.

And the storm clouds gather in an instant. Can I never say anything right?

"What warhorse cannot cross a drawbridge, or what cavalryman cannot ride him without hesitation?" snapped the Tsar. "And it is *not* a fortress, although given the reports of treason that abound, I have every right to be concerned."

"What reports are those, Father?" asked Alexander. "Who has spoken of plots?"

"I am not such a fool to disclose those who tell me what others would keep hidden!" his father snapped. "Mikhailovsky Castle will serve its intended purpose. I have the safety and seclusion I need to confer with my most intimate advisors." Paul gestured to the three military officers who had been standing apart from the father and son: General Panin, Count Alexei Arakcheyev, an old acquaintance from Alexander's childhood days at Gatchina, and Count Pyotr Pahlen, governor-general of St. Petersburg.

"These three," the emperor continued, his eyes boring into his son.

Alexander's skin prickled under his father's scrutiny. He was keenly aware that General Panin had moved and was now standing just behind him, as if allying himself with the young grand duke.

"Yes, my dear son," said Paul, his mouth twitching. "There are plots on my life. Some have even suggested that *you* are suspect. They suggest that you, my own son, would wish to see me dead and yourself on the throne of Russia."

"Papa!" said Alexander. "I wish no such thing, I swear it! Who are the traitors who accuse me—"

"Ha!" said Paul, wrinkling his nose as if he smelt something foul. "As the Englishman says, 'Thou dost protest too much,' Alexander. Did you and my mother not plot? Conveniently blotting me out of my nation's future?"

"I—"

"I know all about it. A manifesto drawn up in September 1796, when you were nineteen. Do not pretend you do not know, Alexander. You have never learned to lie persuasively."

"Yes, I knew of such a document, Your Highness," said Alexander, lifting his chin in defiance. "It was the Empress Catherine's proposal, not mine. I have never wanted to usurp your throne. Never!"

The Tsar's eyes narrowed. His mouth tightened.

"Swear an oath to me, Alexander. Get on your knees and swear by Archangel Michael!"

Paul pointed to the open door, looking down onto his private chapel.

Alexander dropped to his knees, facing the image of St. Michael painted on the vaulted ceiling.

"I swear my allegiance to you, my father, Tsar Paul! I swear it!" He bowed his head and repeated, "I swear my allegiance to our most gracious Tsar Paul, ruler of all the Russias!" He crossed himself according to the Orthodox tradition.

Will he never have faith in me?

Paul looked his son up and down, as Alexander rose to his feet.

"No," he said, closing the door to the chapel. "No, Alexander. You haven't the guts to be an emperor. A tsar must make impossible decisions quickly and decisively. Fearlessly, Alexander! Your sail would flap in the wind, as you stood weighing this result against the other until the beating canvas was torn by the gales."

Alexander's face burned. He ventured a glance at the three officers. All three lowered their eyes in embarrassment at the browbeating of the young tsarevitch.

And the Tsar was not yet done.

"Your blood is too thin, Alexander, your conscience too brittle to command this mighty empire." Paul snorted a derisive laugh. "Your younger brother Nicholas should wear the Russian crown. Now there is a military man in the making!"

Alexander flinched under the comparison.

Nicholas is a child! Four years old! Given to tantrums, breaking toys, and striking out at anyone who defies him. Is this the son my father prefers?

Alexander said nothing.

"There are changes in the wind, Alexander," said the Tsar, taking a deep breath. "I have ordered the British ambassador Lord Whitworth home with his tail between his legs."

Alexander sucked in his breath, aghast.

"Lord Whitmore sent back to London? But the British have been our allies, our international trade depends on—"

The Tsar cut him off with a gesture. "The British are no longer our friends. We will sign a pact with Napoleon. Then we shall meet the British, defeat them, and then on to Constantinople. Napoleon will rule the West and Russia the East. Russia and France! There will be no defeating us."

"Napoleon? But— But what of our allies?"

"The devil take them! We shall rule the East."

Alexander heard boots shuffle and sensed Panin's uneasiness just behind him.

Panin worked hard to establish diplomacy with England. What can he possibly think of my father's ravings?

"You are dismissed, Alexander," said the Tsar, with a flap of his hand.

Alexander bowed to his father. General Pahlen escorted him out the door.

"We must talk, Grand Duke," whispered the general.

Chapter 18

I gave Alcides his head and we galloped in the moonlight toward the Cossack camp. He needed to expend his restless energy from not being ridden—and I needed to put my home and my parents behind as quickly as I could. There was no time for second thoughts, no time for turning back. The autumn wind stung my face as we raced through the dark.

Freedom! A precious gift from heaven.

The road to the Cossack camp led through a dense forest. I slowed Alcides to a walk as we entered the dark silence of the woods. A frigid north wind began to blow and I tucked my chin under the rough wool of my tunic. My fleece hat was pulled down so low I could barely see where we were going. But Alcides was sure-footed and he followed the road. Hours passed. At last, at dawn, he smelled the horses of the encampment and broke into a trot.

In a few minutes, I could smell the toasted warmth of kasha steaming in kettles over the fire. The colonel and officers were gathered in front of the headquarters tent, eating the hot porridge. They were talking intently when I rode up.

Silence fell as they looked up at me. They took in the colors of my Cossack uniform, not blue like that of the Don Cossacks, but the red of the Zaporozhian, from the steppes of the Ukraine, my mother's homeland.

"What's your regiment?" were the first words I heard.

I answered the colonel in the deepest voice I could muster.

"I do not have the honor of belonging to any regiment, Colonel."

The men's eyes grew wide and suspicious. I felt them inspecting me, my uniform, my saddle, and especially Alcides.

"I don't understand you. You are not enrolled anywhere?"

"No, I'm not."

"Why not?"

"I haven't the right."

"What! What does that mean, a Cossack without the right to be enrolled in a Cossack regiment! You wear a *cherkesska*. And Cossack boots and fleece cap. What kind of nonsense is that?"

The men began to murmur and mill about me. I wondered if they had guessed I was a girl, an impostor. As they pressed closer, I wondered if hands would reach for me, pulling me off my horse.

"I am not a Cossack," I said.

"Well, then who the hell are you?" demanded the colonel. "Why are you in Cossack uniform and what do you want?"

"Colonel," I said, reining Alcides away from the men who gathered close beside me, "I desire the honor of being enrolled in your regiment until such time as we reach the regular army."

The murmurs grew louder.

The colonel grunted. "But just the same I have to know who you are, young man. And are you not aware that nobody can serve with us except native Cossacks?"

There was a growling laughter from the men. I felt my childish dreams shatter.

No! I cannot have risked so much to be refused!

"And I have no such intention, Colonel. I am only asking you for permission to travel to the regular army in the dress of a Cossack serving with you or your regiment. As to your question about who I am, I will only say what I can. I am from a noble family. I have left my father's house and am on my way to serve in the army without my parents' knowledge or volition. I cannot be happy in any calling except the military. If you won't take me under your protection, I'll find some way to join the regular army on my own."

The colonel took in my words. Something I said must have struck a chord. "I haven't the heart to refuse him," said the colonel, turning to another Cossack who had remained silent, seated in the shadows. "Anatoli! What shall I do?"

The Cossack rose. He was one of the tallest men I had ever seen. He looked at me with shocking green eyes. I felt as if I had been shot.

The tall man scrutinized me, drinking in my features as his eyes ran across my face, my body. I saw his nostrils flare, the muscles of his face tense.

Then the faintest trace of a smile.

"And why should you refuse him? Let him come with us. He is but a boy."

"He might make trouble for us."

"Let him join us. His parents are nobility. They will be grateful to us for giving him refuge. With his hardheadedness and inexperience, if you turn him away he will surely come to grief. These forests are dangerous, especially for one as young as he."

I saw the tall Cossack was giving me an advantage. I plunged in. "I will ride alone if you do not take me. I shall not turn back, I swear it!"

The colonel looked at me, shaking his head.

"Very well, young man. But I warn you that we are now on our way to the Don, and there are no regular troops there in the Ukraine."

"I don't care. I beg you to take me with you."

"Shchegrov! Give the lad a horse from our stables."

"Yes, sir," said a small man beside him.

The tall Cossack moved toward Alcides and me. He ran his hand over Alcides's forelegs and then his hindquarters. Alcides quivered under his touch.

Then he moved to take my horse by his reins. "I'll take him, lad. I like Circassian bloodlines."

"Get your hands off my reins," I snapped at him. He looked into my eyes with anger. I met him with the same.

"Colonel!" I said. "I have a horse, a good one here. Circassian. I'll ride my own, if you will permit it." The colonel burst out laughing.

"So much the better, so much the better. Ride your own horse. What's your first name anyway, my gallant lad?"

"Aleksandr Vasilevich Sokolov," I lied, taking my father's and brother's name in one mouthful and inventing the surname.

"Aleksandr Vasilevich, on the march you will always ride with the first troop where I can keep an eye on you. You will dine and be quartered with me. Go on now. Eat some kasha to warm yourself. My orderly will take your horse for water and forage. We will be moving out almost immediately."

The tall Cossack finally let go of my reins and I surrendered my horse to Shchegrov, who had another inferior horse in tow. I felt the tall Cossack's eyes scrutinizing Alcides's conformation as he was led off.

Alcides whinnied at parting with me.

"A fine horse," he said. "He likes you. I trust you are a good enough rider to do him justice?"

"We do all right together," I said.

How will we do in the battlefield? What do I really know about a Cossack regiment?

"Aleksandr Vasilevich Sokolov," said a voice. It was the burly cook who gave me a metal cup full of steaming buckwheat. I took a wooden spoon from his hand, shoveling the porridge into my mouth. Never had anything tasted so good.

Half an hour later I was mounted with a heavy saber in my hand. It was nothing like the imaginary weapon I had wielded, running through our gardens in Sarapul, shouting, "Charge!"

My muscles were not accustomed to such weight. Every muscle shook with exertion. I could not hold my saber properly but tried with all my might to lift it high when the colonel and captain rode by me.

The strange dialect of the Cossacks, their laughs, and jokes were foreign to me. They spat and cursed. Every once in a while I'd see a soldier's hand reach for his privates, scratching an itch.

As I urged Alcides forward, he pranced, flicking his ears at the new sounds of the horses around him, the flapping banners, and the lance point on his right flank.

"You sit your horse well, Aleksandr," said the green-eyed Cossack from my left flank. "You have a fine Circassian waist that sets off the horse."

The other men laughed.

"He does indeed! Comely as a girl," said one rider.

I blushed, the rising heat scorching my neck and cheeks. I turned around in my saddle to see my tormenter, the green-eyed Cossack, as tall as Peter the Great.

He laughed, riding his horse flank to flank with Alcides.

"Aleksandr Vasilevich, indeed!" he whispered in my ear.

My blood froze.

He knows I am a girl. A single word from him and I will be sent home. This man, this one could ruin my life.

"Who are you?" I asked him.

"Your worst nightmare, Aleksandr Vasilevich," he said, spurring his horse forward. He called over his shoulder, "My name is Anatoli Denisov. Don't you remember me?"

"Should I?"

Denisov threw me a curious look, his brow furrowed. Then he laughed.

"To the right by threes!" shouted the captain.

The men in the front section burst out in song, their rich voices singing the Don Cossacks' favorite song, "The Soul Is a Good Steed."

Despite the cold morning, dust spun up on the road under the horses' hooves. Alcides arched his neck, sensing the excitement. He was my only connection to home.

As we moved southwest toward the Don plains and the Cossacks' homeland, I left my childhood behind forever.

The officers and I were all quartered together. The canvas tents were set close to one another. I was assigned to the colonel's tent.

I waited until dark to make water. I felt as if I would burst even though I had been careful not to drink too much from my canteen. I walked from camp in the cover of night to make sure no one could catch sight of me as I squatted in the woods.

As it was already late autumn, I did not worry about undressing in front of the two captains and the colonel who shared the tent. I hoped that I would not dream or call out in the night. I fingered the short tufts of my hair reassuring myself that I looked more boy than girl.

No one spoke when the lantern was snuffed for the night. The men passed gas freely, insulted each other coarsely, and laughed in gruff voices. But there was no real talk. My companions fell asleep immediately. I listened to their raucous snores until I, too, fell into a deep sleep.

Before light had pierced the canvas, men stirred beyond our tent flaps. I heard the gurgle of the water poured into the enormous samovars for tea and boiling kasha, and the crackle of the fire. I could hear the stamp and snort of the horses, tethered to their picket lines. As I rubbed the sleep from my eyes, I heard the creak of the hinges of the hay wagon as the feed was pitched to the nickering horses.

My new life had truly started.

I walked down to the stream to wash the soot and dirt from my face. I cupped my hands into the icy water, dousing my face and neck in water. Far downstream I saw a movement. In the pale sunlight was a nude figure, clothes in a heap beside him. It was Denisov bathing. He shook the water from his blond hair like a dog and began rubbing himself dry with his tunic. His muscles formed knots in his back between his shoulder blades, his waist curved in like a scimitar. His left ribs were marked with a pink scar, running from his chest to his back.

I turned my back on him, splashing my face until my cheeks stung. When I looked back he was gone.

We had little time to eat. The kasha was mostly millet and buckwheat, but every day it was different depending on what had been procured from villages as we passed through. Just like the horses' fodder, our diet depended on what could be requisitioned along the way from begrudging farmers. Often enough our kasha had bits of twigs and chafe in it, even sand and small pebbles.

Still the grains sustained us and I grew lean and muscled. The first few days I saw little of Denisov since he was, as I learned, a scout who rode ahead of our regiment.

At night he squatted in the shadows beyond the light of the campfire, watching me silently, his green eyes hungry as a wolf.

Chapter 19

Alexander's bedroom at Mikhailovsky Palace looked out over a grove of linden trees. The torches on the drawbridge below leapt, flaring with gusts of wind. The dancing flames reflected in the dark waters of the moat, orange-yellow against black.

The young grand duke moved away from the cold window and returned to his book, Voltaire's *Brutus*, a play greatly admired by his old tutor La Harpe.

Voltaire, the old radical, had maintained a friendship and correspondence with Catherine the Great. Wistful both for his grandmother and for the guidance of his tutor, Alexander read the play to while away the long Russian night.

Now he drew a deep breath, expelling it into the cold air of the room. He remembered a long-ago night, a father and his young son nestled snugly under bearskins, their ears and noses red with the cold.

Alexander was yanked from his reverie by the crash of doors flung open. He jumped to his feet, lunging for his sword. He recognized two personal servants of his father.

And right behind them, the Tsar himself burst through the doorway.

"What are you up to?" demanded Paul. "Planning my demise?"

"Father!" Alexander said, dropping the sword. "All I am doing is reading!"

"Ha! Let me see," said the Tsar, seizing the book. He scanned the spine. "Ah! Just as I suspected. Voltaire, my mother's old friend. I know the play too well."

"Perhaps you can tell me the ending, then," said Alexander, shaking with both fear and rage. "For I have not finished it, Papa!"

Paul ignored him, flipping through the pages. His hands were brutal, like a dog scratching wildly to unbury a bone.

"Ah! Here it is. 'Rome is free: that is enough. . . . Let us give thanks to the gods!'"

"I beg your pardon, Your Majesty?" said Alexander, his fingernails digging into the palms of his hands. "What has that got to do with—"

"Treason! Words to incite rebellion—are you plotting along with others?"

Paul hurled the book to the floor and departed.

Alexander stood stunned, staring at the little book on the Persian rug. He picked it up, holding it with trembling hands.

My father is truly mad!

A few minutes later, Ivan, Paul's servant, returned.

"Pardon my intrusion, Grand Duke. The Tsar has commanded that I read you a few pages from *The Life of Peter the Great.*"

"Now?" asked Alexander.

"Yes, Your Excellency. At once."

Alexander sat down in a chair as the servant remained standing.

"The tsarevitch resented his father. . ." he began in French.

Alexander immediately recognized the passage. The story of the Tsarevitch Alexis, accused of rebellion against his father, Peter the Great.

"You do not have to finish. I know very well what became of Prince Alexis! I am not wholly ignorant of my family's—"

The servant continued his reading.

"Tsar Peter persuaded his son to return from sanctuary in Austria under the care of Charles—"

"Yes, yes. The tsarevitch is duped and returns to Russia, thinking his father has forgiven him. Alexis is imprisoned and tortured. He dies in prison. By Christ's name, stop!"

But Ivan did not pause in his reading until he had finished the passage detailing the exquisite torture and death of Tsarevitch Alexis. When he was done reading the gruesome scene, he closed the book with a thump and bowed as he backed out the door.

Alexander slept little that night. He thought of Pahlen's conspiratorial whisper, Panin's glittering eyes.

My father may be mad, but he is right. A plot is afoot, I can smell it. I should join them, what choice do I have? My father will never abdicate. He will murder me first.

My dearest Elise,
I send my brother with this missive in the utmost confidence. My lips pressed the paper in anticipation of touching your beloved hands.

How I grieve not to be by your side and stroke the black curls of our darling baby girl.

My brother tells me that she indeed looks like me, an identical image.

Our baby girl! Never have I had such joy as you have given me. How I long to hold my daughter in my arms again. To hold you, my dearest Elise.

Sardinia's charms lie not in the court, but the enchanting blue sea that surrounds this island. And the green hills dotted with white sheep remind me of Tuscany.

If only we could walk hand in hand here. I walk the coast alone, the wind tugging at my jacket. I look north, across the sea toward Russia. The wind here blows from the west, but occasionally it turns and comes from the north, fresh and clean—from St. Petersburg, I fancy. It is your breath it carries in its whistling sigh.

Ah, and when I was in Rome—its grand beauty—I thought constantly of you. As I did when I walked along the Arno in Florence. Let me take you to every great city on this planet!

Alexander has written me of another plan, should he become tsar. He wishes to abdicate the throne, not to Constantine but to Nicholas! Then he would divorce you and marry Maria Naryshkina. They would sail on to America where they could live in peace.

And we would be free to marry, my darling Elise, and remain in Russia—or Poland if I could so convince you. I would live anywhere with you, my love.

Please be my wife.

Yours in love always,

Adam

The little Ethiopian door servant was ordered to stand outside the grand duchess's door. In her hand Elizabeth clutched Adam Czartoryski's letter, shaking it in rage in her husband's face.

"Alexander!" The grand duchess began, her voice rising in anger, as soon as the last servant had left her bedchamber. "How dare you confer with Adam Czartoryski before you address me with your plans!"

Alexander walked toward his wife, taking the letter from the grand duchess. He cupped her hands in his.

"What news do you have of our mutual friend? Has he proposed to you?" said Alexander, a broad smile on his face.

Elizabeth dropped her mouth open, aghast.

"Is this really how you intended to break the news of a divorce? How dare you—"

Alexander squeezed his wife's hands gently.

"Elizabeth! I have been honest with you from the beginning. I have no wish to be tsar. I see what it has done to my father—he's raving mad, crazed with power! I want to live a simple life."

Elizabeth stared at her husband, incredulous.

"Along with Adam Czartoryski, I have no truer friend than you," he said.

Elizabeth tore her hands from his as if they were on fire.

"I don't want to be your friend, Alexander! I don't want to be left behind in Russia, a divorced empress. Take me to America, not that Polish whore!"

"I will not allow you to insult her, Elise," said Alexander, the kindness melting from his face. "She and I live together as man and wife. She will have a child soon."

Elizabeth turned away, hiding her face.

"How you torture me, Alexander! You do this because I cannot conceive with you. But you are so rarely in my bed, how can I?"

Alexander's face contorted in anguish.

"Elise!" he groaned. "How can I make you understand! I do this because I am not meant to be an emperor. You know me, my darling. I am not the strong man Russia craves, the iron fist she needs!"

"But what of the reforms you planned?"

For a moment, a smile touched his lips.

"Yes, Russia needs reforms . . . badly. Oh, Elise! Don't torture me. You know how I love my country."

"Yet you talk of abandoning it!" she said. "And running off with a Polish countess who is already married."

"I can't stay here and rule. I'm not my grandmother, strong and ruthless. I'm not even my father, who is an impossible tyrant. Russia has grown accustomed to a rough hand on the reins.

"I want to live a simple life, free from the wars and the politics that a tsar must contend with every second of his life. And I want to be monogamous—"

"Oh, Alexander! How long will that last?" Elizabeth jerked her tear-damp chin up at him. "Until you see a pretty actress or a new lady at court you have not bedded down?"

Alexander's jaw tightened. He began to pace the room, his hands clasped behind his back.

He stopped, looking into his wife's eyes.

"Do you not love Adam Czartoryski?"

Again Elizabeth tried to hide her face.

"Look at me, Elise!" he said, grasping her by the shoulders. "I will do you no harm, but I will have Maria Naryshkina as my lover. Just as you have Adam. Look at the precious daughter you—"

"You *thrust* me into Adam Czartoryski's arms. And him into mine. Do not pretend you did not."

"Do you love him, Elise? Answer me that. This situation must be remedied."

"Yes! Yes, I love him. But I love you best, Alexander. I always shall. I cannot leave you, my husband. Ever."

Alexander regarded his wife, chewing at the inside of his cheek.

"Did Maria Naryshkina put you up to this?" asked Elizabeth, her face coloring with rage. "You owe me this much."

"She wants me to divorce you, yes."

"There it is. She would be empress. Empress, yes. But would she really sail to America with you without a royal title? Would she leave all she owns, her prestige in St. Petersburg's court, to marry a man who could be tsar but refused?"

"Stop, Elise!"

"No! No, Alexander, I shan't stop until you answer me! Do you really think that Princess Naryshkina will sacrifice everything in order to leave Russia with you?"

"She would. She loves me passionately."

Elizabeth uttered a bitter cry.

"You are a fool, then. You do not know women—certainly not *that* woman—as well as I do. I tell you she will be unfaithful to you in the future even if you *are* tsar of all Russia."

"Stop!" commanded Alexander. "Stop this now!"

Elizabeth shook her head bitterly. "Oh, no! She will leave you for a better lover, Alexander. One with passion!"

Her chin jutted in rage.

"You aren't the most artful lover, my darling husband. And an ardent whore—a Pole!—like Maria will need more between her legs than a quick poke by a bloodless fool."

Alexander stormed out of the room, pushing aside the Ethiopian serf who waited on the other side of the door.

There was no more talk of divorce or of Czartoryski's proposal. Fortunately, her baby girl Maria still filled the grand duchess's days with joy. She gave the baby a German nickname, "Mäuschen," little mouse. The child had a heart-warming smile, her black eyes sparkling with laughter. The grand duchess's ladies-in-waiting were enchanted by the beautiful baby.

Elizabeth wrote to her mother in Baden constantly, informing the new grandmother of every stage of Maria's development.

> *Even if she is unwell, she is such a nice girl. She is teething but behaves bravely and is of good temperament. All who see her remark of her good nature.*

Oh, Mother. She is my life! I want nothing but for her to love me the way I did you. The greatest delight of my childhood was sitting next to you, going for a walk by your side, playing hide-and-go-seek under your watchful eye. How can I instill this love in my Maria? The love of a daughter for her mother is a sacred gift.

The letters continued even when Maria Alexandrovna was sent into quarantine at the Marble Palace, where royal children who were not vaccinated against smallpox were taken for their own protection until they could receive inoculations. Grand Duchess Elizabeth accompanied her baby there, forsaking her royal apartments and husband in order to spend every moment with her baby girl.

It was one evening in the Marble Palace that Elizabeth received a parcel from Italy.

The grand duchess stopped breathing. She knew Adam Czartoryski had followed the exiled Sardinian Court to Rome.

She opened the leather and velvet wrappings to find an exquisite box made of polished walnut with gold hinges.

A letter was enclosed.

For our dearest Mouse. Teach her to love the image under the velvet, even if she is never to know its significance to her.

Elizabeth pulled back the plush velvet. In brilliant enamel was the image of a yellow knight in medieval armor astride a warhorse. The rider brandished a sword pointed skyward.

The Czartoryski family shield.

"My God!"

Elizabeth shrieked at the sight of her beloved daughter writhing in her crib.

"Send for the doctor . . . and my husband. At once!"

Alexander rushed in, not far behind the court physician.

"What is happening?"

"Convulsions, Your Highness," said the doctor, leaning over the crib. "The baby has a fever."

"But I kept her away from smallpox—"

"It is not smallpox, Grand Duchess. But a dangerous fever all the same."

Alexander took his wife into his arms as she sobbed.

"Elise!" he whispered. "Oh, Elise! I will get word to Adam."

"Do not tell him yet," she cried. "He will be here immediately— and the Tsar will kill him."

Just days later, Maria Alexandrovna, barely thirteen months of age, died in her mother's arms.

The grief-stricken young mother could barely shed tears. She locked herself in her apartments in Pavlovsk Palace, refusing to participate in court. Instead she wrote to her mother.

> *Oh, my dearest Mother! I have never felt such an abyss of sorrow. I am alone in the world, my adored Mäuschen no longer exists. As long as I live I shall never overcome this pain.*

Grand Duchess Maria was buried in the tomb of the Annunciation of Alexander Nevsky. The tiny white coffin was a toy boat adrift on waves of sorrow from the ladies-in-waiting who had come to love the little girl with the enchanting smile.

The Grand Duchess Elizabeth was inconsolable. In deep mourning, her letters to Adam Czartoryski stopped.

Alexander knocked quietly at her bedchamber.

A lady-in-waiting answered, bowing deeply to the grand duke.

"I would like to address the grand duchess in private," he said, entering the antechamber.

"Of course, Your Excellency. Pardon me while I notify the grand duchess of your request."

She backed out the door still bowing. In a matter of minutes she returned and opened the door for the grand duke.

Alexander strode into Elizabeth's bedchamber. He stopped mid-stride upon seeing how grief had transformed her face.

The heavenly radiance, the sparkle of her blue eyes that he had taken for granted since she was fourteen, had disappeared. In its place was the gray skin of the dead, grieving eyes dull and ringed in red.

"Oh, my darling Elise!"

"Alexander," she said. Her voice was flat, emotionless. She turned away from him, looking toward the gardens of Catherine's palace. "Look how they bloom, the roses. Oblivious to death, to the end of life."

"Perhaps that is why we send them to those in grief. A rose in bloom is resurrection."

"Resurrection," mumbled Elizabeth. "How can a child so young find her way up from the cold wet earth to heaven?"

Elizabeth stood up, staring at the roses. She raised her right hand to her mouth.

"She will get lost! My poor little Mouse!"

Alexander took his wife in his arms, embracing her.

"Cry, my love," he said. "Let her spirit go. She will be in Jesus's arms, I swear it!"

He felt his wife's body melt, bending into his own.

Then for the first time in days, Elizabeth began to weep. She wept convulsively, her body shuddering like a sail in a storm.

"Adam Czartoryski has written me," said Alexander, stroking back his wife's blonde hair. "He is sick with grief. He tells me he has received no letter from you since Maria's death."

"I cannot write to him," said Elizabeth. "I cannot bear to think of Adam. My little Mäuschen looked so much like him, Alexander. I can't . . . I can't."

"It's all right, Elise. It's only that he worries about you."

"I cannot. Do you think, dear husband, that God has punished me for loving Adam?"

"Oh, my darling Elise. No!" he said, pressing her close to his chest. "It was I who wanted my two best friends to love each other. The God who is all-merciful would never take a child in revenge. A child who was loved by all of us!"

Elizabeth looked up at her husband. The rough gold braid of his uniform had left a red welt on her cheek.

She sniffled, reaching into her sleeve for a handkerchief.

"I should go now, Elise."

Elizabeth nodded solemnly. "You are indeed my angel husband. I don't know if I can bear to see Adam ever again. I will always see our little Maria in his eyes."

Chapter 20

Count Nikita Panin waited until Alexander was settled at the Winter Palace. What Count Panin had to say could not be uttered within Mikhailovsky Castle.

"What does he want?" asked Elizabeth, when the count sought to be admitted to the grand duke's private apartments. "Why should he want to speak to you here and not at court?"

Alexander sipped a glass of his favorite Burgundy. "We will find out soon enough."

The tsarevitch was already certain of what Count Panin would propose. He made sure only his most trusted servants were on duty when he admitted the vice-chancellor to his study in the Winter Palace.

"Good evening, sire," said Count Panin. "It is most gracious of you to permit me to visit you."

"I am sure you have ample reason, Count Panin."

"Have you heard that the emperor has made more overtures to Napoleon? He has encouraged Napoleon to declare himself king."

Alexander nodded. This was not a complete surprise—not after his father had announced that he planned an alliance with Napoleon.

Panin continued. "Your father and mother were close friends of Louis XVI and Marie Antoinette. They gave sanctuary to the French royal family here."

"I am aware of that, Count Panin."

"Yes, sire, but that is my point." He took a deep breath and then plunged ahead. "Tsarevitch Alexander, your father is acting in a most contradictory—forgive me for speaking candidly—a most *mad* way. He has turned his back on all his former allies. He is suspicious of everyone."

These words were treason. If Alexander did not call the guards and denounce Panin on the spot, he too would be guilty, just for having listened. He swallowed, clearing his throat.

"Pray continue, Count Panin."

"His Majesty Tsar Paul has imprisoned a thousand British seamen who happened to be in port, thus destroying most important commerce with England. He has dispatched twenty thousand Cossacks to the Indus River to join the French in an invasion of India, a mission that is surely doomed. We will be at war at once with Britain."

Alexander could only nod, yet again. He didn't trust himself to speak. His brother Constantine had said at dinner the night before, "Our father has declared war on common sense, firmly resolved never to conclude a truce." Alexander wondered if Constantine had been paid a visit by Count Panin as well.

Panin continued. "There can be no further delay. Our troops in India threaten mutiny. Admiral Ribas supports us, as do most of the Imperial Guards. Tsar Paul destroys the heart of Mother Russia. Our nation bleeds. Since the death of our beloved Tsarina Catherine, we have lost all grace, beauty, power. Only you can stanch the blood, Grand Duke."

Alexander stared at the count. He steepled his fingers, pressing them hard to his forehead.

What must I do? Can I stand aside and let Russia be destroyed? But to betray my father . . .

"I beg you, do not hesitate, Tsarevitch. An empire turns its eyes to you, imploring your leadership. Otherwise . . ."

Alexander raised his hand, interrupting him. "But, Count Panin. I have not the qualities Russia seeks. You know of my love of democracy, of reform."

"Forgive me, Your Excellency. You will outgrow that—they are youthful notions. Russia needs you! Napoleon will seize power if you do not."

Alexander's lip curled at the thought of Napoleon as king. "Napoleon would certainly make himself emperor if he could! He is brazen and arrogant."

"And your father encourages an alliance. Which will only last until he changes his mind again—perhaps next month? In the meantime our Mother Russia will be committed to war on all the eastern fronts, alienated from England and all the rest of its allies. We will be vulnerable on every frontier," said Count Panin. His eyes swept the vicinity, checking that they were alone. He lowered his voice.

"And ruled by a madman."

Alexander drew in a deep breath, making the gold braid on his uniform creak. But he still said nothing.

"You must come to Russia's aid, Grand Duke. If you hesitate it will be too late."

"I will take all you say into consideration, Count Panin," Alexander said at last. "But my father must be allowed to live out his days in peace."

The count bowed his head solemnly. Alexander could not see the curve of a smile on Panin's lips as he lowered his gaze to the floor.

General Pahlen hesitated outside the door of the Tsar's private office. The general had cultivated Tsar Paul's friendship and trust through the years, and was the head of the state police, the Semyonovsky Life Guard Regiment. He had to play his part perfectly—the penalty for even the slightest mistake was death.

And even a flawless performance could end with imprisonment, torture, and death.

The Tsar was balanced on the precarious brink of madness—and all of Russia was there with him.

By now, with the first hints of spring still far off, more than sixty people had joined the circle of conspirators, including aristocrats, senators, members of the emperor's inner circle. But it was General Pahlen who led the plot.

The general swallowed hard and marched confidently to meet the Tsar.

He was hardly inside the door when the Tsar bellowed: "What do you know of the conspirators who threaten me? Is there a coup being planned? Are *you* involved, sir?"

General Pahlen looked solemnly at the Tsar.

"Yes, Your Majesty."

"Yes?" The Tsar's eyes bulged. "You say *yes*?"

"A conspiracy is indeed developing. I myself have joined it to be fully informed on all its aspects."

Pahlen watched the Tsar carefully. Paul tightened his bulldog jaw.

"You have nothing to fear, Your Majesty," said Pahlen calmly. "All is under control."

"My two sons, Alexander and Constantine. Are they involved in any way?"

This was the moment he had waited for. If he could force Alexander's hand, give him real reason to join the conspiracy . . .

"It grieves me to say . . ."

"What?" roared the Tsar. "Are my sons involved in the plot?"

General Pahlen took a deep breath. If this went wrong, if word of this lie were to escape, the Tsar would have him killed. Alexander would have him killed. He exhaled and threw his life into the game, onto the bonfire.

"Not only your sons, Your Highness. But your wife as well, the empress Maria Feodorovna."

The color drained from Tsar Paul's face. His right hand trembled. Then all the color came back—and more—until his face was purple with rage.

"I knew I smelled a traitor in my family! Now you say there are three rats gnawing at my entrails! No, four! From even beyond the grave my mother haunts me!"

"Your Highness, we must act rationally. Stealthily—"

"By God, no!" the Tsar said.

"The best plan is—" said Pahlen.

"Silence! Arrest them at once, both my sons!"

My God. What have I done?

"My Tsar! To arrest royal dukes, I must have permission from the courts. I must have a signed affidavit and show proof."

"You have given me proof enough. Damnation! Can I trust no one? You are all snakes. Even you, General Pahlen!"

The Tsar did not believe anyone. He issued warrants for vast numbers of arrests in St. Petersburg—including his sons, Alexander and Constantine.

General Pahlen raced to warn Alexander.

"Grand Duke, even your mother is in danger. The emperor suspects she may be privy to the conspiracy."

"My mother?" said Alexander, his lips losing all color. "That is outrageous! The Tsar is truly mad!"

"We must act immediately."

Alexander clenched his fists.

"So be it." Alexander could resist no more, wait no longer. "But there must be no violence, no blood spilt! You give me your word, General Pahlen! Give me your word."

"Of course, Your Excellency. But we must act at once."

Paul pulled back the heavy curtain of his bedroom. It was a cold morning, another storm threatening, gray clouds hanging low. The ceramic stoves were struggling to keep the palace warm.

No sign of spring. It feels like the dead of winter.

His grim mood was interrupted by an unexpected visitor.

"Why do you disturb me, General Pahlen?"

"Your Majesty," said the count, bowing low. "You must relieve the horse guard, Colonel Sablukov, of his duty."

"Colonel Sablukov? He is one of my most trusted officers."

Pahlen gave the Tsar a knowing look. "Your Majesty, your life is in danger. I beg you to take my advice."

"Leave me, General Pahlen. I lose patience."

"But Your Majesty!"

"At once!"

Tsar Paul sat, staring at the gilded moldings. The winding vines of gold seemed ominous, as if they'd slither down from the wall and wrap around his neck, strangling him.

He stared at the interior door that communicated with his mistress's, Lady Gargarina, apartment.

"Ivan!" He called to his servant. "Tell a carpenter to nail shut the door between my bedroom and Princess Gargarina's. At once! There shall be no other entrances to chambers but the front hall, and that must be guarded at all times."

"Yes, Your Majesty."

"You are dismissed. Go!"

The Tsar sat down at his writing desk. He looked over his shoulder to make sure he was alone. He opened a drawer, pulling it completely out of the desk. He opened a hidden compartment at the back of the drawer and took out a sheet of paper covered with numbers.

Referring frequently to the sheet, he painstakingly composed a coded message.

He would send it after dinner, when no one was watching.

That evening Tsar Paul dined with General Mikhail Ilarionovich Kutuzov, hero of the Turkish war. The dinner was splendid and the Tsar joked with the general's eldest daughter.

Alexander watched his father's easy relation and admiration for Kutuzov.

My father has issued orders for my arrest! Yet look how charming he is with that fat toad of a general.

Paul studiously ignored his family. He gave his full attention to Kutuzov and his stories of crossing the Alps on horseback in the dead of winter.

"We dragged the caissons and cannons up the rocky cliffs, hauling them with ropes up precipices higher than the Winter Palace," said Kutuzov, spooning sugar into his champagne before draining the glass. "Snow was up to the horse's flanks as we made our way down the mountains."

"Now here is a man who loves Russia!" declared the Tsar, raising his glass to Kutuzov. "A man I can trust!" He flicked a glance at Alexander, seated across the table.

The Tsar held out his glass for the servant to refill.

The candlelight glimmered against the cut crystal of the wine goblet and reflected brightly in the large mirrors, whose imperfect glass twisted and distorted the light before sending it back again into the room.

As Tsar Paul laughed at a remark made by General Kutuzov's daughter, he caught a glimpse of himself in the mirror.

"A most peculiar mirror," he said, nodding at his reflection, "I see it wringing my neck!"

Platon Zubov, the last lover of Empress Catherine—and four decades her junior—made his way through the dark, rainy streets of the city. It was just past midnight and St. Petersburg seemed to be holding her breath, waiting for the conspirators to strike.

The wet wind off the Neva River lashed Zubov's face with a mix of brackish water and sleet. He looked up at the Winter Palace in the distance, now dark and barricaded. He thought of the lively soirees and the lovemaking Empress Catherine had given so generously.

His face tightened.

At the residence of General Talyzen, a servant opened the door only slightly. Then, recognizing Zubov, the attendant ushered him in and offered a glass of brandy. The hot fire warmed the wet wools and furs of the men who were gathered in groups, drinking brandy in hurried gulps. Zubov glanced around, nerves on edge.

This room smells of wet animals, nervous sweat, and hard liquor. It reeks of danger.

"Platon! Over here!" called a voice.

Zubov's two brothers had already arrived. The three formed a tight knot next to the fire.

"Are you ready, Platon?" asked one brother.

"Never have I been more eager," Platon replied. "I could storm Mikhailovsky Castle alone!"

"Such hot blood! We will share in the task, my brother."

Several other men, including General Pahlen and General Talyzen, had heard Zubov.

"Listen to Platon Zubov! Now there is a man!" said General Pahlen. "Who else has passion? Who else is a true Russian?"

The men roared, swigging their cognac, their eyes burning from the alcohol's fumes.

Tsar Paul retired to his bedroom, his little dog Spitz at his heels. He scowled at the sentries outside his door. The dog, sensing his master's unrest, made a low growl.

"Send for Colonel Sablukov!" the Tsar ordered his manservant.

Entering his bedchamber, he inspected the carpenter's work, sealing the door to his mistress's bedroom. He ran his hand over the door frame to ensure the boards were secure.

Spitz looked up at his master with a quizzical cock of his head.

"We cannot be too careful," the Tsar muttered, patting the dog on his head.

His two valets stood ready by the dressing room. One silently held out a white nightshirt for the emperor.

"No, Karl. I will wait until after I have spoken with Colonel Sablukov."

There was a knock at the door of the antechamber.

Colonel Sablukov wore a bewildered expression. "Your Majesty! Is everything in order?

"*Vous êtes Jacobin!* Traitor!" shouted the Tsar, his face red with rage.

Sablukov dropped back a step, his face contorting with surprise.

"I do not mean you personally, you idiot," protested the Tsar. "I mean your regiment, my personal guards. I want them disbanded immediately. At four o'clock tomorrow morning I want the entire regiment mustered and sent to another post, do you hear me? Send them to Siberia!"

"But your son, Alexander, is the colonel-in-chief," protested Sablukov.

"I am well aware of that! Send every man in the regiment! Every man. Do I make myself clear?"

"Yes, Your Majesty!" said Sablukov, blinking.

"And send away the guards outside my door. I will have my valets take guard duty."

"Your valets, Your Majesty?"

"I trust none of the soldiers in this regiment! Send them all away!"

The two valets look at each other in stunned silence.

"Damn it all!" said the Tsar. He saw the coded note on his writing desk.

Now there is no one I trust to deliver the message to her.

The band of conspirators—drunk with vodka, fear, and bravado—stumbled through the freezing rain, trampling the slushy snow. They made their way through the park toward Mikhailovsky Castle. Their movements startled the hundreds of crows roosting in the branches of the linden trees, and they let out a shrieking cry, winging away in a black cloud. The men froze, certain that the emperor would have heard the cacophony and that guards would arrest them on the spot. But silence fell again and the men moved on.

Half the conspirators—a group of twelve, including Platon and Nikolai Zubov, Colonel Bennigsen, and Count Panin—went through the Christmas gate at the corner of the palace grounds and raced upstairs to the Tsar's apartments.

Stunned to find only two unarmed valets stationed outside the Tsar's door, the men pushed them aside and rushed to the bedroom, only to find an empty bed and rumpled sheets. A small dog barked wildly at the intruders.

"He has escaped!" cried Platon Zubov. "We have come too late!"

But Colonel Bennigsen, who had consumed far less cognac than the others, spied two bare feet peeking out from behind a red satin screen.

Bennigsen pushed the screen aside, revealing the Tsar in his nightshirt, bed jacket, and nightcap. The dog, seeing his master collared by the intruders, raced to the rescue, biting at Bennigsen's ankles.

The colonel kicked hard and sent the dog limping away, yelping in pain.

"Your Majesty," said Bennigsen. "Your reign has ended. Alexander is now our emperor. We are arresting you on his orders. You must renounce your throne. Be reassured, no one wishes to harm you. I'm here to see to that. Accept your fate, for if you offer the least resistance I cannot vouch for your safety."

"What have I done to you?" asked Paul. "To any of you?"

An answer was shouted by one man in the group, "You have tortured us for four years!"

"Shut up," said Bennigsen. "I'll do the talking. You must abdicate, Your Majesty—"

Outside they heard a scuffle and voices.

"The guards!" hissed someone. "They've returned!" The conspirators ran to escape. Only Colonel Bennigsen was left, his sword pointed at the Tsar's chest to keep him from fleeing.

The fleeing conspirators ran out the door leading to the hall only to meet face-to-face with the other half of the group, who had lost their way in the castle. Together they returned to the emperor's bedroom, drunk and clumsy. In the confusion a fire screen fell over, snuffing the one candle that lit the bedroom. In the dark and chaos, Tsar Paul tried to escape.

"Where do you think you are going," slurred Platon Zubov. "You are under arrest, Pavel Romanov!"

"Arrest! Arrest! What does this mean?" Paul retorted in the darkness. "I will never abdicate! Traitors!"

A conspirator lunged for him in the dark. Paul could not see his face. He smelled brandy on his attacker's breath. A pungent nervous sweat filled the small bedchamber. Animal instinct gathered force, each drunken man driven to murderous rage. The veil of darkness gave them a feeling of impunity.

Furniture crashed to the floor, wood splitting.

"What have I ever done to you?" screamed the Tsar again, rolling to the ground as an unseen man grappled with him.

A hand snatched a silk sash from Paul's bedpost and wound it around the Tsar's neck. The crowd of men pressed forward, trampling on him. The sash pulled tighter. The Tsar choked, gasping.

In the melee, the sash loosened and the Tsar shouted again, "Traitors!"

Bennigsen fought his way through the confusion and into the hallway. He returned moments later, flaming torch in hand. Shadows leapt, and the walls moved with distorted monsters and grasping hands.

"Do not harm him!" shouted Bennigsen.

"Traitors!" shouted the Tsar. "You! Get your hands off me, Zubov!"

"Why do you shout so?" bellowed Nikolai Zubov, a giant of a man. The drunken Zubov struck the emperor on the hand, like a parent admonishing a child.

Insulted that he had been touched, Paul pushed away Zubov's hand.

"Get your hands off me, you disgusting pig," he shrieked. "How dare you touch the Tsar of Russia with your filthy hand!"

Zubov's mouth twisted in hatred. He seized a heavy gold snuffbox and smashed it against the emperor's head, sending him sprawling on the floor.

The Tsar, stunned and bleeding, gazed up at the faces of his tormenters. He thought he saw the fair hair and face of his son Constantine.

"Constantine? You are here?" he cried. "*Et tu?*"

The Tsar looked about for his eldest son. Blood blurred his vision, his head whirled. He felt consciousness slipping away.

Is Alexander here too? Son, my son! Do you remember the cold troika ride through the snows on that long-ago Christmas? I held you tight. You would not stay under the furs, your head popped out like a jack-in-the-box. You wanted to see the first glimpse of Gatchina . . .

Gatchina. Our refuge.

"Get him!" shouted a voice.

"Tyrant! We will show you justice! For Russia!"

Your little hand sought mine, under the heavy furs. "I shall stay with you at Gatchina, Papa? Grandmama will not mind?"

Would that you could have stayed forever, my dear boy.

There in the darkness, hands reached for the discarded sash.

Would you forsake me now? You who swore on your knees an oath to me. "It is yours, the throne, Papa. I do not want it . . ."

He felt his head roughly lifted from the floor and cool silk tied around his throat.

As your grandmother willed it. They murder me in my nightshirt just as my father before me.

Paul's head jerked back as invisible hands violently pulled the ends of the sash. He gasped, writhed. His breath stopped.

As he lay on the floor, the conspirators kicked, trampled, and bludgeoned his corpse. This tsar could never be dead enough.

Grand Duchess Elizabeth paced in her bedchamber. Outside in the antechamber, Alexander could hear his wife's light step.

A tap on the door arrested her steps. A servant went to answer.

"You are dismissed, Ivan," Alexander said as he saw General Pahlen in the antechamber.

Pahlen handed the grand duke a sheaf of papers.

Alexander sat at his desk, his eyes studying the manifesto drawn up by the conspirators.

"Sit, Count," commanded the young duke.

"You are most gracious, Your Majesty, but I prefer to stand."

"By signing this, I become part of the conspiracy," said Alexander.

"Your Majesty, your signature only affirms that you agree to accept the throne after your father's retirement. He will abdicate tonight."

Alexander frowned. "But I should think that would be obvious that I will be tsar. I am the heir apparent."

"Please, I beg you, Your Highness," countered Pahlen. "Lives are now at stake, risking all to save Russia. Your signature shows that you take your responsibility as the new emperor with strong resolve. A smooth transition. That is all."

Alexander picked up the pen, dipping the nib into the pot of ink. With a flourish he signed his name.

"May I?" asked Pahlen. He held the blotter in his hand. He pressed down firmly.

He seals my fate. Why does my heart beat like a rabbit, pursued by a hound? Have I no courage? Have I—

A commotion at the entry of Alexander's apartment sent him jumping up from his chair.

Nikolai Zubov appeared at the door, accompanied by one of Alexander's personal guards. His face was flushed, his speech slurred with emotion and drink.

"The emperor Paul has died in a fit of apoplexy!" he declared.

Alexander's eyes darted to the parchment, now grasped firmly in Pahlen's hands.

"What? How can that be?"

He collapsed back into his chair, his face ashen. His lips quivered, "I cannot . . ." he said.

"Get hold of yourself, Your Majesty," said General Pahlen. "This is a moment for courage."

Alexander felt the cold wind of a long-ago January evening biting his cheek, the bells of the sledge ringing over the fields of snow.

"Abdication—you, Pahlen! You all said *abdication*! Not murder!"

"You must act for all Russia now. Russia needs a strong leader. The people do not care how it came to be! Only that a strong hand holds the reins. What has happened is of no consequence now."

"No consequence? No consequence! You are mad, Count Pahlen! I cannot go on with it. I have no strength to reign. I will resign my power and give it to whoever wants it!"

"Do not behave like a child, Your Majesty! This is no time—"

"Let those who have committed the crime be responsible for the consequences."

Count Pahlen stiffened, rage filling his throat.

"The fate of millions now depends on your firmness, your strength. Go and reign, damn it!"

Grand Duchess Elizabeth flew into the room, the door banging behind her. She covered her mouth with her hand in horror.

She had heard everything from the adjoining room.

"Alexander!" she said. "Oh, Alexander!"

Alexander opened his arms to his wife. He sobbed into her white shoulders.

"Elise, what am I to do?" he cried. "What am I to do?"

"Calm yourself, my darling," she whispered. "Send this wretched man away! We will think together, you and I. Just send him away at once!"

"Count Pahlen! Leave us," said Alexander. "I will send for you later."

"Your Highness, I will remain outside until—"

"Go!"

The door shut behind the count.

Elizabeth pressed her husband's head to her breast. "I will stay at your side, always. We will make a plan, Alexander. Have courage, my love."

He clung to her words like a drowning man.

The next morning, Alexander stood on the balcony overlooking the parade square of the Winter Palace.

Fighting for control of his voice, he addressed the soldiers and guards of the palace.

"My father is . . . dead. He died of an apoplectic seizure. I am now the Tsar. During my reign everything will be done according to the spirit and principles of my grandmother, the empress Catherine II."

Without further remark, Alexander—now Alexander I, Tsar and emperor—withdrew into the castle.

How shall I have the strength to rule, plagued with the constant memory that my father was assassinated?

An hour after Emperor Paul's death, Sir James Wylie, chief physician to the Romanov Court, arrived to prepare Paul's body for viewing. Not long after that, Johann Jacob Mettenleiter, who had painted the delicately adorned panels for the state bedroom in Pavlovsk Palace, was summoned to make the corpse presentable. Escorted by the Imperial Guard, he carried his paints in a canvas satchel.

"Do your best," said the Scottish doctor. "He was your patron— you know how he looked in life. Make him whole again." Mettenleiter stared in horror at the task he had been given. As an artist, he had created great beauty. Now he painted a living face on a dead man, brutally mutilated. He tried to imagine he was painting a portrait on canvas, rather than the dead flesh of the man who had been his emperor. Mettenleiter disguised the gash from the gold snuffbox and tried to restore a normal color to Paul's face. He painted over the many bruises and lesions.

When the artist finally left the bedchamber hours later, he was hunched and pale, visibly shaken. Sir Wylie bowed to Alexander, who was waiting anxiously outside the door.

"I pray you enter now, Your Highness," said the doctor, bowing to the new emperor.

Alexander entered the chamber, falling to his knees beside the exquisitely painted doll who had been his father.

"Fetch my mother, Empress Maria Feodorovna," he whispered. "She has sent word she will not recognize me as emperor until she has seen my father's . . . corpse."

Alexander remained at his father's bedside, the shadows of the guttering candles illuminating the profile of the kneeling man, his tear-streaked face bowed in prayer. His right hand flew across his head and body in the sign of the cross.

Maria Feodorovna entered and stood speechless at the sight. She removed her dead husband's tilted cap, her fingers hovering over the deep gash in his left temple.

She drew in a breath, fingering the wound camouflaged with thick paint.

"Where is the nightshirt he wore?" she asked.

"I do not know—"

"Send an order immediately. I want that nightshirt. Unwashed. I will keep it with me always," Maria Feodorovna said, bending over her dead husband to kiss his forehead.

With the stoicism of a Romanov, she turned stiffly to her son and said, "I now wish you great joy, Alexander. You are emperor." Her mouth puckered as if she were tasting a bitter herb.

"Mama, I—"

"You are covered by the blood of your father!" said Maria Feodorovna.

Alexander collapsed to the ground. His wife and those few others present thought him dead.

Chapter 21

Winter Palace, St. Petersburg
November 1801

Alexander often dined alone in the Winter Palace.

This night he dined with Empress Elizabeth, who desperately tried to soothe her young husband's conscience as he teetered on the edge of collapse.

"Darling Alexander. You must deliver yourself from this abyss. Russia needs your leadership, your enthusiasm for the throne!"

Alexander stared at his plate.

"Even my mother calls me a murderer. How should I find this 'enthusiasm for the throne'?"

"Oh, dear Alexander. Do you not see how she loves you? The shock induced such a rash accusation. She longs for her eldest son to serve Russia with honor. Above all things, she recognizes your good heart. Go to her and receive her blessing, I beg you."

Alexander looked up through the flame of the candelabra at his wife, his lips trying to form a smile.

How good she is to me! I am not deserving of Elizabeth . . . or of Russia.

"You are right. I shall go to my mother. I must have her blessing or perish."

"Emperor Paul was a tyrannical fiend," said Elizabeth, folding her napkin.

"He was my father and I loved him," said Alexander, holding up his hand. He said a silent prayer. When he looked up again, his wife's eyes had dropped to her lap, filling with tears.

She would never hurt me, her heart is golden. How I wish I could leave Russia and take Elise away with me to live in obscurity, raising our children away from the sycophants and murderous schemers of this empire!

But how could I leave my Maria Naryshkina?

"Elise," said Alexander. "I have sent for Adam Czartoryski."

Elizabeth stiffened.

"He has been my closest and most faithful advisor," said Alexander. "The two of you have been friends in the past. Before . . ."

Elizabeth nodded her head woodenly.

"I need him," Alexander said. "I hope that you two can remain . . . friends."

Elizabeth drew a deep breath. She looked out into the dark, where she knew the Neva still flowed through the night.

"Adam Czartoryski is indeed an honorable man," she said. "But Alexander, after the death of little Maria, I don't know if I can suffer any more. I simply . . . can't."

Alexander moved his chair closer to hers. He took her hand.

"I understand. I only want you to accustom yourself to the idea of Adam being close at hand. There are so few men I can trust. I am surrounded by sycophants, every one! I need Adam."

Elizabeth nodded. "For you, Alexander. And for Russia. I will try to be his friend." Then she dipped her head, not looking at her husband. "But every time I see his face, I see little Mäuschen."

"With time you will heal, my dearest Elise. I pray for this."

"But go now, Alexander. Speak to your mother. You will see how a mother forgives all."

A servant approached Alexander with a silver tray. Alexander frowned knowing that only an urgent message would be presented to him while he was dining with his wife. He opened the envelope.

"What is it, Alexander?" said Elizabeth.

"A matter I must take care of immediately. Forgive me, my dear."

"Of course."

Alexander's valet, Boris, stood waiting in the study. He bowed as the emperor entered.

"Forgive me, Your Majesty. My deepest condolences—"

"Boris, what is this urgent news?"

Boris glanced at the door.

"The late tsar's head valet, Monsieur Littauer, has brought a document that was found in your father's bedchamber. He asked me to deliver it at once to Your Majesty's hand."

Boris produced a scrap of linen stationery from a leather satchel strapped around his waist.

"I cannot say what it is, but as it is written in your father's hand, Monsieur Littauer thought you should have it."

Alexander looked at the piece of paper. It had been crumpled, but the creases had been smoothed.

A short string of random numbers were penned in black ink. There were two letters among the numbers: AP. Alexander recognized the flourish of his father's pen stroke.

"It's gibberish," said Alexander.

"Perhaps it is not for me to say, Your Majesty. But I believe it is code."

"Where was this found?"

"On the late tsar's writing desk."

"Thank you for this, Boris. And I shall thank Monsieur Littauer personally for his consideration."

"At your service, Your Majesty," said Boris, bowing.

Alexander stared at his father's lettering.

AP . . . AP . . .

Adam Czartoryski sipped his cognac, looking out over the Neva. He was weary from travel.

I need you, Adam. I need your good counsel, the new tsar had written.

Keenly aware of Russian history, Czartoryski knew a weak or reluctant tsar was an extreme danger to Russia, especially as Napoleon gathered more and more strength, collecting lands and people throughout Europe.

Taking up his pen, Czartoryski wrote to his friend Nikolai Novosiltev:

The grief and remorse that Alexander relives in his heart are inexpressibly deep and troubling. He has mad hallucinations. He sees in his imagination Paul's mutilated and bloodstained body on the steps of the throne which he has to ascend. Our dear friend whom we so heartily encouraged to be tsar has human sensitivity that is in total conflict with being the Strong Man of Russia.

The Pole blotted his letter and set it aside. He stared across the room at a fat fly, creeping along the edge of his plate, still resting on the dinner table.

Lazy winter insect!

Czartoryski waved his hand viciously at the pest and considered what must come next:

We will reverse the course Tsar Paul charted for us! We cannot remain allies with this fiend, Napoleon, or refuse Britain's overtures. We will ally with the Ottomans if we must, but the French shall not be our masters, or our equals!

I shall be the Tsar's ambassador to Napoleon and say as much to his face.

Napoleon wasted no time sending his emissaries to the new tsar. His emissaries sent back reports filled with praise of Alexander. "How perfect is his French, with no telltale intonation of the Russian language. He employs such lofty expressions—obviously the result of a careful education. He knows all the writers of the Enlightenment and is well versed in French literature, music, and culture."

"We shall be allies, this glorious tsar and I," Napoleon declared. "Together we will rule the world."

But the French emperor's entreaties to Alexander were rebuked. Unlike his father, the new tsar wanted nothing to do with the Grand Armée or Paris. When Napoleon heard of Russia's rapprochement with England, he was incensed.

"How dare he!" Napoleon shouted at Alexander's emissary who brought word of the Tsar's refusal. "We were to share in power. How can this man turn his back on so brilliant a future? He is so well versed in French, schooled in liberty and Enlightenment."

The fire had been laid, the tinder was ready, and only a spark was needed. Napoleon provided the spark when he ordered the execution of the Duc d'Enghien, a member of the French royal family. When a commoner dared to touch a royal, all Europe's sovereign families trembled with collective rage. This upstart Corsican had crossed the line, revolution or no revolution.

Tsar Alexander's emissary, Adam Czartoryski, conveyed a message of disgust and condemnation to the French ruler.

And with that, Russia and France were at war.

Empress Elizabeth watched her husband slowly grasp the scepter.

She and the Kremlin advisors had begged him to step forward and fill the vacuum of power before vying nobility could attempt to usurp his right as the Tsar.

And slowly, each day Alexander became stronger, remembering his intentions to institute reform, pledged what seemed like a lifetime ago with his Committee of Friends. He set to work, aligning Russia once more with Great Britain as his grandmother had done.

"You will be a great and good tsar," Empress Elizabeth told him. "You will protect us from Napoleon and unite Europe."

Alexander shook his head.

"I wish I had the iron strength my forebears did. The only force that compels me is duty to Russia. And the need to control this mongrel who has usurped the French throne!"

Chapter 22

St. Petersburg
January 1802

Ekaterina Pavlovna, the Tsar's youngest sister, the most spirited of all
the Romanovs, often sat at her brother Alexander's table. She was given
the honor of sitting at his left, while his mother, Maria Feodorovna, sat
on his right. The dowager empress was moved into the Winter Palace,
now with greater power and influence than she ever had under the rule
of her husband. With each passing day, she forgave her eldest son for his
complicity in his father's assassination, for he was so racked with grief
she was convinced he had indeed taken no part in the murder.

Empress Elizabeth watched the light of the chandelier glint off the
crystal champagne flutes, the silver and gold cutlery. With his mother's
love and his family's encouragement cocooning him from the raw ache
of his father's murder, Alexander emerged shyly but brilliantly in his
new mantle of Tsar of Russia. Seated on the Romanov family dais,
Alexander radiated confidence.

His mother nodded with pleasure as she watched him.

He is coming to life. When he saw his father, strangled, trampled,
a beaten corpse—exactly like his father, Peter, before him—when

Alexander saw that, he died his own little death. But now he laughs, breaking bread with his family, those who share the same blood that spilt from his father's veins.

My son is resurrected.

And as Maria Feodorovna basked in her son's happiness, Elizabeth shrank in her gilded chair, noticing how Alexander's eyes flashed as he exchanged looks across the room with the Polish princess Maria Naryshkina. Despite her extravagant fortune—her villa in Fiesole, her castle in Florence, her residences in Russia—Princess Naryshkina dressed simply in white with no jewelry or adornment. Her black hair seemed to float about her white neck, tendrils spilling gracefully to her shoulders.

Elizabeth shuddered with hatred at the audacity of her husband's mistress.

She had to tell me, when I inquired after her health, with simple politesse, "Ah, I am pregnant, you know." Oh yes, I know. Just as I know the father is Alexander. My husband. I almost slapped her, just to see my red hand print on her white skin.

Amid the warm laughter and smiles of the Romanovs and courtiers, Empress Elizabeth receded in the shadows.

Part 3

Shadows of War

Chapter 23

The Don Steppes, the Ukraine
September 1806

A Cossack's duty is to his horse. Without a horse, we are nothing. With the Cossacks, I learned to saddle and unsaddle my horse—a chore that had always been done by a groom both in the cavalry and at home. On my own, I had almost always ridden bareback.

But no matter his rank, a Cossack cared for his horses personally. Every night we led our mounts down to the water, letting them drink their fill. That was my favorite time of the evening. I watched Alcides's lips meet the surface of the water, breaking the transparent ripples over the gray river rocks. The sun slid through the branches of the overhanging trees and stillness fell, except for the comforting snorts of the horses. Alcides drew the water down his throat, his ears swiveling forward and back with each gulp. I stroked his withers, stretching my arm over his back. I drew in the salty scent of warm horse mixed with the mineral smell of wet river stone.

He nuzzled against me curling his big head over my shoulder to my breast and nibbling at the buttons of my tunic.

I truly believe Alcides loved the Cossack cavalry as much as I did. We both tasted freedom. My body ached, but my soul soared.

"He is a fine animal," said a voice. I turned and saw Denisov behind me. He was chewing on a stalk of dry grass.

"*Da*," I said, turning away from him. The rocks were slippery on the bank and I did not want to embarrass myself by falling in the river.

"Where did you get him?" asked the Cossack.

"He was a gift."

"But where did he get him? He is a Cossack breed, but not from the Don. *Pah!* Most of our herd are ugly dogs. That horse is from the Caucasus Mountains, or at least his ancestors are."

"My father had a friend who rode with the cavalry in the eastern mountains. Alcides was a special gift."

"You sit him well," said Denisov. "He is comfortable under your hand."

"Thank you," I said, turning to face him now.

I caught the sparkle in his eye. Then his face turned serious. "But you are no cavalry soldier," he said, shaking his head. "You have much to learn about riding. Good instincts but not enough instruction. Or experience."

I turned away, shame washing over me.

"You say you want to join a unit, Aleksandr Vasilevich. But you cannot wield a weapon over your head or follow military drills with precision. You haven't the strength, and you haven't the discipline."

"I am strong enough," I snapped back.

He laughed. "No, you are not! And if you are permitted to join a regiment, you will be nothing but a burden. Our captain has a soft spot for young strays. He did not want to see you lost in the woods. But we will be joining the other Don Cossacks soon and then disperse. Then what will you do?"

"I . . . I . . ."

"You do not have a plan, do you?"

"I will join a regular regiment," I said. "I come from a noble house. They will take me as an officer."

"Not unless you become much stronger and not so naive. They cannot play nursemaid to you on the battlefield. You will endanger other lives."

Alcides had finished drinking. He lifted his head, drops spilling from his mouth back into the river. He swiveled his ears toward me, waiting for my command.

I tugged on the rope and he leapt up onto the bank. I wanted to leave, but Denisov wasn't done with me yet.

"You know you will have to travel northeast to Grodno to meet up with the regular regiments. There will be none there on the Don. Just we Cossacks. After our review, we depart for duty in all directions. You will be alone. How will you make it to Grodno alone?"

I stared at him. "I do not know. Not yet."

"You need to have a plan, Aleksandr Vasilevich," he said, turning toward camp. As he walked away, he called over his shoulder. "Think about it."

We reached the Don River and Cossacks began to arrive from all directions. The Cossacks were attached to regiments throughout the Russian Empire, but returned to their roots to assemble and drill as a united tribe.

During the three days of drills and review, Alcides and I roamed the boundless steppe or I walked on foot, carrying a gun. As a young soldier—a boy—I had every right to explore the magnificent Don on my own, with no one to stop me. Half of my blood was Ukrainian and I was at last in my homeland.

Among Cossacks.

I thought of what Denisov had told me. I tried to strengthen my upper arms by wielding my sword over head. I could not begin to match the strength of a man. The sword point dipped dangerously close to Alcides's neck.

On the third afternoon, the review ended. As I practiced maneuvers with my saber, I watched the hundreds of Cossacks on the hillside scatter in all directions, like ants fleeing a disturbed anthill. They were headed home, dispersing across the steppe.

"Aleksandr Vasilevich." Denisov had ridden up quietly behind me.

I nearly sliced my thigh with my saber as I whirled around.

"You haven't the technique at all. Let me show you before I leave for the north."

He grasped his own sword, unsheathing it in a flash.

"Hold the hilt like this," he said, grasping the saber with a practiced hand.

I watched him and tried to imitate him.

"No! Here, let me show you." He sheathed his saber. "Extend your thumb along the back strap of the grip. Then you will have a more forceful downward swinging cut. Watch me."

He unsheathed his saber with a resounding ring. He swung from the shoulder, his elbow locked, a straight line from his right shoulder through to the tip of his sword.

I watched him make a savage upward slice with the weapon.

"That is when a man's guts are spilled. Hesitate and you are a dead man."

Spill a man's guts? I had thought of the thrill of battle, galloping toward the enemy. Beyond that—to kill? To see a man die by my sword?

Denisov moved his horse beside Alcides and grasped my hand. I felt the roughness of his skin, as callused as a field hand's. He moved my fingers around the hilt of the sword, arranging my hand properly. I noticed he let his hand linger on mine. I felt his warmth and sinewy strength.

He reined his horse even closer until Alcides's shoulder met his horse's. His leg brushed mine.

"Then you must keep the blade above your head, giving full range to your blow or to the charge. If your arms are too weak to lift it sufficiently, you must lower it and let blood rush to your arms. To swing the blade as low as you do is dangerous. It is only a matter of time before you gash yourself, Aleksandr Vasilevich. Or worse yet, this marvelous horse."

"I will not harm Alcides!" I said.

"Then practice cautiously, Aleksandr. And often."

I held the sword over my head, swinging it as I had seen my father and the cavalry soldiers do so many times. My arms began to tremble.

Denisov made a deep grunt of disapproval, seeing my right arm and shoulder shake with fatigue.

"Aleksandr Vasilevich, you have led a soft life in your noble house," said Denisov. "Lower your weapon before you hurt yourself. You are no Cossack!"

"I do not wish to be a Cossack," I said stubbornly. "I will join a regular Hussar regiment."

"Hussars? Oh, Aleksandr, you dream large," said Denisov. "Which one?"

Of course I had no idea. I had only wanted to escape home and join the cavalry.

"I do not know yet. I haven't chosen."

"Ah, they must choose you, my little friend," he said, laughing. "You are nobility. I suppose the captains will let you join. But . . ."

"But what?"

"Aleksandr Vasilevich, you have so much to learn. The captains and colonels will have no time to look out for you in the heat of battle. They cannot coddle you the way our Cossack colonel has done."

"I do not mean to be coddled!"

"You won't survive a day in battle."

He was right. Not only would I die, but my beloved Alcides would suffer for my incompetence.

I looked up at him.

"And you, Denisov? Where will you go?"

"After I return to my village for leave, we go to Vilna and on to the border on the Niemen River."

"Then I suppose I shall never see you again, Denisov."

He did not speak for a moment but watched over my shoulder as the last of the Cossacks rode off. The two horses touched heads, Alcides flicking his ears back.

"I should report to the colonel and take my leave," he said.

"We are bivouacking one more night," I said.

Then what? How would I ever make my way north alone to join with a regular regiment? I had little money and did not know how to survive on the land. Winter was approaching, and while it did not snow until December on the Don, the snows would be deep beyond the steppe.

My chest tightened.

"Can't I go with you?" I blurted.

A flash of incomprehension shot across the Cossack's face.

"I wouldn't be any trouble, and—"

"You are not a Cossack!" he said. "You know that is impossible!"

"I . . . I . . ." I had no words.

Denisov listened to my breath, a trace of a smile on his lips. He watched my chest heave under my tunic. His eyes climbed from my tunic to my face, his green eyes scrutinizing me.

"You are not even a man. Why don't you go home, little Aleksandrova?" he whispered. "You are brave, but the emperor would not wish a girl to die in battle with Napoleon."

"How dare you, sir? I am not a girl," I stuttered. "You! You—You take back your insult!"

Denisov's green eyes sparkled mischievously at me. With his hand around my shoulders, he pulled me close, close enough I could smell the tang of his perspiration, tobacco on his breath.

"You may fool some of the men, but certainly not me. But then . . ."

"Then what? Then what?" I demanded.

"I know women better than you think," he said. He pressed his lips to mine hard. I tasted the salty warmth of his mouth.

I made a move with my sword. He struck the hilt with the flat of his hand, knocking the weapon out of my grip.

The saber clattered to the ground, making Alcides jump. Denisov grabbed my reins, steadying my horse.

"Ah, little Aleksandrova! The next lesson is to learn to keep your thumb in the thumb ring at all times you bear arms!" he laughed.

He dropped my reins and spurred his horse, riding off to the hill. And soon, like all the other Cossacks, he disappeared, returning home.

I rode Alcides back to the colonel's tent. Now that the hundreds of Don Cossacks had disappeared over the hills, I felt a wave of loneliness, even desperation.

What was I to do now?

The colonel was sipping tea when I walked into the tent.

"Aleksandr Vasilevich, I haven't the heart to let you go out on your own to certain destruction," he said. "You are the youngest, most inexperienced soldier I have ever known."

I bristled but then thought of the lonely miles ahead, trying to find my way to Grodno. I did not know the road, had little money, and wasn't sure I could even find forage for Alcides. I would starve myself first rather than let my poor horse suffer.

"The marauders would murder you for your horse the first day! Remain here on the Don. You can stay with my wife while I go to join

Ataman Matvej Platov in Cherkassk. My stable is at your disposal. You will not be bored."

I wasn't certain whether to be grateful or insulted.

"When I return, our unit will head north and you can travel with us again to join the regular army. It will not be long. Agreed?"

"Thank you for your offer," I said reluctantly. "I do not want to put Alcides's life at risk."

The colonel laughed and tousled my hair with his rough hand.

"You are a brave lad, Aleksandr. And you value that good horse," he said. "But you are certainly wet behind the ears!

"Come, I will introduce you to my wife. She will care well for you. You will see!"

We rode into the colonel's village. At the outskirts, there were earth and dung brick huts, whitewashed and roofed with tin or thatch. They were surrounded by wattle fences that confined their poultry and other livestock.

At the center of the village was a handful of finer houses with stables, surrounded with brick walls. My colonel's house was a compound with several outbuildings, a small bathhouse, stables, and a vegetable garden.

The colonel's wife rushed out the door to meet us, pulling off her apron. This middle-aged and comely woman put a hand on her husband's knee, not waiting for him to dismount. He bent over in his saddle, kissing her heartily. She was a tall woman, plump, with black eyes, brows, and hair, and a swarthy complexion.

"Ah! Jiula. May I present you to our guest, Aleksandr Vasilevich."

Jiula's hand flew to her mouth.

"So young! And dressed like a Caucasus Cossack!"

Her eyes scanned my dirty red uniform. She stared into my eyes.

"How could your parents allow you to leave their home alone? You can't be more than fourteen. My son is eighteen and I will only permit him to go to foreign lands with his father."

She smiled at me in a most agreeable way, clucking over me as if I were her own chick. After we took care of our horses, we returned from the stables to find that Jiula had set the table with honey, grapes, cream, and sweet, newly pressed wine.

When I hesitated to drink with the rest of the family—three boys—she poked fun at me.

"Ah, you dare not drink, young man! Here on the Don we all drink our wine. Women, even children, drink it like water."

Of course I was afraid I might become tipsy and say or do something foolish that would betray my gender. And I was terrified of overloading my bladder and having to relieve myself publicly, by the side of the road as a man would. I always planned my urination breaks carefully before dawn or in the cover of night.

I had never tasted wine before but at her insistence I did. I felt her eyes scrutinizing me. Women's eyes frightened me. They could catch on too quickly, recognizing their own in disguise.

The colonel replenished his supplies and left me immediately in the company of his wife. I watched him wave as he galloped his horse over the steppes into the horizon.

The next morning as I ate my breakfast, the colonel's wife's eyes were fixed on me.

"How unlike a Cossack you are, Aleksandr Vasilevich!"

I lifted my lips from the rim of the teacup she had handed me.

"How is that?"

"You are so pale, so slender, so shapely—like a young lady," she said, smothering a giggle with her hand.

I quickly took another draft from my teacup to hide my face. I scalded my mouth and spat out the tea on her floor.

"Please pardon me!" I sputtered, looking around for a rag to wipe up the small puddle at my feet. "Let me clean it up."

Her eyes fixed on me again. "Of course not! A military officer cleaning up a spill in a woman's house? No Cossack would do such a thing!"

Certainly a Russian nobleman would not clean the floor. He would leave it for the serfs, I could hear her thinking.

Of course she was right. I settled back into the chair as she brought a rag to clean up my mess.

"Oh, Aleksandr Vasilevich! What a curious boy you are. Do you know what my women think? They have already told me this morning that they believe you are a girl in disguise!"

She burst out laughing, her merry eyes looking up at me from the ground as she wiped up the spill.

I forced a laugh. But I was dying inside.

"Here," said the kind lady. "I have something for you."

She left the room returning with a neat pile of blue linen in her hands.

"My husband asked me to dress you in proper Don clothes. You must not wear the red in our region. You are a guest of the Don Cossacks while under our roof."

She laughed, adding, "And your scarlet uniform is tattered and dirty. It is falling to shreds on your little body!"

I bowed low in thanks. I was proud to accept the Don uniform but blushed hot red at her scrutiny of my body.

"Thank you, madam," I said. "I am deeply honored."

I left the colonel's house as quickly as I could, riding Alcides across the steppe. From that morning on, I avoided the women as much as possible by staying away until nightfall.

A Cossack's life was simple and communal. Every man worked the fields, even the officers. Lieutenants, captains, and even colonels who were not on active duty joined together at daybreak. They worked in long lines across the width of a pasture, their scythes arching overhead in a fluid motion, from right to left, left to right, a unified wave, the rhythm punctuated by the dry rustle of severed stalks falling to the ground. Old veteran officers, once decorated for their feats and courage in battle, now took their place among the rest, beads of sweat on their battle-scarred brows.

I recognized some of the Cossacks from our march. They pulled off their caps, whistling and waving to me as Alcides pranced by.

"Aleksandr Vasilevich! Once we have made the harvest and our captain returns, we will mount our horses and ride together again!"

The field erupted in cheers. I noticed the smiles of contentment on their damp faces.

This manual labor was not shameful to them. On a Russian nobleman's estate, only serfs would do this kind of work. But here, the lands belonged to each and all of them, the bounty of the harvest would benefit all Cossacks of that village of the Don.

But a Cossack was a military animal. Any other chore beyond war and harvest was beneath his dignity. All the men were eager to mount their horses and go to war. It was the Cossack women who planted the crops, tended the fields, cut the wood, raised the children, and kept hearth and home fires burning.

The colonel's wife worried about me, gone away the whole day from the home. I ate my cabbage soup by an oil lamp while she sat by the green tiled stove, knitting.

"You are so curious, Aleksandr Vasilevich!" she said, glancing up at me. "Why do you spend so much time away from our comfortable house? You should rest before the march, but you are always riding your horse, coming back at dark."

"I want to remain fit for the march, madame. A good day's ride keeps me in condition as it does my horse. Is that not the Cossack way?"

She laughed, putting down her knitting. "Yes, you could do with some more muscle, Aleksandr Vasilevich. And some fattening. Look how slender you are, like a fawn! You eat my cabbage soup but don't touch the good fatty meat and sour milk. That and the pancakes with clotted cream would put weight on you."

I struggled not to make a face. To my taste, Cossack meals of cold lamb trotters and hot mutton roasts swimming in soured milk did nothing to pique my appetite. I preferred the standard rations I had grown accustomed to on the march: cabbage soup, millet or buckwheat kasha.

"If you had more muscle and substance, a Cossack girl might take a fancy to you, Aleksandr Vasilevich!"

That settled it. No clotted cream for me.

While I rode through the village at dawn every day, I watched the young boys—some not more than three years old—ride the tribe's horses to the stream. They rode bareback through the marsh grass, the feathered tips of the stalks tickling the soles of their feet. At the stream, the horses stood side by side, their necks extended down, muzzles sucking in the cold water. Meanwhile the boys on their backs wrestled, trying to knock each other to the ground. They roared with laughter as the littlest of them fell backwards off his pony, splashing into the frigid water.

Then they galloped their horses off to play war games. They raced each other along the dirt road from the river to the hay fields to the stables. The men harvesting whistled and urged them on.

Soon enough the boys would help gather the sheaves, but the scything was men's work. Learning to become expert horsemen was crucial.

In the village at sunset, I passed a knot of women leaving the church. They grew silent as I rode by. I felt their black eyes scanning my body, scrutinizing my skin, face, even the new growth of hair along the back of my neck.

I shivered under their scrutiny, the hairs on my neck standing on end. I made up my mind to leave immediately, with or without the Cossack regiment.

As I rode back to the colonel's house, I heard his voice ringing above the voices of other men.

"Ah! Aleksandr Vasilevich! There you are," he said, as I slid off Alcides. "You must make ready, for we leave at dawn."

The Cossack regiment was headed to the Grodno province, where many regular army regiments were gathered.

"You will be able to choose a good regiment," said the colonel. "If they choose you!"

"Thank you, Colonel. I can never repay your kindness."

He tousled my hair. "May God be with you, lad. Now get some sleep."

I saddled Alcides at three in the morning. He snorted at the intrusion in the pitch black of night but settled when he drew in my scent.

"We are riding north, boy," I said, slipping the bridle over his head. "We will be in battle, you and I. Just as soon as I can join a regiment."

When I went into the house to bid good-bye to my hostess, a crowd of family packed the house. There on the floor was the colonel kissing his mother's and father's feet, asking their blessing for his journey.

"Go with God," the parents blessed their son.

I thought of my childhood friend Olga, who had described the Cossacks as barbaric. Ignorant she was and ignorant she would remain.

I heard a rustle of a dress behind me. I turned and saw one of the servant women at my shoulder.

The old Cossack woman leaned closer and hissed in my ear. "And why are you still standing here alone, young lady? Your friends are mounted and your horse is running around the yard."

I turned to her in horror. She nodded, an ironic smile twisting her face.

"We Cossack women are no fools. Go, little soldier girl," she said. "But don't touch our men or you'll be sorry."

Her words haunted me. I hurried out the door to where I had tied Alcides. No soldier had ever been as eager to begin a march.

The new regiment included many of the village Cossacks, but also many others I did not know. These other officers were better educated and remarked on my good manners, indicating my level of upbringing.

The command "To the right by threes!" rang out and we set off, the first unit singing "The Soul Is a Good Steed."

Life on the route to Grodno with the Cossacks relieved my fears. I realized that women were much more intuitive about my sexual identity than the men who wrote me off as a young lad of nobility who neither drank much nor smoked.

At Grodno, my colonel bid me farewell.

"You have much to learn, Aleksandr Vasilevich," he said. "Be frank with any commander you may have. And write immediately to your family for confirmation of your entitlements as a nobleman. Otherwise you will never be an officer."

I bid the colonel good-bye. As I watched the regiment depart, I had an urge to gallop Alcides after them. Suddenly, I was all alone.

I stayed at a roadside tavern. Alcides, hearing the regiment's horses move on, pawed the ground and danced nervously in his stall. Outside the tavern there was a great commotion. Uhlan cavalrymen were playing music and singing at full voice, dancing and leaping about. They swilled vodka from canteens and invited the young lads of Grodno to join in.

As I later learned very well, this was the Verbunok, the military recruiting ritual, much like a traveling circus, enticing young men to join the ranks. I watched the parade of merry soldiers, their arms slung around each other's shoulders. A cadet approached me.

"How do you like our life? It's marvelous, isn't it?"

"Indeed!" I replied, though I found this carnival atmosphere odd and undignified.

"Join us, then!" replied the cadet. "We are the Polish horse lancers. Be one of our uhlans, lad!"

He strode on in pursuit of new recruits.

I learned that the Polish uhlans were recruiting after heavy losses in battle. They needed every breathing body they could find. There were loud dinners where recruits were swayed by camaraderie and vodka. For me, this intimacy and drinking were poison. I wanted only to ride and fight, not be scrutinized by drunken soldiers who might comment on my feminine build.

The next day I saw the same cadet and asked if I could join the Polish regiment—which had an excellent reputation as courageous horsemen—without attending the raucous parties.

He laughed. "You will be in the commander's good graces forgoing the Verbunok! I will take you to see him at once!"

The cadet escorted me to Cavalry Captain Kazimirski's office. On the way we passed through the large public room, typical of any tavern. Drunken cadets and prospective recruits capered and danced, one uhlan catching me by the waist. He spun me across the floor, preparing to dance the mazurka.

The deputy cadet came to my rescue, pulling me by my long Cossack sleeve toward the captain's office.

The captain was about fifty years old. His good-natured face was tempered with a steely look earned from valor and experience in battle. He looked me over.

"State your business."

"My name is Aleksandr Durov," I said, using my father's last name for the first time. "I come to join the Polish uhlans."

"But you are a Don Cossack! You should be serving there."

"My clothes deceive you, forgive me. I am a Russian nobleman but have traveled here with the Don Cossacks. They gave me these clothes. I wish to be part of your regiment, Captain Kazimirski."

"A noble? Can you prove it?"

"No. I have run away from home without consent of my father. At the end of the campaign I will write him. You will see that I speak the truth."

"Your age?"

"I am in my seventeenth year."

He turned to one of the regiment's officers and asked in Polish, "What shall we do? What if he is a Cossack, run away from his unit?"

"He is no Cossack. And he is too young to lie so convincingly. Obviously he is noble born," said a lieutenant. "Look at his hands. Unscarred and uncallused. There is a war on and we need good recruits."

The captain was not convinced. "He is terribly young."

"I have my own horse," I offered.

"Impossible!" said the captain, turning to me. "An uhlan is given a horse from the picket line. If we take you, you will have a chance to sell your horse here in Grodno."

"Sell him!" I said. "God preserve me from that misfortune! I have money. I will feed my horse at my own expense, and I won't part from him for anything on earth."

I saw the reluctance in the captain melt. He was a cavalryman, and my fierce attachment to my horse was the deciding factor.

"I will have to secure permission for you to serve on him. All right, Durov!" He motioned to an uhlan. "Go with uhlan Orlov. He will teach you to ride in formation, wield a saber, shoot, master a lance, and tack your horse with our equipment."

With a curt salute to the captain, Orlov escorted me to a simple cottage where I would be instructed along with all the other new recruits.

Every day at dawn, the new recruits met at the muster room and then went on to the stables. I learned quickly, and the instructor told me I would be a gallant lad.

But brandishing the heavy eight-foot lance! The uhlans' spear was even heavier than the Cossacks'! I didn't have the muscles for it. I hit my head several times as my arm gave way to fatigue. I was not much better with the saber, despite practicing Denisov's technique. I was deathly tired, my arm quivering under the weight. For days my muscles made me feel like some bird whose wings had been stretched to snapping from the joint.

As a nobleman, I was invited to dine with Captain Kazimirski. Although I could barely keep my eyes open during the meal, the captain quizzed me to see how much I had learned in my instruction.

"What do you think of military craft?" he asked me.

I told him I had devoted myself to learning the uhlan exercises and that I considered a cavalryman's calling to be the noblest on earth.

"Most important is fearlessness!" I said. Perhaps it was the glass of vodka forced on me or my fatigue that made me so adamant. "Fearlessness is indivisible from the greatness of the soul, and the combination of these two great virtues leaves no room for vice and low passions."

The room of officers laughed at my passion. But Captain Kazimirski silenced them with a stern look.

"Cadet Durov. Do you really think, young man, that it is impossible to have qualities meriting respect without being fearless? There are a great number of people who are timid by nature and have outstanding qualities."

"I can well believe it, Captain," I answered. "But I also think that a fearless man must surely be virtuous. And it is a fearless man who can serve our tsar."

How I have revisited that conversation! I was drunk on devotion to the uhlans. I wanted nothing more than to serve my country . . . and my tsar.

"Ah! To Tsar Alexander!" shouted the officers, standing and raising their glasses.

I pulled myself to my feet unsteadily, lifting my glass high.

"To our blessed Tsar Alexander!" I said. "The most fearless of all Russians!"

The captain patted me on the shoulder. "Perhaps you are right, Cadet Durov, about the qualities of fearlessness. But let's wait for your first battle—experience can be rather disillusioning."

I heard the grunts of affirmation from the other officers as they drained their glasses of wine and vodka.

How true those words were.

We rode on to Lithuania, toward Vilna. The land was choked with stones, the soil dense with brittle clay. Despite the toil of farmers and serfs, the earth delivered a poor crop. The people were sullen, their faces hollow, their eyes haunted with starvation. The only bread to be had was as black as soot, the dough full of bits of dirt.

At last I was awarded a uniform: my own saber, lance, wooden epaulets, a plumed helmet, and a white cross-belt with cartridges.

Ah, and government-issued boots!

As hard as the lance was to brandish, my boots were the true tyranny! They were like iron traps clamped on my feet. Attached to my heels were heavy spurs that clanked as I walked. Fettered with such footwear I had to stop taking the carefree walks in the woods when we were stationed in a camp—at least until I had developed a fine set of calluses.

In Lithuania, we were stationed at the edge of a swamp in a poor village. Captain Kazimirski assigned me and another young comrade, Wyszemirski, to the first platoon under the command of Lieutenant Boshnjakov.

Wyszemirski was not but a year or so older than I was. He had fair hair and pale eyes, faded as blue fabric left in sun. He knew only a little more than I did but helped me learn maneuvers, how to clean my weapons, where and how to tie Alcides on the picket line. In formation next to me was Kosmy Banka, a stout young man who was as dark as Wyszemirski was fair. He was always first to dinner and drank my ration of vodka that I gave him happily.

"An uhlan who does not drink!" Banka exclaimed merrily, his pudgy hands cradling a tin cup. "I have indeed found a good comrade."

In my spare time after drills and maneuvers, I scavenged the harvested field, searching for overlooked potatoes. I filled my plumed cap with what I found under the clotted earth, my fingernails caked with its brown clay.

My Lithuanian hostess accepted them each day with a scowl. She hated the Russians who occupied her home. Although she cooked the potatoes I brought, she would shove the clay bowl sullenly across the table. On her face was written her deep spite for us, regarding us only as occupiers.

I remembered the babushka who nursed me when I was a dying girl, feverish with smallpox, here in the same land. That good woman had sung of horse spirits and placed horse bones beside my pallet to call down magic to cure me.

I lay awake in bed wondering about these strange Lithuanians whose land we had conquered and annexed. Having recently tasted my own liberty for the first time, I sensed more keenly the bitter hatred they had for the Russians who so casually requisitioned their houses for quarters, turning the owners into servants.

Their independence was worth fighting for! They had once ruled the Russian lands in their own empire. They had conquered Moscow!

But I still became angry when the woman treated my gift of potatoes with contempt. Spiteful woman!

Chapter 24

Guttstadt, Prussia
May 22, 1807

At last! We ride into battle. This is what I had been waiting for. After
months of drilling, action at last! We entered Prussia and faced the
enemy in Guttstadt. I was given permission to ride Alcides. Now I could
prove myself to my country and tsar.

I still could not hold my oak lance as high as I should have, despite
all the will I could muster. But I was ready to face whatever came my way.

I had never heard the boom of cannon fire, nor had my horse.
Alcides jumped sideways, skittering along the rutted road. The roar and
ominous rumble of the cannonballs filled the air.

Our regiment was ordered on attack several times, rotating by
squadrons. I did not understand the tactics and joined each squadron
every time they were called into battle. I rode hard into the attack,
circled around to regroup, and attacked again.

I thought that was how it was done.

A squadron leader—not my own—rode alongside me shouting,
"Get the hell out of here! Go back to your own squadron!"

I rode back, Alcides lathered and heaving. His barrel expanded and collapsed like giant bellows.

"I'm sorry, boy," I said, stroking him.

Our squadron was ordered to rest while the other squadrons pressed on. I thought this a terrible waste of time—why should we not all ride forward together and defeat the enemy at once?

Instead of following orders, I rode Alcides to a nearby knoll where I could better see the battle scene. Suddenly I caught sight of several enemy dragoons surrounding a Russian officer. A pistol shot rang out and the officer fell to the ground from his horse. The enemy prepared to hack him to death where he lay.

Finding a burst of strength, I hoisted my oak lance and galloped Alcides down toward the murderous scene. The dragoons saw the lance pointed at them, approaching at a thunderous pace. They scattered, leaving the Russian officer bleeding on the muddy patch of grass. I rode over to him, Alcides and I blanketing him with our shadow. The officer lay deathly still, his eyes closed.

As the moment wore on, he twitched his eye. I could see he was feigning death, sure I was a Frenchman standing over him.

"Are you all right, sir?" I asked him in Russian. "They have fled. But so has your horse."

"You are Russian!" he gasped. "My horse?"

"Galloped away." I thought for a second. "Do you have need of mine?"

The officer winced, pulling himself up to a sitting position. He clapped a hand over his shoulder, blood oozing through his uniform.

"Oh, be so kind, my friend," he said. "I must get back to my regiment."

I did not think. I slid off my beloved Alcides and tried to help the officer astride.

Weakened from his wound, he could not mount, even with my help. We struggled trying to get him into the saddle, but he was as immobile as a bag of stones.

With luck a soldier from his regiment saw us and offered help. We got the officer into the saddle, though he slumped forward, making Alcides prance.

"Ride off before he falls!" I ordered the soldier. "Return my horse to Recruit Durov in the Polish Horse Regiment."

"Of course, Durov," he said, taking the reins over Alcides's head, leading off the wounded man. "You have saved Lieutenant Panin of the Finnish Dragoons. On behalf of our regiment, we thank you," he said, touching his heart.

He spotted a group of soldiers crossing the edge of the wood. "Over here!" he shouted. "We need help!"

I watched Alcides swing his head toward me as the soldiers led him off. I was left alone in the muddy trampled field. The thud of cannonballs was coming closer, as were the shouts of men.

Alcides! What have I done?

Running through the charges, gunfire, and swordfights, I dashed like a rabbit across the battlefield. Horses' hooves churned up clods of mud and grass, pelting my face and obscuring my vision. I stumbled through the flash of guns, clambered over dead soldiers and horses torn open by cannonballs, their guts slippery underfoot. Men on horses charged by me, once a pair of spurs snagged my uniform jacket.

And I? A cavalry soldier without a horse, scrambling back to my squadron.

Alcides! Where are you now?

When I finally staggered back to my regiment, the captain rode up to me.

"Are you wounded, Durov? Did they kill your horse?"

"That great horse!" exclaimed another. "These French demons!"

When I explained what had happened, the captain shouted at me.

"Get away from the front, you fool!"

I ran further back where I saw lances with the pennons of the Polish Horse Regiment.

Men looked down on me from their horses.

"Oh, my God! Look, at the blood on his uniform!"

"What! Such a young boy to be wounded!"

I looked down on my breast and saw the swath of blood from where I had supported Lieutenant Panin's body against mine. My sleeves too were still wet in blood.

And Alcides was gone.

No one can describe the fatigue that comes from a day at battle. First the fiendish cold! That year spring forgot to appear. I had my greatcoat—a soldier's salvation—stashed in my saddlebags, which had disappeared with Alcides. My uniform jacket was wet, chilling me to the bone. And the cold rain showed no mercy. Wind blew stinging drops sideways until I shivered in spasms.

Grapeshot from the French cannons rained down on us even when we were too far out of range for them to do real damage, pinging against my hat, bouncing off the sleeves of my jacket. The cold of fear, wind, and rain permeated my bones until I ached like an old man. My eyes were swollen into slits from the chill and lack of sleep until I could barely see.

Haunted by the crack of gunfire, the bright red and blues of the French army, the fierce crimson of blood, I fell asleep huddled at the foot of a linden tree.

An infantry soldier from our regiment came by, shaking me by the shoulder. "Vodka, comrade? A piece of bread and lard?"

He obviously took pity on me, a weak child splashed in blood, asleep.

"Eat," he said. "You have seen your share of battle today. They say you have lost your horse."

He offered me a draft of vodka.

"Yes," I said, groaning. I pulled myself up to a sitting position, every muscle in my body rebelling. I drew a gulp of vodka from his canteen and made a face.

"I will give you water," he said. "But the vodka will warm your bones, lad."

He pulled another canteen from his leather bag. I drank greedily.

The soldier squatted beside me watching me chew the food. Even my jaw hurt, though I could not understand why.

"My horse, Alcides. I asked them to return him."

The soldier laughed.

"You are wet behind the ears! Do you think that wounded officer will have the wits to return your pretty horse when we are in battle? Best forget that horse, lad."

Alcides? Forget my best friend, my only link to my home, my father?

I fought back tears, pushing them away savagely with the pad of my thumb. The infantry solider regarded me, offering me another swallow of his precious vodka.

"You need to recover," he said. "You need to eat. You are not a man yet. Our blessed Emperor Alexander would not wish a child's blood spilt in this terrible war."

"I am seventeen," I mumbled.

"You are a liar," he said, spitting on the ground. "You do not look older than fourteen. And if you are seventeen, you are the puniest runt I ever saw. Your mother should have drowned you at birth."

A few days later, after fighting on an unwieldy gelding that did not respond to my heels, reins, or whip, I chanced to see one of our lieutenants, Podwayzacki, galloping away from the enemy position on Alcides.

Alcides saw me and neighed loudly, shaking the lieutenant with his roar.

"He knows you!"

"Lieutenant! He is my horse," I said, jumping off my nag to greet my old friend. "I joined the regiment on him, do you not remember?"

Alcides began to prance and frisk about.

I broke out in a smile, the first since battle.

"Is this really your horse?" said Lieutenant Podwayzacki.

"I gave him to a wounded Lieutenant Panin of the Finnish Dragoons. They said they would return him to me."

"You gave your horse away? You are a fool, Durov! I bought this horse from Cossacks for two gold pieces. And I mean to keep him."

"But—"

"If you are fool enough to give your horse away in battle, you are not intelligent enough to ride so magnificent a mount! I will keep him."

"No!"

"What did you say, Recruit Durov?" Alcides felt the lieutenant's hand tighten on the reins. He threw his head. "Did you contradict me, Durov? You! Who gave away your horse in the heat of battle, you walk across a raging battlefield like a blind dog—"

"I have money, lieutenant! I will give you twice what you paid for him, just give him back to me. My father gave me Alcides. He is the only friend I have!"

Alcides nickered and, ignoring Lieutenant Podwayzacki's hand on the reins, took a step toward me, nudging my shoulder. He made me lose my balance and I fell into the mud.

The lieutenant took a deep breath. He looked down at my blood-encrusted uniform, my smoke-streaked face.

Who else but a horse would choose me for a friend? I was rash, incompetent, pitifully weak.

"You know, Durov, we are fighting Napoleon for our Tsar and country. This is not a child's romp on ponies. I will give you back your horse if you reimburse me my expense. But let me have him now. My horse was killed and I must carry on in the field with my squadron. There is a battle to fight."

"All right," I said, nodding. He spurred forward Alcides, heading back toward the battlefield. "God bless you, Lieutenant."

As he rode off to the blackened, smoking hillside, I called to him.

"Take care of yourself, Lieutenant Podwayzacki! And my horse! Take care of my Alcides!"

Chapter 25

Tsar Alexander left a candle burning by his camp bed. He watched the wax melt and puddle, nearly submerging the wick in its translucent pool. Sleet and snow spat against the windows, rattling the crystal panes.

How I hate them, these generals. These conspirators who murdered my father in cold blood. I cannot abide even their smell, their knowing looks. They rekindle that night's horror with every regard, every sour breath we share in a closed room.

Alexander's hands twisted the sheets. The flickering candle cast absurd shadows against the wall.

Their vile hands, saluting me. Hands that killed my father, bludgeoned him to death, strangled him.

One by one, advisors and generals, the conspirators vanished from Moscow and St. Petersburg. Pahlen was exiled to Courland on the Baltic Sea, while Panin and two other senior officers were banished from St. Petersburg. Nikolai Zubov, who had slammed the gold snuffbox against Tsar Paul's right temple, was deported from Russia.

But a few would remain in Alexander's army as generals. He needed them, their experience in the battlefield.

Still their eyes, lifted from maps of battlefields, would meet his own. *Remember! Remember that March night we murdered your father . . .*

He stared down at their hands, fingers pointing out knolls and valleys, vantage points to defeat Napoleon.

These men forever haunted him with memories. But he needed them to defeat France. For love of Russia he would endure them, for they were good military men.

But he would never forget. His fingers sought the small cloth bag he always carried. The well-worn paper within rustled at his touch.

Austria had been a fickle ally to Russia. Still a coalition had been struck and Alexander's young general aide-de-camp, Prince Peter Dolgoruky, had insisted that because of the alliance, it was certain that Russia and Austria could defeat Napoleon on the Austrian border.

Adam Czartoryski did not trust Dolgoruky and had a visceral dislike for the prince, whom he considered a braggart and a sycophant willing to spill Russian blood in pursuit of glory and honor.

Czartoryski begged the Tsar to delay making a commitment to ally and fight with Austria. In the Tsar's tent, they argued late into the night. Soldiers watched two silhouettes moving in animated discussion against the yellow, lantern-lit canvas.

"May I join the discussion, Your Majesty?" said Prince Dolgoruky, pulling back the flap.

Czartoryski scowled at the aide-de-camp, who was fast becoming a favorite confidant of Alexander's.

"Focus more on your reforms within Russia," he continued, ignoring the intruder. "We have much to do within the country. Tsar, you cannot rely on Austria as a steadfast friend. Nor on Frederick William of Prussia. Insist on a right of passage through the Germanic lands. If they deny Russian troops access to defend us all from Napoleon, seize Berlin. But do not commit Russia's forces to Prussia. As a sovereign and commander, the king is rash—"

"Nonsense!" said Prince Dolgoruky. "You speak like a Pole, while I speak as a Russian prince. I know what you are thinking: 'Seize Berlin.' Of course. Then you will attempt to persuade Our Majesty to make Berlin the center of your glorious independent republic of Poland."

"We will only ask for access for troop movement," said Czartoryski. "How can Prussia deny such a request when asking for an alliance?"

Dolgoruky turned to the Tsar. "I beg you, Your Majesty, do not listen to a Pole's counsel. Napoleon will be defeated with the Austro-Russian alliance. And with the help of the Prussians—"

"The Austrians!" said Czartoryski. "Ha! The Austrians will be absorbed into Napoleon's empire like a hare swallowed by a python. Austria sneers at Russia as barbarians—they would think nothing of deserting you, Your Majesty, in your hour of need."

"Really, Prince Czartoryski," said Alexander. "I think you greatly exaggerate."

"Exaggerate? Your Majesty, those Austrian generals who strut about like overstuffed peacocks will one day meet us as foes on the battlefield, greeting us with their shiny cannons under Napoleon's command. Mark my words."

"Do not listen to this Polish rebel, Your Majesty," said Prince Dolgoruky. "What bad counsel he gives, especially as foreign minister of Russia!"

Alexander could not make a decision. His mind was in turmoil.

What would Peter the Great do? Blast it! I do not know whom to trust.

Czartoryski fumed silently. He could see the vacillation in Alexander's eyes.

"You are dismissed, Minister Czartoryski," said Alexander.

When Czartoryski had left the tent, Prince Dolgoruky whispered to the Tsar: "You cannot listen to him, I beg of you. You are the all-powerful Tsar of Russia, and Czartoryski's allegiance will always remain with his native Poland. Send me in the future to deal with Napoleon. I will let him know not to trifle with a descendent of Peter the Great!"

Two days before his departure to Austria, Alexander visited a venerable mystic, Sevastianov. This Russian starets lived in a small hovel on the Gulf of Finland.

Sevastianov welcomed the Tsar but forbade him to enter with his guards or footmen. Alone, Alexander crossed the humble threshold, ducking low so as not to hit his head on the door frame. The hermit's dark sanctuary smelled of sea and sweat, for the monk was not prone to bathing, no matter the season.

A tallow candle was lit in honor of the Tsar, for the starets was poor and thrifty. The tallow made the Tsar cough, the rendered fat smoking thick and black.

Sevastianov served the Tsar a tea infusion of berries: whortleberries, blackberries, wild strawberries, and some other wild fruit. There was a tartness that the Tsar did not recognize, and when he inquired, the starets only shrugged.

"Your Excellency, forgive me," he said, exposing the gaps in his teeth. "We have our mysteries. Now, my Tsar, please tell me why you honor me with this visit."

Alexander looked about the hovel, drying grasses, herbs, and flowers hanging overhead like an upside-down garden. Roses of all colors gave off a heady fragrance.

I read Voltaire, Kant, Hobbes, Rousseau. I correspond with Thomas Jefferson. To spurn superstition is the hallmark of a liberal education. Why do I return to the Orthodox Church to visit an obscure starets?

"I ask you, Starets Sevastianov, will I defeat Napoleon?"

The mystic looked unblinking past the smoke, his eyes unfocused.

The starets spread his hands wide, like two white starfish in dark waters.

"No. Your time has not come," Sevastianov said, startlingly loud. His voice reverberated in the low-ceilinged room.

Alexander set down his teacup, his brow set in deep furrows.

"I am to be forgiven, I hope, Your Excellency," said the hermit, crossing his hands over his breast. "My Tsar seeks truth. The truth is this: the accursed Frenchman will beat you and destroy your army. You will have to flee in shame. Wait. Get stronger. Your hour will come. Then God will help you destroy the enemy of mankind."

Alexander took another sip of the tart brew, making a face. The strange man said no more.

Ah, but the die is cast! Napoleon has already occupied Vienna, crossed the Danube as far as Brunn. The Corsican wolf is nearly at Russia's front door. Besides, my advisors—other than that recalcitrant Czartoryski!—have endorsed our march against the French usurper.

Alexander cast his eyes about the hovel. There were only a few icons set in the corners, darkened with soot. A string of prayer beads, a simple washbasin carved of wood. A straw pallet and coarse wool blanket lay a stride away. The Tsar leaned back in the crude birchwood chair, making it creak.

He blinked at the queer little monk through the smoke. Despite Sevastianov's unwelcome words, Alexander felt a quiet peace. He lingered over his simple wild-berry infusion in a chipped cup, his eyes taking in the rustic setting.

Alexander's fingers reached inside his breast pocket.

"Starets, I have a coded note. I've never been able to decipher it, though I have had trusted advisors and mathematicians try. Would you look at it?"

"Of course, my Tsar."

Alexander unfolded the paper, putting it into the mystic's hands. There was a long moment of silence.

"Can you understand anything about it?"

Sevastianov shook his head slowly. "Who wrote it?"

"My father, Tsar Paul. The night of his murder."

Sevastianov glanced up at the Tsar. "This is what I can tell you, Your Majesty. This letter signifies a great deal to you. The letters written here: AP. Of course they refer to Your Majesty, Alexander Pavlovich."

Alexander started.

"Keep this letter close to your heart. Do not show it to others," said the starets. "What's done is done. It is for you only to decode, Your Majesty."

Sevastianov passed the letter back to the Tsar. Alexander stared at the mystic.

"Tell me, Starets," said the Tsar. "What is life like for you here?"

Sevastianov's eyes sparkled now. He leaned forward, his voice full of joy.

"I have never known such contentment." He stroked his white beard. "I am with God day and night. Imagine my joy!"

"Thank you, Sevastianov," said Alexander, rising, though he longed to linger in the hermit's cabin. There was a palpable peace that hovered in the air, despite the smells of dirty linen and tallow.

Instead, Alexander's nose sought the pervading odor of the dried roses overhead, dangling from the ceiling.

He let out a great sigh of satisfaction.

"Perhaps we will meet again, Sevastianov."

"In God's kingdom surely," answered the hermit, snuffing the candle. "If not before. Until then, my Tsar, may the Lord guide you. And Russia."

Chapter 26

Alexander listened to Prince Dolgoruky's advice, but he did not entirely forget Czartoryski's either. Two Russian armies had amassed on the western border. The first—fifty thousand troops—was commanded by General Mikhail Ilarionovich Kutuzov. The second—ninety thousand troops—under the command of General Mikhelson stood at the ready to fight against Prussia if necessary, should it not willingly allow the Russian troops to cross its borders.

The Tsar left St. Petersburg on a morning so shrouded in fog that he could not see the Neva from his office at the Winter Palace. Alexander shivered as he thought of the starets's prophecy.

Despite the starets's words, good fortune awaited the Tsar in Prussia. Napoleon had invaded southern Germany. Outraged, King Frederick William III invited Russia's troops to cross Prussia's borders to fight their common enemy.

Alexander was feted with an elaborate reception in the Prussian Court. Queen Louise, famous for her beauty and notorious for her sexual appetite, was taken by the young Tsar, declaring him "perfection among men."

While Alexander was flattered by her attentions, he was more interested in cultivating a strong alliance with Prussia than bedding the Prussian queen.

"I propose a toast," he said, lifting his glass of Riesling. "To your predecessor. To the spirit of Frederick the Great, one of the finest warriors of all time."

The three lifted their glasses, the two Prussian royals naturally flattered.

Alexander, smiled, drinking deeply. Replacing his glass on the table he regarded his hosts.

"I wish to pay the great man homage. In person."

There was silence in the dining room except for the hiss and creak of the enormous ceramic stove.

Queen Louise, her face flushed with warmth, wine, and love, asked, "Homage? What do you mean, Your Excellency?"

The fatigue of travel and the sweet Prussian wines may be coaxing me from reason. Is it the ghost of my father who drives me to pay respects to a dead man?

Am I honoring Frederick? Or my murdered father?

The candle flames blew sideways, a sudden draft chilling the room. Queen Louise pulled her ermine collar tighter around her neck.

"I wish to bow my head in prayer at the foot of Frederick the Great's tomb. And pay my respects to the man my forefathers held in such high esteem."

King Frederick William raised his eyebrows. Alexander studied his face.

"Of course!" the Prussian king said, his chin lifting from his stiff collar in assent. "What a great honor you do Prussia. We shall visit the crypt right after dessert."

A pale-faced Queen Louise cloaked in black accompanied the Tsar and the king across the empty courtyards of the Potsdam castle to the churchyard. She had imagined Alexander in her warm bed in the throes of lust, not in a cold tomb! As the spell of champagne slowly ebbed, the beautiful queen shivered at the thought of visiting a long-dead corpse.

The three descended by torchlight into the crypt. Resting his head on the foot of the tomb, Alexander paid his respects to the man his father had so revered. He kissed the tomb, saying, "Frederick the Great, good friend to my father, grandfather, and Russia, aid us now in our fight against the Grand Armée and Napoleon."

The king and the Tsar solemnly swore an oath.

"To the mutual defense of Russia and Prussia!" said Alexander, his words echoing in the musty vault.

He could feel the cold hand of his dead father, clapping him on the back. Then he thought of the ominous words of the queer little hermit, Sevastianov, and he shivered.

Chapter 27

Near the Village of Austerlitz
December 1805

Tsar Alexander arrived in Olmutz in Moravia, fiercely determined to lead his Russian troops. Not willing to talk with anyone who might try to change his mind, he immediately relieved General Kutuzov of his duties.

"I shall make the tactical decisions," the Tsar informed the general. Kutuzov, an old bear of a man, knew he could not oppose the Tsar even if he thought him an exquisite fool, vainglorious, and misinformed.

"Your Excellency," Kutuzov protested. "Please allow me to use my experience in the field. I have fought many battles."

"No, General Kutuzov," said Alexander. He thought of the last night his father was alive, entertaining the fat general, the two of them laughing together. "I along with General Weyrother, and my aide-de-camp"—he nodded to Dolgoruky, standing beside him—"shall issue the orders. You will execute them according to our wishes."

"General Weyrother! An Austrian?" gasped Kutuzov. "We should at least wait for reinforcements, Your Majesty. Our troops are exhausted, living on frozen potatoes with no salt. They haven't the strength to defeat the Grand Armée."

"It is thinking like this that assures me I am making the right decision," said Alexander. "You haven't the grit! Of course we will defeat Napoleon! *Toute de suite!*"

Kutuzov rubbed his blind eye in frustration. He could foresee the bloodshed that awaited them.

After Kutuzov was dismissed, Czartoryski begged Alexander to reconsider.

"Listen to General Kutuzov, Your Majesty! Do not attack unless we have reinforcements, I beg you. Wait for the other regiments to reach us. And for God's sake, Your Excellency, let Kutuzov take command of his troops! He's a seasoned soldier, a great commander—"

"Bah! General Slowpoke, the fat old man. That's what our younger Russians call him," countered Dolgoruky. "The soldiers shall be inspired to have their tsar lead them. No commander has done such since Peter the Great."

"Hurrah!" said the sycophants who always clustered around the Tsar. "Tsar Alexander shall lead us into battle as Peter the Great did a hundred years ago!"

Czartoryski looked in disgust at the young officers—Lieven, Volkonsky, Gargarin, and in particular Dolgoruky.

These men in their glittering gold braid and spotless uniforms are just new arrivals, cocky and well fed, unlike the starving soldiers who have just marched here, dead with exhaustion.

"You are dismissed, Minister Czartoryski," said the Tsar.

Czartoryski jerked his chin up with indignation. "Yes, Your Majesty." He bowed and threw a quick look over his shoulder at Prince Dolgoruky, who sneered at the departing foreign minister.

On the eve of battle, Alexander sent Dolgoruky as emissary to Napoleon.

Prince Peter Dolgoruky rode to the French encampment dressed in his spotless blue uniform, his gold braid shining.

"I requested a meeting with Tsar Alexander himself," said Napoleon, surveying the arrogant officer who barely tipped his hat as he approached the French emperor.

"Our Supreme Tsar Alexander of Russia will not attend any negotiations with you, sir," answered Dolgoruky.

"Do not address me like some common soldier, you wet-eared nincompoop!" bellowed Napoleon. "You are addressing the emperor of France."

Prince Dolgoruky ignored the remark. "Tsar Alexander demands you renounce your claims on the Kingdom of Italy, the left bank of the Rhine, and Belgium. You must evacuate Vienna immediately. Only then will the Tsar of Russia consider meeting you in person."

"Enough of your arrogance," snapped Napoleon. "Tell your tsar I am not accustomed to dealing with underlings, especially one with the manners of a cowherd. We shall meet you and your tsar on the battlefield in the morning. Alexander shall rue the day he sent you in his stead!"

A rider in a red-trimmed green uniform, a plume drooping now with soot and scorch, urged his horse forward against the surging tide of men retreating.

"Advance!" cried Tsar Alexander, though he could barely control his horse amid the grapeshot, falling bodies, and roar of cannons. "Advance, I command you!"

Above on the Pratzen plateau the French artillery fired, cannonballs exploding in thick curtains of black dirt. Russian soldiers threw down their guns to run faster, the torrent of mankind crushing the officers who barked orders in vain from their warhorses. Banners heaved and fell into the trodden earth.

Alexander's mare moved through the broken bodies, bloody hands rising blindly to supplicate for help, forming a sea of waving arms. "Help me!" they cried, as his mare picked up her feet in a dainty dance to avoid their writhing bodies.

"Over here, Your Excellency!" cried Adam Czartoryski. He maneuvered his horse toward the emperor.

"They are—our army is retreating!" cried Alexander in wonderment. "They are retreating!"

"They have no choice, Your Highness," Czartoryski shouted over the roar of cannons and screams of dying soldiers. "The casualties! We have lost almost a third of our men."

A half dozen horses beyond them on a picket screamed. A cannonball had landed squarely on the center of the line. The first few fell like toys to the ground, silent. Some reared in panic—others, white eyed, rolled in pain, their intestines spilling out.

Alexander shuddered, vomiting into his rein hand.

"Follow me!" shouted Czartoryski, tugging at Alexander's rein. "We'll find cover and I'll fetch the physician."

Czartoryski left the Tsar in the care of the imperial physician, James Wylie. Then the Pole wheeled his horse around and galloped back to the Russian battle line.

Alexander sat hunched by an icy ditch under a linden tree, his head buried in his hands, sobbing.

"Your Majesty?" asked Doctor Wylie.

Alexander choked. This doctor, this voice. The hands who had dressed the corpse of his father.

"Please remount, sire," said the doctor. "We must move from this spot."

"Leave me be!"

The doctor looked at the young squire who stood nearby, holding the Tsar's mare.

"There is a hamlet just a few versts away," said the young squire. "Please, I beg you to remount, Your Majesty."

The sobs had turned to convulsions, the Tsar now desperately ill.

"We have to get him to shelter," said the doctor to the squire. "I will prepare a potion to calm him. His Majesty is ill." He turned again to the Tsar, authority creeping into his voice. "You must remount. The Grand Armée is advancing."

Little by little the doctor and squire managed to coax the Tsar onto his mare. The squire jumped his horse back and forth across the little ditch as an example, urging the shaken emperor to follow close behind.

Then the squire rode on to find shelter in the hamlet.

"This is all we can manage?" asked the doctor when he arrived with the Tsar at a peasant's hut that the squire had found.

"The Austrians have requisitioned all the other buildings," said the young man.

"Outrageous!" said Doctor Wylie. He turned to see the Tsar hunched in his saddle, listing to one side, about to fall.

"All right. Strew the floor with straw. Keep watch while I find wine for the medicine."

King Charles of Austria was housed in the same town. The doctor pounded on the door of his temporary residence. "Open up in the name of Tsar Alexander of Russia!"

After several minutes the door finally unlatched.

"Please!" said an Austrian aide-de-camp. "I beg you not to make such noise! The king of Austria sleeps."

"Give me wine and I shall stop my bellowing. I need to prepare the Tsar's medication."

"Wine? Oh, no, sir!" said the officer. "I cannot procure wine from the king's storeroom without his express permission. And I cannot wake him, of course."

"You must! This is the Tsar of Russia, your ally!"

"Please go away. The king of Austria must not be disturbed."

"Did you not hear me? The wine is for the Tsar of Russia, Alexander I!"

"Go away, I must insist!"

Doctor Wylie rode away, his heart pulsing in rage. A few minutes away he found a campfire surrounded by Cossacks.

"Please!" he implored the men. He looked at their dirty faces, scarred and bloody. One had lost his eye, and another writhed on a filthy blanket.

"Please give me a draft of wine that I might make the Tsar a potion!"

The eldest man, dressed in a dirty blue *chekmen*, nodded. He lurched to his feet in agony, staggering forward. He reached for a bladder tied up in his leather kit, giving it to the doctor.

"To our Tsar's health," he croaked, his arm shaking wildly as he made his offering.

The doctor nodded solemnly, accepting the old Cossack's gift to an emperor.

Back at the hovel, he prepared a draft of opium in the wretched wine.

"Drink, I beg you, Your Excellency," the doctor said. "You will wake refreshed."

The first news that reached St. Petersburg was that Austerlitz was a Russian victory. As Alexander rode back into the capital, citizens lauded him and peasants kissed his boots.

It was not long before the truth became known. With thousands of casualties, the defeat hit Russia hard.

Czartoryski penned a letter to his friend Tsar Alexander, reproaching him for pushing General Kutuzov aside and for his own vainglorious but useless presence on the battlefield. Alexander received the missive and read, his hands shaking with emotion:

> . . . *instead of moving ahead to the advance posts, or later exposing yourself in front of the columns, Your Majesty, far from helping, if I may speak the truth.*

The Tsar closed his eyes, shaking with emotion. Of course that impertinent Pole would speak the truth. He always had—even to the detriment of their friendship:

> *You only upset and impeded the generals. It would have been better had Your Majesty stayed clear and let the army march forward without you. You were a distraction and the charm of your accompaniment lost its power. It was precisely at that place in the battlefield of Austerlitz where you rode that the rout was so immediate and complete. Yes, Your Majesty had his share of that chaos, but you ought to have hastily ridden away from the engagement without demonstrating your terror. To see your predicament only increased the sense of panicked retreat and general demoralization.*
>
> *Your servant,*
> *Adam Czartoryski*

Tears of humility sprung to Alexander's eyes.

He's right. No one else on earth would tell me the truth. They would kiss the manure from my boots, toast my immortal name and all tsars of

Russia before me. But only Adam Czartoryski would ever dare to show me my error. No one else in the world would have the courage to berate me like this in order that I might alter my course of destiny.

No—there is one other who tells me the truth. One other whom I can trust.

Alexander turned toward his secretary, who was standing in the antechamber.

"Please tell Her Highness, the Tsarina Elizabeth, to expect me to sup with her this evening."

Chapter 28

Berlin
October 1806

The French soldier smiled broadly, exposing the gaps in his rotten teeth. Warm sun, bright for so late in October, lit his face.

He bit off a chunk of bread and hearing the whining of the dog that accompanied him, threw him half his piece.

The sun glanced off the soldier's bayonet. From his musket hung a goose, dangling wildly from its broken neck on a piece of twine. Like all the French troops, this soldier was not shy about taking the spoils.

The soldier grinned, blinking into the tart autumnal air, his skin red and oily. He looked up at the nearby statue of Frederick the Great and shook his head. The Frenchman and his comrades had defeated the Prussian army—a quarter million strong—and battled their way into the Prussian capital. They had won the right to take whatever they could find. He looked down at his toes, emerging caked with dirt from the holes in his boots.

He sniffed the air, enjoying the wafting aroma of the enormous cooking pot on a flatbed wagon just ahead of him. The army was accompanied by vast cauldrons attached to wagons, kettles large enough to feed hundreds at a time. The cooks and stokers worked around the clock. The cooks concocted stews and soups to feed French stomachs so far from home, while the stokers kept the fires burning constantly despite inclement weather or raging battle.

As the soldier enjoyed the thought of a hot meal, Napoleon reined in his stallion and surveyed the city of Berlin from the shadow of the statue of Frederick the Great. Watching his troops march through the arched gateway, he noticed the jolly soldier with his tattered uniform and battered boots, a goose swinging from his musket.

"Now he's a sight," said a staff general, reining his horse next to the emperor. "What a disgrace to the Grand Armée!" As the general moved to reprimand the soldier, Napoleon held up his hand, staying him.

"Leave him be. He's not that far, not that long from the battlefield of Jena. These Frenchmen. My countrymen. They can fight, *Mon Dieu!*"

Napoleon nodded toward the soldier.

"Let him hang a goose from his bayonet. He enters Berlin a French victor. He'll look livelier for the next battle."

Napoleon turned to his brother-in-law, Murat.

"I want to pay my respects to Frederick the Great," he said, tucking his right hand into his shirt, his fingertips on his heart.

"The Prussian?" said Murat, wrinkling his nose in disgust.

"Ask Caulaincourt to locate the crypt. I intend to pay my respects before I settle into quarters."

"And what about the king and his beautiful queen?" asked Murat, smirking. "Will you pay your respects to her? Or only to her defeated husband?"

"Queen Louise of Prussia is a beauty. But both she and her husband Frederick William are fools." Napoleon leaned over from his horse to take an apple offered by a staff sergeant. He bit into the fruit with a crisp snap.

"Good autumn fruit," he said. "It has been a good season." The emperor smiled, dabbing apple juice from his mouth with his gloved hand.

"Why, they thought they could defeat France and the Grand Armée without a single ally standing along them. Stupidity! Arrogance!" Napoleon said. "If they had waited until Alexander moved his Russian army to the battlefield, then we would have had a battle to test our strength."

Murat grunted in agreement.

"The Russians weren't much use at Austerlitz, were they? Rumor has it Alexander relieved General Kutuzov of command just before the battle."

Napoleon smiled. That great victory would always remain sweet. And yet, victory or defeat, there was always another battle to be fought. He sighed.

"Alexander suffers from inexperience and youthful arrogance," said Napoleon. "As for these Prussians, they are brave and quite skilled, but they have some incompetent commanders. That's why I pay my respects to the greatest warrior of them all: Frederick the Great."

He looked up at the statue above him. "If he were alive we wouldn't be here. Don't doubt that for a minute, Murat."

In the street, the soldier started whistling a tune, a bawdy song from a Parisian tavern. The dog trotted along at his side, his tongue slung long and panting from his mouth.

"Find Caulaincourt," Napoleon said, referring to his former ambassador to St. Petersburg, now his master of the horse. "He'll know where the crypt is. I hear Tsar Alexander visited the tomb a year or so ago." The victorious emperor of France chuckled. "A lot of good it did him. He must have offended the great warrior."

Chapter 29

Battlefield of Heilsberg, Prussia
May 1807

I can barely hold my pen, I am so exhausted:

> *Dear Papa,*
> *Since our ignoble defeat at Austerlitz seventeen months*
> *ago (28,000 noble Russian soldiers slaughtered!) our*
> *Polish uhlans have been ordered to the battlefields of the*
> *East in Heilsberg to defend Prussia.*
>
> *Prussia! Their vile King Frederick William antago-*
> *nized Napoleon, challenging him to war on the battle-*
> *fields of Jena and Auerstadt. What stupidity! Together*
> *we could have defeated this French ogre. But instead of*
> *waiting for us to join the Prussian army on the battle-*
> *field, Frederick William declared war and stood against*
> *Napoleon. Alone.*
>
> *Now their country is sliced into tidbits at Napoleon's*
> *whim.*

I swear my allegiance to our supreme Tsar Alexander I. I shall die for him. I shall die for Russia. But for Prussia?

Heilsberg. I see many men as white as sheets, I see them duck when a shell flies over as if they could evade it. Evidently in these men, fear has more force than reason. I have already seen a great many killed and maimed. It is pitiful to watch the wounded moaning and crawling over the so-called field of honor. What can ease the horror for a common soldier? For an educated man it is a completely different matter; the lofty feeling of honor, heroism, devotion to the emperor, and sacred duty to his native land compel him to face death fearlessly, endure suffering courageously, and part with life calmly.

As I dipped my pen in the bottle of ink, I wondered, *What did the infantryman really feel?* So many serfs were forced to fight, "given" by the wealthy aristocrats as their contribution to the cause, Mother Russia, to our tsar. So cheap are their souls, offered so freely by their masters! These serfs were the ones who pressed forward, who fell face first into the mud, one after another to fight, to die winning just another patch of mud, foot by foot against the French. Their war was a bloody game of dominoes, one dead comrade falling against another.

The infantry had no horses to carry them into victory or to gallop away in retreat. Battles were won by the foot soldiers, not by the cavalry. We owe them a great debt.

But I could not write that to my father.

So I simply signed the letter:

Your loving son,
Aleksandr Durov

I sat and stared at that letter for a long time. How long, I could not say. Then I carefully tore it into tiny pieces and scattered them to the wind.

Alcides lost a shoe. The imbalance would make him lame if he didn't bruise and tear his hoof first.

As I rode through the explosions, heavy smoke, and rain of grapeshot, I was wondering how to find a good farrier in the heat of battle when a grenade exploded under Alcides. He leapt with wild surprise. Shrapnel whistled around us, showering us in dirt so that I saw nothing. I responded the only way I could, by digging my seat deep into the saddle and clamping my legs around Alcides's barrel.

"You've been hit by a grenade," shouted Nestor, a new recruit, riding next to us.

"What?" I could not comprehend.

I leapt off Alcides, examining him from head to tail, running my shaking hands under his belly.

"Get back on him," screamed another uhlan. "Race for the hill! We are under artillery attack!"

It was not until we were over the knoll that I thought of examining myself.

"Are you wounded, Durov?"

"No," I said, not comprehending.

"It is impossible," said Nestor to the others in my squadron. "We saw the grenade explode under the horse's belly."

"No, I examined him! He galloped soundly and swiftly. Not a false step."

"Impossible!" repeated Nestor. "We all saw the grenade explode!"

"What strong angels guard over you," said Oleg, who rode directly behind me in our regular formation. "Think now of your angels and those who pray for you, that you might recognize their power and give thanks."

Still dumbfounded, I thought of my father and old grandmother. My mind flashed on the old Lithuanian babushka who cared for me when I was dying.

And of course Astakhov, who gave me Alcides.

The order was given to pull back. Our regiment suffered many casualties, and the groaning survivors were carried in an endless parade of litters to tents or simply laid in the trampled grass. The echoing screams of amputation made the horses white eyed with fear, rearing and pulling back on the picket lines.

I needed no looking glass to imagine my physical state. I regarded the faces around me. Young men, aristocrats, moving with the stiffness of ninety-year-old men. Knuckles swollen as big as pig trotters, faces haggard. I heard the chatter of teeth that matched my own.

But worst of all, their eyes! Haunted. Seared by images too horrible, blocking the natural light of their young souls. Their eyes were dull, deadened to the world around them. These soldiers moved merely in order to survive, automatically stuffing stale brown bread into their mouths, dampened by the pouring rain. Their hair was either plastered to their skulls or spiked in dozens of directions like madmen's.

They were no longer alive, just phantoms wandering the earth.

I received permission to ride to Heilsberg a verst away from the battlefield to find a farrier. I had to find food as well. In battle we are required to carry our own rusks. Mine had disappeared with my saddlebags.

The rain had begun the night before, soaking the ground where we slept. Rain dripped down my helmet, splashing my chafed breasts, forming rivulets at my collar that worked a chill down my spine. The rain even made its way into my boots, soaking my already-freezing feet. I quaked like a birch leaf and could not control my shivering body.

At Heilsberg I found a blacksmith who was shoeing some Cossacks' horses. He agreed to shoe Alcides. I walked a short distance to a roadside tavern. A Jewess ushered me to a large leather chair, where I flopped down in exhaustion. She agreed to find me bread and rusks. I could barely manage to dig my frozen hand into my purse for money.

I gave her the coins with my stiff fingers and fell instantly asleep. The warmth of a fire, the comfort of the old stuffed chair, lulled my aching body and mind into a numbing slumber.

I dreamt of a man in the dark touching me, in intimate places. His hands were huge and rough. I was riding Alcides in my nightgown. The man seized my shoulders, lifting me off my horse's back.

He forced me astride, facing him in his own saddle, a bolster almost as large as a chair. His tongue ran over my neck, my breasts. He grasped at the ribbons of my nightgown.

I strained to see his face in the darkness. He pressed his shoulder against my mouth so I could not scream.

"Shh! Little horse girl," he said. "I will not hurt you."

I awakened to a soldier shaking my shoulder.

"Honorable sir! You must wake up!"

The room was black, with only the embers of a fire glowing orange. It was deserted except for the soldier and me.

"The cannons are getting closer," he said. "Cannonballs are falling on the city!"

I raced back to the blacksmith and found Alcides still standing there. Wet from the rains, unfed and unshod. The blacksmith, the tavern owners, had all fled.

"Oh, Alcides!" I muttered, burying my face in his neck. I felt his body shivering.

I mounted my poor horse, moving him toward the city gates. But we were fighting against the tide. Throngs of wounded were pushing their way into the city, along with men, women, and children all surging through the gates to find shelter from Napoleon's troops.

Alcides kicked against the pressing crowd. I knew he would rear if he could find space. We stood like a rock in a river, immobile in the flood of humanity fleeing the French.

A troop of Cossacks pressed through the crowd as only Cossacks could. I followed in their wake, Alcides's head to the rump of the Cossack in front of me. My knee was crushed against the side of a wagon. I was pulled sideways in my saddle, clutching Alcides's mane to keep from tumbling off. Hanging over my saddle, my shoulder struck against the struts of a carriage.

I was certain I had broken my shoulder. The pain rendered me weak and useless. I was astonished that I still straddled Alcides's back, my left hand entwined tightly in his mane.

As we were spat out beyond the city gates, I had no choice but to urge my tired, unshod horse into a gallop toward my squadron's last station. I knitted my fingers even deeper into his mane, my body unsteady but spurring him on. I had to find my platoon's new location.

The night was as dark as a coal mine. I could not see beyond my horse's ears. I loosened the reins, hoping his sense of smell would locate my platoon's herd of horses. I surrendered myself completely to Alcides's instinct.

We blundered up a steep embankment and then another. I smelled the rot of death but could not see anything. Alcides shied and jumped away from unseen obstacles. I clung tighter to his mane, mumbling prayers into his coarse hair.

Finally after an interminable time struggling upwards, Alcides plunged down an embankment. I was thrown forward but used what remaining strength I had to ease myself a little back in the saddle, taking the weight off his exhausted forelegs.

But the incline was steeper than any imaginable. To save both of us, I leapt off him, my hand clutching the reins. I tumbled forward taking him with me, barely avoiding his hooves from crushing my skull.

Hot pain shot through my shoulder. But I had realized by this point it was not broken.

With my shaking steps I led Alcides blindly down the cliff, clutching at shrubs to keep from slipping. I bent close to the ground to inspect each footstep forward. At this incline I could take a false step and plunge into an abyss.

Where have you taken me, Alcides?

We stepped at last into level ground and I remounted. The moon had finally risen, illuminating a ghastly vision.

Alcides had taken me to a field of death: the scene of the retreat from Heilsberg on the road to Friedland.

Corpses lay everywhere. An officer's gold braided uniform was washed in red, his neck slashed. Blood curdled like red whey in the mud. Bodies littered the field in awkward positions, some impossibly contorted, others like boys curled asleep in the torn grass. A young Don Cossack had died with his mouth stretched in yowling surprise. Flies buzzed lazily in and out of his mouth.

This boy was a Don Cossack but I don't know his regiment. Was he a comrade of the cheeky Cossack scout who had stolen a kiss from me? Will I find Denisov's body here in the same battlefield?

Alcides dropped his nose to a dead man, snorting, then leapt over him, bolting up so abruptly I nearly lost my seat in the saddle.

Beyond the field toward the right I saw the yellow embers of campfires. I quickly calculated where Alcides had taken me. Those must be the embers of our platoon!

I urged Alcides forward toward the fires. Though he moved forward he fought me to bear left.

"Enough, Alcides!" I said.

I spurred him forward over the mayhem. Dawn was approaching but the moonlight still played on the ghastly scene. Alcides jumped the corpses, each time landing to the left, pulling me off center in the saddle. I yanked his reins to the right and we crabbed toward the soldiers' cook fires.

I heard the clatter of horses' hooves beyond me.

"Halt!" cried a voice in Russian. "Who goes there?"

My spine relaxed, my shoulders sagging forward.

"A Polish uhlan," I answered.

"Where are you going?" shouted a general, reining his horse toward me.

"Oh, Your Excellency! I am returning to the Fourth Platoon."

"But the Fourth Platoon stands behind us!" he answered, pointing in the direction Alcides had been determined to take. "You are riding toward the enemy, uhlan!"

The general and his men galloped off in the direction of Heilsberg.

I climbed up my horse's neck, kissing his ears. He was so exhausted from lack of feed and verst upon verst of hard riding, he allowed me to caress him.

"How could I doubt you, old friend?" I murmured. I gave him his rein once again. He felt the looseness of contact and broke into a gallop toward the encampment with a roaring neigh that resonated through my entire body.

When we reached the camp, my platoon was already mounted and prepared to move out.

"To the right by threes!" ordered the captain.

Alcides, despite his hunger and fatigue, neighed with gusto, taking his place among the ranks. He—and I—were back with the herd. We had survived.

Wyszemirski and my other comrades' faces lit up when they saw me. Wyszemirski leaned over his skittish horse to clap me on the back.

"We thought you done for," he said. The others in the regiment nodded solemnly, for many of our men had indeed been lost forever.

After a few versts we stopped to water our horses at a stream. Alcides sucked up the water, his ribs working under me like a giant bellows.

A corporal rode up to me. "Durov! The sergeant major orders you to report to him immediately."

I exchanged looks with Wyszemirski. He just shook his head.

"You do foolish things, Durov!" the sergeant major roared. "You won't keep your head on your shoulders. You gave away your horse on the battlefield. You left yourself exposed like a rabbit amongst a pack of wolves! You went to Heilsberg, requesting only minutes to tack on a shoe on your horse and what? You fell asleep? With the French pounding artillery all around you?"

"Sir, I—"

"I do not care how old you are. There are some standards of sense that are required no matter whether you are seventeen or seventy. I advise you to stay on your horse, who is a great deal more intelligent than you are. Die on your horse, Durov. Die with honor or you will be taken prisoner, murdered by marauders, or worst of all, considered a coward. Do you hear me?"

"Yes, sir."

I left in the persistent rain that drenched me. I had not eaten in two days and had ridden through the night and now day. Having lost my wool greatcoat along with my other belongings in my saddlebags, I suffered mightily with the wet weather, shivering with spasms that rocked my body.

We rode three abreast but when we approached an obstacle such as a narrow bridge we negotiated it single file. During these halts I took advantage of the delay by dismounting Alcides and throwing myself on the ground to catch a few moments sleep. My comrades would call to me to mount as we proceeded.

I dragged my oak lance with me, pulling myself up weary with exhaustion.

The sergeant major saw these interludes and shouted at me. Even my comrades were angry, for we were all exhausted.

"Look at us, Durov," Wyszemirski said. "We too are sleep deprived. Do what we do and sleep in the saddle. Knot your fingers into your horse's mane."

"Next time you dismount we won't wake you," grunted Oleg. "Stay mounted, Durov. We won't be covering for you any longer."

"If you die, there will be no extra ration of vodka for me," said Kosmy Banka, wagging his big head sadly. "Take care of yourself, Durov. I'm fond of the drink."

"All right," I said, though my eyes were so swollen with lack of sleep I could barely make out my comrades.

I stayed in the saddle throughout the night. I mistook trees for uhlans and uhlans for trees. I buried my face in Alcides's mane, waking with a jolt. Several times I found long strands of my horse's mane in my teeth, his neck wet from my saliva.

At dawn we at last came to a halt.

"You may kindle small fires to heat your kasha," said the sergeant major.

I had nothing to eat but lay down to sleep by our fire for my ten campmates.

"No sleeping, Durov!" said Wyszemirski. "The sergeant major ordered us to let the horses graze in the pasture. Take the curb bit from your horse's mouth and lead him to the grass."

Horses came first. My responsibility—my life—depended on Alcides.

The grass was thick with dew. I huddled in a ball, pulling my knees tight to my chest to try to warm myself.

"What the devil is wrong with you, Durov?" asked Wyszemirski, losing his patience. "Are you ill?"

"No, I am chilled until death! I lost my greatcoat with my saddlebags. The Cossacks sold the horse but kept my supplies."

"This won't do," said Wyszemirski. "You are the youngest among us. A Russian cavalryman cannot survive without a greatcoat. Here, go speak to the sergeant major. There are bundles of greatcoats gathered from dead soldiers on the battlefield. They are on the wagon train. He can procure you one."

All I could do was shiver an acknowledgment.

"Look, I will look after Alcides. And here," he said digging in his pocket, retrieving a green-tinged piece of hardtack. "Here is a rusk to eat, but I have very little myself. You go now and speak to the sergeant major."

But there was no time to approach him. He was meeting with the other officers and within an hour's time, we were ordered back into our ranks.

As we marched, the sun came out drying my uniform. I turned my face up to the sky, my throat warming in the sun. If only I had something more to eat!

At the next rest I walked Alcides into the grassy meadow along with the rest of the uhlans. A few old seasoned men pulled out hard rinds of cheese to eat. Their old teeth bit into their food and they smacked their lips. My knees were weak with hunger.

I began searching on my hands and knees for wild berries in the grass. When I found a few, I stuffed them into my mouth with greedy hands.

The sergeant major rode his horse among us, checking the condition of the horses. He saw me rooting through the grass, my face smeared with purple juice from the few berries I had found.

"What are you doing?"

"Searching for berries, sir."

"Have you nothing else to eat?"

Wyszemirski, hearing the conversation, answered for me.

"Sergeant Major—no, Durov has nothing at all. His supplies were confiscated by the Cossacks. He has no greatcoat, no food. Nothing but the bare saddle."

The sergeant major raised his eye to the heavens and gave an exasperated sigh. "Follow me. I will see that you are fed enough, you two whelps. How you wiggled your way into the army is beyond me. Well, come along."

"And us?" grumbled one of the older uhlans. "You provide this useless child food and we who carry our weight, nothing?"

"You old fools!" shouted the sergeant major. "You may be seasoned soldiers, but why do we fight a war if we cannot care for our Russian children? Look at these two—they should be playing at home, not fighting a battle!"

This gruff man now smiled at us.

"Come along, children. You will dine on soup, roast meat. Ah! And white bread."

Chapter 30

Friedland, Prussia
June 1807

With my belly full on officers' food, I grew warm and drowsy. The sergeant major had given me a greatcoat that was a few sizes too big but made of tightly woven wool. I thought of the big man who must have worn it before me.

The cold rains ceased, the skies cleared, and I soon had no need of the coat. In fact, as summer in the interior of Russia often can be, it was now unbearably hot. I stashed my new coat in my kit bag and took Alcides back out to graze again.

The flies buzzed now in the heat, attracted by the horses' sweat and dung. The insects' buzzing and our mounts' snorts were a lullaby to me, as I had not had any real sleep in days. I closed my eyes.

I woke to hear "Curb your horse!" the call to tack up and mount immediately. The uhlans around me bridled their horses, swinging up on their backs.

Alcides was nowhere to be seen!

The sergeant major was already mounted and inspecting the uhlans as they rode into formation. I caught sight of a strange movement in the river just beyond the ranks, a dark form breaking the ripples of the current.

Alcides was swimming to the far bank.

"Why are you standing there without your horse, Durov?" shouted the sergeant major.

I looked up at the officer and ran to the river. With my bridle over one shoulder slung from right to left I swam toward my horse.

The water soaking my jacket and boots threatened to drag me under. The river carried me downstream as I struggled against the current. I pulled myself to shore, exhausted. Alcides, who had reached the other bank before me, walked over to me, water sluicing off his back.

I stretched up my arm when he bowed his head toward me. My fingers entwined in his mane and he pulled me to standing. With quivering hands I slipped the curb bit into his mouth and mounted. We had to ford the river again to reach the ranks of soldiers.

I chewed my lip thinking of the admonishment from my superior officer.

As I rode into my rank, water puddling under Alcides's belly, the sergeant major said, "Well, at least that was a plucky recovery." He was smiling.

As we rode toward Friedland we passed through the village of Schippenbeil. Great God, what a horror! The houses were charred heaps of splinter and ash, and pottery shards littered the road. We tried to avoid treading upon the sharp bits and smoking embers to protect our horses' feet, though this proved difficult in formation.

Not a soul remained there. How many had been burned to death?

I exchanged looks with Wyszemirski. His pale blue eyes stared, haunted.

Friedland—just that simple word still chills my blood.

Half our regiment was pulled under this great tide of battle, a surging sea of bullets, cannonballs, bayonets, grapeshot. We advanced, we retreated, we reformed ranks, noting the comrades who were missing. We advanced again, each time washing back on shore from the sea of battle, bloodied and diminished. The shrill whine of bullets unnerved me. Alcides galloped on, shying when solid banks of dirt were thrown up by cannonballs, racing through the whizzing bullets. The sky was gray with lead.

How puny were we with our oak lances, we uhlans! Yes, we charged ahead at a gallop, usually pitting cavalry against cavalry. But it was the infantrymen who won or lost the battles for us. Oh, our vainglorious charges, lances fixed or sabers gleaming. But we slew so few in comparison with our brave infantry! They marched into the field shoulder to shoulder, their eyes trained on their enemy. Their faces were set with intense determination, resigned to kill or be killed. The cords strained in their necks, veins pumped blue, the bone of their jaws defined in battle. What advances they reaped defined our regiment's glory and honor or shameful losses and ultimate defeat. Either way I stared down in horror from my horse to see fallen bodies bleeding in the mud.

Grapeshot and bullets showered us, but they were nothing to the nightmarish roar of the cannons. In an instant, five or more of our uhlans and horses were blasted sideways. I shielded my eyes as Alcides reared and whinnied. Bits of earth, pieces of leather from their saddles, hit us. The uhlans lay on the ground, some dead outright, and others crawling blindly toward their dead or wounded horses.

A fellow uhlan still rode, his head wounded and bandaged from a previous injury. He rode in circles, clearly out of his mind. We trotted up to him and I asked him which squadron he was from. He could not remember and swayed like a drunk in the saddle, at the verge of toppling to the ground. I tied his reins to Alcides's neck and with one arm tried to pull him toward me as we rode side by side. I brought him to the river, where I hoped the cold water would refresh him, bringing him to his senses.

When I let go of him, he toppled out of the saddle to the muddy shore.

Gunfire and cannonballs whistled all around us. The pennons of my squadron were no longer in sight. I felt a frantic twist in my gut, a cold shiver of fear. But I could not leave this comrade to die.

I dismounted, ducking low, and filled my helmet with water, pouring it over the wounded man's head. The water diluted the blood and it ran down his face, coloring his pale skin and collar a rosy pink.

"Oh, God have mercy on me, lad! Do not abandon me here! I will get on my horse somehow."

I could barely hear him through the gunfire and explosions. I cupped my ear, struggling to make out what he said.

"Just walk me back behind the army's lines," he said. "God will reward your human kindness!"

With great difficulty, mustering every muscle I could command, I managed to help him up on his horse, the poor beast bleeding profusely from under its belly. I took his reins, leading him alongside Alcides back to Friedland.

The few remaining denizens of Friedland were fleeing. Soldiers—some of them deserters from the battlefield—screamed, "Flee! Save yourselves. All is lost!" I scowled at them—how they terrorized the civilians who were already horror-stricken.

It wasn't until I saw the caissons retreating that I realized what the first wave of soldiers was saying was true. Our Russian army had been defeated—badly.

Now I was alone without my squadron and with a critically wounded comrade.

As I watched the artillery pieces pass, I turned to him.

"Would you consent to traveling on a caisson? You won't be able to stay astride your horse much longer."

He nodded, a pathetic jerk of his neck.

I pulled him and his horse along with us as I sought the artillery commander through the rising dust and smoke.

"Will you let this wounded man ride along in the wagon? Will you take along his horse, wounded?"

"Yes, of course," said the mustached commander. "Sergeant! Move this man to that wagon. Spread out a blanket. See that his horse is taken care of."

The uhlan smiled weakly to me, then grimaced as two men pulled him down from his horse and carried him like a sack of potatoes to the wagon.

As he disappeared, I was swept with such joy as I had not experienced since I left home. The freedom! I no longer had the burden of a wounded comrade. Now I had no one to care for but myself and Alcides. But where to find my squadron in the retreat?

I followed the road out of Friedland along with the retreating army. For hours, I asked everyone where my squadron might be. Some said they thought I should continue to look farther ahead and others said my comrades had turned left off the road just beyond Friedland.

Nightfall was approaching. I had to give Alcides a rest and a chance to graze. Alongside the road I saw a group of Cossacks around a small fire.

"Friends! May I spend the night next to your fire?"

"Yes, of course," said the oldest Cossack. "You may share in our kasha as well." He handed me a carved spoon made of birchwood.

"God bless you. I want to water my horse first," I said dismounting. "I need to let him graze as well. But he will wander, I've learned that."

"Then do what we do, uhlan! Wrap a rope around his legs to hobble him and then tether that to your arm. If he wanders he will wake you up when the strap goes taut. He will pull you out of a dreamless sleep!"

The other Cossacks squatting around the fire grunted a laugh.

"Don't expect us to wake you. We will leave before dawn, ulhan," said the old man.

I thanked him for his advice and went to the stream to let Alcides have a long cool drink. I searched my pockets but I had nothing that resembled a rope to tether.

Then I thought of my handkerchiefs, the ones my Ukrainian grandmother had embroidered. I took them out, long and elegant, made of white linen. I cherished them among the few belongings I had from my past. But I would have to sacrifice them now.

I tied them end to end, making a tether. In the meantime, the old Cossack filled my bowl with kasha.

The kasha was toasty hot and filled my cold belly. I heard the bloody tales of the battle, how the French had thrashed our armies into retreat.

"Are you with Don Cossacks?" I asked, though by the way they were dressed, I was fairly sure.

"Yes," said the youngest, who stoked the fire. "You know Cossacks?"

"I rode with a regiment from Sarapul to Grodno."

Four pairs of eyes flashed at me.

"You? You rode with the army of the Don?"

"Impossible," grumbled one. "This one is a liar!"

"As far as Grodno. I met a scout who was with Ataman Platov's regiment. Anatoli Denisov."

Now all the dark eyes burned across the glow of the fire.

"Denisov!" said the one who had accused me of being a liar. "Denisov is a brave man. You knew him?"

"We heard he was injured in Friedland," said another. "A bullet through his shoulder blade."

"Is he all right?" I asked, startled to hear my voice rise an octave like the girl I was.

"We do not know if he survived or not," said the eldest.

My eyelids had grown swollen and heavy. I was dog tired and the thought of Denisov dying on the battlefield along with so many others made me feel lonely and empty inside, like a sack turned inside out.

I felt a compression in my chest, a nagging ache. I reached for my chest with my right arm, rubbing it.

The old Cossack said, "Get some sleep, soldier. You have seen too much, too young."

I spread out my greatcoat on the ground a little ways from the Cossacks where I could still see the glowing embers in the darkness. I did not take off Alcides's saddle because in the precarious position of a retreat, I needed to be able to mount at a second's notice. But I did loosen the girth as much as I dared. I tied the kerchief to Alcides's forelegs making a loop and then tied the trailing end to my arm.

The night was starless and as dark as the inside of a coal stove. I fell asleep immediately. When I awoke, the Cossacks had already left. Their horses were gone.

And so was Alcides.

Chapter 31

Beyond Friedland, Prussia
1807

Now I was once again a cavalry soldier without a horse. And again, the saddlebags and my provisions were gone. I fought back tears of frustration, berating myself for my situation.

I walked for a half hour and spied a bit of white in a pasture off the road. It looked odd, like an ivory bird nesting in the grass. I took a few steps toward it, then a few more. I broke into a run. It was a shred of my grandmother's embroidered kerchief!

A neigh broke over the meadow. It was Alcides! He galloped toward me, trailing the tattered remains of the handkerchiefs that had so unsuitably served as a hobble.

But as he trotted to me I saw he had no saddle, no bridle.

A squadron of dragoons were breaking camp near us. I walked over to them, my horse following like a dog behind me.

"*Dobre utra*," I said. Good morning.

"*Dobre utra*," an officer said to me. "Well-trained horse you have. Where is your tack? Your provisions?"

"All has been stolen," I said. "I have nothing to ride him in."

The officer raised his eyebrow. Several other dragoons turned toward me.

"I can give you a leather strap, lad," said one. "I am sorry I cannot do better. But you can make it serve as reins. Tie it to that leather halter and see if it will hold."

The strap he gave me was of rotting leather, spotted with white mold. I thanked him for his offer and went to work tying it fast and hard as I could to the halter.

For the remaining day of our march I rode bareback, attracting the stares and comments of dozens of soldiers and civilians.

At last I reached my squadron. What would the sergeant major say this time?

Ah, but it was not the sergeant major who first saw me approach, but Captain Kazimirski.

"Cadet Durov!" he roared. "What is the meaning of this? You disgrace our regiment by riding your horse without a saddle, without your lance? Where are your supplies?"

I explained to Kazimirski what had happened when I took pity on a wounded uhlan, giving him my horse.

"You left your squadron on the battlefield? You purposely deserted our company."

"But sir, he was dying—"

"First you ride in circles, joining every squadron you can to fight in battle without being called. Then you dismount on the battlefield to give your horse to another, leaving yourself on foot scampering across the battlefield in the heat of conflict. Then, after being reprimanded you once again leave your squadron to rescue an uhlan. You show up here, days later, without a saddle, lance, even a bridle!"

"But sir . . ."

"No! I have had enough of your childish pranks. Give your horse to the sergeant major for safekeeping. You get onto the wagon for the rest of this campaign."

"The wagon, sir?"

"You do not deserve the fine horse you ride or the honor entrusted to the Polish uhlans," he said, red faced with anger. Then he sighed.

"I am doing this for your own good, Durov. You will not survive long at this rate. I want to preserve you to fight with the daring you so foolishly display. A few years' maturity and experience will keep your head on your shoulders. We need soldiers of your caliber of courage—but tempered with common sense to fight another day."

Never had I imagined a punishment more severe. I felt lightheaded, bloodless. I stared, my mouth open in horror.

"Aide! Take the boy's horse."

I dismounted, pressing my face into Alcides's neck and cried hot tears. For once I did not care if my emotion tipped off the general and the other officers that I was a girl. Besides, I had seen men cry in battle, men's dirty, bloodied faces streaked with meandering rivulets, as they called out for help and mumbled last words to send to their loved ones.

To be sent back from the battlefield, stripped of my horse and in the flatbed of a supply wagon was worse than death.

"Durov," said the general's aide. "Let go of the reins, Durov. Let me have him."

My tears and phlegm glistened on Alcides's black mane as the aide led him away.

Chapter 32

As I climbed into the wagon I was shocked to see Wyszemirski sitting on a bag of oats. I didn't dare speak to him—he looked angry enough to hit me and so distressed, he could easily burst into tears.

For once I kept my silence. I rocked along in the supply wagon, my spine jolted by each rut in the road. In the distance I could see Alcides, tied to one of the stable wagons, along with the other reserve mounts. He pulled against the tether, indignant.

"Why did you get ordered off your horse?" I finally asked Wyszemirski.

He shrugged.

"I do not know. The general said, 'No child's blood will be spilt under my command.'" He looked accusingly at me. "A child! I am nearly eighteen. I always obey orders. Not like you, Durov—"

"Shut up."

"It is true! Falling asleep, riding away from the squadron, giving your horse away on the battlefield—"

"I told you to shut up! I gave up my horse once to a man who was dying—"

"An uhlan is nothing without his horse. It is a disgraceful act and—"

He did not have time to finish his sentence. I leapt on him, punching him hard in the stomach.

"Ugh!" He bent over, convulsing.

I expected a fight from him, a tussle. But the punch had hit the top of his stomach where the muscles converge. He doubled over and vomited.

"Wyszemirski!" I said. "Are you all right?"

"Leave me alone, Durov."

"I—I did not mean to—"

He vomited again, long sticky threads hanging from his mouth.

The wagon pulled to stop, making us both lose our balance. We tumbled to the floor of the flatbed. I struck my elbow hard on a barrel of vodka and winced.

"What is going on back here?" shouted the driver. He coughed in the spinning dust still settling from the abrupt halt.

"Nothing," said Wyszemirski wiping his mouth with his sleeve.

"What was that commotion back here? Yelling and moving about. You scared the horses."

Wyszemirski bent over the wooden rails of the wagon, throwing up what was left of his morning kasha.

"You aren't carrying disease, are you, soldier?" said the driver. "We will quarantine you—"

"It is just we are not used to riding a wagon," I said quickly. "The motion over the ruts makes us both queasy."

"You're sick from the rocking, lad?" said the driver, mirth dancing in his eyes. "The general is right. You two are babes in the woods! Better in wagon than on horse."

He spat merrily into the dust, climbing back to the platform. We took off with a lurch.

"I am sorry," I said to Wyszemirski, offering him my canteen. "Will you forgive me?"

He took a long swig.

"I will consider it, Durov," he said.

He stoppered the canteen, handing it back to me.

"You have one hell of a punch for a baby-faced cadet."

"You—" I said and then I squinted. From the left flank rode several squadrons of riders in blue. Don Cossacks.

Leading them was a blond captain who sat bolt straight in the saddle, so unlike the rest of the motley horsemen. His shoulder was bandaged in a sling.

He swiveled his head toward us.

"Aleksandr!" he shouted. He spurred his horse into a gallop approaching us.

"Oh, Mother of God!" I said, shrinking down against the splintered panels of the wagon.

"Aleksandr!" he said, riding alongside the jolting wagon.

"Are you injured?"

I shook my head.

"Where is that magnificent Circassian horse of yours?"

I pointed to the end of the wagon train where the reserve horses were tethered, trotting along the dusty road.

"Tell me you are not—"

"Cossack!" shouted Kazimirski. "Return to your squadron at once."

Denisov scrutinized my commanding officer. He leaned over deliberately and slowly. He spat into the dust.

"You take care of yourself, Aleksandr," he said to me. "Promise me that. Keep your head low." Without a word to the officer, he reined his horse back to the Cossack division.

Why did he have to see me in disgrace?

"Who was that?" asked Wyszemirski.

"No one," I said.

"But he—"

"Shut up," I said, sinking down against the bag of oats. I felt as I had been punched in the stomach too.

From the back of the wagon I had my first glance of Tilsit. My first reaction was astonished delight. A village that had not been burned to the ground, its inhabitants alive and busy. After battlefields of dead men, gaping holes, charred remains, the simple wooden houses and stone streets reminded me of a normal life I had forgotten.

I spied something in the middle of the river. It looked like two small white houses afloat. There were boats sailing toward it from either bank of the Niemen.

"What's that?" I said, pulling at Wyszemirski's sleeve. "Look!"

The boats flew flags—one the imperial standard of Russia and the other Napoleonic French.

"Lads!" said the driver. "This is the end of the road."

We turned to see our sergeant major riding toward us.

"Get your horses and mount up. The emperor has ordered a review of all troops!"

I mounted Alcides and rode to formation. I noticed a new uhlan next to me, and my vodka-swigging comrade missing from behind. It could only mean Oleg and Kosmy Banka had fallen in battle.

My breath caught in my throat. I thought of my two merry comrades, nearly as young as I, dead on the battlefield.

"The emperor is meeting with that Corsican devil?" asked a gray-bearded uhlan next to me. He gripped his oak lance so tight I could see the white bones of his knuckles.

"Shhh!" said a coronet next to him. "Careful what you say."

"I do not care!" said the uhlan. "My best comrades died in the battle of Friedland!"

I thought of Oleg and Kosmy Banka, feeling the cold wake of their absence in the ranks.

Jolly Kosmy! Drinking my ration of vodka. Maybe I would drink it myself now.

"My brother and cousin both died in Heilsberg and Austerlitz," said a young cadet, his voice raising an octave. "How can he—"

"Shut up, I am warning you all!" said the coronet. "The emperor will do what is right for Russia."

"Making peace with the French butcher?" countered the old uhlan.

"What are they talking about?" I asked Wyszemirski.

"I just heard," whispered Wyszemirski. "The Tsar is meeting Napoleon midway in the Niemen River on a raft. Those were the little white houses we saw floating on the water. The emperor and Napoleon are negotiating a truce of some kind. A treaty—"

"A truce!" I said. "How can we have a truce after . . . losing so many comrades? The villages and towns burned to the ground—"

"I know," said Wyszemirski. "But watch what you say. It is our honorable tsar."

"For what, all these deaths?" I said, nearly in tears. "The burned villages, the sacrifice—"

Wyszemirski held up his hand that held his reins, making his horse swing into Alcides. "It is the end of the campaign, Durov, if the Tsar agrees. No more battles. No more death."

I stared off toward the blue streak of the Niemen, shaking my head in wonderment.

A truce! All those souls lost on the battlefield, their bloody flesh and shattered bones. For what? To shake hands with the French Satan? The crumpled bodies of our comrades still lay rotting in the fields, unrecovered corpses lying among their dead horses. And our emperor is sitting across a table from their murderer.

The trumpets sounded, an order rang out, and we lowered our lances in respect for the Tsar. He cantered a fine bay horse up to our ranks. His eyes were an imperial blue with blond eyelashes. Yes, he was that close. Eyes that shone with his noble soul. Lips as rosy as a woman's, pulling at a benevolent smile. He is one of us. He will not sell the Russian soul to the French demon.

Would he?

Alexander trotted his prancing horse among our regiment. His mouth twisted in sorrow—or shame—as he spied me and Wyszemirski among the ranks.

He gave us a benevolent nod. He stopped and wheeled his horse around, riding back to say something to Captain Kazimirski. Then he cantered on, thin lines of worry etching his brow.

Chapter 33

Tilsit
July 1807

Tsar Alexander dressed in his imperial blue uniform and crimson sash stood erect on the small sailing vessel that carried him to the middle of the river Niemen. French carpenters had worked frantically to build the rafts and the pavilion for the meeting. As Alexander's sailboat tacked in the capricious wind, he stumbled backwards, catching a line to balance himself.

Nothing is more revolting than making peace with this little Corsican demon! He dares to declare himself emperor. Not a drop of noble blood—he has peasant lard in his veins. Now I must greet him as an equal.

Alexander swallowed, his nose wrinkling at the sour taste in his mouth.

Alexander's boat docked at the rafts anchored midriver. The French flag, blue, white, and red, waved triumphantly from Napoleon's vessel. The two boats had set sail from opposite banks at the same moment, by agreement, but Napoleon, of course, had sprinted ahead and was already on the raft, waiting to greet his defeated enemy.

The white pavillion on the rafts housed a mahogany table and chairs, with six windows so that guards could watch the actions of both emperors.

Alexander squinted at a wreath of laurels on one side of the pavillion, encircling the initial *N*. A wreath on the opposite side, identical, but noticeably smaller, was marked with a capital *A*. Pale-green banners of silk brocade festooned either side of the entrance. Napoleon did not smile at Alexander. He stood stiffly in his cutaway blue uniform, startlingly white riding breeches, and waistcoat, his black tricornered hat held in his left hand, the white plumes dangling like tail feathers.

Alexander stepped onto the float, the platform bobbing with the weight of his foot. He could not help but admire the style and flourish the French had produced so quickly.

How do I address this little man who has decimated my armies—and those of Austria and Prussia? He will never be my equal, yet I must secure peace.

"I hate the English as much as you do," said Alexander, addressing Napoleon without as much as a salute.

"In that case," said Napoleon, "peace is as good as made."

Chapter 34

"How could you make peace with that barbarian!" said Ekaterina, throwing a gold-plated fork to the ground. A servant scurried to recover it. Another swiftly gave the princess a new one.

"Katia!" admonished the dowager empress. "Your manners. The servants observe us."

Ekaterina's round face took on a fierce aspect. "How can you embrace this Corsican who demeans nobility, murders our—"

"I have no choice, Katia," said Alexander, putting down his fork. "Our armies and the Prussians were destroyed by Napoleon's Grand Armée—"

"Don't call it that!" said Ekaterina.

"What?"

"Grand Armée! It's as if you tip your hat in obeisance every time you say it! And how could our Russian army be defeated by the French? I simply do not understand."

"No, you don't," said Alexander. "You did not see shreds of flesh, shards of human bones sharp enough to cut into the horses' hooves.

You did not look down into a bloody hole that was a soldier's head just minutes before. Or children younger than you fighting among the front ranks."

"Alexander!" said the dowager empress. "We are at the dinner table."

Empress Elizabeth made a move to catch her husband's hand. He snatched his fingers from her grasp, clenching his fists in emotion.

"I cried, Katia! I held my head in my hands and wept! I led the Imperial Army into battle, haughty and full of bravado. Instead of a victory, I opened the bloody door of hell for tens of thousands of souls. One by one they died for Russia, for me. I led them into hell."

Alexander pressed his knuckle into corners of his eyes to stop the new flood of emotion.

"Yes, dear sister. I made peace with Napoleon so that a serf could return home to his family. I signed the filthy treaty and drank champagne with a monster so that a nobleman could once again oversee the lands to bring in the harvests so that hundreds of thousands don't starve. I made peace in Russia's name so that we might survive another day."

He wadded his napkin, hurled it to the floor, and strode out of the room, his riding boots clicking on the magnificent parquet.

"The Tsar wishes to be received," said one of Ekaterina's ladies. The duchess looked up from her book of Kant, the German words still filling her head.

"Of course, show him in at once." She placed her book on the table among the many others written in an array of foreign languages.

As her brother entered her study she remained determinedly seated, arching an eyebrow at her visitor.

"Ah!" said Alexander, kissing her cheeks three times. "I see you do not observe proper court etiquette by standing when the Tsar of Russia enters the room, Katia."

"I see that you have done everything to abolish proper court etiquette and the court itself, dear Alexander, " she replied.

Alexander took a seat next to her, settling back into the stuffed chair.

"Did you put our mother up to writing that damnable letter?" he said, pulling the paper from the pocket of his jacket.

"Which damnable letter do you refer to?" she asked, laughing. "I cannot accept blame for every letter our mother writes. Do let me see it."

Alexander passed the letter to her. While she read, he examined the pile of books on her table.

"I see you are reading Kant," he said. He lifted another book, scanning the spine. "Rousseau. And what's this? Locke and Hobbes?"

"Shhh!" said Ekaterina. "Yes, I am reading. Ah! Here she makes reference to me. A motive for respecting myself by attending balls—which she means meeting a future husband, I am sure. Oh, that is rich!"

"Did you say as much?"

"No!" said Ekaterina. "I simply notice your absence. You have withdrawn from all of us, not just the court. But yes, a ball or two might enhance your popularity amongst the nobles."

"Bah! The nobles. They hate me as do the commoners since the Tilsit accord."

Ekaterina cocked her head. "And Mama is right. We do miss Grandmama's elegant parties."

Alexander smiled. "You enchant me, little sister."

"If I so enchant you, dear brother, then I ask you, why do you not spend more time with us?"

"I need time to think," he said, shaking his head. "To pray."

"What? Pray? To whom?" Ekaterina laughed. "To your Polish mistress, perhaps?"

He shook his head vehemently. "You are too young to understand."

"Alexander! Do not be a fool. I am nineteen years old."

Alexander looked down at his hand. "Which brings me to business." A shaft of light cast his profile into shadow.

"Oh, no. You are about to be serious, aren't you, dear brother? If it is about marriage, I mean to marry Francis of Austria."

"No!" said Alexander, dismissing her with a wave of his hand. "Do not talk nonsense. I would never consent to it. He is nearly forty years old! Besides Austria is a fickle ally."

"I would be the empress of Austria and of the Holy Roman Empire, Alexander! Yes, I know Francis is no Adonis, but he is a decent man."

Alexander shook his head vehemently.

"I forbid it," he said. He leaned over and took his youngest sister's hand. "I could not bear to have you be unhappy."

"You have read too many French plays, I think," said Ekaterina, though she did not withdraw her hand from his warm grasp.

"You are my conscience, my rudder in all these turbulent seas of war, of leadership," he said. "Ah, I see in your eyes you think me flattering you."

"Only because you will not allow me to be empress of Austria," she said, pressing his hand. "I think you rather selfish."

"Ah, dear sister. Your spirit, your light is beyond me. I cannot fathom its depths. You share my blood. I see myself in you, our father, and most of all our grandmother, God rest her immortal soul. You have her vivacity, her wisdom—"

"So am I to remain a spinster then, good brother? So that you can worship at my feet, Alexander? Really. Do you think I have no ambition?"

Now he dropped her hand, ever so gently.

"I do have a proposition for you, dearest Katia. You say you have ambition. All right. Prepare yourself."

Ekaterina crinkled her eyes at him, laughing.

"Whatever must I prepare my—"

Alexander waved his hand for silence.

"The emperor Napoleon has asked for your hand."

"What?"

"He has divorced Josephine in order to find a wife to give him an heir. He wanted to wed our little sister Anne, but Mama of course protested."

The blood drained from Ekaterina's face, her jaw slackening in horror.

"You cannot be serious, Alexander!"

"Yes. I mean to discuss it with Mama this afternoon."

"But! No, I will not! I would rather marry the lowest Russian serf than that Corsican!"

Alexander drew a deep breath into his lungs. He held it for several seconds before he expelled it, his shoulders shrinking.

"You know that if we refuse, our tenuous alliance with Napoleon will rupture. We will return to the battlefields where—"

"You will not marry me to that monster! You who said I was your conscience. You are in great need of a conscience this very minute!"

Alexander rubbed his brow hard. "Your refusal will be war. He will take it as a colossal insult, a rejection of our alliance."

"I do not give a damn what Napoleon thinks! Do not pander to that boastful peasant! Russia shall prevail."

"We haven't the troops, Katia! We cannot defeat—"

"You disgrace our ancestors, Alexander! You would prostitute your own sister to that Corsican swine?"

Alexander said nothing. He stood up and walked to the door. As always an Ethiopian serf turned the handle, opening it for the Tsar and bowed low.

Alexander spoke to Dowager Empress Maria Feodorovna that afternoon.

"Mama, you must speak to her. Convince her it is for the sake of Russia."

"No! Categorically, no!" she answered. "I will not have my brilliant daughter married to that peasant. We have discussed it."

"Then how shall we approach Napoleon?" Alexander asked. "What excuse can we give him that he does not engage us in war?"

"Stand up to him, Alexander!"

"Mama, you do not understand. It would mean the slaughter of our army, a massacre—and still we would not win! Napoleon would seize Russia."

The dowager empress turned away, gazing out the window toward the Neva. Then she looked from her son to the little gold casket that held Tsar Paul's bloodstained nightshirt.

She raised her eyes slowly again to her son's.

"I shall make it impossible!"

"Mama! You can't!"

Maria Feodorovna shook her head, dismissing his protest.

"Do not contradict me, Alexander. I will arrange a marriage this very day. Who is available?" An idea brightened her eyes. "Ah, Count George of Oldenburg!"

"Mama! Her first cousin? Hardly an attractive man. Nor very imposing," sniffed Alexander. "He is too old for Katia."

The dowager empress glanced at her son. "I would almost think you jealous, Alexander, dear."

"Nonsense!" said Alexander. He rubbed his forehead aggressively. "It is just the comparison of Napoleon to a Prussian count is, well—"

"The Count of Oldenburg is a decent man and will make a good husband. I shall write to him immediately." She rang a bell, immediately soliciting a servant. "Please send for Duchess Ekaterina immediately."

The dowager empress Maria Feodorovna looked at her son, whose shoulders were huddled in defeat.

"I know how you love her, Alexander. At least this way she will be safe from that tyrant. My beloved daughter shall not be a sacrificial lamb to that Corsican usurper!"

Alexander threw up his hands. "How can I negotiate peace now?"

Maria Feodorovna stared at her son as a crow eyes a button on the ground.

"What, Mama?"

The dowager empress shook her head. "What worries me now, Alexander, is how you are changing. Where are your ethics, your moral grounding?"

Alexander shook his head vehemently, his cheeks scorching under his mother's rebuke. "I have seen death. I have seen the horrors of war firsthand. I'm trying to maintain peace for Russia, Mama!"

The dowager empress met his eye. "At the cost of your very soul."

Alexander blanched under her withering look. He watched his mother's gaze shift to the golden casket and closed his eyes in anguish.

Part 4
A Namesake

Chapter 35

Polotsk, Russia
August 1807

After the Treaty of Tilsit, we returned from the Lithuanian frontiers to old Russia.

Peacetime required a new etiquette from all of us, one that I never learned when we were thrown into battle. The captain sent for Wyszemirski and me. He instructed us to observe all formalities of rank, coming to attention for officers and presenting arms to them—drawing our sabers—when we were on duty. We had to respond to roll call in a barking gruff voice, something I was forced to practice, as it did not come naturally.

We were required to clean the *placowka*—the square where sentries assembled in front of the guardhouse—and to stand watch, guarding the church and powder magazine.

Our regiment, the Pskov Dragoons, was combined in one camp with the Ordensk Cuirassiers. The tents—instead of housing only ten— were as big as ballrooms, with a platoon in each. Among so many men I kept to myself, working hard to disguise my gender by changing my underclothes silently in the cover of night. I washed my intimates in the river when I watered Alcides, stuffing them inside my jacket—and then rolling them tight in my wool blanket and letting them dry while I slept.

They were never completely dry and chafed me, especially the linen pads for my monthlies. I developed a rash that itched like the devil. I longed for quarters where I might have more privacy to tend to my personal hygiene.

As I stood sentry or cleaned the *placowka* with a spade, my mind wandered to my parents, to my home in Sarapul. The captain urged me to write to my father to confirm my station as part of the nobility so that I might be given an officer's rank. Without proof I was condemned to never rise above the rank of Cadet Durov, essentially an enlisted soldier.

How I longed to write my father! And how long could I endure being a common soldier, especially in peacetime?

Finally I decided I had to write him, if only to let him know I was still alive.

Alcides frisked about now, well rested and putting on weight after battle. I had a difficult time keeping him under control as I led him to the river for water.

"Ah, Alcides!" I said to him, stroking his neck. "You deserve an officer astride you, noble Alcides! How we survived Heilsberg and Friedland is a miracle. Let us hope Papa is proud to have a . . . son, serving the emperor."

Alcides seemed unconcerned, nibbling at the sweet grass growing in clumps along the riverbank.

I was summoned to report to Major General Kachowski's headquarters.

"Durov, I want you to tell me the truth. Do your parents know that you enlisted in the army?"

I swallowed, biting my lip.

"No, sir," I admitted. "They never would have given me permission."

"I see," said the major general. He drew a deep breath, saying nothing more. He went to his desk, leafing through some papers.

"You are to be sent to Vitebsk, accompanied by my adjutant Neidhardt. Please surrender your saber, lance, and pistols."

"Sir?" I gasped. "Yes, sir."

I fought back tears. Was he sending me back to my parents? Had my father demanded my return?

General Kachowski looked at me with such compassion I almost embraced him. But I stood rooted to the carpet.

"You are a brave soldier, Durov," the general said. "Despite your bad judgment, you have proved that to all of us. We will miss you."

He turned away from me, looking out the window. I was sure he had tears in his eyes.

"Dismissed!" he said, without turning around.

Neidhardt and I left Polotsk by carriage, Alcides tied to the back. At first Neidhardt did not speak with me—he appeared aloof and dined alone in the post stations, leaving me outside to watch over the change of horses.

I wondered what he might know or even where we were going, but I dared not ask.

By the time we arrived in Vitebsk, Neidhardt's demeanor had softened. I was invited to his quarters, and he hosted me to coffee and breakfast. Though we still had not exchanged any meaningful words, I felt more camaraderie.

"Durov," he said. "I must leave you to report to the commander in chief, Count Buxhowden. Please ready yourself to meet him this afternoon."

"Count Buxhowden!" I said. "But—why?"

"This is a matter I cannot discuss," said Neidhardt. I must have looked as desperate as I felt, for he added, "If it comforts you at all, I am ignorant of the matter. I am simply obeying Major General Kachowski's orders."

I checked a sob that rose in my throat, turning away from Neidhardt. I already suspected I was being sent home.

Chapter 36

Adam Czartoryski requested a private audience with the tsar.

"What brings you here so formally, my friend?" asked Alexander.

"Exactly that, Your Highness," said Czartoryski. "I want to talk to you as a friend."

Alexander waited silently while Czartoryski gathered his courage.

"I think you have been misled by your advisors, particularly Prince Dolgoruky."

Alexander raised his chin.

"I do not like your tone, old friend. One might think you are jealous of your comrades-in-arms."

"Your Majesty! My sources inform me that he was deliberately rude to Napoleon before the Battle of Austerlitz. A battle that swept away nearly thirty thousand lives."

"Austerlitz? Why return to old history? We are at peace with Napoleon."

"Peace? What kind of peace can Russia have with that tyrant?"

Alexander held up his hand, stifling any further comment on his new ally.

"What do you mean, attacking Prince Dolgoruky?" he asked.

"You sent him as an envoy, instead of me. He stuck his finger in Napoleon's eye."

"Dolgoruky is not a sycophant to—"

"Sycophant! He is precisely that to you, Alexander. You surround yourself with *faux amis*! At Austerlitz, you seized General Kutuzov's command with their urging and flattery! You galloped to advanced positions, to the front of the columns."

"We have already discussed this. I want all my generals to lead by example—at the front of our armies."

"You should have left the army in the hands of an experienced commander in chief."

"Kutuzov? That old blind bumbler—"

"He tried to warn you not to proceed with the attack until reinforcements arrived. He tried to save the Russian army—"

"Czartoryski! You have made your point too many times. You are dismissed. Permanently. I am replacing your position as foreign minister with Baron Andre Budberg."

The Polish prince drew in a heavy breath, stunned.

"I see," he said. "I am no longer in favor, since I speak the truth. Paul Stroganov and Nikolai Novosiltsev warned me as much. We cannot speak the truth to Alexander as we once did. But I cannot stand by quietly while Russia crumbles."

Alexander winced hearing the names of his two old friends. A memory of cognac-fueled toasts and dreams of reformation sifted through his mind, then disappeared.

"Our drunken talk was just that! Pipe dreams among boyish friends."

"I thought—as did the others—that reform in Russia was more than a mere pipe dream, Your Majesty."

"Russia! You always defended Poland, Adam. Could it be that our alliance with Prussia is the real reason for your bitter criticism? The Prussians are no friends of Poland."

"They are no friends of Russia either."

Alexander was slow to anger, but when piqued his temper could burst into flame.

"How dare you attack my staff and motives for making peace with France!"

"Your Majesty knows peace with Napoleon will never last!"

"You come to me, spoiling for a fight, Adam. What do you want me to say?"

"Stand up to Napoleon!" shouted Czartoryski. "Don't listen to bad counsel, Alexander!"

"Adam! What possesses you to address me in such a tone?"

Czartoryski shook his head.

"Is this outburst solely rooted in politics," said Alexander "Or . . ."

"Or what?"

Alexander glared at his old friend. "Or is it perhaps the Empress Elizabeth who provokes you to such diatribes? And her liaison with Captain Okhotnikov."

Adam Czartoryski's eyes blazed. His mind flashed on Elise, his lover, her blond hair strewn over his chest. For a moment he was at a loss for words.

The Tsar drew nearer.

"It is Elise, then," said Alexander, now more gently. "You are too wise to be jealous, Adam. Don't make the mis—"

"I understand I have been dismissed, Your Majesty. I shall take my leave, begging your pardon."

"No. Stay here, Adam. We need to talk," said the Tsar, his eyes flicking to the closed door. "First, I am assigning you to another post—in Poland. You will be groomed for a leadership role in your own country when reforms take place. Secondly"—Alexander put his arm on his friend's shoulder—"I do not approve of my wife's current choice of lover—"

"Anymore than the tsarina approves of Maria Naryshkina," snapped Czartoryski.

"Damn you, Adam! You know I have my lovers and the empress has hers. But her relationship with you was distinctly different. You are a man of character and morality. But this Alexis Okhotnikov tarnishes her brilliance. The captain is boastful and he jeopardizes Elise's reputation. I do not believe he is as discreet and loyal as you."

Czartoryski's nostrils flared. He looked beyond Alexander at a gold clock ticking the minutes, to avoid the Tsar's eyes.

Do you know how you are wounding my heart, speaking of her lover? A bullet could do no more harm.

"What's more, Okhotnikov poses a grave danger," said Alexander. "My brother, Grand Duke Constantine, despises the man. He warns me daily of the scandalous gossip of the tsarina's affair circulating amongst the army and in the streets of St. Petersburg."

Czartoryski stood deadly still. "Can you not send the captain to Siberia?"

"A sudden assignment like that would be a tacit acknowledgement of his relationship with Elise. There would be trouble. She is smitten with him."

Alexander looked his old friend in the eye—and in an instant, the fate of Russia, which had driven Czartoryski to demand this meeting, was swept aside.

"Adam—Elise is pregnant."

The opera had been short of brilliant. No matter. Alexis Okhotnikov had indulged in vodka and champagne during the performance, which put him in a good mood, despite the dismal October weather. His thin aristocratic lips pulled up in a smile, making his handsome face turn cruel.

Ah! The slaps on the back, the camaraderie of the regiment. How Okhotnikov's popularity had risen since the rumor of Tsarina Elizabeth's pregnancy! Next month he would be the father of a grand duke or grand duchess. No one would dispute paternity, especially not Tsar Alexander. Russia could not risk the disgrace.

A cold rain lashed the stone walls of the Imperial Kamenny Bolshoi Theatre. Okhotnikov turned up his collar to the wet wind coming off the city's canals.

The brick pavement was slick and he could hear the roughshod horses—already prepared for the snowy winter—resound in a chorus of clicks and clatter as the carriages rolled away from the theater. Voices rang out in laughter, a few words in Russian—several vulgarities— rough and muscular amid the French language. The coach lanterns threw erratic pools of light on the wet road as the voices faded away.

Okhotnikov headed toward a tavern where he could find other officers from his regiment. The strong drink had affected his stride—not staggering, but less than perfectly coordinated.

The vodka and heat of the crowded theater had made him randy. He thought of the Tsarina Elizabeth and her creamy white skin, so smooth under his touch. He sucked in his breath thinking of her bosom and the sweet smell of his lover, pregnant with his child.

I can't risk entering the Winter Palace at this hour. Under what pretext? I've seen how Grand Duke Constantine's eyes burn with hatred whenever he sees me. Ah, but to touch Elizabeth's breast, to press my mouth to her lips, to her neck. Everywhere!

How delicious to make a cuckold of our tsar!

Captain Okhotnikov thought back to that morning: how he stood straight and still under the Tsar's inspection of the regiment. But Okhotnikov had dared to swivel the tip of his tongue back, licking his back molar at some sweet taste left from breakfast. It was a minute movement. But he was sure Tsar Alexander had seen it. The emperor had said nothing—really, what could he say without drawing attention? Everyone knew he was being cuckolded by Alexis Okhotnikov.

How divine! A tsar who bedded down every woman who caught his fancy, who proclaimed emancipation in his marriage—and now his tsarina was pregnant with a cavalry officer's child. If he be a boy, he would one day inherit the Russian throne.

The Tsar had met Okhotnikov's eye and then passed to the next soldier in the ranks.

The cocky Okhotnikov had stifled a smile that died on his lips as the Tsar moved on and revealed Grand Duke Constantine's stormy face, his eyes burning with hatred. The grand duke did not move with his brother but continued to stare at Okhotnikov.

The Tsar was harmless. But the brother.

Alexis Okhotnikov, so deep in reverie, did not notice the dark figure behind him in the rain. He turned only when he heard the racing boot heels strike the wet stones. He saw the gleam of the knife and reached for his sword, but too late.

The stranger's blade sank deep between Okhotnikov's ribs, then twisted and forced its way upward within his chest.

The assailant walked off into the darkness, leaving the wounded Captain Okhotnikov lying in the freezing rain.

The room smelled of fetid wounds and death. Tsarina Elizabeth sat by the bedside of her lover who had lain here in fevered pain for two and a half months. The Tsarina dismissed everyone from the room except her lady-in-waiting.

"Alexis! Can you hear me, my darling," she whispered.

The injured man could only moan.

"You are a father, Alexis. You have a little daughter now. She is beautiful, my love."

"What is . . . her name?"

"Elizabeth. I call her Lisinka. You must see her, you'll—"

Okhotnikov writhed. "No. They—He—tried to kill me."

She flicked a glance at her lady-in-waiting. "Who? Who was it, Alexis?"

"Assassin. He was sent."

"Sent by whom?"

"The grand duke. Constan—Oh! Oh!" shouted Okhotnikov.

Elizabeth placed her fingertips to her mouth. "Fetch the doctor," she said to her servant. "At once!"

The doctor rushed in. He saw the fever burning in Okhotnikov's eyes. "Forgive me, Your Majesty. It is better if you leave."

"Of course," said Elizabeth, gathering her skirts as she rose.

Alexis Okhotnikov died in early January, just days after Orthodox Christmas. It should have been a joyous time, especially after the christening of a new child, the daughter of Tsar Alexander and Tsarina Elizabeth.

But Alexander's mind was on Napoleon, and Elizabeth could think of nothing but the murder of her lover, father of her child.

Elizabeth had a mausoleum built over Alexis Okhotnikov's grave: a mighty oak split by lightning, a woman weeping at the foot of the tree.

After the funeral, she refused to leave her apartments in the Winter Palace.

Maria Feodorovna summoned the Tsar.

"The tsarina must accompany the Tsar to functions," complained the dowager empress. "You must insist, Alexander. You must appear together. She must watch the parades and attend dinners and balls by your side. Otherwise tongues will wag."

"Mama. Elise is a new mother. She must care for the baby, the—"

"Nonsense! She has nursemaids to attend the child!" snapped Maria Feodorovna.

"Mama. She suffers—"

"Suffers! Elizabeth has disgraced us!" she hissed. "Disgraced *you*! She is mourning for the captain who fathered that child, that bastard! The two of you bring shame to the Romanov name—"

"Shame?" said Alexander, stiffening. "A fine example my grandmother set. Some of her lovers were almost as young as me! Or my father with Princess Gargarina!"

"Alexander!"

"I beg you, Mama. Leave Elise alone. Never mention this affair again." He stomped out of his mother's apartments.

Alexander sent a card announcing that he would visit his wife in her apartments. When he was ushered in, he was stunned at the sight of Elizabeth, her face pale and drawn from lack of nourishment and sleep. Her eyes were swollen red from fits of weeping.

In her arms was the sleeping baby.

"Oh, Elise!" he whispered.

She looked up, her blue eyes spilling tears.

"You see, I can't stop crying, Alexander." She forced a smile and then looked down at little Lisinka. "She is a darling baby and I am such a sad mother."

"Then let me hold her," said Alexander, his hand resting on Elizabeth's shoulder.

Elizabeth turned her face up toward her husband.

"You want to hold her?" she said. "After—"

"Of course, Elise," he said, reaching out for the baby. "She is my daughter."

Elizabeth began to cry again. But this time her smile showed through her tears like the sun through a passing rainstorm.

Chapter 37

Our carriage pulled up in front of a splendid house where uniformed guards stood sentry.

An adjutant was waiting by the door.

"Good luck, Durov," said Neidhardt.

"Thank you," I said, puzzled more than fearful.

I was led to Count Buxhowden's study. He stood immediately from his desk.

"Durov!" he said, smiling. "But where is your saber?"

"All my weapons were confiscated, sir."

"I shall order them all returned to you immediately. A soldier should never be without his weapons."

I was still a soldier?

He asked me to sit down and regarded me with an avuncular smile.

"How old are you, Durov?"

"I am in my eighteenth year."

"Eighteen!" he repeated. "I've heard much about your bravery. Your commanders have reported nothing but the best from you."

He put a hand on my shoulder.

"Now what I am about to say should not alarm you."

I was immediately alarmed.

"I must send you to the emperor."

The emperor! What had I done?

I felt my knees start to buckle.

"No, I told you, do not be alarmed. Our emperor is the embodiment of grace and magnanimity—"

"But, sir! He will send me home. Your Excellency, I will die of sorrow!"

The count shook his head.

"Have no fear of that. The emperor wants only to recognize your fearlessness and honorable comportment. I will add my own report to those of your commanders, Captain Kazimirski and Major General Kachowski."

"Major General Kachowski wrote a report?"

"A very glowing one, indeed," said the count, smiling at my amazement. "So you see, Durov, I don't think the emperor will take away the uniform to which you have done such honor."

Chapter 38

Alexander unfolded the wrinkled letter yet again:

> *Please, I beg you, my Tsar, Your Highness. Help me locate my daughter Nadezhda. Return her home to the father who loves her most dearly.*

Alexander looked out the window of his study, onto the Neva River. Chunks of ice floated in the water, knitting up into solid frozen blocks anchored to the banks below.

Who is this girl who defies her father and runs away from home to fight for Russia? This mere girl who dashes into the bloody battlefield. To imagine her amid the death fields of war. A girl fighting Napoleon!

Alexander looked down at the bare-branched linden trees that lined the north face of the palace. He longed for spring, to see crocuses lift their garish colored heads from the snow.

My people despise me for making peace, when all I meant to do was save Russian lives.

A dove-gray and black crow settled in the branches of a linden. It scratched its beak against the bare twigs. Its perfectly tailored suit earned a half-hearted smile from the Tsar of all Russia.

I need the strength to resist this French tyrant who threatens the entire world. And here is a girl whose heart beats with Russian blood of courage, defiance.

If only I could muster the same courage.

"Your Majesty? Recruit Durov has arrived."

"Yes, show Durov in," said Alexander. "See that we are not disturbed. We will speak alone."

I stood erect, saluting the emperor and then bowing, not quite sure of the etiquette. He walked over to me and took my hand. For a moment—what a moment!—he looked directly into my eyes.

He spoke in a gentle voice that might have dispelled my anxiety—except for the words he spoke.

"I have heard, Durov, that you are not a man. Is that true?"

I couldn't breathe. I looked down at the glorious Persian rug, wishing I could hide in its red and indigo designs, its intricate swirls.

When I looked up again, I met his blue eyes.

"Yes, it is true, Your Majesty."

I saw that he was blushing.

A sob of remorse welled up in me, for I was so ashamed. I threw myself at his feet, begging forgiveness.

"Your Majesty! Forgive me for my deceit."

My face met the polished leather of his boots.

"Rise, soldier," he said.

I wiped the tears away with the back of my hand and rose. When I looked up into his face, his blue eyes twinkled.

"Such courage! You fought in Friedland. I have never heard of a similar feat—a girl in one of the fiercest battles of all our history! Your commanders list your honors, your sacrifices. I have read how you saved officers, risking your own life. You swam across a raging river to secure your horse. You and your horse engaged in every battle. You survived without food, supplies, or adequate clothing."

He smiled.

"What is your real name, maiden?"

I swallowed. "My father gave me the name Nadezhda Durova. As a recruit I go by Durov. I beg of you, Your Majesty, please address me as Durov, not Durova . . . I—"

"You shall return home with honor—"

At the word *home* I threw myself once more at the emperor's feet, groveling like a serf.

"Home? No!" I pleaded.

"Mademoiselle Durova! Whatever is wrong?"

I winced at the feminine name—Durova—the name, the world, I would return to as a woman.

"Don't send me back! I should surely die there! Don't make me regret that there was not a bullet marked with my name."

My tears streaked the leather of the emperor's boots.

"Rise, Durov," he said.

He called me Durov—the masculine form of my name. I said a silent prayer.

I felt his hand under my shoulder. I met his eyes. They too had tears.

"What is it that you want, then?" he said.

"To fight Napoleon," I answered. "To wear a uniform and bear arms for Russia. That is the only reward I want. I was born in an army camp. The call of trumpets was my morning hymn."

I crossed my arms over my breast as before an icon.

"And now Your Majesty wants to send me home? If I had foreseen such an end, nothing could have prevented me from seeking a glorious death in the ranks of your warriors!"

The emperor remained silent for an endless minute. I could see he was contemplating my words, my fate. At last his countenance brightened.

"If you presume that permission to wear a uniform and bear arms is your only possible reward, you shall have it!"

His face was so animated, so full of goodwill I could not help but gasp with joy.

"And from this moment on, you will call yourself by my name, Alexandrov!" he said, taking my hand.

Son of Alexander.

"Your Majesty!"

He was like a boy, his face lit with joy. "And I have no doubt that you will make yourself worthy of the name we will now share."

I was beside myself in astonishment. To carry our tsar's own name?

"I will promote you to lieutenant and you will be enrolled in one of our finest regiments of noble families: The Mariupol Hussars, a most valiant corps."

The Mariupol Hussars! Me, an officer! My ears hummed as if I had been struck a great blow to the head.

Then he bowed to me. Yes. Alexander, the Tsar of all Russia, bowed to me.

He pulled something from his desk. I recognized it immediately, once my eyes caught the colors, the bright orange and black stripes.

The Cross of St. George!

"The highest honor Imperial Russia can bestow," he said. With his own hands, the angelic hands of our beloved Mother Russia, the Tsar threaded the ribbon through the buttonhole of my jacket.

"I hope," he said, "that it will remind you of me at crucial moments in your life. We share the same name now."

His eyes lingered on my cross.

Was he remembering something? Saying a prayer?

"Go, Alexandrov," he said finally. "Serve the Hussars nobly. And never forget that this name must always be above reproach, and I will never forgive you for the shadow of a stain upon it."

I mouthed my new name. *Alexandrov.* The son of Alexander.

The emperor rose to his feet. "Go now. Until we meet again, Alexandrov."

I nodded and bowed. I turned for the door but could not work the handle.

The hand of Alexander reached past me and opened the door. It may as well have been divine intervention, the hand of an angel.

As the emperor opened the door to the antechamber, he saw Adam Czartoryski standing in the smoke-laced room.

He will depart two days from now to Poland. I have banished my best friend from the Russian Court.

"Czartoryski!"

"Your Excellency," said Czartoryski, striding across the room.

"I want you to follow the Polish uhlan to his horse. Talk to him. He is the most unusual lad I have ever met. You will not regret meeting him."

"Brave, Your Excellency?" said Czartoryski, raising an eyebrow.

"Beyond brave. I just awarded him the St. George Cross. His name is Alexandrov," said the Tsar, pronouncing the name with satisfaction.

He smiled. "Alexander Andreevich Alexandrov. Go on now. Exchange a few words with him. You will never see the likes of him again."

Czartoryski bowed to the emperor.

"Adam," said Alexander. "Meeting Alexandrov makes me remember priorities in my life. Forgive my cross words with you. I shall miss you when you return to Warsaw."

As Czartoryski turned to leave, the Tsar reached out and placed a hand on his shoulder to hold him there a moment longer.

"You remain my most faithful—and honest—friend."

An equerry stood holding my Alcides for me as I exited the Winter Palace. My faithful friend nickered, recognizing me at once.

"That is a stunning horse you ride, soldier," said a voice behind me. "From the Caucasus?"

"Yes, he is," I said. "He is a brave horse, too."

The man approached closer. With dark curling hair and velvet eyes, he was the most handsome man I had ever seen.

"The emperor has told me you are brave," he said. "I am Prince Adam Czartoryski, minister of foreign affairs." He winced when he said this as if he had bitten the inside of his mouth. "Former minister," he added.

"I am . . ."

"Alexander Andreevich Alexandrov. Congratulations, Alexandrov. It is usual when the emperor awards the St. George Cross of Honor for the recipient to drink with the Imperial Guard. We would like to toast your honor, your bravery. Please come inside."

I froze, looking at him.

How shall I disengage myself from such a cordial man—a minister of the emperor's! But I would surely blush and stammer, and reveal my gender.

"I am sorry, Your Honor. I must return to quarters immediately. It is quite urgent."

I swung up on Alcides, nodding to the equerry to let go the rein.

The prince approached a step closer. He wore a look of astonishment on his face at my refusal.

"At least let me exchange a few words with you, Alexandrov! It is not every day a uhlan receives the St. George Cross, especially at such a young age."

I realized I had been unforgivably rude to refuse the officer's toast and congratulations.

"Forgive me, sir. Yes, of course, the matter can wait a few minutes more. I only regret not accepting your invitation to celebrate."

Prince Czartoryski ran his open hand along Alcides's neck. "You belong to the Polish uhlans, the emperor told me. What brave lancers they are! I am originally from Poland, as you might tell from my accent."

Suddenly I realized just who he was. This was the emperor's closest confidant!

"You must have done something extraordinary to merit the emperor's highest honor," he said, clapping my kneecap in camaraderie.

His hand lingered there. He smiled up at me in the saddle.

"Are you sure you won't indulge us in a toast, Alexandrov?"

"Quite sure, Your Honor," I said, fidgeting with my reins. "I really must go."

Those velvet-black eyes met mine. He studied my face—cheekbones, throat. He nodded.

"Very well. It was an honor to meet you, Alexandrov," he said, removing his hand from my knee. "Fight bravely for Russia. My regards to my old countrymen, the Polish uhlans. *Odwaga!*" he said in Polish.

Courage.

"Yes, sir," I said, reining Alcides away from the Winter Palace. I left Czartoryski standing there, watching me in the gently falling snow.

I returned to the apartment where the emperor's aide-de-camp Captain Zass hosted me until I left for the Mariupol Hussars' regiment. Madame Zass fussed over me until I almost couldn't stand it.

I was taking a cup of tea one afternoon when we heard a knock at the door. An orderly answered and I heard another voice, vaguely familiar.

"May I see Recruit Durov of the Polish Horse Regiment?"

"I am Durov," I answered, at once standing. An old man entered, hat in hand.

I stared. He was my father's young brother, Nicolaj Durov.

My uncle approached me and then gave me an embrace. He whispered in my ear.

"Nadezhda. Your mother is dead."

When we were out of Zass's apartment on the street, I finally trusted myself to talk. His words had pierced my heart.

"Dead?" I said. I trembled, my face drained of blood.

"Nadezhda, come home with me," Uncle Nicolaj said, motioning to his sleigh. "I will tell you all there."

I nodded, being guided like a half-wit. The rush of grief and shock robbed me of all senses. I settled into the black leather seat. I ducked my face into my greatcoat so that the residents of St. Petersburg wouldn't see me cry as the sleigh glided by.

"Your father received the letter you wrote," said my uncle, guiding the horse through the snowy city streets.

The letter! I had written to my father to obtain his word that I came from a noble family so that I might become an officer. I had begged him to forgive me for the unbearable suffering and sadness I must have caused him.

I had told him how life with my mother's scrutiny had become unbearable, how I would rather die than live under the restrictions she proposed for me.

My uncle could see that I could not bear more. He said no more until we reached his apartment, not more than twenty minutes from the Winter Palace. It was another world, a grim building of broken stucco, the red brick exposed like wounds. His rooms smelled of boiled cabbage. My uncle Nicolaj had fallen on hard times.

He lit a single lantern and put a kettle on to boil over the embers of a feeble fire.

"Your father was beside himself trying to find you and get you back, Nadya." He looked at me sadly across the grimy table. "In his hysteria, he showed your mother the letter, not thinking of how its contents would affect her."

Oh, no!

"Your mother was already quite ill. Your condemnation of her pushed her over the edge. She said, 'Nadezhda blames me?'"

He reached across the table and took my hand. "Then she turned her face to the wall and died."

My face crumpled in agony and I sobbed like a child. Behind the tears, my mind was whirling at the unfairness of it all.

Why is he telling me this? Is he trying to torture me? My mother never loved me. She never said a kind word to me. I only wrote the truth in my letter—if the truth killed her, why am I to blame? How was I to know that my father would show her the letter?

"Let me finish, dear niece," said my uncle. "There is good that comes along with tragedy. Your father, who loves you, realized you were alive. He sent a letter to me, trying to find your regiment. I showed it to various generals in the Ukraine and again here in St. Petersburg. Finally he wrote to the emperor himself."

"That is how the Tsar knew!" I said. "He knew I was a woman, Uncle Nikolaj."

"The letter moved Tsar Alexander to tears, Nadya," he said. "He contacted me. He wrote your father. The emperor also asked for a full report on your comportment from your commanders. Every officer gave a brilliant commentary to your valor and conduct."

It was all too much for me to comprehend. I didn't know what I could say.

"Your father is very proud of you," my uncle said. "When he hears the emperor awarded you the St. George Cross, he will cry with joy, Nadya!"

I fingered the St. George Cross attached to my buttonhole.

"Call me Alexander Alexandrov, Uncle," I said, thinking of my dead mother. "The girl Nadya died the day I joined the cavalry."

Chapter 39

St. Petersburg
February 1808

My uncle wanted me to return to my father's home immediately, but I told him that it was not possible. I refused to tell him of my new assignment in the Ukraine with the Mariupol Hussars. He badgered me mercilessly, but I did not want him or my father to interfere with my military career.

"I will visit my father when the time is right. Tell him that now I must serve my tsar and Russia."

Emperor Alexander paid for my Hussar officer uniform: two thousand rubles! Only a son of wealthy nobility could pay such a sum. I was given a travel pass and regimental orders to travel to the Ukraine—my mother's homeland. That cast a slight shade of a bitter joke on what should have been a joyous voyage.

The other bitter joke was that the Tsar—despite his overwhelming generosity—had not thought to give me money to pay for my trip.

When Alcides and I finally arrived, dusty and weary, I had only one ruble, one single coin, to my name—now Alexander Alexandrov, a name I carried with pride, despite my empty pockets.

I delivered my orders, issued by Count Lieven of the Imperial Court, to the battalion commander, Major Dymchevich. He lifted his eyes from his paperwork, scrutinizing me.

"Did you meet Grand Duke Constantine, the Tsar's younger brother?" he asked gruffly.

"No," I replied. "Only the Tsar himself."

"Hmm." He nodded. I thought he should have been impressed, but he didn't show any sign that he was. "Go to the regimental adjutant and give him these papers," he said with a flourish of signature.

I was immediately given command of the Fourth Squadron until the return of the regular commander away on leave. This squadron was based in a hamlet of Berezolupy, where I was given quarters with a woman landowner, Pani Staroscina. She treated me as if I were one of her grandsons, giving me a cup of warm milk for breakfast.

"You are too young to be an officer!" she said to me. "What are the Mariupol Hussars thinking, giving a command to you."

"I am nearly nineteen," I protested. "I fought in the Battle of Friedland!"

"Well," she said, suppressing a smile. "At least wipe the milk foam from your mouth before you address your new squadron."

A junior officer, with all the pomposity and gas of a rotten melon, greeted me. "Fine horse," he boomed. Then he looked about. "But where are the rest of your horses?"

"I was told I would be assigned another from the regiment."

"Yes, but you are an officer! You must have one for your pack and one in reserve, of course. And you must have an orderly."

I groaned inwardly.

"I have no money," I told him. "I cannot possibly buy another horse, let alone pay an orderly."

"You are a Hussar now!" he roared as if I had been accepted into Olympus as a new god. "You can buy a horse on credit. I know a man who has one to sell you."

I was sent to see the horse in question, a lop-eared gelding, whose conformation and wit could not compare with Alcides.

But what horse could?

I bought the horse at the price of one hundred rubles silver, paid on credit until I received my wages. I named him Lop Ear.

I wasted no time writing to Count Lieven in St. Petersburg. Tsar Alexander had instructed me to write if I required anything.

I asked for the loan of five hundred rubles to begin my career. I wrote with regret that I had not a ruble to my name.

My request was answered immediately, and I paid the horse dealer his one hundred rubles.

And now it seemed as if my military training had to begin anew. With the Polish uhlans, I had learned—painfully—about lances and sabers. Now I had to master a new weapon: the carbine.

I had to train with old Grebennik, the flank Hussar of my platoon.

"Order arms! Slope arms! Present arms!" He rattled commands while my head spun.

I was hopelessly clumsy. My hands were slow and awkward when Grebennik commanded, "Slope arms!" or "Present arms!" But when he barked "Order arms!"—with the carbine butt on the ground and the barrel in my hand—I failed even more miserably.

"Don't worry about your foot, Your Honor!" he insisted. "Toss the gun more boldly!"

"I'm trying!"

"Don't worry about your foot, damn it!"

I gritted my teeth and tried not to worry. The heavy gun stock crashed down on my instep. I limped for a month. My new squadron fought smiles as they watched me dismount from my lop-eared horse, wincing.

But I had learned the carbine drill.

"You are to present your regiment to the divisional commander, Count Suvorov."

"Suvorov?" I repeated in wonderment.

"Yes, the son of the great general."

There was no name more revered in Russian military history than Suvorov—except for Peter the Great. In sixty battles over his lifetime, General Suvorov had never known defeat. His victories against the Turks had saved Russia in the Ottoman wars, lest we all be subjects of the sultan. Every Russian knew his name: the general who had crossed the snowy Alps with his army as only Hannibal had done before—and then driven Napoleon out of northern Italy.

My first review would be an inspection by the son of Russia's hero.

My colonel's voice pulled me from my reverie. "Make sure your squadron is perfectly drilled, Alexandrov."

The name Suvorov echoed in my ears as I made certain that my squadron was turned out perfectly in their white dress uniforms, gold trim, and white-plumed shakos. As we stood, arrayed and waiting, I could not help but think we resembled ladies at a St. Petersburg ball, especially the youngest of us with our fresh faces and slender waists.

I rode Lop Ear, wanting to save Alcides for the final inspection the next day by our corps commander Dokhturov. Besides, I needed to expose the new horse to drills to give him the training he needed.

Unfortunately, Lop Ear decided it was I who needed training.

I realized quickly that Lop Ear must never have ridden at the front of the ranks before, for when I urged him forward to the lead role, he kept backing up and shying sideways, working his way back into formation. I spurred him forward and he reciprocated by arching his neck and rearing.

Count Suvorov rode past our regiment, inspecting our formation. I held my breath, my spurs at the ready at my horse's side. The count moved ahead and gave the command, "Honorable officers!"

At this command the entire regiment charged forward at a full gallop to their commander. Lop Ear refused to budge, despite my spurs. I gave him a few hard whacks with the flat of my saber. He responded with a languid gallop, his donkey ears waving like banners.

Count Suvorov waited patiently until I had rejoined my squadron. Then he proceeded to call out the orders we would perform the next day for Commander Dokhturov.

"By the platoon, to the right, wheel!" he called.

Lop Ear would have no part of it. He arched his back, snorting, jumping sideways, knocking aside my subordinates' horses. Seeing that there was no good end in sight, I ordered my sergeant to take my place before the platoon.

I smacked my mount with the broad end of my sword, making him race full speed down the Lutsk road.

My platoon watched me disappear, riding the vinegar out of old Lop Ear.

Count Suvorov observed wryly, "The young officer doesn't appear to want to drill with us."

That night I was invited to dine with this gracious count. With impeccable manners he avoided all reference to my hasty exit down the Lutsk road.

Lop Ear proved a disastrous purchase. Six weeks passed while I tried in vain to train the obstreperous horse. Finally Captain Podjampolsky gave me one of his string, a frisky young stallion.

Oh, that Podjampolsky! He must have laughed up his sleeve when he assigned me that horse!

Our maneuvers were proceeding well when I gave the final command.

"From your places charge—*charge!*"

My stallion reared and then surged ahead. The abrupt lurch ripped the scabbard of my saber loose from its front strap, leaving it dangling between my horse's legs.

As the scabbard whacked him, my horse bucked at full gallop, loosening me from the saddle. On the third galloping buck, I fell hard to the ground, losing consciousness.

What happened next was almost my undoing.

The officers picked me up from the ground, unhooking my tunic. They undid my necktie, calling for the regiment physician to bleed me immediately.

I slowly regained consciousness feeling the cool air on my bare skin as they prepared to undress me completely!

I struggled up to a sitting position. "I am all right. All right, I say!" batting their hands away from me.

"Fetch my horse, I shall remount immediately!" The world was still spinning, but I could not risk my identity being discovered, even if I stood a chance of killing myself on the wild-eyed stallion.

This was not the end of the adventure. After the maneuvers, Major General Dymchevich, the battalion commander, sent for me. He rode with me apart from the other cavalrymen.

"Alexandrov! You fell off your horse!"

"Sir, the horse threw me. Captain Podjampolsky mounted me on a half-broke stallion! The scabbard tore from—"

"Alexandrov! *You fell from your horse.* A Hussar only falls with his horse, not off it!"

I made up my mind to ride only Alcides from that day on. To hell with these other nags!

⚔︎ ⚔︎ ⚔︎

I wrote to Count Lieven to ask the emperor for leave. It had been three long years since I had left my father's house. I knew that since I had been so recently attached to the Mariupol Hussars, there was little chance of being granted leave without some special intervention.

I took my chance writing to the emperor, but he had instructed me to let him know of any desire I had.

This did not play well with the new commander in chief, Baron Egor Meller-Zakomelsky. He ordered me to headquarters, asking why I had bypassed the chain of command to apply for leave to the emperor himself.

"The emperor requested—no, sir, ordered!—that I keep him informed of any requirement. I knew that this was the only way I could be granted leave as soon as possible."

The commander in chief was astonished at my candid reply. How could he argue with the Tsar? He was left sputtering.

"Report to Count Suvorov in Dubno for your travel orders."

As I left, I heard the commander remark to his orderly: "Lieutenant Alexandrov hides behind the Tsar's coattails."

The remark struck me like the flat side of a saber.

I vowed then and there I would never depend on the emperor's protection again. I would be my own man.

I reported to Count Suvorov, still embarrassed about my last encounter with him when I had disappeared down the Lutsk road astride old Lop Ear.

"Ah, Alexandrov! We meet again," he said, clapping his hand around my shoulder. "Yes, I have your travel orders. But they won't take effect until the day after my grand ball. You shall be my special guest. It is a Moroccan affair, you see. No chance I will let you slip away before that!"

He clapped me once more on the back and strode away.

Indeed there was much going on about us as we spoke. Dust spun with the sweeping and cleaning of the mansion. I joined many officers of my regiment, and we stood drinking tea.

"Please move back, gentlemen," said a serf.

"What now?" said a colonel next to me.

To our surprise a cartload of straw was unloaded in the room. Serfs raked the straw evenly, and then Moroccan rugs were spread on top of it. Velvet cushions were strewn here and there. Suddenly we stood in an Arabian palace!

I thought of how playful this count was, how eccentric. His father, the best-known general in Russian history, had defeated the Eastern invaders, while now his son entertained his troops and Polish and Ukrainian society with Arabian trappings.

The count charmed everyone. The Polish women, fine ladies dressed in their evening gowns, flocked around Suvorov, despite his occasionally bizarre statements. He did not seem to censor anything he said.

Noticing me not dancing or even approaching the beautiful women, the count inquired what was the matter with me.

Before I could answer, my commander, Stankovich, interjected.

"Alexander Alexandrov approach the ladies? Oh, no, Count. He is afraid of them, you see. I think he knows nothing of relations with them."

I blushed purple. Stankovich winked at the count.

"You see!"

I shall kill you in your sleep, Stankovich!

"Really?" said the count. "Well come along with me, Alexandrov. We will have to remedy the situation."

Oh, God of mercy!

I followed the count as he approached one of the most charming ladies there, the young princess Lubomirska.

Bowing to her, he presented me saying, "*À la vue de ses fraîches couleurs vous pouvez bien deviner qu'il n'a pas encore perdu sa virginité.*" With one look at his fresh color, you can easily tell he has not yet lost his virginity.

I winced, shrinking up inside my uniform like a scalded snail.

The princess took this all in jest, a faint smile visible on her lovely face. She rapped the impertinent count on his forearm with her fan.

The first chance I could find, I retired from the ball. It was well after midnight and I was exhausted—and frightened. Stankovich was right in saying I feared women. I really did. A woman seemed able to stare at me for only a minute and guess my secret.

I was determined to try to avoid contact with them. My future in the cavalry was too much at risk from women's prying eyes. I hurried away from the hall, anxious to return to my pallet, taking refuge in sleep.

That night I dreamt of the stranger again, the strange images and sounds returning.

Hands grope for me in the dark, seeking my nipples through my nightdress. "You play at being a boy astride a horse," he says. "I'll show you how much a woman you are."

He kisses my lips, my neck, my breasts. I shiver in the cold mountain air.

I don't refuse. I am transfixed. No one has ever shown me such passion. Ever.

He cups my buttocks with his hands, pushing himself into me. I throw back my head and cry out, but the only sound is the sudden flutter of wings of the frightened birds overhead, roosting in the thick foliage of summer.

My nightgown is torn and bloody. I don't know how I will explain this to my maid Ludmilla or to my mother.

But all I can think of is, will I ever see him again.

Dreams so real I could swear they were truth.

Chapter 40

Sarapul, Russia
March 1810

Three and a half years had passed since I left my father's home. Riding Alcides in the darkness, I reached the hill looking down on the town of Sarapul. It was after midnight but still far from dawn. The stars shone bright and clear over the silent town and the slow-moving river.

I reined in Alcides, gazing down over the sleeping town.

"Do you remember when we left this place, Alcides?"

Obviously he did. He pawed anxiously with his left hoof.

I gave him a loose rein and he trotted ahead, knowing the way home.

We arrived in pitch darkness. The gates were locked. I tied Alcides to a post and prowled the walls. Along the palisade I found my old escape hole, where four stakes were loose.

The memory of a little girl in a white linen chemise slipping out in the night . . . I smiled as I crawled in my Hussar uniform through the gap. Now I was swarthy from the sun, my face more oval and my body muscular. I had lost any traces of softness and femininity I had in my youth.

I brushed the soil from my precious uniform and unlocked the gate. I put Alcides in the stall and made my way up to the house.

All the windows and doors were locked. I didn't want to rap on the shutters of my little brother or sisters' room as I would scare them.

Our two dogs, Mars and Mustupa, charged me, but their growls dissolved into joyful squeals of recognition. They leaped up to lick my face, entwining themselves in my legs. I knocked on doors as the dogs scratched the wood. After long minutes, Natalja, my mother's maid, answered.

"Who's there?"

"It's me, Natalja! Nadezhda."

She opened the door, then froze staring at me.

Her eyes wandered from my saber to my Hussar uniform to my face. Then back to the uniform.

"Aren't you going to let me in, Natalja? Some homecoming!"

"Is it really you, mistress?"

"Don't you recognize me, Natalja?"

"Recognize you?" she gasped. "Never! If it weren't for your voice, I would not believe it to be you at all. What rich clothes! Are you a general?" She reached out to touch my gold braid and fur-lined collar. Her fingers lingered on my uniform as if she were blind.

"Natalja . . . Please. Could you make up a bed for me? I am cold and exhausted."

"Tea, miss . . . Madame? Oh, dear . . . what shall I call you?"

"What everyone else does. Sir."

She gave a worried look. "I don't think I shall ever get used to that, miss. Or sir."

She wandered off, muttering, to prepare the tea and see to the bed.

In the morning, after a few hours' sleep, I went to the parlor in my white uniform with gold braid. My father sat in his old embroidered chair, drinking his tea. He gasped as I entered.

I fell to my knees, embracing his feet. I kissed his hands. Overcome with emotion I could not utter a word.

He pulled me to his breast and hugged me tight. "You don't look like a woman at all, Nadya! How you have changed! Your uniform—the Cross of St. George!"

My little brother Vasily came in. He threw himself into my arms, his eyes wide in wonder.

"Look at how you've grown, little brother!" I said. "In three years time, I'll take you with me to join the Hussars!"

"Will you?" he cried.

"No," said my father. "God forbid! You have followed your chosen path, my daughter. Leave Vasinka here with me for the consolation of my old age."

I pressed my lips together tight. I felt the emptiness in the house, the palpable absence of my mother.

"I'm sorry, Papa," I said. "I never told either of you good-bye."

As I turned to leave the room, Vasily whispered in my ear. "I will go with you!"

I nodded my head, not uttering a word. After all the heartache I had caused my father, I was going to take his only true son away to war.

Chapter 41

Winter Palace, St. Petersburg
January 1811

A blond boy rides his pony alongside a black-clad stranger. No matter how he tries, the boy cannot not see the face hidden under the stranger's dark hood. They ride to a knoll overlooking a battlefield.

Bloody corpses lie strewn in the early summer grass. Crows circle overhead, a few daring to light on soldiers' bodies. The cannons blast, blowing holes in the ground, unexpected geysers of black earth. Horses and cavalrymen disappear into the clouds of dust, erupting from the blasts. When the dust settles, horses and riders lie still, like wooden toys knocked down by an angry fist.

Then there are no soldiers, no horses. Only silence and death.

The boy turns, hearing the three-beat gallop of a single horse.

A single slender-waisted uhlan rides his mount forward through the ghostly plain, screaming, "Hurrah!"

The boy looks up to the hooded horseman, his brow knit in inquiry. "Who is he?"

Finally the shrouded man speaks: "One who deceived her father, but did not murder him."

The boy draws back in horror, his heart thudding in his chest. He looks up at the shrouded man.

The rider draws back his hood, exposing his battered face and a fat, purple tongue that slurred his words. "You hold the reins, my son. What is your plan?"

The boy looks down and sees the reins crumble to chunks of mud in his hands.

"Was it worth my sacrifice?" wails the man. "Now you have made peace with Napoleon, just as I did!"

Alexander woke, choking out a half-born scream. His eyes snapped open to see a white flash and then a dark shadow scuttle just beyond the foot of the bed.

"Who goes there?" he shouted.

The guards always present at his door heard his shout and burst into the room, guns and flashing sabers at the ready.

"Your Majesty!" said one. "Is everything all right?"

The valet sleeping in the adjacent room turned up the wick in the gas lamp, sending giant shadows of the guardsmen leaping on the walls of the bedchamber.

"A dream, I think," said Alexander. He ran his fingers through his hair, trying to collect his thoughts. "Yes, a nightmare. Send for—"

"Your Majesty?"

"Send for—"

Adam Czartoryski.

"No one. Never mind!" said the Tsar, running his fingers through his sweat-drenched hair. "I am fine. Leave me."

There was no one to tell. Alexander had dismissed his three most trusted ministers. His Committee of Friends was dissolved. Adam Czartoryski was banished to Poland.

There was no confidant—other than the tsarina—whom he trusted with so intimate a memory.

Alexander's hand shook with rage as he held the letter from his sister Ekaterina.

> *My Dearest Angel Brother,*
> *What are we to do? The monster Napoleon has seized*
> *the duchy of Oldenburg from my father-in-law. We*
> *have become French subjects overnight! What of my*
> *family, my children? You can see that appeasement and*
> *overtures to this French beast have rendered us helpless.*
> *Did you not secure a guarantee that Oldenburg would*
> *remain free?*
> > *What can be done? For my children's sake!*
> > *Your loving sister who adores you above all others,*
> > *Katia*

Alexander's teeth clenched until his jaw ached. Despite their accord, Napoleon had pushed further to the north and east into Poland, and now the duchy of his sister's husband.

Two can play at duplicity. The devil with Napoleon!

Chapter 42

Palais des Tuileries, Paris
January 1811

Sleet panged against the tall narrow windows. Napoleon looked out at the puddles forming on the brick pavement. Long wet fingers of water running down the glass distorted the view of the trees and the perfect symmetry of the Tuileries gardens just beyond the gate.

At the entrance to the palace, horses had left mud behind on the bricks as they returned to the stable. Their hooves had carried soft, wet earth from some unpaved Parisian street to the very doors of his palace. The muck was shaped into small pools from the impression of horseshoes. The emperor smiled as he gazed down at the small muddy mounds smeared across the pavement.

He thought of the thousands upon thousands of hoofprints, churning up the loamy soil and grass of the battlefield.

Napoleon sniffed the air of the palace and wrinkled his nose.

The air is stale. Even the potpourri smells ancient, like the incense in Notre Dame. Old and dead.

I am not a man for palaces. I wrap myself in red velvet and ermine and wear a crown for a portrait. I am the emperor of France! But my bones ache to lie in a canvas bed, close to the snorting horses, soldiers' talk, and the crackling fires the night before a battle.

Too long in Paris, I become Samson shorn of his hair.

Napoleon touched his fingers to his scalp.

I must return to the battlefield. I need to smell the piss of horses, the acrid smell of gunpowder. I need to hear "Vive l'empereur!" from the soldiers, dying for me, for France!

The emperor swallowed and moved his tongue in his mouth trying to taste the pungent flavors of war, of battle. That taste, gunpowder and smoke, had always meant victory to him. Napoleon had a craving for that sweet savor.

A deadly craving.

Coming back to Paris after a victory filled Napoleon with satisfying glory, like a good meal filled his belly. Seeing his pretty young wife, Marie Louise, and their infant son—the king of Rome—gave him a depth of pleasure and tenderness he thought he was not capable of, a battle-scarred general in his forties.

But after a fortnight or two he found himself longing for the sounds, scents, and sights of the battlefield. He felt his stature shrink, a small man in Paris. Astride a horse he was taller and mightier than any general alive.

I shall invade Russia, damn them! If I do not conquer the northern bear, our Grand Armée will at the very least decimate its troops. Then I shall have no more trouble with Tsar Alexander.

Summer. Early summer, when the rivers have thawed and our army can live off the land. We'll be home in Paris before autumn.

Napoleon smiled down at the wet bricks below. The mud had diluted in the downpour, its last traces slowly washing away.

Armand de Caulaincourt, the French ambassador to St. Petersburg, was recalled to serve as aide-de-camp to Napoleon. The emperor needed his intimate knowledge of Russia and Tsar Alexander in order to plan his new war.

For five hours, Caulaincourt tried to dissuade the French emperor.

"Your Majesty! The Russians, their devotion to nation—they are like no others. They will never capitulate. Never, Your Majesty!"

"Alexander has capitulated before. He shall again."

Caulaincourt bowed. "With all respect, sire. I think it will be different if we invade their homeland. The tsar is sure the serfs and all Russians alike will fight in militias in addition to the regular army."

"What impertinence! Did you sit in the tsar's presence and let him prattle on? Tell me you objected, or I shall think you do not represent France's dignity!"

"Tsar Alexander said, 'I shall not be the first to draw my sword, but I shall be the last to sheathe it.' I excused myself from dinner at these words, but the sentiments are clear."

"Empty threats! I know Alexander. He hasn't the character nor courage to withstand the Grand Armée. He has proved that more than once."

Caulaincourt shook his head. "My emperor, I dare say Alexander has changed in the years since Tilsit. He challenges you by aligning with England and breaking the embargo. He stands up against us for the duchy of Oldenburg. I beg you not to underestimate him or the Russian people. Or the Russian winter."

"We shall attack quickly and defeat the Russians. I will wait until summer to commence. The Grand Armée will not feel the pinch of a Russian winter for we will have finished the war long before the leaves change. One good battle, a decisive thrashing, will see the end of all your friend Alexander's fine resolutions—they will be battered like sand castles under a wave!"

Napoleon poured himself a glass of cognac, draining it without offering Ambassador Caulaincourt a drop.

"You seem to have become more Russian than French in your lengthy residence in St. Petersburg. What else did your precious Alexander say regarding possible war?"

Caulaincourt drew a breath recalling the last formal dinner at the Winter Palace, before he was recalled to Paris.

"Our spies report that Tsar Alexander knows our soldiers are brave and our Grand Armée strong. But he is confident that Russia's winters will win the war. He says we cannot afford to cross his borders into the vast lands that are Russia, so far from Paris. Nor can we stay and fight his people for years."

"For years!" roared Napoleon. "Fool! We shall defeat Alexander in a matter of weeks, a battle or two. Our forces far outnumber his and are better trained. We will crush him!"

"But Your Majesty and his generals don't know the Russian countryside."

"You are mistaken, Caulaincourt," said Napoleon. "How could you so underestimate your emperor? Let me show you."

He opened a wooden coffer and withdrew a scroll. With a devilish smile he spread out a map of the whole of western Russia, clear to the border of the Ural Mountains. Names of even the tiniest villages were written in French, transcribed from Russian.

"Have you ever seen such a detailed map?" said Napoleon, rubbing his hands together. "I've had a team of spies working for over a year on this."

Caulaincourt blinked down on the magnificent *carte*.

"Not that we will ever use it, except for the westernmost fringes," said Napoleon. "We will defeat Alexander's army just as we did at Friedland and Austerlitz. I have no intention of entering into the damned Russian interior. We will finish off Alexander and have him suing for peace soon enough. Right here."

Napoleon thrust his thumb down on the blue line of the Niemen River, at the border of the old Lithuanian lands, sixty miles from Vilna.

"The beginning and the end of this war will be right here."

"I beg you, Your Majesty! War with Russia would be a catastrophe."

"*Ça suffit!* Enough, you are dismissed, Monsieur Caulaincourt."

The staccato click of boots echoed through the halls of the Tuileries Palace as the generals answered Napoleon's summons. General Ney looked beyond the windows at the falling snow silently blanketing the gardens.

"Surely Napoleon would not order us all to report to him at once if he did not intend war," said General Eugene to Ney. "But how can we move an army against Russia in the winter!"

General Ney gave a curt nod.

"The blight on wheat triggers food riots in Normandy," said Davout. "How will we fill a soldier's belly without bread?"

The three generals were careful not to let General Murat, Napoleon's brother-in-law and king of Naples, overhear their conversation. Any doubts or criticism of the emperor's plan could be considered treason.

Together, the four generals entered Napoleon's study.

"This Tsar Alexander is a duplicitous rascal!" fumed Napoleon. "I offer him my hand in alliance and he spits upon it, trading with England and others. He takes me for a fool!"

The generals focused their eyes straight ahead, listening to the emperor rant. Clocks sounded the hour—tinkling, bonging, chiming down the long halls of the Tuileries Palace.

"We shall endure no more from this Romanov. If it's war he wants, war he shall have! Begin preparing for our campaign against Russia!"

The generals bowed their heads in respect.

"The Grand Armée will crush the Russian rabble and take Moscow. I cannot wait to see Alexander's face when we turn twenty thousand Prussian soldiers and Austrian cannons against him! Then we shall take St. Petersburg." Napoleon's right hand dived under his waistcoat. "Eternal allies, indeed!"

Chapter 43

Never have I been more proud than when I wore the imperial blue uniform of the Mariupol Hussars for the first time and then was given command of my own squadron. I loved my comrades, my commanders, my platoon, my regiment. I wish I could say that my career in that glorious regiment carried on until I fell in battle.

But that was not the case.

As the storm of the Patriotic War of 1812 approached with its crash of thunder, I realized that I was not suited for the Hussars. Quite literally.

I could not afford an orderly. Or another supply horse. More important, a Hussar's uniform must be impeccable, requiring meticulous care and replacement when it is torn or badly soiled. The Tsar had bought my first uniform and I simply could not afford to purchase another.

The truth is I mismanaged my money. And two thousand rubles for a new uniform would have been an impossible expense.

I dared not write the Tsar for more money—Alexander was engaged in planning a war against Napoleon. I could not bother him for money when Russia's fate hung in the balance.

I transferred to the Lithuanian Uhlans Regiment and I relinquished my Hussar uniform for a simple blue *kolet* with red facings. I was a lancer once more.

We were sent immediately to Dąbrowica, southeast of Warsaw. My regrets at leaving the Hussars dissolved as I saw the uhlans and their lances, heard men speaking Polish and Lithuanian, mixed among the Russian. The bright pennons waved atop the regiments' lances, bringing back my memories of my first taste of freedom, when I joined the Polish uhlans.

As luck would have it, I was assigned to serve under a colleague from the Mariupol Hussars, Captain Podjampolsky—the same rascal who had given me his frisky stallion who bucked me off.

Podjampolsky leapt off his horse to embrace me.

Then he stepped back to take a quick survey of my body, wrinkling his brow.

"The Hussars did not feed you very well. You certainly haven't grown much. And you have no beard at all!"

I ducked my head in embarrassment that quickly ignited into fury.

"Can you still hold a lance?" asked the captain.

"I should think so!" I said, the heat rising from my collar.

Don't treat me like a child!

The captain laughed. "Of course you can. Alexandrov, how good it is to see you again."

He clapped me on the back. My shoulders relaxed.

"We will let you get your bearings," said Podjampolsky. "We will be at war soon enough."

War! I was going back to the battlefield, as I was in those first years as an uhlan. I felt a thrill of reliving my past. No more drilling or endless cleaning of weapons, uniform, and quarters for inspection. We would meet Napoleon again in battle!

"In the meantime, until we have our orders, the chief of the regiment, Count Plater—Stanislaw Manuzzi—and his wife, Countess Plater, host the most glorious parties. Dancing until four in the morning, magnificent breakfasts. Rest up, tonight you shall see."

Magnificent indeed! The Plater mansion was a three-story affair with a copper mansard roof, a white-columned entrance, and an enormous coat of arms over the doorway. The chandeliers were ablaze, the ballroom festooned with ivy garlands and white bows. Music filled the rooms, and women dressed in silk gowns sashayed through the great hall on the arms of dashing young men in uniform.

The young Countess Manuzzi had come home to visit her parents, Count and Countess Plater. What a black-eyed beauty! She sent our uhlans into a frenzy of adoration. They danced, leapt about like goats, twirling their mustaches. Some doused themselves so thoroughly in scent that in the closed ballroom we could barely breathe. Others confessed they had washed themselves in milk in the bathhouse.

Uhlan after uhlan bowed to the young countess, spurs jingling, waists cinched with sashes *à la circassienne*.

All tried to win her heart but with no success.

But when our regiment commander, Colonel Tutolmin, returned, it was the countess's turn to fall in love. The dashing officer left her head spinning.

The next few weeks the handsome couple were inseparable, as Countess Plater hosted evening after evening of entertainment for us all.

To love an uhlan! It was a dangerous adventure for this young beauty, especially as Napoleon approached Russia with the Grand Armée.

One night, the music stopped abruptly. A hush and then a buzzing murmur filled the room. A knot of commanding officers congregated at the corner of the dance floor. Count Plater emerged from the tight knot of men and spoke to his wife and daughter.

Then I heard the sound of a woman's weeping.

And the announcement was made: we move out in twenty-four hours!

A tremendous cheer erupted. We pounded each other's backs, embracing one another.

Countess Manuzzi, inconsolable, bade farewell to her newfound love.

He left her for another love, a deeper love: the love of battle.

I listened to the countess's sobs and thought how I would feel if a man I loved had left me behind to go to war.

I would follow . . .

I watched the tears slide down her face. To leave loved ones behind with the prospect of never seeing them ever again.

Ever again!

I was riveted to the spot where I stood.

"Are you all right, Alexandrov?" said a voice.

I turned to see Captain Podjampolsky. "We move out tomorrow at 20:00 hours. You should pack your kit and be ready. We will ride all night. Get some sleep now."

I managed to nod. Only then did I realize my cheeks were wet with tears.

"Yes, sir."

I cast one last look at the grieving woman and exited the room.

The saying goes, whenever Russian troops move out, every sort of foul weather travels with them. That blustery March, storms lanced us with pelting sleet and sharp crystals of snow. My face chapped so mightily it turned scarlet and began to bleed.

Captain Podjampolsky had to deal with accounts and requisitioning for the march, which left me in charge of the squadron. I spent time reviewing the uhlans, seeing that all the sabers and lances were sharpened. I personally inspected the horses to see that there were no stone bruises or ill-shod mounts. I ran my hand over the horses' backs, checking for aches and saddle sores.

The men murmured to each other how attentive I was to the horses, how well prepared we would all be to meet the Grand Armée.

"Napoleon! We'll show him a lance in his fat French gut!"

"I'll spear him through like a Turkish brochette!"

Such bravado. Foolish braggarts! A shiver overtook me. I had seen Napoleon's Grand Armée and the destruction they could wreak.

"Inspection!" I ordered. "Show me your kit!"

I made them show me their greatcoats, to prove they were in good condition without need of mending. I did not share with them the story of how I almost died one cold rainy August, not from wounds in battle but for the want of a greatcoat.

Nor did I mention how brave Napoleon's Grand Armée was on the battlefield, how shrewd their general, who always sought to divide his enemy and destroy them one regiment at a time. Or how the French rained hellfire down from the high ground Napoleon always managed to capture.

We are on our way northwest to Bielsk. Three days into the march, Captain Podjampolsky was called to ride ahead and meet with the generals for a few days. During his absence I was housed in a hamlet with a Polish priest and his gracious wife. She served me coffee, cream, and sugar wafers every morning while her husband had to make do with warm beer and cheese.

As the priest sat across from me, glaring, his wife kept up a ridiculous banter.

"You must be Polish!" she insisted. "Your manners are so noble. You speak with such a pleasant voice."

This insult to my Russian heritage annoyed me, even if I did have Polish blood.

"Is it really your opinion that noble manners and good conversation are the exclusive property of Poles?"

She laughed. "But there are other good graces you have that are Polish . . . or at least certainly not Russian!"

I had to admit that I am half Ukrainian on my mother's side. And yes, my father's blood was part Swedish . . . and yes, Polish.

It was clear she had no use for Russians. Now she turned her attention to Swedes!

"You see—a Swede!" she said, clapping her hands. "I adore Swedes, their forthright character, their courage."

The priest glowered, a hateful look in his eye.

Now I need to explain that, in that part of the world, for some inexplicable reason, the melted bits of lard served on a hot bowl of kasha are called swedes. And just then, the priest's wife set a bowl of kasha in front of him—and the priest began howling, smacking the bits of fried lard in his buckwheat kasha.

"I hate swedes!" he screamed, bits of lard flying about the room. "I hate swedes!"

The bowl of kasha smashed against the log wall.

"Oh my God!" gasped my hostess. "He has gone mad, completely mad!"

I was relieved when Captain Podjampolsky returned home that day and we resumed our march. The war was sending all of us—even civilians—into the nether regions of madness.

Our march to war began but lasted only until our supplies ran out and the captain was sent back to headquarters while we remained in a Lithuanian hamlet. It was a poor village and we officers had the vilest of quarters in a barn.

Corporal Czerniawski, and the brothers Tornesi—Ivan and Cesar—were to become my closest friends in the months to come. We commanded our own squadrons, though Ivan Tornesi outranked us all. Together we would see the worst of the battles of the great Patriotic War.

While waiting for Captain Podjampolsky to return from meetings with the generals, we officers whiled away the time reading after finishing our reviews of the troops and camp. Corporal Czerniawski read Racine while I read and reread my copy of Voltaire's tales. Cesar Tornesi smoked his pipe incessantly, placing a plug of aloe atop the tobacco.

"That's the way the Turks do it," he said. And since his father had participated in the Turkish Wars with General Kutuzov, we believed him.

His older brother Ivan indulged him. Cesar was the baby of the family and Ivan was gentle with him no matter his boasting or antics. Young Cesar became our personal clown, dancing ballet for our amusement. His favorite was Ariadne on the island of Naxos.

"You are the buffoon, aren't you?" laughed his brother. "Ah, but we turn to you for entertainment in these troubled times, little brother."

My heart warmed to see the fraternal love between the two. What comfort to have a loved one on a march.

After too many ballet performances, I threw aside my Voltaire, having read it for the hundredth time, and turned to reckoning the accounts. I realized that we did not have enough oats and forage for the horses to travel but fifty versts.

I wrested Czerniawski from his Racine, Cesar from his pipe and visions of tutus.

"We must see what supplies can be requisitioned for the horses," I said.

My two comrades pulled disgusted faces. They scowled at the windows, splattered with raindrops and dried leaves. Neither one of them wanted to venture out.

"You heard Lieutenant Alexandrov," affirmed Captain Tornesi. "He's next in command. Get on your feet. That's an order."

Reluctantly they walked out in the pouring rain. When they returned at the end of the day without hay or grain, I realized it would be my turn as soon as Captain Podjampolsky returned and I surrendered my temporary command.

It was my luck that Podjampolsky returned the very next day. Czerniawski and Cesar Tornesi slapped me on the back, wishing me luck.

"You'll find forage, Alexandrov. Anyone would take pity on your baby face," they joked.

In the Russian army, officers could requisition oats with vouchers, payable at headquarters for money. At least in theory. But landowners knew it wasn't that easy to get paid and they needed what little stores they had for their own estates.

I went from one estate to another. The Poles had hidden their grain and negotiation was fruitless. I became more and more agitated realizing that Napoleon had already crossed the Niemen and that we were stuck in a muddy village, unable to move because we had no forage for our horses.

Wars are won and lost by such factors—without fit horses we would never defeat Napoleon.

I pushed on further up the road.

It was then I noticed the smoke. I should have been aware of it long before, but my preoccupation with finding fodder distracted me.

Billowing black clouds lay ahead, a horizon of flames.

I rode a verst more and came across a landowner of about sixty. He had a sad cast about him, his blue eyes blurred with tears.

I asked him about the fires, but he didn't answer me directly.

"Come in lad," he said, instead. "I will make you a cup of tea—the samovar is bubbling. Sit at the table with me."

I thanked him for his trouble, taking a seat at an elegant birchwood dining table. I ran my hand across the grain, admiring it.

My host noticed me.

"Poets say that a Russian's heart is made of birch. There is no more noble tree."

"I have loved them," I admitted. "Since I was a child."

He watched me, his head slightly cocked as if he were listening to a faint tune.

"They are a soft wood at heart and burn fast," he said.

I thought this a curious remark because birch is actually quite hard but said nothing.

"I know why you are here," he said, his eyes lost again in sorrow. "My, you are young. My son's age, I would reckon. You are here to find grain for your horses."

"How did you know?"

"Your colleagues were here a few days before. I had rolling fields of oats, barley, and rye. Oh, you should see the rye in the summer. My son would ride through the fields on his stallion. You could barely see his cap."

I withdrew the vouchers from my pocket.

"I will buy all the grain you can sell me."

He waved away the vouchers. "Useless," he said. "My fields have been burned. Napoleon is coming. Our generals have ordered the crops destroyed rather than feed a marching French army as we retreat."

"Oh," I said, confused. "Forgive me. I must go—"

"I wish you would stay, young man. My son was fighting near Vilna, on the front lines against Napoleon. They brought his body back in a wagon. I buried him yesterday."

At this those faded blue eyes finally shed their tears. They fell one by one on the birchwood table.

The next day I found a fierce retired cavalry officer. He knew the fate of his neighbors, how the fields were being burnt to starve out Napoleon.

"But I still have oats and rye. The torch has not been set on my fields and I have some stores set by," he said, twisting the ends of his mustache. "And what will you give for them?"

"I have vouchers," I said.

"Vouchers," he said, snorting. "Useless pieces of paper."

"It is all that I have," I answered.

"And if I refuse, what will you do?"

He knew full well that I had the power to confiscate the grains for my troops in the name of Mother Russia.

"Nothing," I said. "I will go back empty handed."

He stopped fingering his mustache and looked into my eyes. I saw a flicker of patriotism in their depths, a man who loved Russia more than life itself.

"You are younger than I even thought possible," he said. "*Kochany kolego!* Dear comrade! You have a job to do, Lieutenant Alexandrov. Your horses and their brave riders are all that stand between Napoleon and us. I'll give you twenty quarters and send you on your way to fight."

"What about your own needs? Your farm—"

"Our motherland first," he said, rising from his chair. "We have no time to waste. Take what you need before it is torched." As he took the first step toward the door, I could see his severe limp.

"I was wounded in both legs in Austerlitz," he said. "Go slow with me. I'll point out the fields and storehouses of grain to you and your sergeant. You can start filling your wagons at once."

Then he turned to me.

"One favor for an old man," he said. "Stay with me a day or two before your regiment moves out. Your blooming youth, energy, and high spirits remind me of my own soul in the days of my boyhood. I'll invite the families of the neighboring estates. We all need to remember youth and joy, for hard times lie ahead."

I bowed my head. I, a girl, reminded this old veteran of his youth on the battlefield. What greater tribute could I ever earn?

I agreed as we walked through the beautiful gardens and blue lake toward the grain fields and the uhlan wagons.

I ordered my uhlans to fill their wagons at his granaries. I listened to the rustle of dried oats spilled against the wooden planks. I rubbed my eyes, the stinging soot of burning fields making me cry.

Chapter 44

Belarus and Eastern Poland
July 1812

Our regiment had been ordered to join the Russian Second Army under General Petr Bagration to defend the southern frontiers. With a five-hundred-kilometer border where the French might have entered Russia, Napoleon had chosen the Niemen and driven a wedge between our forces. Our First Army, standing alone under General Barclay de Tolly, had been forced to retreat, overpowered without the Second Army's support. Divide and conquer. That was Napoleon's way. The generals of the two Russian armies were desperate to regroup.

Our regiment was stationed on alert on the banks of the Narew River, west of the Second Army's position near Volkovysk.

We were quartered in a tiny village. Every night, half of the squadron stood guard in the village while the other half rode out on patrol. We slept during the day—or should I say we closed our eyes. True sleep was hard to come by.

Those July evenings my senses were sharpened. I listened hard, through the constant chirp of the crickets, the gurgle and flow of the river, ebbing against the banks. My eyes peered through the moonlight that gleamed on the ghostly white birch. We listened, waiting for the jingle of caissons, the creak of cannons over the rutted roads, the snort of horses. Our eyes strained in the darkness for the flicker of campfires. I sniffed the air for smoke when I walked alone to wash in the creek.

I submerged myself in the black water shadowed under birch trees. The leaves trembled overhead, etched above me where they were bathed in moonlight.

I knew it was only a matter of time before Napoleon destroyed our peace. I thought of how my life had changed since that day I rode away from home on Alcides.

Not all injuries come from cannonballs, bullets, and sabers. One afternoon, we passed through a hamlet where our regiment had to cross a little dike. The first detachment encountered some obstacle and halted. We all backed up behind them, crushed by more squadrons coming from behind. Our horses, packed tail to head, began rearing and kicking. We tried to maintain them in position to avoid falling into the steep trenches on either side.

The horse in front of me kicked. His iron shoe slammed into my leg.

The pain! From the recesses of my soul I gasped.

When we made it to camp, I removed my boot. My leg was bloody, bruised, swollen. It ached from my toe to my knee.

Riding was torture. For the first time in my career I was grateful for the two cups of wine allotted each day to soldiers. Eventually, I had to give in to the pain and I rode in a carriage. But each hour my injury grew more ominous. The skin turned black as coal.

The next night, in camp, I confessed that the pain was unbearable and they called for the regiment physician.

He was a stout man, with a grizzled beard and dirty hands. I winced at his touch as he cut away my lower pant leg to examine my wound.

He grunted.

"Alexandrov. We will have to amputate this leg."

Chapter 45

"Will General de Tolly never stand and fight! Retreat! Retreat! Every report indicates a retreat!" Alexander's finger rapped the paper in his hand. "Can you explain this, Arakcheyev?"

"De Tolly does not have the army to defeat Napoleon. Not yet," said the war minister, Count Alexei Arakcheyev. "He draws the enemy further and further into the heartland."

"And closer and closer to Moscow!" said Alexander. "What game is this?"

"It is a game of saving lives until the Russian army has the advantage." Count Arakcheyev had known Alexander since he was a small boy. He did not suffer the Tsar's criticism lightly.

"He is a coward!"

"No, he is shrewd," said Count Arakcheyev. "Napoleon undoubtedly planned on returning to Paris before midsummer. Now September is only days away. The French supply lines are attacked and destroyed daily, making his return route a wasteland. Napoleon has no forage for his horses and must be dangerously low on food."

"If Napoleon reaches Moscow—" began Alexander. He could not find words to complete his sentence.

"Before Moscow there is Smolensk," said Count Arakcheyev. "With its fortified walls, I can think of no better place for our armies to stand and fight."

Alexander's stomach clenched to think of Napoleon ever setting foot within the city walls.

Chapter 46

Volkovysk, Belarus
August 1812

"No! No amputation!" I shouted.

Never ride again? Returning home to spend my life enclosed in a house embroidering pillowcases?

"Leave my leg alone!"

I would rather die!

"Have it your way, Lieutenant. I've got other soldiers that need my care," said the doctor, leaving me writhing on the stretcher.

I was alone with my pain. The doctor never came again. A day passed, perhaps more. Then suddenly, amid great commotion, I was carried out of the tent and loaded into a wagon. We set off at a fast clip, jolting over the rough, rutted roads. I screamed in pain, confident that no one could hear me over the drum of hooves, the creaking wood and hinges of the flatbed. I fainted, then regained consciousness and fainted again.

We were retreating.

As days passed, fresh blood slowly returned to my limb, flushing out the blackness.

I returned to mount my horse after ten days, always alert not to jostle against another uhlan's mount or brush against a tree. I was in anguishing pain but I still had my leg and I could ride.

But just barely.

We lost our beloved regiment commander Tutolmin to sickness. Those dinner dances and fetes of Countess Plater seemed like another lifetime, a glittering fantasy. Now the beautiful Countess Manuzzi would weep forever, her lover and our commander taken from us all.

Another commanding officer took his place, a Lieutenant Colonel Stackelberg from the Novorossiysk Dragoons. He was German, a stickler for rules and regulations. Our company hated him.

After our hasty retreat through a trackless forest we were ordered to stand guard in shoulder-high hemp fields. It was midsummer and the heat rose in puffs from the earth like the breath of a dragon. Under the broiling sun, the green hemp gave off a pungent scent that overwhelmed us.

I rocked sideways in my saddle, about to faint from the heat and the pain throbbing in my leg.

"Alexandrov!" said Colonel Krejts, our brigade commander, riding next to me. "Snap to!"

I grabbed the pommel of my saddle, to avoid tumbling to the ground.

"Sir!" I said.

"Are you all right?"

"Yes, sir!"

Krejts ordered me to fetch water with fourteen uhlans under my command.

"It will give you a chance to bathe and refresh," he said. "And cool your injured leg. But be careful! The enemy is near."

"If the enemy is near, why aren't we on the attack?" I demanded, the heat prickling me with irritation.

He waved me off toward the river. "Just wait, Alexandrov. You'll get your share!"

I ordered the uhlans to fill pots with water, wash, drink, and refresh themselves. I walked upstream a half a verst to undress and plunge into the indescribably delicious water: cool, fresh, a current ebbing against my back, carrying away the dust, aches, and soreness.

My refreshment was short lived. Shots rang out.

I was out of the river and into my clothes in seconds. The last thing I wanted Napoleon to find was a naked Russian girl in the water. I ran back, buttoning my jacket, my feet wet inside my boots. We gathered up the pots of water and returned to our posts.

Colonel Krejits ordered us to remain quiet but alert. That night, I commanded a half squadron on patrol while Podjampolsky kept watch with the others in a village.

I commanded my uhlans to ride on the grass, pressing their sabers to the saddle with their knees to keep them from jingling and with enough space between their horses to keep their stirrups from clanging. My new auxiliary horse Zelant had a bad habit of neighing, but on this deathly dark night he seemed to sense that silence was demanded. He held his breath and trod so lightly I could not hear his hoofbeats.

I stared into the night, the sheds and peasant hovels ominous, deeper black within the dark background. Each could hide an enemy. Our uhlans rode around the hamlet making sure it was quiet, and then we ventured out to the foot of a rocky hill where sentries had been posted.

I chose two uhlans to relieve the sentries and told our bristle-haired sergeant to take command of the rest of the men while I led the replacement sentries up the hill.

As we were getting ready to ride up the hill, the sergeant approached me. I could smell hair oil in the heat of his scalp.

"We hear something in the fields, Your Honor. And shadows keep sweeping across the fields, something looming up. Possibly men on horseback."

The French! Combat at last . . . and us only a half squadron!

"I need to get these sentries in position above, Sergeant. I leave you in charge of the men. Fire on anyone who fails to give the password when challenged."

I signaled for the two relief sentries to follow me. We trotted into the darkness, the sergeant's horse prancing, wanting to follow us.

Once I had inspected our positions and settled the two new sentries into place, I headed down the hill with the two uhlans who had been standing sentry. We moved stealthily, listening for any sign of the enemy.

To my astonishment I saw a figure walking toward me.

"Halt! Who goes there?" I said.

But I already recognized him before he spoke. It was a young Lithuanian soldier I had left at the foot of the hill with the sergeant.

"Why are you on foot! What happened to your horse?" I asked.

"The French attacked us. The sergeant you left in charge ran away. There was nothing we could do. My horse reared and threw me, then ran off."

"And where the devil are the French?"

"I don't know," he said.

"Find your horse!" I commanded him and rode on with my party of three. As we came out of the woods I spied a group of mounted men milling about in the field. As we rode toward them, I heard them talking among themselves.

They were speaking Russian.

"Who are you?" I challenged them. "What are you doing here?"

"Cossacks," replied one. "And we were getting ready to chase you down and attack you. You ran away from us just now! Like cowardly French."

"That was not me, it was part of the squadron I left on sentry."

"Fine sentries!" scoffed the Cossack. "They all fled! If you had not hailed us, we would have struck you down with our lances."

"We were all set to give you a warm welcome!" sneered an older Cossack.

Damned Cossacks!

"Our uhlan lances are harder than yours," I answered, gritting my teeth, "and our regiment is close at hand!"

I left the Cossacks, chagrined.

I could already envision the dispatch to headquarters, reaching the hands of the Tsar: "A picket under the command of Lieutenant Alexandrov was routed by the enemy who, by this action, broke through the forward line of the vedettes." How he would tremble in rage, in humiliation having given his name to me, thinking, "That damned Lieutenant Alexandrov is either a coward or a blockhead who let himself be routed without defending himself or alerting the reserves."

I crumpled in my saddle remembering the Tsar's words: *Even the shadow of a spot on the name of Alexander will never be forgiven!*

The two uhlans and I rode forward into the night, back to the pickets.

Suddenly thundering hoofbeats pierced the silence. In the dim light I could just make out the horsemen.

Cesar Tornesi raced ahead of all of them.

He pulled up in front of me.

"Thank God, Alexandrov! For God's sake, what happened?"

"Our cowardly uhlans ran like hares from our own Cossacks without raising a weapon!"

"What? Captain Podjampolsky is distraught. Your squadron sergeant reported you had been taken prisoner and—"

"Prisoner?"

"And the entire squadron butchered."

"Butchered! The lying—"

"We were on our way to rescue you, even at the cost of the entire squadron," he said.

When I got back to camp, I reported to Captain Podjampolsky. I told him how the blockhead sergeant had deserted his post. The captain nodded.

"I will deal with the sergeant myself," he said. "And the rest of the cowards. Return to the picket, Alexandrov."

The entire night I was haunted by doubts.

Would this story reach the ears of the Tsar?

I had been in charge. Didn't I alone deserve censure and punishment? The half squadron was under my command. Why had I left them with an inexperienced sergeant who had never been in battle? I could not get this thought out of my head.

I still blush to remember this night.

God bless Captain Podjampolsky's soul. He never reported the incident. He would have preferred that the entire squadron die rather than admit to the cowardice of men under his command.

We were retreating again! Further and further back into the heart of Russia. The French Grand Armée followed us into our deep forests. Could Napoleon not realize what de Tolly was doing? Drawing the insect into the deep hole, like a ground spider.

Napoleon! Rash, too confident. Arrogant. Uninformed. He didn't know or bother to understand the Russian people. He did not fathom the Russian soul. Bonaparte expected the serfs—the majority of the Russian populace—to embrace him when he promised them freedom: "You slaves, you will be free, you will be educated! You will belong to the Republic of France as freemen."

"Frenchmen?" thought the serfs. "We'd rather be Russian and slaves than Frenchmen. Our souls are tied to Russia."

No. Napoleon didn't understand Russians. While some did join him, most of the serfs chose to fight for Mother Russia. They formed rag-tag militias using birch clubs if they had no better weapons.

To remain Russian—that was all that mattered to their souls.

And the French?

Keep following us, you fools of blind ambition! Follow us into our heartland and we will show you a Russian welcome—your bones scattered across our countryside, your bodies left to rot.

We kept moving, marching day and night toward Smolensk, stopping to bivouac every night or two. Some of the men could sleep on horseback. I never could and if I had had a million rubles, I would have traded them all for a good night's sleep. No one who hasn't been at war can understand the toll sleeplessness takes on a soldier. There was a point when I didn't care whether I lived or died, just as long as I could lay down my head.

I studied my reflection on the blade of my saber. An aged stranger, a pale phantom, stared back at me. No luster in my eyes, my skin parchment white. I tried walking alongside Alcides rather than riding, to keep my eyes open. Then I barely had the strength to remount.

Captain Podjampolsky took Cesar Tornesi and me aside to criticize us for letting our platoon doze in the saddle.

"I see their heads swaying, the helmets dropping to the ground. See that they look lively and alert. The French are on our heels!"

Cesar grumbled to himself, resenting this chastisement.

"I do what I can with my squadron. But we are human beings, deprived of days' and nights' sleep. Of course our uhlans will doze!"

Ah, but we had our revenge. The day after this harsh reprimand we both spied Podjampolsky riding along with his eyes closed, despite his prancing, high-spirited horse.

"Watch!" said Cesar, with a devilish grin. "You stay here and just enjoy some fun."

He reined up his horse and then galloped ahead, racing past Podjampolsky. The captain's horse bolted ahead a full run, spooked by the commotion. Captain Podjampolsky struggled to gather up the reins, which had fallen from his hands as his horse raced ahead, willy-nilly.

Cesar and I kept straight faces—and we never discussed the incident with the captain.

We finally camped about fifty versts before Smolensk, receiving orders to halt until further notice. We joined with other regiments. I spread out my greatcoat in a stack of hay and slept ten hours. When I emerged, my short hair studded with grass and seed, it was near sundown.

The camp was lively with cuirassiers, uhlans, and Hussars walking about, discussing if we would have, at last, a chance to fight the enemy. Soldiers squatted near campfires, cleaning their firearms, sharpening their sabers or lances. Our regiment's band attracted throngs who yearned to hear a merry song.

At nightfall I climbed a hill, still able to hear the chatter of the soldiers. Hundreds upon hundreds of campfires lit up the countryside below me. I could hear the snorting and stomping of horses tied to their pickets.

Then I descended the ridge on the other side. Stillness enveloped me. The sound of peace. I stood listening to my own breath.

Tsar Alexander sent his orders: "The emperor will no longer restrain your valor and frees you to take revenge on the enemy for the tedium of involuntary retreat which until now has been essential."

"Hurrah!" shouted the regiments, loud enough I thought to terrorize the French.

Never had I been so wrong.

When I heard the distant rumble of cannons and saw the flashes of light reflected from shining bayonets, a shiver of excitement coursed up my spine. Bracing fresh was the memory of the battles of Friedland and Heilsberg, before our tsar had made peace with the French enemy. The smell of smoke, acrid and pungent, struck memories so vivid, they seemed only yesterday.

All around me, our soldiers were freshly shaved and dressed in their finest parade uniforms. Battle was dirty business and those fine uniforms would suffer—but they knew that death hovered close at hand for all of us and they wanted to look their best if they were called to meet their God.

Waiting outside the walls of Smolensk, ready for battle orders, we heard the cheers of the inhabitants.

"Rout the enemy!"

"Show the French what a Russian soldier is!"

"Save our dear town, our Smolensk!"

We exchanged proud smiles. We had been waiting months—no years!—for this revenge. Finally we'd be able to meet the Grand Armée in battle, rather than retreating ahead of Napoleon.

It was the old men's wishes, shouted down from the walls, that haunted me. They knew what battle was and what awaited us.

"God save you!"

"God help you!" Their old voices cracked in solemn tones.

Our first order was to delay the enemy, engaging them in skirmishes. Ivan Tornesi was the first to volunteer.

He rode out with twenty uhlans under his command to lead the French away on a chase. But instead he rode full gallop into a large squadron, eager for battle. No matter how loud the uhlans called to him to come back, he did not heed them. Brandishing his saber, he charged the French, slashing left and right.

Surprised initially to finally be engaged in battle by at least one Russian, the Frenchmen hesitated. Then annoyed, they engulfed the brave officer, killing him instantly. He tumbled from his horse, slashed to death.

Our regiment was ordered to wait at the top of a knoll until needed. We watched the course of battle from our hilltop: the spiraling plumes of cannon fire, the rain of dirt, the flash of bayonets, and the ever-widening sea of fallen bodies both men and horse.

Our regimental priest Wartminski—the bravest man among us—came dashing up the hill, waving his crop, the only weapon he had.

"Look!" he said, pointing behind him.

There was the enemy galloping toward us!

Captain Podjampolsky shouted, "Second half squadron, left wheel! Take command, Lieutenant Alexandrov!"

I knew my role. I was ready. Now I was the battle-hardened veteran. "From your places! Charge! Charge!"

Then, even as we began our charge, the captain shouted.

"Back! Back!"

He had reassessed the situation. We were outnumbered.

I looked over my shoulder to see my half squadron galloping at full speed back the way we had come. I was left behind.

I was riding Zelant, my auxiliary horse. I wheeled him around. Zelant had a bad habit of flinging his head in the air and catching the bit in his teeth when I reined him in. Now, he reared up, wasting precious time.

I spurred him back toward my regiment, the half squadron I commanded now far ahead of me. I heard the pounding of hoofbeats behind me and glanced over my shoulder.

There were three or four French dragoons right behind me, one just three feet from my flank. I could hear the jingle of the hilt as he brandished his broadsword.

I could have turned to fight, like Ivan Tornesi, but, like him, I would have been slaughtered on the spot and the Frenchmen would have been free to pursue my squadron.

I raised my sword, but instead of engaging, I brought the broadside down hard on my horse's rump. Zelant dashed forward like a tempest leaving the dragoons to chase us hopelessly.

In the few minutes I had diverted the enemy, the squadrons had reformed. "Charge!" came the command and our uhlans rushed forward, making the French pay for their impetuous attack. The uhlan's pennons fluttered in the wind, a forest of lances rushing to meet Napoleon's men. Now it was their time to retreat and run, but our fast horses formed flanks around them. They fell one by one or raced away to safety, thoroughly thrashed.

After the battle we returned to our post where we were to protect a nearby fortress. Captain Podjampolsky looked over at me, shaking his head.

"What is it, sir?"

"We almost lost you, Alexandrov!"

"It was my horse, sir. Zelant reared up when I checked him."

The captain shook his head again, looking out into the distance. The cannon smoke wafted over the landscape, strong enough to choke us.

"We should have advanced by now," he said. "The French draw nearer and nearer."

To punctuate his words, bullets showered us. They fell short, harmless chunks of lead at the end of their trajectory. One of our regiments was engaged in battle just beyond us.

Podjampolsky watched the lead fall from the sky, pelting his uhlans and their horses. "Alexandrov! Ride to Smolensk and ask Colonel

Stackelberg what his orders are. We cannot stand until tomorrow. The bullets will find their targets soon enough."

We heard a groan and one of our uhlans slumped in his saddle.

"Go!" shouted Captain Podjampolsky. "As fast as you can ride, Alexandrov!"

I galloped Zelant to the walled city four versts away and found Colonel Stackelberg.

"Why does he send you, Lieutenant Alexandrov?" the German colonel said. "You are an officer in command. He should have sent a courier of lesser rank, one without a platoon to lead. And he must never question an order. His order is to stand!"

I galloped back to my squadron gritting my teeth. How could I deliver such a death sentence? We were to stand and die, without the satisfaction of a fight.

"Well?" shouted Podjampolsky from a distance. "What does he say?"

I felt the eyes of all my brother uhlans on me. Their horses shifted nervously.

"Colonel Stackelberg says to stand," I shouted over the boom of the cannons.

"Stand?" Podjampolsky rubbed his eyes in the thick smoke. He wheeled his horse around to face the troops.

"Colonel Stackelberg has commanded us to stand. Stand we will," his voice rang out.

The uhlans straightened their backs and shouted, "Yes, sir!" The skirmish with the French earlier in the day had filled their veins with fresh blood and courage. They would stand.

The battle raged before us and still we stood.

Toward evening, my half squadron was given permission to dismount and rest. I took advantage of this time to approach Captain Podjampolsky. Something had been bothering me since I was dispatched with the message to Smolensk.

"Why, sir, did you send me instead of the sergeant with the message to Stackelberg?"

Captain Podjampolsky didn't answer. His tongue poked a bulge in his cheek, smudged with smoke and grime.

"Is it because you were afraid the bullets might hit me?" I asked, guessing his motive.

Podjampolsky brought his hand to his head, as if in pain. "*Da.* It is true. Ah, Alexandrov! You are still so young. In the midst of this ferocity, all gun smoke and death, you are so innocent. When I saw you lead your half squadron on the attack, it felt as if I had loosed a lamb into a pack of wolves. Blood rushed to my head—a senseless sacrifice, a murder of a child."

"But I am *not* a child—"

"I cannot help what I think, Alexandrov! I have a little brother in the Mariupol Hussars. I remember you in the Hussar blues. I suppose I see him in you."

Podjampolsky turned away from me. I suspected he did not want me to see tears in his eyes. There was no braver, no more soulful, officer in our regiment.

"Now get an hour's sleep, Lieutenant Alexandrov," he commanded. "And do not question my orders again."

I fell asleep and awoke when a spent bullet slammed into my helmet. My eyes flashed open and I saw bullets scattered around me. I collected them into my hand as a child would marbles and carried them over to show the captain.

Podjampolsky laughed, staring at my handful of bullets.

Any one of them could have killed me. Or my comrades.

"Do you find it really such a wonder, these French bullets? We are in battle whether we stand or not!"

I stared at the French bullets in my palm, turning one over with my finger.

"Stop playing with ammunition, Alexandrov. Get back on your horse. We just received orders to retreat."

Retreat? We have surrendered Smolensk!

But not before our army set fire to the entire town and the crops in the fields.

Smolensk was ablaze, the black smoke choking us as we fell further back toward Moscow.

Chapter 47

Borodino, Russia
August 1812

We rode toward Borodino, a village on a rolling plain spotted with knolls and forests. We rode through rain and muck. My uhlan greatcoat was not near as good as the Hussars' uniform. It had no lining and my *kolet* was made of flimsy cloth. I was yet again shivering as if it were winter, for the wind was blowing hard from the north.

This boded ominously for the winter to come. It was only August.

"Cheer up, Alexandrov," said Cesar, riding beside me. "The rain will stop one day."

A shiver rocked me in the saddle. I decided losing my temper would warm my blood.

"It's not the rain. It's this bitter north wind. I can't feel my fingers or my toes, Cesar!"

"Better that way," he said, scratching his neck. He drew his collar tighter.

"Why the devil weren't we given the order to fight?" I said. "Why weren't our squadrons ordered into battle? We stood like stuffed scarecrows on the battlefield."

"You squawk like a wet hen," said Cesar. "A battle isn't won by counting the last body dropped."

Cesar drew a sharp breath. I guessed that he was thinking about his brother.

"General de Tolly must have felt there was too much to lose," he said. "That's why we retreated."

This answer angered me even more. I had the smoke and soot of the holy city of Smolensk in my eyes. Alcides's nose ran with black phlegm and he had a bad cough.

"You mean we Russians couldn't beat Napoleon in the heart of our own country? I want to stand our ground and fight."

"De Tolly has seen hundreds of battles," said Cesar. "He is not vainglorious. I think he's set on drawing Napoleon as far into Russia as he dares."

"What? And let him into the gates of Moscow?"

Cesar scratched his head under his helmet. "Maybe. Maybe even that."

I drew back in revulsion at the image of the French in our sacred ancient capital.

That night Captain Podjampolsky gave me orders to procure hay. "And find something for us to eat. I'm so tired of kasha. A chicken or a goose!"

It was harvest time, the second cutting. The rain had stopped, though the wind still bent the stalks of rye still in the fields. I took a few uhlans with me and a hay wagon. Three versts away there was a village with fields piled high with haystacks. The serfs had finished scything the hay fields and fled before threshing the grain.

I left my men to load the wagon.

It was twilight and darkness was descending. I scouted around and found a ghostly sight: a farm with the doors of its house, shed, granaries, barns, and stalls all left agape. Cows were wandering about the garden, munching on cucumbers and melons, trampling the cabbages. Chickens, ducks, and geese pecked at bugs and rotting vegetables as if they owned the place.

I remembered my captain's wish for fresh meat. I caught a goose by the neck. It squawked, trying to peck my hands.

I lifted my saber over the struggling fowl. With a quick move, I sliced off its head.

I stood there, not able to move.

I've killed it!

There was warm blood on my hands, the animal just seconds before so animated and squawking, hot-blooded with rage and fear. Now its lifeless body was cooling in my hands.

I heard the far-off boom of a cannon. Then another.

As I looked at my bloody saber I shook with emotion. *Battle-hardened veteran, hah!* I had never killed anything in my life before this moment. Now, with my noble saber, I had cut off the head of an innocent bird.

How could I ever kill a human being?

I came back with the limp goose swinging from my saddle to find that the uhlans had loaded the wagon full of hay and even tied up great sheaves behind their horses' saddles.

"Good God! Don't you think that's enough hay?"

"Hay is light, sir," answered one of my squad.

"Light as air," chuckled another. I noticed his mare was agitated, prancing about under him.

"That hay must be scratching her flanks," I said. "Well, let's ride on. It's getting late."

We had ridden only a verst when an orderly galloped up to me.

"Orders from Captain Podjampolsky! You are to abandon your mission. We are ordered to leave camp."

"What?"

Just then one of the mares who had been protesting her cargo of hay reared up. To my surprise a sheep fell out of the hay and off the horse's rump!

The sheep began to baa and set off a chorus behind every uhlan's saddle. The horses began bucking and rearing, hay cascading off their flanks. Sheep rained down from the horses' hindquarters, forming a wild-eyed flock that darted this way and that.

"Get yourself in order!" I shouted. "The captain has ordered us to resume our march! Look lively!"

"But, sir . . ."

"Leave the livestock. We are to rejoin the regiment at once!"

The men pulled long faces.

"Kasha be damned!" said one. "I can't stand another day of it! I feel like I'm eating dirt."

"I can taste the roasted shank—and smell the mutton grease on the fire!"

"Get on, you lads!" I ordered. I flung my dead goose in the road just to make things even for all of us. It landed with a flop in the dust.

We left the decapitated goose among the flock of bewildered sheep and trotted off toward Borodino—the last stand we would make to defend Moscow.

Captain Podjampolsky was in a foul mood. We were all cold, miserable—the sluicing rains soaked us. The biting, unseasonal wind was brutal, like none I had ever known.

Can winter be closing in so early? What will winter bring if this is a harbinger?

We were on the march again. But when we were ordered to halt late that night, I heard the news that brought howls of joy from the troops.

"They say de Tolly had no choice. The scorch and retreat tactics have caused such humiliation to our troops, he had to do it—"

"I heard one officer say de Tolly was an agent of Napoleon."

"Rubbish!" said Captain Podjampolsky. "Idiots will babble whatever mounds of dung flow through their minds. De Tolly was a brave general who had no other choice but retreat, given our odds."

"We could have stood and fought!" said a young officer from another regiment who visited our fire.

Captain Podjampolsky's eyes glittered in the firelight.

"And lose every last one of us? Perhaps we could have won a battle but it would have decimated our troops. Who, tell me, would fight the next battle, and the next, and the next after that?"

The young officer lifted his chin in defiance. "Forgive me, sir. But brave men should have the chance to fight for Russia. Our cavalry hated General de Tolly for depriving them of the honor of dying for our country and tsar—"

Cesar jumped in, his face animated with joy. "Wait until the regiments hear about de Tolly's replacement. We will hear the roars of joy! "

Replacement? Could it be?

"Who is it?" I asked. "Who is to replace General de Tolly as commander in chief?"

"General Kutuzov," said Podjampolsky. In the flickering light I could see my commander's sooty face crease with fine lines. He was smiling too.

The great Kutuzov!

I let out a girlish squeal of delight that made the other officers stare at me.

But I didn't care.

Captain Podjampolsky stretched out his hand and ruffled my hair.

"There's the lad," he said. "All soldiers need heroes. We deserve a Kutuzov to stir the blood of our men."

"Kutuzov will let us fight at last!" I said.

"*Da!*" said Cesar. "Our men would rather stand their ground for Russia than run like scurrying rats. If I hear 'Retreat!' one more time, I'll . . . I'll . . ."

Podjampolsky gave his subordinate officer a curious look. Cesar reminded me of myself that first dinner with officers before the battles of Heilsberg and Friedland, when I had talked so proudly about the valor of a Russian cavalry officer.

What a fool I had been!

Like Captain Kazimirski, Podjampolsky's face was kind and indulgent. He saw that Cesar could not complete his sentence and held up his hand to stop him from trying.

"Remember that General de Tolly was a good and honorable commanding officer," he said, resting his hand on the officer's shoulders. "His orders to retreat saved many lives. Maybe you and I—and Alexandrov, here—are alive because of his orders."

"We ran away like cowardly dogs," said Cesar. "Our men were aching to fight and we were ordered to retreat. Captain Podjampolsky! We lost the battles!"

"But not the war," said Podjampolsky, extending his other arm over my shoulders. He held us tight like beloved children. "Not the war. Remember that."

Chapter 48

Peterhof Palace, St. Petersburg
August 1812

Empress Elizabeth could find no peace. She paced the great Peterhof Palace like a cat, rankled with heat and restlessness.

Finally she sat at her desk to compose a letter to her mother in Baden. The tsarina dipped her quill into the ink pot.

> *I am sure you are badly informed as to what transpires here in Russia. Perhaps you have heard the rumors that we have fled St. Petersburg for Siberia as Napoleon hunts us like a wolf after lame prey.*
>
> *We are far from cowering. We will not flee! We are ready for anything except negotiations.*
>
> *The more Napoleon advances, the less the chance for eventual peace. All Russia is united in that respect: peasants and noblemen alike.*
>
> *This is what Napoleon did not expect. He was wrong about this, like so many other things. How could a Frenchman ever understand a Russian?*

Each step he takes in our vast Russia is a step closer to the abyss. We will see how he bears the winter!

Elizabeth signed her name and then blotted the paper. She gazed at the extra ink and indentation her quill had gouged in the paper on one word: *winter*.

In early September, we united the armies once more near Borodino. We took the Kolotsk monastery after a thirteen-hour battle and those of us in the rear guard took up position southwest of Borodino, near the village of Shervardino.

"Our army is too heavy on the right flank," said Cesar, pointing to the bright campfires that lit up the battlefield like stars on a moonless night. "De Tolly's army is over there along with Platov's Cossacks."

"General Platov's regiment?" I said.

Denisov would be there.

"Cossacks aren't their best on the regular battlefield. They hunt like a pack of wolves, attacking when there is vulnerability."

"And now?"

"They'll be at a real disadvantage. Cossacks don't fight in formation—they descend helter-skelter like a swarm of hornets upon the enemy in an ambush. But on the battlefield Napoleon's army will mow them down with their artillery."

I stood blinking out into the darkness punctured with thousands of small glittering lights. Somewhere out there was Denisov. I don't know why I worried about that man who had treated me so roughly.

"But I don't care about the Cossacks," said Cesar. "I'm worried about our position. Napoleon will be determined to capture this redoubt and the high ground. They will pound us mercilessly."

We were stationed between a heavily fortified artillery position, a mound called the Raevsky redoubt and three minor fortifications—the flèches—just south.

The wind didn't cease—its blasts chilled me to the bone. There were no fires lit for two nights. I shook inside my unlined greatcoat, trying to shiver myself to sleep.

At dawn the next day, the signal cannon rumbled, a sound that resonated in my chest. Its roar filled the plains and hills, haunting us. As the army awoke around me, I stared into the gray that wasn't still night, but wasn't yet day.

I thought of the gathering storm, the human beings who would lose their lives over the course of the next few hours, the next days. Not just Russians.

The Grand Armée hears the same cannons—are their Catholic prayers the same as our Orthodox? So many different nations make up Napoleon's army now. The conquered are impressed. Soldiers who just months ago fought against the French now are part of that same French army. They were our allies before, but now they will kill us or we will kill them. But they don't hate us. We Russians are not their enemy. If the Austrians, Poles, Italians—a dozen nationalities—could manage it, they would desert Napoleon and his Grand Armée. But now they are deep in Russia, almost at the gates of Moscow. If they run away, they will be shot or starve. If they stand, then we will kill them.

None of it makes any sense. We are enemies only on the battlefield. A soldier in the Grand Armée is not fighting for Napoleon, he's fighting for the chance to return to his homeland, to embrace his wife, hold his child, kiss his aging parents.

War. There is nothing so filthy.

The French marched toward us in dense columns. We watched from our redoubt as our Russian troops moved to meet them, regroup, and battle again.

Another hellish day! Now we were fully engaged.

I was nearly deaf from the explosions from both artilleries. The ground rocked under us, and our balance was shaken by the constant thunder of cannons in our ears. Bullets rained down on us, whistling, hissing, pelting us like hail. We ignored them. It was the roar of cannons that rattled us, made us jump, even in our saddles, with the threat of instant destruction from the shattering impact of the iron balls.

Our squadron went on the attack. Even in the heat of battle, that strange, unseasonable wind was freezing, stealing the warmth from my body. Without gloves my hands were so numb that I could barely bend my fingers around the hilt of my saber. Between attacks I replaced my blade into its scabbard and dug my hands under my greatcoat to warm them against my body.

Sitting on Alcides between attacks I whispered to him, "What have we gotten ourselves into, old boy?"

He stepped sideways, swinging his head toward my right stirrup, the way he used to when he'd nibble on my bare feet on our nightly rides years ago.

This was not what I thought war would be. Yes, I loved my horse, the adventure of riding all day and sleeping in a tent at night—the freedom from the tedium that is the life of a woman.

But I realized that I had lost the overwhelming courage that had made me so bold before my captains. Having fought in Heilsberg, Friedland, Smolensk, and now Borodino, I no longer had a youthful edge, that biting, innocent, ignorant hunger for war.

I would simply be thankful when I could feel my limbs again. I was so cold and numb. I wished with all my heart to escape from this freezing hell.

And my wish was granted. But as our Russian tales tell us, a wish is rarely granted without a curse.

I shall tell you what happened, though I desperately don't want to. I cannot bear to remember.

Half of Platov's Cossacks—twenty-four hundred or so—crossed the Voina north of Borodino and attacked the French left rear. The French overreacted and sent seventeen cavalry regiments to counterattack. Platov's heroic move bought time for the Russian army to maneuver and reinforce its right flank.

I thought for a moment of Denisov. Had he survived?

But just as Cesar had predicted, Napoleon was still determined to capture our redoubt. We were pounded by artillery.

And then—I almost do not have the courage to tell you any more . . .

I shall tell you what happened, but only once. I cannot bear to remember. My heart shrinks up like a wound splashed with vinegar when I recall that day.

Alcides and I were hit by a cannonball. I heard his scream and saw the earth flying up around us. I fell to the ground half under him but he rolled away from me.

Cesar saw me fall. He disengaged from the enemy, galloping over to me.

"Alexandrov!" he cried. "Are you wounded?"

"Alcides!" I screamed. My beloved horse writhed beside me in agony.

His guts spilled out of his abdomen and he screamed, a piteous high-pitched whinny.

"Alexandrov! Are you wounded? Answer me!"

"Shoot him!" I screamed. "Shoot my horse. Don't let him suffer, I beg you. Cesar!"

He did not even dismount. We were still in the thick of the battle. But I saw his hand reach for his pistol. A shot rang out. Alcides lay suddenly still in the midst of the infernal movement and whistling artillery of the battlefield.

Absolutely still.

"No!" I cried, crawling over to embrace his neck. I pressed my lips against his long jawbone, kissing it over and over. His glassy eyes stared back at me.

"Sergeant Major!" shouted Cesar. "A fresh mount for Lieutenant Alexandrov at once!"

It was only as I struggled to stand up that I realized I was wounded. Although the skin was not punctured, I had been hit. My knee and lower leg had been smashed by the cannonball that killed my beloved Alcides. I had no control over my leg. I tried to stand, but my leg crumpled uselessly under me.

I fought to make my leg obey me and suddenly, as if something had snapped in place, I gained control of it. I could stand, even walk— although the pain made me feel faint.

I was helped by a sergeant major to a spot behind our lines and given a fresh horse, the feisty Zelant. I saw no blood on my leg and no evidence of broken bones. I decided I was ready to return to battle.

When I rode out to the front, Captain Podjampolsky glanced at me.

"Alexandrov! What are you doing back?"

"I'm fit to fight," I answered. "Permission to take back command of my half squadron."

We continued to hold our position until nightfall. My blood was ice and the pain in my leg unbearable, a constant throbbing torment.

I was finally forced to be relieved from duty. Captain Podjampolsky sent an uhlan to accompany me into the village of Borodino.

Each trotting step jostled my leg, sending me into agony. At stretches, the uhlan rode alongside me, grabbing my coat to steady me in the saddle. When we reached Borodino we found even the tiniest cottage jammed with wounded.

I was unable to dismount and remount, so my uhlan companion went from house to house, asking for permission to take shelter. We were turned away everywhere.

Finally I decided to enter a large peasant cottage without asking permission. I opened the door and was greeted with the dark and stink of the grave. Soiled, wounded flesh blasted an acrid cloud from the warmth within.

But it was warmth.

Voices greeted me. "Who's that?"

"What do you want?"

"Who came in?"

"Shut the door, you devil!"

"I am from the Lithuanian Uhlans, an officer," I said, answering the unseen men in the darkness. "Lieutenant Alexandrov. I am wounded. Let me spend the night with you. I'm freezing."

"Impossible!" shouted several voices. "There is no room! Go away."

I limped forward. "You should find it in your heart to help a wounded comrade!"

A voice called through the darkness. "Well, stay if you like. But there is no room here for you to lie down."

I signaled for my uhlan to stay outside with the horses. I moved forward slowly, my eyes slowly accustoming themselves to the darkness. I crawled with my leg as stiff as a board to the stove and lay against the corner of it. I still wore my weapons, even my helmet. I was cold, hungry, and in extreme pain. My limbs began to warm and the pain lessened. I fell asleep in a minute.

Sometime during the night I must have tried to turn over or shift my weight. My saber clanked against the iron stove. A chorus of voices filled the room in great fright: "Who goes there?" "Who is it?"

I could hear the anxiety in their voices. We were all wounded and unable to defend ourselves. We were struggling to stay alive.

"Who is there, damn it?"

A voice of what passed for reason under the circumstances rang out.

"It's just the uhlan officer fussing about, the one the devil delivered us last night."

The voices died down and soon returned the snores. I could not return to sleep, however, because the pain had returned and I had a high fever.

The smell of the unwashed and wounded—fetid and sour—nauseated me.

A few hours later, the pink light of dawn seeped through the cracks in the shutters.

How dare the dawn still be pink after all that has happened?

I made my way across the room to the door, dragging my injured leg across grumbling soldiers. My uhlan was asleep in the saddle outside the door.

He awoke with a start and then helped me mount Zelant. We rode further on to the wagon encampment. There, one of my companions, the regimental paymaster Burogo—a face and voice I knew, for we had fought together, faced death together—greeted me. He placed me in a big chair by the stove, wrapping me in his sheepskin coat, and handed me a cup of soup. Then he wrapped my leg in alcohol-soaked bandages.

"Alexandrov!" he said. "Why did you let the French do this to you? You weren't so careful, were you?"

I smiled for the first time in days. Then I remembered Alcides. I drank up the best soup in Borodino, my tears salting the broth.

Chapter 49

Outside Moscow
September 1812

After two days, I regained my strength and returned to the battlefield. Captain Podjampolsky gave me command of a small detachment—two dozen uhlans—to bring our depleted squadron up to strength.

Too many faces were unfamiliar. Most of my squadron had fallen in battle.

I forbade myself to think of them, just as I could not think of killing the damned goose.

Or Alcides. In order to survive I had to push all I loved and cared about aside.

I was a soldier fighting for Russia—that was all that mattered.

Despite our hopes after the battle, we retreated yet again. Our new encampment was just ten versts from Moscow. I asked permission to ride to Moscow, where I could have a warm coat tailored for me. I planned to stay in the Kremlin with my father's old comrade-in-arms Colonel Mitrofanov. I was given permission to ride in a supply wagon to Moscow's gates.

Inside the city, I stopped to stare up at the majesty of the white walls of the Kremlin.

The Muscovites were as frantic as bees after a foolish boy has thrown a rock at their hive. They were packing their belongings and boarding up the windows. There was little left in the stores. I found a tailor who agreed to fit a warm coat for me. In the meantime I went in search of Mitrofanov's house.

He had left—like so many Muscovites—but when I stood, stymied outside his building, I was taken in by a young merchant's wife.

"Come in, sir!" she said at once, seeing by my uniform that I was an officer.

"Monsieur Mitrofanov is a dear friend of my father," I told her. "They served many years in the cavalry together."

She clapped her hands.

"A friend of Colonel Mitrofanov! Oh, please do us the honor of staying with us, sir."

She asked me to take a seat next to her on the sofa and then bade her young daughter Katenka to make tea. She asked her younger daughter Anna to bring some butter and bread, a satisfying black rye.

Katenka's eyes were blue as chips of a sunny sky. She was a sweet girl whose eyes flashed open at each bit of news she could glean from me.

"The enemy—Napoleon—how near is he to Moscow?"

"Twenty versts at most. But he is regrouping his army," I said. "As are we. I will only be here as long as it takes to get my coat made."

"We hear Napoleon forces his enemies to convert," said Anna. "He brands his prisoners over the heart with the Catholic cross."

I took a bite of my buttered bread and nodded solemnly.

"I have heard the same, though I don't think it's true. Fear breeds tales like a fire stretches shadows. But Napoleon surely has no regard for our Orthodox religion."

The young girl clapped her hands over her heart as if Napoleon were wielding the branding iron then and there.

"Oh, dear sir! You won't let the French in to Moscow, will you? Our army will protect us, won't they?"

And seeing her frightened face and angelic pose, reminding me of an icon on a church wall, I made a promise.

"Of course we will! The Corsican will never be permitted into our capital. The military governor Rostopchin and his army will protect the walls. Our army will keep the French away. Do not cry, little Anna."

Now I know that I lied that day. But at that moment we all believed Moscow would never fall.

How could it?

When my new jacket was finished I set off to find a livery to take me back to camp. Every coach and buggy, every wagon and old nag, was engaged as Muscovites fled the city. I was forced to walk on my wounded leg.

I had gone only three versts when the throbbing in my leg forced me to stop. I lay down in the grass. Fortunately a supply wagon loaded with saddles, saddle blankets, canteens, and knapsacks came rumbling down the road.

The officer made room for me, taking me back to camp.

When I got there, I found that my reserve horse—now my main mount—Zelant had been sent along with the reserve horses to another village five versts away. I was given a hideous Cossack horse with a thin, elongated neck. He was past his prime and had neither speed nor spirit. The saddle I was given had an enormous bolster in front of it, making it as clumsy as riding a camel in an overstuffed armchair.

On this horse I am to lead my squadron into battle?

But again the orders came. "Retreat. Retreat."

Rostopchin's army had deserted Moscow! Our ancient capital was left defenseless, with no one guarding the gates and walls.

I saw the stunned look in my comrades' eyes as they went through the motions of tightening their horses' cinches, mounting up, and staring at the great white walls of Moscow.

Defenseless. Only we, the defeated, stood between Napoleon and Moscow. There would be no further battle. Kutuzov had ordered a stand-down.

Our regiment rode through Moscow. Wagons and carts still choked the streets, though the majority of inhabitants had already fled. Civilians who had no horses or means of transportation cried out to us.

"Do not surrender Moscow! Protect us!"

"Defend our ancient capital! Do not let Napoleon defile our city!"

Kutuzov rode ahead in his carriage, pulling down the canvas shades on his windows.

We camped two or three versts beyond the walls, while the main army was stationed even further away.

One of my uhlans suddenly turned in his saddle, looking back to Moscow.

"Look!"

All eyes swiveled. Bright yellow and red flames leaped amongst the wooden houses in one corner of the city. It was not long before the smell of smoke filled our nostrils.

"The demons!" said one of the uhlans.

"It would have been better to perish to a man than to sacrifice Moscow!"

"This is how our General Kutuzov defends Russia!" said another.

"No, this is how Rostopchin leaves our sacred capital. He was ordered to stay and fight. Instead he leaves the city in ashes!"

"Shut up," hissed a soldier. "You'll be facing a firing squad if you keep up that talk."

He was right. The words were treasonous. But I'd wager my soul that everyone in our squadron—the entire regiment—was thinking the same thing.

"What barbarians are these French," said another uhlan, turning the conversation away from Kutuzov. "Why would they set fire to Moscow after fighting so hard to get here? What will be left for them?"

"They will ransack our churches," said the one who had complained so bitterly about Kutuzov. "Mark my words: Napoleon has no respect for our religion."

Captain Podjampolsky rode up.

"Hold your tongues and move out, soldiers!" he said.

He must have seen the emptiness in my eyes, the supreme sense of loss.

"Kutuzov has not forsaken Russia. Napoleon will find as winter approaches that his soldiers cannot eat gold."

My donkey of a horse set off at a trot only after I gave him a smack with the flat of my saber. His jolting action threatened to loosen my teeth from my jaw. A cavalry soldier is only as good as his mount. With this Cossack nag I could neither ride to meet the enemy nor run away from him.

Colonel Stackelberg charged me with forage detail, to procure hay for the regiment's horses.

All I could think of was Alcides. No horse would ever be the same as he—so brave, so willing. How he trusted me. And I brought him to this war.

I forced myself to stop thinking of him, at least for minutes at a time. The vision of his suffering rendered me immobile, useless. Lost. A danger to myself and everyone around.

I set off with a detachment and two hay wagons toward a little hamlet. My sergeant pointed beyond our destination.

"That's where the reserve horses are kept, sir," he said. "It is about a verst beyond."

Zelant! Only a verst away. Minutes from me!

"Load up your wagons and then wait there in the forest edge to hide. I will be back immediately."

But Fate has no mercy. The uhlan reserve horses were stationed another three versts beyond. I spurred my unhappy nag into what one could not call a gallop but a "galumpf." Then it stopped, resisting my kicks and traveling only at a snoring walk. If I had the choice of fighting two more battles of Borodino or riding this beast two more days, I would have chosen the former.

As I approached the camp, I spied Zelant on the picket line and threw my reins to the attending solider.

"Take this horse!" I said. "Give me a decent saddle and I'll gladly give you mine. Zelant there, that is my horse."

It took a few minutes for the sergeant to find a saddle but within a quarter of an hour, I was on my way.

When I finally reached the edge of the forest where my detachment should have been waiting for me, I found no one.

The soft grass was churned up by galloping horses. I thought the worst. I raced back to the encampment.

When Colonel Stackelberg saw me riding into camp alone he turned blue with rage.

"Where is your detachment, Alexandrov?"

I explained the situation.

"You left your troops! How dare you commit such a stupid act?" he shouted. "Now they are lost and the enemy has occupied the forest. Go find those men and if you return without them, I shall report you and you will be shot!"

Stunned, I reined Zelant back to the forest. When I reached the edge I encountered an officer I knew from the Imperial Guards standing in the front line of our skirmishers.

"Where are you going, Alexandrov?" he said.

I told him my story of woe and that I was sent to return with the foragers or face a firing squad.

"Not to worry, brother. I'm willing to bet that your detachment took cover and went the long way to safety. Ride to the hamlet where we're keeping our rearguard reserve horses. You'll find them there."

"But that's where I came from!" I said.

I galloped away along the road, skirting the action in the forest. When I reached the picket line, there was my detachment.

"Why didn't you wait for me?" I asked.

"We heard galloping and gunfire in the forest, sir," said the sergeant. "I ordered the wagons down the road away from the action. We thought we'd meet up with you."

"Well, Colonel Stackelberg has threatened to shoot me because of this escapade!" I said. "Let's return to camp and hope Stackelberg isn't aiming a pistol my way when we get there."

I was angrier than I have ever been. Damned German! I didn't go looking for Stackelberg to make my report. Using a pencil stub in my pack I dashed off a note on a rag of paper to Captain Podjampolsky:

Inform Col. Stackelberg that I am not eager to be shot. I'm going to the commander in chief and try to obtain a post on his staff.

Kutuzov. I would apply directly to General Kutuzov, commander in chief of the entire Russian army. It seemed I still had an endless supply of sheer brash nerve.

I rode to the commander in chief's temporary headquarters several versts down the road at a Muscovite's country estate that Kutuzov had requisitioned.

The attending sergeant directed me to the main house, where adjutant generals hurried in and out the doors like ants.

I entered the anteroom, which was filled with the masculine smell of tobacco, leather, and cognac—far more appealing than our officers' hovel.

There was a group of adjutants. I studied their faces and went up to the one who had the kindest face, a colonel.

"Please, sir, I must speak to the commander in chief," I said.

"About what?" asked the colonel, raising his eyebrows. His face wrinkled with amusement. "You must know he is waging a war against Napoleon."

I pressed my lips tight with determination. He did not take me seriously.

"Please, Colonel!"

"Tell me your business and I will relay the message."

"No. I must speak to him personally without witnesses. Please do not refuse me this favor," I said, bowing.

He gave me a curious look, tangled with irritation.

"Let me see what I can do," he said.

He entered Kutuzov's room. A minute later he returned.

"If you please," he said, holding open the door.

I entered a room thick with tobacco smoke. With my first step toward the gray-haired veteran, the legendary leader, venerable hero of Russia, I felt my heart hammering.

General Kutuzov looked at me like a jovial crow out of his one good eye. He gestured with an open hand. "What can I do for you, my friend?"

My friend—the great Kutuzov's first words to me.

Overcome with awe I stood dry mouthed before him. The general stared at me. I was just one among hundreds of thousands of soldiers he commanded. How did I have the nerve to demand a private interview?

"I have come to ask you to grant a great favor. I would like the good fortune to be an orderly for the rest of the campaign."

Kutuzov's fleshy face drew up, wrinkling.

"What's the reason for this extraordinary request and, more importantly, for the manner in which you propose it?"

"Colonel Stackelberg has threatened to have me shot."

I launched into my story of how I had been born into the army and had only one desire in life—to be in Russia's cavalry.

"Since my birth, I have consecrated my life to the army, to the cavalry, forever. I am ready to shed my last drop of blood defending the welfare of the emperor. I revere him as I do God. I do not deserve to be threatened with a shot to the head by a German."

"Colonel Stackelberg actually threatened you with death?" asked the commander in chief.

"Yes, sir."

I told him of my previous campaigns: Heilsberg, Friedland, Smolensk, Borodino, and the skirmishes in between. He nodded his head once or twice, surveying me.

"I see you limp. Were you wounded?"

"Yes, sir. In Borodino."

Finally I told him the tragedy of losing Alcides, the hardest blow of all. It was the only time I became overcome with emotion. I checked myself and changed the subject, but not before my voice cracked.

"You are indeed a brave officer," said Kutuzov.

A hot wave of blood flooded my face, burning my cheeks.

"In the Prussian campaign, Your Honor, all my commanders praised my bravery. I tell you that only to prove that I do not deserve to be executed by a German officer."

"You served in the Prussian campaign? Can you really have been in the army then? How old are you? I assumed you were not more than sixteen."

"I am twenty-three, Your Excellency. I began service in the Polish Horse Regiment."

In all this time, I had not pronounced my name. I felt General Kutuzov's eyes boring into me.

"Tell me your name," he said.

"Alexander Alexandrov, sir."

Kutuzov hauled himself to his feet and embraced me. "How glad I am to have the pleasure of meeting you in person. I have heard about you, Alexandrov. The emperor has spoken to me personally about your bravery. And your—unusual background."

Kutuzov knew. I straightened my back, standing erect and stiff, but I did not drop my gaze as the general inspected my physique and uniform with his one good eye.

"As for the threat to shoot you," said General Kutuzov, "you shouldn't take it so much to heart, Lieutenant. Those were empty words, spoken in anger. This war makes us all testy. But go now to Adjutant General Konovnitsyn and tell him you are to be a permanent orderly on my staff."

"Yes, Your Honor!"

I thanked him profusely and walked toward the door.

"You are limping badly, Alexandrov," he said. "Tell my doctor to examine you immediately."

"Oh, it's not bad," I lied.

"A contusion from a cannonball? Do as I say, Alexandrov. Immediately."

"Yes, sir," I said. Filled with joy, I closed the door quietly behind me.

We lived in the village of Krasnaja Pakhra not far from Moscow. We orderlies were relegated to a plank hut, drafty and damp. We huddled against the cold. It was true that my wound was not healed. I had a fever and quaked like a birch leaf.

Adjutant General Konovnitsyn remembered me from my Hussar days. I was the quickest to deliver a message. Ah, those days with my brilliant Alcides!

Now, to my great misfortune, any time there was a message to be delivered he would ask for that "uhlan orderly." With my poor health "that uhlan orderly" looked like a pale vampire dashing between regiments and even sometimes between wings of the army.

Finally General Kutuzov sent for me.

He took my hand as soon as I entered the room.

"Well, Alexandrov. Have you found it more peaceful here with me than under Colonel Stackelberg? Have you rested up and healed?"

He looked closely at my face.

"My God, you are pale! And thin. What on earth is wrong with you, Alexandrov?"

I was forced to tell him the truth. My leg had not healed and I had to cling to the mane of my horse to stay in the saddle.

"I am ordering you home to your father. Rest, recover. Then come back."

Go home!

"How can I go home when not a single man is leaving the army? Russia needs every soldier to fight Napoleon."

"That is an order, Lieutenant," he said. "We've stopped here without action for the time being," he said, as he looked out the window at the flapping banners. "Perhaps we will be here for a long time. You go home or I'll put you in the camp hospital."

"Yes, sir. Thank you, sir. Your Honor, may I bring my little brother back with me? He is fourteen and it would be an honor for him to start his career under your aegis."

"*Da*, Alexandrov," said General Kutuzov. He smiled to himself, my name bringing him satisfaction. "Bring him back with you. I will be like a father to him."

Chapter 50

Alexander strode into his war office and threw his gloves on the desk in disgust.

"Rostopchin deserted Moscow?"

"Those are the reports we have received, Your Majesty," said Count Arakcheyev. "Rostopchin's guards were to hold the city if possible, but they were gone when Kutuzov's army got there. The city was almost deserted. Kutuzov had no choice. He marched straight through Moscow and out the Kaluga gates."

"Rostopchin simply left Moscow? The scoundrel!"

"There is a report that he has rigged the chimneys and stoves with powder kegs. When the French try to set a fire to warm themselves or cook, they will be blown sky high!"

"And destroy Moscow. The blasted traitor!"

"Without reinforcements Rostopchin felt he could not protect Moscow from Napoleon."

"Hah! He didn't even wait for Kutuzov, did he?" The Tsar sat at his desk, anger and disappointment clear on his face. "Tell me, how are the people in St. Petersburg taking the news?"

Count Arakcheyev lowered his gaze to the silvery-white marble floor.

"They cannot believe it, Your Excellency," his head still lowered. "Many are stockpiling food and preparing to give shelter to their Muscovite friends and family. The gossip on the street is that Napoleon has set his sights on St. Petersburg. He will not be satisfied until all Russia is under his thumb."

The Tsar rose again, unable to sit and listen any longer.

After a moment, the adjutant general spoke again, trying to calm the emperor: "I don't think Napoleon will go any further, sire. He doesn't realize it yet, but he is trapped—caught between our armies . . . and our winter. Kutuzov is blocking the southern route on the Kaluga road. Napoleon's only way out of Russia is back through Smolensk— which is burned. All the crops and food supplies are cinders and ash. There will be no forage for horses, or victuals for men. Russia will suffer, but we can withstand the pain, Your Majesty."

The weary Tsar returned that night to the Winter Palace. The tsarina rushed to meet him as he entered the door.

"Is it true, Alexander? Has Napoleon really taken Moscow?"

Alexander embraced his wife, tears sparkling in his eyes.

"Yes."

"Oh, Alexander! How can this be? How could we let the wolf in the gates?" Elizabeth pressed a hand to her lips. "What will become of the Kremlin? The churches! He and his soldiers will defile them—"

Alexander shook his head vehemently. "I don't know how this happened. Rostopchin deserting, Kutuzov marching through the city but not defending it."

Elizabeth watched her husband's face wrinkle in pain.

"Kutuzov must have weighed the risks. If he knew his army would be defeated, he—"

"Are you defending Kutuzov?" said Alexander.

"As if the general needs me to defend him!" said Elizabeth. "I'm simply trying to fathom why Moscow was deserted."

Alexander pressed his hands to his temples.

"It is a disaster! My grandmother Catherine must be shedding bitter tears in heaven. The French in Moscow!"

"Come, Alexander. Have a glass of Burgundy—"

"Burgundy! I hate all things French."

Elizabeth touched her husband's hand, saying nothing. Alexander's fingers unfurled, taking her hand in his own.

Chapter 51

Outside Moscow
September 1812

Two days after ordering me to return home on medical leave, Kutuzov sent for me again.

"Here are your travel orders," he said. "And money for horses."

He pressed his lips together tightly, as if debating whether to speak further.

"I have been in contact with our emperor. He sends his blessings and concern about your injuries. You have earned a special place in his heart. You bring honor upon his name, Alexandrov."

I almost wept at these words but controlled myself. Despite my throbbing leg it was my heart that I felt, a deep warmth expanding in my chest.

"Go with God! If you should ever need anything, write directly to me and me only. I'll do all in my power to help you. Farewell, my friend."

My friend!

The great Kutuzov, commander in chief of all Russian armies, embraced me with the tenderness of a father.

From General Kutuzov's embrace to my father's was a journey of a week. Because I traveled under a courier's orders, the coach drivers galloped their horses from post station to post station. The crimson stripes of my uniform and the whispered name of Kutuzov resulted in a jolting ride, as I muffled my cries of pain.

"Trot is appropriate," I told them over and over again. "You do not have to rush!"

But given the courier orders coming from Kutuzov, they assumed that the fate of Moscow and Russia overrode my pleas as we covered ground at lightning speed toward Kazan, and then onto Sarapul—where I collapsed into my father's embrace.

At length, he stood back and looked at me.

"My God! Nadya! Look at you. You are but bones and skin."

He fingered my uniform, scorched, sooty, and riddled with bullet holes.

"Are you really my Nadya?" he whispered, pressing me close to his breast again. We may have both shed tears in that embrace.

"Now go to the bathhouse at once. Natalja!" he called to our maid. "Heat the water as hot as you dare, beat her skin with birch strips, and then see she rolls thrice in the snow. We must dislodge the vermin. We will have no lice in this household!"

I gave my old uniform to Natalja, who made a dressing gown out of the venerable rag after it was boiled. My father hung it in his wardrobe to remember me during my future absence from home.

Papa did not want Vasily to leave home.

"Is it not enough that I give my beloved daughter to Russia in this war? Vasily is not yet fourteen!"

"But Papa!" protested Vasily. "I will be fourteen in the spring. And there could be no better start for me than to be under the commander in chief's auspices!"

My father paced the floor. I could see he was tortured with this decision.

"*Da*," acquiesced Papa. "But only on one condition. You must wait until spring. I will not have a thirteen-year-old son of mine sent away in winter to fight the French. Vasily will wait until the snow thaws."

What could I do? My leg had not mended properly and my brother needed my escort to Kutuzov's headquarters.

I wrote to General Kutuzov. He answered:

> *Lieutenant Alexandrov:*
> *You have every right to carry out your father's will. You are not obliged to account for your absence to anyone but me. I permit you to remain at your father's side until spring. At that time report back to my headquarters with your brother.*
>
> *You will lose nothing of the men's opinions by remaining home a few months. You have fought bravely in the bloodiest battles of the campaign. Your father should be proud.*
>
> *General Kutuzov, Commander in Chief of the Russian Army*

I showed my father the letter. Tears welled in his eyes as he read it.

That letter that I would have treasured was confiscated by my proud father, who showed it to everyone he knew. To him the missive merited the same respect as my Cross of St. George. It soon became smudged with fingerprints from being passed from hand to hand.

Part 5

The Tide Turns

Chapter 52

The Kremlin, Moscow
October 1812

Napoleon had not had a good night's sleep since arriving in Moscow. He woke several times a night in his canvas camp bed, his eyes squinting in the darkness as he waited for the message he knew must be coming.

Night after night, he waited for a message from Tsar Alexander.

How long will it take this Russian to sue for peace? We have captured his most cherished city, his holy capital. Moscow! Does he not understand that he has lost? That France has won the war?

But that correspondence never came. Night after night he twisted the linen bedsheets in wrath. Then dread.

This Russian dog! We have won! Is Alexander so stupid he does not understand that?

But Napoleon remembered gazing long and hard at Alexander when they had signed the peace treaty of Tilsit. He remembered Alexander's blue eyes, quick and soulful, that exquisite mind that grasped Rousseau, Voltaire, and all the progressive thinkers of the day. Capricious, indecisive, yes. Stupid, no. Never.

Then what is his game?

The ticking of the clock was all he heard in the night. His steward silently entered the room.

"Who's there?"

"It is I, Your Excellency, Guichet."

"Have you brought me word from St. Petersburg? From Tsar Alexander?"

"No, I am sorry, Your Highness. I have only brought you blankets—the night is so terribly cold. It has snowed again, Emperor. Drifts as high as my thigh have accumulated in the last two hours."

Snow. And it is only early October.

"With your permission, Your Excellency," said the steward. "May I add the extra blankets?"

"And fetch a bed warmer. It is as cold as a dead man's teeth under those sheets!"

Napoleon rose from his bed, his bare feet on the cold marble of the floor.

"And find a rug to put at my bedside! I shall lose my toes to frostbite."

All this marble! Where have they hidden the Ottoman carpets, those bastards!

Puffs of vapor burst into the air with Napoleon's agitation. The steward lit a taper, handing it to the emperor, who moved closer to the ceramic-tiled stove that radiated heat.

"Move my bed closer to the stove, steward."

"Of course, Your Highness."

The candle cast an elliptical pool of light. Napoleon saw his novel lying on the table where he had left it earlier that evening.

Reduced to reading novels in the Kremlin while the Tsar refuses to admit he has lost!

After his morning ablutions at daybreak, Napoleon, clean shaven and angry, summoned General Caulaincourt, his master of the horse.

"How are the fires?"

"There are still some burning in the Kitay-Gorod district. The Kremlin site here is secured."

"Have more of the Russian arsonists been arrested?"

"Yes, Your Excellency. At least ten more in the past two days have been taken prisoner. They proclaim their innocence."

"Innocence? I suppose they suggest spontaneous combustion for destroying three quarters of the city?"

"The prisoners maintain it is our French soldiers who have torched their sacred city."

Napoleon stroked peevishly at his chin, where he felt a minute patch of hair he had missed when shaving.

This Caulaincourt has spent too much time in St. Petersburg as ambassador! I sense too much empathy with the Russians.

"And the horses? How fare they?"

Caulaincourt shuffled his feet. "There is very little forage, Your Majesty. It is a very bad situation, indeed! I have sent squadrons out to search for stores of grain or hay, but I fear to send them too far abroad, with Kutuzov's army somewhere to the south and the Cossacks and peasant militias lurking beyond Moscow's walls."

"Damn the Cossacks! Take care of the horses, General. That is your job."

Napoleon's left cheek spasmed with rage.

We are the prisoners! Incarcerated in Moscow.

"Many of the horses are wounded and the cold weather takes a toll on them. I fear we will lose most of them or they will not have the strength to press on—"

Napoleon's face turned purple with fury. "Give the horses shelter in the churches of these infidels!"

"Your Majesty! Horses within the churches?" said Caulaincourt.

"Make an enormous fire in the sanctuary of that big cathedral in front—"

"The Cathedral of the Annunciation?"

"It will keep our soldiers and horses warm. That is all I care about. And while they have the fires going, they can melt down all the silver and gold in the churches. To the devil with their pagan beliefs!"

Caulaincourt lifted his chin to stifle a deep swallow.

"What's wrong with you, Caulaincourt?" snapped Napoleon. "Move! That's an order!"

"I shall send three squadrons out this morning to scour the countryside for forage, Your Excellency," said Caulaincourt.

"And transfer those horses who need shelter into the churches. No French horse or soldier shall suffer from this miserable Russian cold."

Two days later General Caulaincourt opened the cathedral door. He took a step back, his hand flying to his nose. The stench of stale piss—both human and horse—assailed his nostrils. A second later the heavy fetid odor of manure registered.

The bare beauty of the cathedral—its spacious open floor for the standing congregation—was now occupied with horses, dirty straw, and an enormous cauldron over an open fire. Soldiers hung from ladders, prying silver and gold from the moldings while their comrades gathered frames from holy icons, chalices, and chandeliers to throw into the pot, melting down the precious metals.

A soldier pissing in the corner turned to Caulaincourt. Recognizing Napoleon's master of the horse, he quickly saluted, his penis still flopping from his pants.

Caulaincourt turned away, looking up toward the empty altar.

What sins we have committed here in this holy space! God will never forgive us!

"General Caulaincourt!" said a colonel, supervising the destruction.

"Do me the favor to tell me, please," he said, lowering his voice. "Is it true that our emperor plans for us to winter here in Moscow?"

"Why do you ask, Colonel?" said Caulaincourt.

"Two squadrons of my regiment were sent to gather cabbages from the fields—the only thing the Russian bastards did not burn! They were ordered to make sauerkraut."

"Choucroute?"

"Yes, *choucroute*! And I am from Alsace, monsieur. I know that choucroute takes many weeks to ferment. Why would the emperor order us to make choucroute if he were not planning to be here when it is ready?"

Caulaincourt took one last look around the smoke-filled cathedral. His eyes took in the emaciated horses, the boiling cauldron, the piles of holy icons stripped from the walls and dumped in a corner.

"I can tell you I have no earthly idea what our emperor plans next. Excuse me, Colonel."

Caulaincourt turned away toward the door he entered, his boots resonating on the marble floor. He pressed his thumbs to his watering eyes as he walked blindly ahead into the sunlight.

Snow collected on the corners of the window. Napoleon looked out across the city, silently cursing.

He threw the novel he was reading across the room. It thudded against the oak box that held his traveling library.

Why have I not had word from St. Petersburg? Did Kutuzov not deliver the message to Alexander? It is outrageous to refuse my offer to go personally to the Winter Palace.

But Napoleon knew very well what Alexander and Kutuzov were thinking. Moscow was a cold stone—no nourishment, no sustenance would it give. They were like rats on a block of wood in the sea.

Napoleon thought of Corsica and the battles against the French in his father's time. The Corsicans knew their territory, the island's rocks hiding their ambushes. But the Corsicans were few and the French prevailed.

Russia was different.

"Send for Caulaincourt! Send for all my generals!" ordered Napoleon. His icy brow turned hot with passion.

"We shall leave for Paris at once!"

Chapter 53

Warsaw, Poland
November 1812

The late autumn sunlight filtered through the gauzy drapes of Adam Czartoryski's study. In his hand, he held an enameled portrait of Alexander, sent by the Tsar himself, and he peered at it closely, examining his best friend's face.

He is changing. Those eyes that looked at the world with kindness and optimism. Napoleon has murdered that innocence forever. This war has left its scars. Like the trickle of water on limestone. I can see the lines of worry, the pinching of his forehead—even as the artist tries to flatter him.

Does he even remember the reforms we spoke about? Rousseau, Voltaire. The liberation of the serfs! The independence of Poland! Nothing more than pretty thoughts now, like silk ribbons in a young girl's hair. The smoke of cannons choke him, death surrounds him. To defeat the enemy, to survive each day, those are the only thoughts that can register in his brain.

Czartoryski looked out his window over Warsaw's Castle Square, the red marble column of Sigismund piercing the sapphire-blue sky.

Forty-five miles outside of Minsk, Napoleon saw that the Russian armies had destroyed the two bridges crossing the Berezina River, blocking his retreat. The bitter cold of late November had cast blocks of ice in the water, a crystalline lacework edging the shore. The waters of the Berezina flowed sluggishly, the ice not yet hard enough for a crossing.

"*Mon empereur? Vos commandes?*"

"Build a bridge!" ordered Napoleon. "Two bridges. At once!"

The order was a death sentence for many of the four hundred bridge builders who plunged into frigid waters. Breath-sucking cold and exhaustion claimed their lives, their bodies lying stiff and frozen on the banks of the river or floating with the broken ice downstream.

And yet those hundreds of deaths were scarcely noticed, a tiny fraction of the many thousands—tens of thousands, hundreds of thousands—who had died on the bitter retreat from Moscow. Without food, without warmth, without hope, harassed by Cossacks and forced into battle against the massed Russian armies, the Grand Armée was broken and battered.

And still, here at the Berezina, two pontoon bridges were built, despite artillery fire from the Russians.

With his vanguard, Napoleon crossed first. His sixty thousand imperial troops rode across the river, the pontoon floats shifting and bobbing under the horses' weight.

"Blow up the bridge. At once!" ordered Napoleon, reaching the other side. "The Russians will use it and destroy us all."

"But my emperor! The troops behind us. Thousands—"

"Blow up the bridge, General. Now! That's an order!'

Soldiers who had battled loyally across Russia to Moscow and then back again to this frozen hell shouted in disbelief as their passage was blocked and sappers set the charges.

"*Arrêtez!*" shouted General Oudinot, who had already crossed the bridge. "Stop! By order of the emperor Napoleon! The bridge is to be exploded!"

"Don't abandon us!" cried a lieutenant, barely able to cling to his saddle. "We stand loyal to the emperor! Don't forsake us!"

Horsemen rushed the bridge and were shot by the Imperial Guard from the safety of the other bank.

"Save yourselves!" shouted General Oudinot. "Stay off the bridge!"

An echoing cry grew, stretching kilometers beyond.

"Emperor! My emperor!"

Panicked riders spurred their near-dead nags, charging the bridge as it blew up, hurling metal, wood, and ice into the frigid air. Remaining fragments left a snake of fire winding across the river. On both banks soldiers looked on horrified, hearing the dying cries of their comrades and the whinnying of horses as they sank below the surface of the Berezina.

Napoleon turned his horse toward Paris, his collar turned up against the cold and the roar of pitiful cries from the far side of the river.

The remnants of Napoleon's Grand Armée who had managed to cross still had to face the Russian army of General Chichagov. But with the desperation of those already dead, they battled their way through the Russian forces and continued their retreat toward home.

And even as they marched on westward, Cossacks harassed them, stealing their already-diminished supplies, picking off small groups as they straggled toward Smolensk.

On November 7, the temperature plummeted to thirty degrees below zero centigrade. The snow shrieked under the feet of the soldiers, spittle crusting their lips shut. Half-mad drivers ran their wagons over their comrades who fell exhausted in their path. Fingers, toes, and genitals blackened and withered, plagued with frostbite. Soldiers wandered aimlessly, stricken with snow blindness.

Frenchmen staggered and fell in the snow. Their comrades stripped their still-living bodies of their clothes. Thousands of ill-shod horses slipped on the ice, breaking their legs. The starving soldiers fell upon them like wolves, their mouths bloody with raw horseflesh.

Shrill wails pierced the air, cursing the name of Napoleon. The Grand Armée reeled forward, madmen lost in the driving snow.

On the fifth of December, in the little town of Smorgoniye, known only for its academy of dancing bears, Napoleon was told there had been a revolt in Paris. General Claude-Francois de Malet had forged a document declaring the death of Bonaparte in Moscow. General Moreau had been appointed interim president.

"A coup? What has become of my son, my wife?"

"They are safe. The coup has been crushed, the perpetrators imprisoned. But, Your Majesty, there is great unrest in the streets of Paris."

"The French are like women, damn them!" said Napoleon, his hand chopping the frigid air. "You mustn't stay away from them for too long. We must break with the army and travel directly to Paris."

"Yes, Your Majesty."

"Murat! I leave you in charge."

General Murat, the emperor's brother-in-law, looked around at the pathetic troops, limping, shoeless, dressed in rags. He saluted the emperor.

"Caulaincourt!" Napoleon said. "We must travel fast as possible. What will it take—two weeks?"

"On our own, without an army—possibly, Your Majesty."

"Take the swiftest, strongest horses. We must reach Paris!"

In little time, the small group broke away from the French forces and headed west.

"Our emperor deserts us!" shouted an officer, shivering in the cold, despite having wrapped himself in a crimson evening gown of shredded satin, looted from a Russian landowner's mansion along the route of the retreat. Frozen spit glittered on his ragged fur collar.

"March on, Lieutenant!" snapped General Murat. "Or you shall be shot."

And so the final fragments of Napoleon's Grand Armée, shredded like that satin gown, headed on toward the Niemen River, where they finally crossed into safety. Of the six hundred fifty thousand who had begun the invasion, perhaps sixty thousand were still alive to again set foot on their native soil of France.

Chapter 54

Bunzlau, Prussia
January 1813

Kutuzov followed the Russian army in his carriage, his bloated body thrown from side to side as they traveled the rutted road. Just a few nights before, Alexander had awarded him the Cross of St. George for his leadership in the battles following Berezina. He looked out of the coach at the pine trees shawled in snow, the lavender light of the three-o'clock dusk casting long shadows across the northern countryside.

Nightfall pounced upon the winter world.

Kutuzov's footman lit the carriage lanterns. Light glinted off the medal on the general's chest. He looked down at the orange and black ribbon and the gold medallion. He fingered the medal, his fingers stiff with the cold.

He thought of the hundreds—no, thousands—of white mounds across the Russian steppes, like bushes or shrubs covered in snow. Frozen soldiers—both Russian and French—finally blessed with slumber. Eternal slumber.

And the living envy the sleep of the dead. How long can we go on?

But the old general followed the Tsar as they pursued Napoleon. Even though he disagreed with him.

"We can chase Napoleon beyond our borders. We can fight," he told Alexander. "But we will return with our faces bloody. For what?"

"We must finish this madman!" said Alexander. "Any lasting peace must be signed in Paris. Europe must rid itself forever of this tyrant!"

Alexander's words seemed fresh and naive.

Our tsar has been in St. Petersburg, warm and comfortable, studying maps and figures all winter. We soldiers are nothing to him. He can't feel our troops' exhaustion, the nightmares they suffer remembering their comrades' deaths. Thinking of their own.

Our army is weary. I am weary.

The old patriot shrugged, his shoulders now bent with age and hardship. He accepted the Tsar's command, taking the Russian army as far as he could until he collapsed ill and exhausted in the Polish lands of Prussia.

Kutuzov had been dying since the late winter, and it was now April. The Russian army had left their commander in chief in Prussia to press on, pushing Napoleon back to Paris.

Winter had turned to spring. The general tossed on his canvas camp bed, stained with sour sweat of an old man.

I have overstayed my welcome on this earth.

His breath was hoarse, a raspy whine.

I'm surrounded by men who speak Polish or German at best.

Why must I die here, like Moses forbidden to enter the Promised Land? I am no Moses.

What was the name of that girl . . . the girl who fought with us?

Kutuzov tried to moisten his cracked lips, but his tongue lay fat and helpless at the corner of his mouth.

I am dying. The retreating tide is pulling at my soul. Why must I be bothered with these small things. What trivial nonsense—cracked lips that need licking. These minutiae keep my spirit anchored here on the rocky shoals.

"General, please take some water."

At least he speaks Russian.

The doctor's aide gave him the edge of a linen rag, sopping wet.

"Suck on this, Your Excellency."

The old general gummed the towel. His gut twisted as the moisture slid down his throat, a few drops at a time.

"That's enough, General," said the aide, pulling the cloth away. "Let go of the cloth, I beg of you."

The border of the cloth snagged, with Kutuzov's jaw clamped down in a spasm. He was powerless to open his mouth. The aide yanked the last centimeter free.

So many men, so many sacrifices . . .

Kutuzov wrinkled his brow fighting to remember.

What happened to the girl? Did she survive? What was her name?

A voice in his ear. "The priest is here, General Kutuzov."

A priest in dark robes, his long beard stiff with winter grease, stood beside the bed holding an icon. As he raised his arms, a whiff of odor from his unwashed body wafted over Kutuzov's nostrils, making them wrinkle in disgust.

The stench of rancid pork lard and self-righteous sweat! Wretched man, go away. Leave me in peace.

"In the name of the Father, the Son . . ." chanted the priest. "Let my mouth be filled with thy praise, O Lord, that I may sing thy glory and majesty all the day long."

Napoleon. Will we ever be free of this French curse? Will his stain be washed from our land?

"Holy God, Holy Mighty, Holy Immortal. Have mercy on us."

Who will inherit my estate? My eldest daughter. Her husband . . . Tolstoy.

My lands shall go to the Tolstoys. May they remember me with kindness.

"Let my mouth be filled with thy praise, O Lord, that I may sing thy glory and majesty all the day long."

Look at the light lingering on my hand. Spilling from the window. Is it spring at last?

"Our Father who art in heaven, hallowed be . . ."

Will this man not leave me in peace!

"Lord, have mercy!"

The girl. How could a girl survive such a war? She told me of a horse. A brave horse lost in battle.

"Lord, have mercy!"

Mercy. Mercy for the girl who disguises herself. Mercy to my daughters who lose a father.

"Look on my suffering and deliver me. For I have not forgotten your law. Many are the foes who persecute me. But I have not turned from your statutes."

My guts are jelly. This hairy priest torments me.

Kutuzov's jaw dropped open in a gasp.

"Is this your confession?" asked the priest, bending close over the dying man. "Absolve yourself of this earthly burden, that you may know God!"

Leave me in peace. What shall happen to Russia? Alexander . . . can he . . .

"Confess your sins and you shall be absolved," said the priest, hovering over Kutuzov's ear.

I can stand this no longer.

Kutuzov closed his eyes for the last time.

Chapter 55

Sarapul, Russia
May 1813

At last when the snows receded, my brother and I left for Moscow. My father begged us not to leave.

"Never start a trip on a Monday!" he said. "Stay until tomorrow, I beg you."

"Papa, you promised we could leave when snows melted. We cannot delay any longer."

So we left that same day, but my conscience bothered me. Why could I not wait one more day to ease the worried mind of an old man—my father.

And then, part way to Kazan our carriage rolled off a slope and smashed to bits. Vasily and I were thrown into a ditch, but luckily not injured. We were forced to travel in a farmer's cart to Kazan. How wrong I was not to heed my father's warning!

When we reached Moscow I received the news from General Mitrofanov, my father's old friend, that Kutuzov was dead.

"Dead?" I whispered. "Dead?"

"He perished of illness in Prussia. He was tired. Tired of war, tired of seeing so many brave men die. Our tsar had removed him from command. Perhaps the great General Kutuzov felt he had fulfilled his duty on earth."

I fought back tears.

"It is all right to cry, Lieutenant Alexandrov." Mitrofanov placed his hand on my shoulder. "All of us have. General Kutuzov loved his soldiers. He loved us like his sons."

I explained that I had brought Vasily here under Kutuzov's protection. He was already enrolled in the Department of Mines and we left without asking permission. If Kutuzov were alive, this would have posed no problem. But now, without written permission from the general himself, how would I explain Vasily's absence?

General Mitrofanov sighed. "I would advise you to send your brother home," he said, looking regretfully at Vasily.

"No, Your Excellency!" said Vasily, full of the Durov impetuous nature. "Nothing on earth could force me to return home. I will stay here and serve in the army like my brother."

Mitrofanov smiled at him. "If you are half the soldier your brother is, you will serve Russia honorably. Stay with us, young man."

We followed behind the French on their way back to Paris.

We followed their ghosts, the traces of their last moments—a scent more malodorous than any stench on the earth.

"Those are the Frenchmen rotting in the forests," said the wagon driver. "It will get worse on the warmer days, now that spring has come."

I looked up at the crows circling like a funnel of black smoke, diving into the woods in a cacophony of caws.

On the Smolensk road we passed Borodino. I pointed out to my brother the redoubt where we had been ordered to stand: "Here so-and-so met his death. Here I was wounded by a cannonball."

"Here Alcides died."

The smell, the rot! Our own Russian peasants were ordered to collect the bodies, both French and Russian, that had been buried under the snow. But here it was mostly French bodies, one after another, soldiers who succumbed to our harsh Russian winter and starvation.

Poor wretches! They were punished for their emperor's presumption and conceit.

At a post station I saw a young girl whose sweet face reflected the joy of life, of the springtime. I was so exhausted with the stink of death that it was pure joy to see such a tender child and be reminded of once-carefree days.

The little girl turned up her face to kiss the station mistress. In turn the woman embraced her.

"What a beautiful child," I said. "Is she your daughter?"

"No," answered the mistress. "She's French, an orphan."

I studied the little girl's face until she turned away shyly, burying her face in the station mistress's bosom.

"And how did she come to be here?" I had to know what strange tragedy had brought such an innocent child to this distant place—and as an orphan.

"The French came through here after the Smolensk battle. They were so sure of themselves that they started little settlements, moving their families into homesteads. This little girl came from one of those settlements right there in the forest," she said, pointing to the edge of a dark woods.

"It was the beginning of the winter. Russia's revenge on Napoleon. Ah, but others suffered too. One night, as they were cooking supper, they heard the blood-curdling whoop of the Cossacks. Platov's Cossacks!"

The little girl began to whimper.

"I should not speak the word—*Cossack!*" the woman whispered to me. "It terrifies her."

"The family scattered in all directions. This one here ran to an impenetrable thicket. She crawled through the snow and finally out onto the highway you travel now. She wore only a thin white frock. A Cossack officer—one of Platov's men—rode by and saw the white bunch of rags in the road.

"She cried out to him and when he stopped, he saw it was a child, her frock in tatters. She was half-naked on the frozen ground. And that hardened Cossack, who hated the French with all his heart, picked up this little girl and brought her here, to this post station. Can you imagine a Cossack taking pity on anyone?"

"What did he look like?" I asked.

"Tall, with green eyes. Handsome, but all flint and bone."

Denisov! Could it have been?

I stopped breathing. The woman didn't notice, she was caught up in her story.

"'Do me a favor,' the Cossack had said. 'Take this child and care for her.' I protested that I had my own children to feed and care for. 'Then I'll dash her brains out right here before your eyes,' he said, 'for I will not let this little one suffer any more.'

"I rushed to grab the unconscious girl from the front of his saddle. She weighed no more than a feather pillow.

"The officer galloped off and for two months this child lay at death's gates. She was badly frostbitten. Skin peeled in long shreds from her arms and legs. Her glorious hair fell out. But she survived. We taught her Polish and found out that she is from a noble family in Lyon. I have spoken of her returning to France—"

"No!" shouted the little girl, breaking into the story, balling her birdlike hands into a fist. "Mama brought me back to life; I will never leave her!"

The little girl buried her face again in her new mother's bosom. The station mistress began to weep, wiping tears from her eyes with her sleeve.

This scene moved me to the depth of my soul. A simple act of kindness in the face of an innocence that somehow survived in the midst of war had forged loyalty—no, love—between two bitter enemies. Inseparable now.

And . . . Denisov!

I was promoted, a lieutenant no more. With the promotion came new orders—ones that would separate me from my little brother.

"Captain Alexandrov," said my senior commanding office. "You have received orders to ride to the Ukraine."

"The Ukraine?"

"A special assignment, Alexandrov," said my commander. "You leave at dawn tomorrow."

I was forced to leave Vasily behind. My companions promised to look after him and treat him like a brother.

I rode south and east through the territories of Belarus and then down into the Ukraine. I was stationed in the beautiful Ukrainian lands of Lapshin, surrounded by forest and crystal-clear lakes.

Ah, the Ukraine! Half my heart and blood is yours. At the sight of your graceful landscape I feel a quickening deep in my soul.

My quarters were a spacious shed, its floors strewn with sand and walls decorated with sweet garlands of flowers and green grasses. Four stumps with plank boards served as a couch, cushioned with sweet hay and covered with a velvet rug. There I read, slept, and thought, far from the booming of cannon and the stench of rotting bodies.

My mission was simple: taking care of horses. I was charged to revive the exhausted, emaciated, and wounded horses that had fought so bravely in the war. To start, I was assigned one hundred fifty horses along with fifty uhlans to help me with my task. More and more horses arrived each day. And every day I thought of my Alcides and I cried—I cried in grief for his loss and I cried in gratitude that I could bring new life to others who had served like him.

Ah! Could there be a better balm to my soul than to watch our injured, emaciated horses graze breast-high in July grass? To see their saddle sores, their gashes and powder burns, heal a little every day! And when they at last lifted their heads and tails, galloping in play across the Ukrainian pastures, once more full of life I thought of our wounded soldiers, praying that they could recover as these horses had.

But could they? Wounded in both body and spirit—could those men ever heal? Hundreds of thousands had died on the battlefield, and those who had survived their wounds had lain writhing next to their comrades' corpses. Did they envy the stillness and sleep of the dead man who suffered no more? Or did they crawl over their bodies, screaming for help?

Or death.

How did a man ever forget? How could they ever heal, remembering such horror?

We fed our herd on sweet grass and oats. Their heads buoyed up gradually, a spark came back to their dull eyes, eyes that had witnessed and endured what no man or beast should. Perhaps they would forget what a human could not.

In the evening, I would wander through the grassy fields checking on our herds and then sit beside the river, marveling at my good fortune. Away from war, an interlude of peace.

Instead of watching a bullet tear through a comrade or a cannonball shatter the bones of his mount, I saw a horse take its first tentative step toward healing. I watched an emaciated steed feed on good oats. My fingers traced my horses' crests, the top line under the mane. I felt good fat slowly accumulating there and smiled. The horses snorted contentedly and closed their eyes under my touch.

I often took my rest in the evening with the horses under a grove of beech trees, listening to the call of the cuckoos. Ah, the peace! The snorting of the horses nosing through their hay and the chuckle of the stream just beyond the paddocks was the balm that soothed my soul after the horror of losing my beloved Alcides.

Caring for animals, this is what I was meant for. After years of the battlefield, I realized I was not a killer.

I loved the cavalry marches, the hours on horseback, the camaraderie with my brave friends. But I have seen enough of bloodshed for a lifetime.

Chapter 56

Lapshin, the Ukraine
August 1813

My respite in the Ukraine was finished at the end of that glorious summer. I was ordered to turn over all my recuperated horses and my squadron of uhlans.

"The horses and uhlans are needed now," I was told. "Tsar Alexander is pursuing Napoleon into France."

I was reassigned to a unit of our regiment commanded by Staff Captain Rszesnicki.

"Hello, my dear Alexandrov," said Rszesnicki. "I have been expecting you. Did you have a good assignment in the Ukraine?"

"Yes, sir," I said.

I already missed my charges—the herd of horses I healed.

"Good. We move out immediately. We are to blockade the fortress of Modlin. Our Majesty Tsar Alexander has Napoleon on the run."

"Napoleon forced from Prussia!" I exclaimed.

"And our tsar in pursuit. He swears he will not stop until he has taken Napoleon prisoner."

"Even into France?" I asked.

"*Da.* Even into Paris itself."

The decision of our great tsar to pursue Napoleon would mean extra months, maybe years of war for Russia—and for me. So I was not finished with war and bloodshed quite yet.

And I owed Alexander everything.

We arrived at our position overlooking Modlin Fortress in March. We were at the confluence of the Vistula and the Narew rivers, just north of Warsaw. Rszesnicki stationed us at posts at two-verst intervals, with me in the center, living in a small cave dugout, in charge of the entire picket. I commanded our uhlans to be on the ready with half standing by their saddled horses and the other half at rest.

I rode back and forth between the posts, making sure the assigned guard was ready. At my signal, sorties rode out.

Modlin Fortress evidently had a good supply of cannonballs and powder, if not bullets. When our men rode out into the field, the French would immediately open fire—with cannons only! This struck me as comical. Can you imagine trying to hit a single rider with a cannonball?

But the French were desperate. Cannonball by cannonball we disarmed them, galloping our horses across the open field as they fired in vain.

After weeks of dodging the damned cannonballs—which our uhlans began to think of as a game—Modlin was captured. Then we were off to Bohemia, continuing west in support of the Tsar as he pursued Napoleon.

We spent the end of autumn on patrol in the Bohemian mountains. I shall never forget looking down from a high peak, watching our Russian squadrons file down the narrow road, a misty sinuous strip through the brilliant red- and golden-leaved trees of autumn.

Then, with the first edge of winter, we descended into the Bohemian capital.

Prague. Oh what joy! I marveled at the buildings, the perfect squares, pastel colors, and dollhouse-like charm of this exquisite city: the tall buildings painted in pastels lined up cheek-to-cheek like the painted toys. Our heads swung around to take in the beauty of this Bohemian treasure with its candy-colored architecture and pristine roads. How our horses' shoes rang out proudly on the cobblestone streets, throwing sparks!

The weather turned fiercely cold. The Bohemians said our Russian weather had followed us—and had they known we were to be stationed there, they would have laid in more peat.

We feasted on succulent roast goose and red cabbage, spiced with copious quantities of caraway, washed down with the finest dark ales I'd ever tasted—though I was not much of a drinker.

I've rarely loved a city as much as Prague. The city of Prague and countryside of the Ukraine reminded me of peace, of fine civilization without war. Would we ever find such elusive peace again?

Our sojourn there was too brief, before we, along with the rest of Bennigsen's army, were ordered on the march again. We headed north and west to contain the French general Davout outside Hamburg.

Chapter 57

Sommepy, France
March 1814

On the thirteenth anniversary of his father's murder, Alexander attended a memorial mass, an occasion he dreaded each year. Before the service, the Tsar calmed himself by holding Elizabeth's Bible to his heart.

Oh, my Elise! Where are you when I need your counsel?

He pressed the Bible close, as if branding his soul.

An aide knocked at the door. "Your Majesty, forgive me. It is time for the service."

Reluctantly, Alexander left the Bible behind and walked to the chapel.

The words of the Mass tumbled, predictable and rote, from the priest's mouth. But Alexander, still thinking of Elizabeth's Bible, couldn't help but be caught up in the ritual that ran through his life from childhood to this very moment.

With the chanting of the priest resonating in the Tsar's chest, he wept as the brutal memories of that terrible night in Mikhailovsky Palace—the night Alexander became the reluctant tsar of all the Russias—slapped him in waves.

The Tsar shivered like a child as he stood praying.

My father, my beloved father. Please forgive me. Guide me to do the right thing. Give me the strength I need to defeat Napoleon.

He prayed as he had never prayed before.

I have no enemy in France but him. I seek no revenge. But I pray, God our Lord, guide me. If I must fight to save Europe, I shall!

I will sleep in Paris, I swear it!

"I will speak with Field Marshal von Diebitsch!" Alexander ordered as he dismissed the Austrians who had deserted Napoleon but were now trying to persuade the Tsar to abandon his pursuit of the French forces. Napoleon had managed a series of victories in pitched battles, and many allies were urging Alexander to declare victory and return to Russia.

"I will have no more talk of falling back," Alexander declared. "We will press on to Paris and rout Napoleon in his den."

Hans Karl von Diebitsch was Prussian born but loyal to Russia and Tsar Alexander. He fought alongside the Russians and had been wounded in the Battle of Austerlitz. He was as experienced and brave as any officer Alexander knew, now that Kutuzov was dead.

"Well?" Alexander asked the general. "Am I mad to ignore the Austrians?"

"If Your Majesty wishes to reestablish the Bourbons on their throne, the best thing to do is to march on Paris."

"To hell with the Bourbons!" said Alexander. "It is a question of Napoleon!"

General Karl Wilhelm von Toll, who had been standing by eager to speak, was unable to contain himself any longer. "We must march upon Paris," he interjected. "But we must be wary. We should have ten thousand cavalry keep pursuing Napoleon south of Paris. We will lure him into engagement to disguise our intentions. Then the rest of the army will pour into Paris before he has a chance to double back."

"Exactly, Toll!" said Alexander. "Brilliant! We shall march on Paris but employ your ruse."

That night Alexander was awash with doubt. He thought of Kutuzov.

Alexander opened the Bible to the book of Ecclesiastes. He read, moving his lips silently: "A time to kill, and a time to heal; a time to break down, and a time to build up."

He clasped the Bible close to his heart. "Please O Lord, guide me. I have been conceited, haughty, and unwilling to listen to wise counsel throughout the years. I swear I shall dedicate myself to you in whatever is left of my life. I ask you tonight, Lord. Be with me."

God be with me. Be with us. Be Russian!

The Russian cavalry unit commanded by General von Wintzingerode rode hard against Napoleon's forces, drawing them away from Paris. The French met the Russians and engaged.

Instead of artillery, the ring of swords filled the battlefield, hard metal against hard metal. Not a single rifle was shot. Cavalry fought against cavalry.

Napoleon looked down from the heights upon the battlefield. A general emerged from the battle, followed by a scout with a lathered horse.

"*Mon empereur!*" gasped the rider. "The Russians have moved their main armies to the outskirts of Paris! We have been lured away by a single cavalry unit!"

Napoleon's eyes snapped wide open. "What?" It wasn't really a question, though. The brilliant strategist already understood exactly what had happened.

All eyes riveted on him. His face transformed to an emotion akin to admiration. "A beautiful chess move! I should never have thought them capable of it!"

He shook his head, as if to clear it. "We move north immediately!" he snapped, although he knew it was already too late.

Alexander's great uncle Colonel Michael Orlov, the illegitimate son of Catherine the Great, was entrusted to carry a plan for peace to Paris. He was ordered to negotiate with French Marshal Auguste Marmont and Napoleon's former foreign minister Charles-Maurice de Talleyrand and ignore Napoleon's brother Joseph, who was officially in charge of the defense of the capital.

"Tell them we have no quarrel with the French people," said Alexander. "I offer peace and tranquility to France, to Europe. If the French troops surrender, I offer them the right to leave the capital. And I will give my word that our troops will be only peacekeepers. We will not allow looting or ill conduct. The Parisians shall be rid of Napoleon and we will inflict no harm."

Orlov took a sheaf of papers that Alexander had prepared and rode toward Paris.

While Orlov negotiated with Marmont, the battle raged outside Paris.

"You are in a precarious position," said Colonel Orlov. "General Wellington has forced the French from Spain. All Europe now surrounds you—foremost Tsar Alexander Romanov of Russia."

Marmont sniffed.

"And if we do not accept your terms?"

"Alexander and his coalition will be forced to ride through Paris with no regard to your people, your architecture, your art," said Colonel Orlov, leveling his eyes at Marmont. "Paris will be at the mercy of the Cossacks and the rest of the allied soldiers who have suffered greatly under the war Napoleon imposed upon them. Paris could suffer the same fate as our beloved Moscow—"

"Cossacks!" said Marmont. "Burn and sack Paris?"

Orlov steadied his steel-blue eyes at the Frenchman.

As you French did Moscow.

"It is certainly not the wish of Tsar Alexander Romanov. Our great tsar reveres Paris. If you surrender peacefully he guarantees the welfare of the French nation. Our emperor has only one enemy in France. Napoleon Bonaparte."

Napoleon and the remnants of the Grand Armée raced to Paris.

"How could I have underestimated Alexander!" said Napoleon to Caulaincourt. "He was so inept at Austerlitz, helpless at Tilsit. Could this possibly that same callow, half-deaf bungler?"

Caulaincourt, who had long admired the Tsar, did not answer. King Joseph, Napoleon's brother, burst into the tent.

"Your Majesty," said Joseph. "There are reports that Tsar Alexander himself is embedded in the horse troops."

"The Tsar? Engaged in battle?"

"His presence has aroused the Russians. Their cavalry fight like madmen."

"What the devil is an emperor—"

A cannon boomed, snatching the rest of Napoleon's words.

Alexander watched from the vantage point of Buttes-Chaumont. From the heights he waited to see who emerged the victor from the mingling colors of uniforms scaling and descending the hills of Montmartre. It was impossible to determine who was winning.

The Tsar returned to his tent to read his ever-present Bible.

"God, I promise you everything I have. I have been foolish, inconstant, and arrogant. I am your humble servant in destiny."

The next day at dawn Colonel Orlov entered Alexander's room. The Tsar was still in bed.

"What news do you bring?"

Orlov bowed. "I bring you the capitulation of Paris, my Tsar."

Chapter 58

Paris
March 1814

Alexander rode into Paris in the blue uniform of the Chevalier Guard. The sun reflected off his gold epaulets, his blue cordon of the Order of St. Andrew stretched diagonally across his chest.

Flanked by King Frederick of Prussia and the Austrian general Schwartzenberg, Alexander sat tall on his light-gray thoroughbred, Eclipse, a gift from Napoleon in earlier days. His expression carefully balanced the pride and satisfaction of victory with his sorrow at the death and destruction. The allies paraded through the streets of Paris and marched beneath the yet unfinished Arc de Triomphe, ordered by Napoleon to honor his victory at Austerlitz.

Cheering Parisians, many thin and hollow eyed from the hardships of war, thronged the streets, climbing into trees, hanging out of windows. The women waved white handkerchiefs.

"Long live Alexander!" shouted a voice, then another and another.

"I do not come as an enemy," said the Tsar. "I come to bring you peace and commerce!"

"We've been waiting for you for a long time!" shouted a man in a tattered coat.

"If I didn't come sooner, it is the bravery of your French troops that is to blame."

The crowd erupted in cheers.

A group of nationalists tried to agitate for the Bourbon royal family.

"Long live the Bourbons!" shouted one loyalist. "The rightful heirs to France!"

A scuffle broke out as a French citizen pushed the loyalist aside.

"*Merde!*" shouted the citizen, waving his emaciated arms. "The Bourbons fled. It is a Russian who has freed us."

"Long live Alexander!" came a call that reverberated down the Champs-Élysées.

Alexander thought, "Paris is mine." Then he stopped himself. "No," he thought. "Not mine. Paris belongs to the world—and foremost to the French. They alone should determine its future. Napoleon is defeated. I have achieved my goal."

A twelve-year-old boy crept up to a campfire on the Champs-Élysées. He had seen these strange men, in loose fitting pants and tunics, their tanned faces all bone and sinew. He gawked at them as the other Parisians did as they rode bolt upright in huge saddles down the boulevard.

Their strange mutterings and fierce bearing had entranced him, for this young boy Pierre Verne had an insatiable thirst for adventure.

The horses were tethered to the trees, gnawing at the bark. The smell of animal fat, horse manure, and soured milk emanated from the campsite. Wet laundry flapped from the railings of the palaces that lined the Champs-Elysées.

Pierre was not alone. He could see in the firelight whole families who had crept near the Cossack camp to watch these wild men who slept in their saddles, smoked pipes, and played cards.

Another boy touched Pierre's elbow, making him jump.

"Better than a circus!"

"Shhh!" said Pierre.

"They won't hurt us. I've thrown a rock at 'em and they laughed. Threw it right back at me, hitting me right here on the shoulder," he said, touching the spot. "They laughed again really hard. No harm done."

"You are stupid but lucky," said Pierre, watching the Cossacks. "I heard they are under strict orders to behave. Otherwise they would have speared you with one of their lances. Or cut off your ears faster than a Les Halles butcher."

The boy pulled at his earlobe, thinking.

"They are fierce looking," he said, nodding.

"That's what it took to defeat Napoleon," said Pierre, his eyes still riveted on the men. "Those Russians and their tsar."

Chapter 59

While our tsar was completing his glorious conquest of Paris, we were still stuck outside Hamburg, battling the stubborn General Davout. Despite the news of Napoleon's surrender, Davout held on to Hamburg in the name of the Bourbon king Louis XVIII until late May.

Despite the defeat of Napoleon, which allowed the Bourbons to regain the throne they had lost during the Revolution, Louis XVIII did not want to cede an acre of land the Corsican had conquered.

I thought General Davout was a blockhead but a brave soldier nonetheless. At last he capitulated and rode away under the protection of the Tsar's Imperial Guards.

The Germans were jubilant, opening their houses to us. Families brought out their good silver and dishes, sharing all the food and drink they could offer us. We were offered soft beds—with clean bedding—to sleep in.

A family—not wealthy, but fine-mannered peasants—took me in, along with other officers. They served us as if we were royalty.

"Our king has ordered us to treat Russians well," the patriarch told me. "Everything we have is yours to share. If it weren't for the Tsar's armies, we'd all be speaking French now!"

What fine food they served us! Succulent pork with stewed apples, the finest dark rye bread I'd ever tasted. Dry white wine and plenty of coffee with cream. Our meals were served on china dishes with silver spoons and saltcellars, fine crystal goblets. The tables were spread with delicate embroidered tablecloths, fit for a king. The Germans could not do enough for us after we liberated them of the tyrant Napoleon.

Our troops were billeted in Holstein, Prussia. We Russians honored Holstein as the homeland of Catherine the Great, grandmother of our magnificent Tsar Alexander. As I walked the peaceful land, I thought of the bravery of our emperor, taking Paris. Now he was in Vienna, orchestrating talks to settle an enduring peace for all Europe.

The "Holy Alliance" he called it. I marveled at the thought of all the nations of Europe coming together to work for peace. Surely our tsar was the first to conceive such a brilliant notion!

Did the other nations realize the deep sacrifices Russia made to put an end to Napoleon's tyranny? Would they teach their children and future generations of the battles of Smolensk, Borodino, Berezina, and the final fierce battle at Leipzig, the largest confrontation ever fought on European soil? Will the pages of history books be filled with images of the burning of Moscow or the glorious ride through the Arc de Triomphe of Tsar Alexander?

What sacrifices Russia has made to defend all of Europe! Russia defeated Napoleon. It is an achievement that should never be forgotten.

And yet, I wonder: Will our sacrifices—my comrades fallen in battle, my horse torn to pieces by a cannonball, those deaths of hundreds of thousands of Russian souls—will they be remembered?

I wonder.

Part 6
Can Wounds Ever Heal?

Chapter 60

Island of Elba
September 1814

Napoleon Bonaparte looked down at the smooth stones two meters under the salt water of Portoferraio. The sea surrounding the island of Elba was so crystal clear, it resembled water from a mountain lake.

An Austrian guard stood on a rock just above him. He held his rifle in his hand.

"It is not so bad being held prisoner here, is it, Your Majesty?" said the guard.

Napoleon tossed a stone out into the gently lapping waves.

"I am an emperor. I am a prisoner. I despise this place."

"Have it your way," muttered the guard, turning away as he added, his voice even lower, "You shouldn't have started a bloody war!"

Bonaparte could make out the misty coastline of Italy from where he stood. He watched the seagulls circle and dive over the wharf. There, just across the water, were soldiers still loyal to him. His villa here, the hundreds of men and servants who surrounded him, even his six hundred French Imperial guardsmen—it all meant nothing. France was calling, waiting for his return. He was certain.

Would my brilliant commander General Ney join me? Ney, who openly declared he would like to see me brought back in an iron cage. Ney, who breakfasted with Tsar Alexander in Paris! Does my best soldier really despise me so much? My faithful general who served me better than any. Shrewd and brave. Surely he would stand with me once more.

Wouldn't he?

Napoleon squinted at the coastline again.

We could take back Tuscany! March on to Paris, gathering troops as we go. I know the Frenchman's heart. I know the Parisians. They would rally around me. "Vive l'empereur!" *I can hear the cry.*

A small fish darted by just a few inches under the water.

At least Elba is in the Mediterranean. So close to France.

The guard spoke again, shaking Napoleon from his reverie.

"They say the Russians lost more than a quarter of a million soldiers in the war. Across Europe, five million lives—"

Napoleon threw up a hand.

"Perhaps. Monsieur, I was not present for the count. I was otherwise occupied," Napoleon sniffed.

The guard tightened his grip on his rifle.

"You destroyed Moscow, they say. Burned it to the ground."

Napoleon ignored the man.

Ignorant bastard! Of all the adversaries I had, Alexander is the one I respect. True he was a vainglorious nincompoop at Austerlitz. But it was a youthful folly. Eight years later he led his army into Austria and the Battle of Leipzig—and then into Paris. Riding the stallion I gave him!

Ah, Alexander. I never wanted war with Russia, only for you to stop meddling in Europe.

We wanted the same thing. Reforms and freedom for our people.

The cries of two circling seagulls overhead made him shade his eyes and look skyward. The sun glanced off their yellow beaks.

But we've changed, we two. We are not the same men at all. The war is to blame.

Time and power have worn us down.

Our dreams of enlightenment, of democracy. Where are our reforms? Where is the brotherhood of liberty, the precepts of revolution?

We grew fat with power. Our dream, the bright coin of enlightenment is tarnished metal at the bottom of a once-sparkling fountain.

We have shed those dreams like snakes shed their skins. But I can still dream.

Of returning.

Chapter 61

Vienna, Austria
January 1815

Tsar Alexander convened the Congress of Vienna, gathering the royalty of Europe to form a lasting alliance that would eliminate the threat of another great war in Europe.

The Tsarina Elizabeth's mature beauty and grace made an impression on the courts of Europe, although her husband paid her no attention at all. Instead, he flirted and consummated relationships with the most dazzling princesses and noblewomen of Europe.

Elizabeth, who had grown accustomed to her husband's philandering over the years, stood by his side at fetes, balls, and banquets, her head held high.

But her greatest admirer, Adam Czartoryski, knew how she suffered. Adam Czartoryski, whom she had refused to see in more than fourteen years, was once again infatuated, the embers of his love ignited.

At a dinner the Tsar and tsarina hosted, Czartoryski caught her eye from across the crowded room and raised his glass in silent toast.

Later, Czartoryski wrote feverishly in his journal:

I see her very much changed but to me she is still the same because my feelings for her have not wavered (perhaps some of their warmth has diminished but they are still strong enough that the possibility of not seeing her at all is torture to me). I have seen her only once so far. Having been ill received, I am experiencing a bad day.

Second meeting: Ah! She is, as always, my angel. I want nothing more than to secure her happiness. I have forgiven her infidelity with all my heart.

The two lovers had reunited. Neither one had tasted such happiness in many years.

Amid the dizzying round of royal fetes and balls in Vienna, the Tsar and tsarina of Russia hosted the heads of Europe at a magnificent dinner. An indoor riding arena was converted to a vast banquet hall. Three hundred and sixty guests were invited, including two emperors, four kings, and thirty reigning princes. Tsarina Elizabeth was seated at the right of Emperor Francis of Austria and Tsar Alexander next to Empress Maria of Austria.

At tables glittering with a veritable bonfire of candles, plates were adorned with pineapples and cherries from greenhouses in Moscow, truffles from Perigord, oranges from Palermo, strawberries from England, and grapes from France.

"Look at her majesty the tsarina!" exclaimed the French writer Madame de Stael, leaning closer to her dinner companion, Auguste-Louis-Charles de La Garde de Chambonas. "An angel. No other . . ." Her voice trailed off. Between these two old friends sentences scarcely needed to be finished. An elegant shrug, a raised eyebrow said so much. The tsarina was beyond compare.

De La Garde concurred. "Her hair. Her eyes. The purity of her soul."

The writer smiled. "And the arts . . ." She shrugged. "Beethoven."

Her companion shot her a puzzled look. He didn't know! Now there was a real tale to tell. Madame de Stael leaned as close as her gown and elaborate coiffure would allow.

"You haven't heard? Beethoven wrote a violin sonata for the Tsar and he couldn't be bothered to pay his debt."

De La Garde raised an eloquent eyebrow. Royalty never paid, did they?

"So the tsarina paid it for him," de Stael went on. "And Beethoven has written a piece expressly for her to show his gratitude. *Fur Elise* he calls it. That's certainly clear, isn't it?"

They both smiled.

"The toast of the continent," said de La Garde.

And they exchanged an arch look.

What a shame her husband is such a philanderer!

The Russian courier's horse stumbled into the Viennese courtyard, half-dead with exhaustion.

"I must see the Tsar at once," said the young man, his legs buckling under him as he dismounted. An imperial squire grasped the courier's arm, pulling him to his feet.

"Stable boy! Take care of this horse at once."

The squire turned to loosen the ties on the leather satchel.

"Don't touch it!" snapped the courier, regaining his strength. "It is a confidential letter for the Tsar. Only I can deliver it."

The courier did not take time to wipe the mud and dirt from his face, clothes, and boots. He was admitted to Alexander's office at once. The Tsar was seated at his desk conversing with the tsarina.

"A letter for you, Your Majesty. From Paris," said the courier, bowing.

Elizabeth stared at the weary messenger. *No good can come of this.*

Alexander slipped a knife under the wax seal. As he read the words the color drained from his face.

"What is it, Alexander?"

The Tsar looked at her, barely able to speak.

"Napoleon has escaped from Elba. He is mounting an army in the south of France."

Alexander inspected his face in the mirror.

I am balding. But the hair I have left still has color. My sideburns are thick enough.

The Tsar rubbed a piece of ice over his face, tightening the skin and bringing out the natural rosiness. It was a ritual he repeated each morning.

Peacetime has made me a bit stout. But I can still dance the night away.

He smiled, thinking of the dizzying array of flirtations, including the ravishing widow of the war hero General Bagration.

Ah, Madame Bagration. She has bewitched me . . .

Then an image of the battlefield flashed in his mind.

Alexander saw the body of a young soldier in a Russian uniform, a bullet through his temple. His pale mouth sagged open in surprise.

Napoleon had escaped. It all could happen over again.

Alexander's rosy complexion faded and he heard the drip of the melting ice in the basin.

He looked back to the mirror. A middle-aged man growing stout and wattled stared back at him.

"Boris! Inform the Tsarina Elizabeth of my intention to dine with her tonight," he said. "A private dinner, just the two of us."

"Yes, Your Majesty."

Boris lingered, noticing his master's slumped shoulders.

"Your Majesty," he said gently. "Are you quite all right?"

Alexander looked at his loyal servant and his graying hair. He thought of the faraway days in the nursery of the Winter Palace. *Ah, Boris. How I've changed since those innocent days.*

Who are you now, Alexander Pavlovich Romanov?

"I play a part in a play, Boris, but I detest my role. I seem to have forgotten my lines."

"Your Majesty, have patience with yourself. The last years have been cruel."

"Cruel? To all of us. But my heart aches."

Maria Naryshkina left me for another lover. Millions of souls have perished on the battlefield. Moscow has been burned to the ground.

All Europe turns its eyes to me to secure lasting peace. Yet I still play the part of philandering tsar.

He dashed the remaining shard of ice against the porcelain basin.

"Boris! Tell the tsarina I need to see her."

The servant opened the double windows.

"I think I feel the first breath of spring," said Tsarina Elizabeth. She smiled. "Freshly turned earth and first growth. Can you smell it, Alexander?"

"Spring comes much earlier here in Vienna, but I can't say I can detect it."

She sighed and breathed deeply.

A servant appeared carrying a lacquered tray with an envelope sealed with red wax.

"Your Majesty, a letter for you."

The Tsar flicked his eyes toward his wife. She was such a graceful consort, admired by all Europe. But for comfort of a more carnal nature he had turned to the widow of General Bagration.

She should know better than to send communication here. I can't have a scene with Elise.

Alexander picked up the envelope inspecting the seal. The image of the medieval knight on a rearing horse.

"Adam Czartoryski," he murmured.

"What?" said Elizabeth. She walked quickly over to her husband.

"What would Adam want to talk to me about now? He knows my stance on Poland," said Alexander. "Poland will have its government and civil rights, but I shall be king. I've made that quite clear."

He turned to his wife. Elizabeth had gone deathly pale.

"Elise? Do you know anything about this?" he said, accepting the letter knife from the servant.

"Alexander—I . . ."

He looked at her quizzically and then withdrew the letter from the envelope.

"He requests a private audience with me this morning. The devil with him! Does he think I can spare time from the Holy Alliance? Napoleon has escaped Elba. The tyrant is on the loose again! I do not have time for Polish politicians."

"Your Majesty, Prince Czartoryski waits in the anteroom.

"Show him in."

Tsar Alexander continued signing documents. The scratch of the quill pen punctuated his response to his visitor. He barely looked up.

"What is it, Adam? I've made my points clear on Poland. Already I hear that I give Poland more liberty than the Russians themselves experience—"

"Your Majesty . . ."

"Please dispense with formalities. We are alone. But be brief. I must meet with the Austrian ambassador to finalize—"

"Alexander. I have come to ask for Elise's hand in marriage."

Alexander's mouth snapped tight, his hand shook. A fat drop of ink pooled where his pen lay motionless on the page. *Alexander Pavlovich Roma—*

"You know how much I love her," said Czartoryski. "We have rekindled our love. All has been forgiven. I only wish to have her as my wife."

"Elise! Marriage? You—you must be mad, Adam!"

Prince Czartoryski shook his head. "I was mad to ever leave her, even with your father's threat to my life. I have always loved her from the day I first saw her, so many years ago. I want to take her to Poland."

Alexander rose from his chair. "Adam! How could I ever give you permission? I would have to divorce her—could you imagine the damage to the House of Romanov and my reign? The instability of Europe—"

"You cannot love her and give her the happiness I can, Alexander!" said Czartoryski, tightening his hands into fists. "Everyone knows of your liaisons: Princess Liechtenstein, Princess Esterhazy, Sophie Zichy, Princess Auersperg, Madame Bagration—"

"That is none of your affair!"

"I don't claim it to be. I only want to take Elizabeth away from her unhappiness, to love her with all my heart as my wife."

"No, Adam. What are you saying? The scandal would topple the Holy Alliance. And the future of your beloved Poland! It will undermine all that you have worked for all your life."

Czartoryski uncurled his fists. "How could my marriage possibly affect Poland?"

"Don't be a fool, Adam! Consider: the Tsar of all Russia has granted Poland liberties unparalleled in Russia. And now the Tsar offers his wife, the tsarina, to the Polish prince most likely to lead revolt against us for independence? I might as well shoot myself in the head now."

"Alexander! This is political banter. I speak of love, of happiness. You don't love Elise."

"You are wrong, Adam!" said Alexander. He walked to the window looking across to the Ballhausplatz. "I do love her and I always have. But now I realize—I need her. I need her counsel, her wisdom."

"Does she not deserve to be happy?"

"You think me selfish."

"Utterly!" said Czartoryski. "Selfish and cruel."

"Cruel? Because I do not visit her bed? You think we have no relationship, Elise and I? But of course we do. There has been no greater comfort to me. It was Elise who pressed a Bible in my hand as I fought back Napoleon."

"Napoleon? I speak of profound love of your wife and you—you speak of Napoleon!"

"I speak of worldly consequences, Adam! You misjudge me. And Elise. She has given me counsel and directed my spiritual path. She alone understands me. I need her now more than ever."

"And for this understanding you would destroy her happiness?"

Alexander turned away, wincing. Outside the window in the brilliant sunshine, he could see carriages rolling along the cobblestones, driven by men in top hats. The formal draft of the Holy Alliance would be presented within the hour.

"There are matters more important in this world than an individual's happiness. I represent all Russia, the power that defeated Napoleon. And now the villain is on the loose again, raising an army. More blood will be shed but I stand for the Holy Alliance, the pact of powers sworn to uphold peace throughout Europe. If I divorce Elise, that power is finished. An eagle with a broken wing! I would be considered a fool. This Congress, Poland's future, Europe's security! All would crumble."

"Alexander, I beg you—"

"No, Adam," said the Tsar, raising his open hand to block any further discussion. "I shall never divorce the Tsarina Elizabeth."

Chapter 62

On the road to Lithuania from Polotsk, Belarus
April 1815

Napoleon Bonaparte's escape from Elba put all of Europe on the march again, damn him!

Our uhlan pennons fluttered once more, and our lances flashed in the sun. Our horses' spirits were high, inhaling the excitement of movement and battle. All of this made my heart race as it always had. But after years of war, there was a new sentiment that cut into the excitement.

I had been a cavalry soldier from the cradle. But now I had seen too many deaths, too much blood and suffering. The menacing beat of the war drum, the sight of gallant lads galloping their mounts to meet the enemy, their lances or sabers flashing, filled me with both reverence and overwhelming dread.

How strange I still found it that one moment, the moment of wringing a goose's neck—such a simple task any farmwife would do!—had brought a profound realization up from the depth of my soul.

I hated killing. And war meant death. Always.

But I was still a cavalry officer and I packed my emotions away. Perhaps during peacetime I could reexamine them. But not during war.

And so we marched to Kovno, in Lithuania.

I commanded new recruits who had seen little or nothing of battle. They were eager "to defeat Napoleon once and for all."

But they were as ignorant as they were excited.

We veterans were tired of war. How could the allied monarchs have allowed Napoleon to escape? What of the French, who had sworn to protect the Bourbon monarchy? The Austrians stationed on the island? The British frigate keeping watch on the sea? And our glorious tsar—may God forgive any untoward criticism—why did he and the allies not send the devil packing to the middle of the Atlantic?

But what was done was done—and we were on the march westward as our allies mobilized. Word came that England and the Prussians were amassing their armies to stand against Napoleon.

My new recruits lacked discipline. They thought nothing of pillaging, stealing. Once at midnight, I passed a field sown with oats. I saw something white flit among the stalks of grain.

"Who goes there!" I demanded.

I heard a rustle in the grain and then a face appeared in the moonlight.

"It is I, Captain Alexandrov. Recruit Golsky from the Fourth Platoon."

"What the devil are you doing there in the dark, Golsky?"

"I'm trying, your honor."

"Trying"—the Russian equivalent of taking what is needed. In order to fatten up his horse, Golsky was stealing oats!

"You must stop this instant! Back to camp, Golsky!"

As I rode to my quarters, I heard a whacking sound. Voices cried out for mercy. I pushed my tired horse into a gallop and soon saw Lieutenant Kolovsky's soldiers beating several of my platoon with a rod.

"Desist!" I ordered.

"Ah! Alexandrov," said Kolovsky. "Excuse me, but I was taking care of this chore for you. Your soldiers were accused of stealing eighteen jugs of vodka from a Jew. Don't be angry, brother."

"Why should I be angry at you," I said, my rage turning in a moment against my own men. "On the contrary, I am grateful. Scoundrels! A disgrace to the name of Tsar Alexander. Continue the punishment!"

I was sick of war. I was miserable trying to train young rascals who had no idea of what sacrifices our Russian soldiers had already made on their behalf, on Europe's behalf.

Then word came that the Duke of Wellington and General Blucher of Prussia had defeated Napoleon at Waterloo.

The hundred-day war had ended.

And instead of sorrow at missing action and a chance for new glory, I felt only relief. Relief so deep it was almost painful.

I was given leave to spend time with my uncle in St. Petersburg. I attended a concert at the Philharmonic Hall. The auditorium was filled with society women all dressed in their finest. I loved to inspect their gowns made of silk, flowered embroidery, taffeta, deep plush velvets. They were fine birds indeed, but my uhlan officer's jacket was far more admirable. I would not have traded it for the world!

As I studied the women around me, I noticed one particularly gaunt and swarthy face, her eyes luminous with intelligence and character. Although she was dressed in fine lavender silks and a rose beret, I knew instantly that woman's skin had seen nature's forces: wind, storms, sun. This was no ordinary lady.

I whispered to an uhlan captain who was sitting beside me. "See the woman seated next to General Khrapovitsky."

"You mean his wife?"

"Ah! Is she the woman who rode beside him—"

"Into Paris? Yes, she fought in the war dressed as a page and received a medal for the taking of Paris. There are not many like that one!"

I felt a prick at my pride.

"I hear that there was another," I said. "One who fought since the beginning—"

"Oh, that one. Nadezhda Durova," he said. "No, she died. She couldn't take the hardship."

I had died? I couldn't take the hardship of battle!

"I see that you don't believe me," said my companion. "Well, consider. Madame Khrapovitsky there had her husband to look out for her. That young Nadezhda Durova joined the army and fought at Guttstadt, Heilsberg, Smolensk. Even Borodino. And she was all alone, what can you expect? At least Madame Khrapovitsky was a page riding beside her husband, a general. Durova was on her own. Of course she couldn't last."

As I considered my growing legend—and my demise—I began to think of my father, alone at home. My sisters had married, and my brother was an officer in the army.

I was a legend but a ghost already.

A sudden feeling for my roots, for my old family home, seized me.

Not long after that evening, I announced my intention to leave the army.

Chapter 63

In the first years after the Patriotic War of 1812, Alexander enjoyed the adoration of the Russian people, but that adoration went to his head.

He did not heed his long-ago tutor's lessons about reform and freedom. Alexander was finished with his Committee of Friends. His faithful counselor Adam Czartoryski never returned to Russia. The Tsar, who had defeated Napoleon, lost the strength to rule. Exhausted, he tossed the reins of power into the unworthy hands of Count Arakcheyev, who changed the tenor of Alexander's government, billeting soldiers in Russian homes, crushing freedoms, and exiling or imprisoning opposition.

The despotic tone of government was mirrored in Poland, under the rough hand of Alexander's brother, Grand Duke Constantine.

Adam Czartoryski wrote: *"My Lord, the Grand Duke Constantine seems to have acquired a hatred for this country and everything that goes with it. An enemy could not do more harm to Your Imperial Majesty."*

But the Tsar did not bother to write back. Alexander had ceased to care. His beloved sister Ekaterina had succumbed to a vicious infection of the skin and finally pneumonia. She died in 1819.

Alexander grieved mightily. He developed the same wretched skin infection as his sister, on his left leg. He spent more and more time either traveling or hidden away from Russian society. Finally, sensing his own desperation, he decided to go back to the starets Sevastianov to seek his advice.

Entering the starets's hovel, Tsar Alexander recognized the earthy smells from long ago as he ducked his head to avoid brushing against the bundles of dried flowers and herbs that hung from the low ceiling.

The mystic Sevastianov had aged mightily since the year of the Battle of Austerlitz. The holy man stared at the Tsar with milky eyes, unseeing. He waved his hand in greeting, motioning to a chair.

"Your Majesty, approach. Please sit next to me," the starets croaked. "Forgive me for not rising—I would only topple over. I have a young boy who attends me but I have dismissed him for our meeting."

"Thank you for receiving me in private, Sevastianov."

"It is my great pleasure, Your Majesty. I've waited for you to return for seventeen years. They tell me you defeated Napoleon."

This man speaks of Napoleon as if he were of as little consequence as a weed in a cucumber patch.

"Yes, he is imprisoned now in the middle of the Atlantic," said Alexander. "Thousands of miles of salt water on either side of him. He shall not be raising an army ever again."

"That is good."

"You were right, Sevastianov, that I would not defeat him right away," said Alexander. "In 1805. How did you know?"

The holy man shrugged. "I know what I know. It is not for me to question. Why do you return to me, Tsar?"

Alexander hesitated. He looked away from the starets's eyes even though he knew the man was blind.

"I am lost, Starets," said Alexander. "I was miscast as tsar. A tsar must rule with an iron fist and I have not that character."

Sevastianov fingered the ends of his long gray beard.

"Your Majesty, did you follow my advice? Did you surround yourself with good advisors?"

Alexander again looked away from the sightless eyes and up at the dried flowers and berries hanging from the roof.

"I did for a time . . ."

"And now?"

"I . . . I fear I have chosen poorly. I am surrounded by threats, assassins, and plots! My minister Alexei Arakcheyev snuffs out the spark of rebellion. But he is harsh, I know. His hand is heavy on the people."

The starets nodded, moving his lips in silence.

"But does this Alexei Arakcheyev represent your will?" he asked after a few moments.

Alexander ran his hand over his face.

"I never wanted to oppress my people. But the Tsar of all the Russias must wield an iron hammer over dissenters."

Sevastianov ran a pale tongue over his wrinkled lips.

"Are you that iron hammer?" he asked.

"No, Sevastianov. I am not."

"But you assign ministers who have the stomach for despotism."

Alexander frowned.

"I suppose I am emulating my ancestors—"

"Your father?"

Alexander nodded.

He reached around his neck and withdrew a small cloth bag attached to a leather cord. Untying the knotted sack, he extracted a scrap of paper.

"This is the coded note my father wrote the night he was murdered," Alexander said, placing the paper into the starets's hands. "I asked you to decipher it before and you could not. Can you try again now?"

"But Your Majesty! I am blind."

"I know. I thought by the holy spirit . . ."

"There are some things that are simply beyond even a starets's power," said Sevastianov. He touched the paper with his fingertips.

"It is very creased," he said. "It has been folded and unfolded many times."

"I cannot help but read it over and over again," said Alexander. "It is a mystery that haunts me."

"It haunts you? Why?"

Alexander dropped his gaze from the starets's eyes staring blindly at him.

"I—I don't know. It could have been my father's last message before he was murdered. What was he trying to tell me? Or say about me?"

The starets reached out and handed back the scrap of paper.

"Forgive me, Your Majesty. I still think you are the only one still living who could possibly answer that question."

Alexander folded the paper, tucking it back into the bag. He stifled a great sob.

"I promised God that if I could defeat Napoleon, I would be a servant of his will. But what am I to do? Throw the Romanov family, the scepter, and the future of Russia to these hungry wolves? The men who thirst for my power would destroy our country, snarling and ripping at one another's throats. There would be no democracy, only anarchy until another strong man emerged, worse than any Romanov."

"Your Majesty, you say you promised to serve God's will. Have you found him in St. Petersburg? In the battles against Napoleon?"

Alexander threw up his hands. "I have sought spiritual guidance everywhere. I've studied the Quakers, the Masons, mystics . . ."

Sevastianov grunted.

"I founded the Bible Society," offered Alexander.

"I have heard of your Bible Society. Pietism, Illuminism, Martinism . . . and Freemasonry—all cults."

"I explore all avenues to find God," said Alexander.

The starets drew a deep breath. When he expelled the air, Alexander heard the rattle of age from his throat and lungs.

"Your Majesty," said Sevastianov. "Have you considered finding God on your own?"

Alexander cocked his head, leaning toward Sevastianov with his good ear. "On my own?"

"Without spiritual leaders or their philosophies. Dedicate yourself to God in the purest form, approach him as the poorest pilgrim."

"Like you?"

"Perhaps."

"But I am Tsar of all Russia! I can't live like you as a hermit. I have the gravest responsibilities."

"Yet you made a promise to the Almighty. Is there no higher purpose?"

Alexander did not reply. In the silence he listened to the call of the seagulls over the Gulf of Finland.

That night Tsar Alexander wrote to the Prince of Orange, husband of his youngest sister, Anna Pavlovna. Since the death of his sister Ekaterina his brother-in-law had become his new confidant:

> *I shall forsake the throne when I reach fifty. I know myself well enough to feel that by then I shall no longer have the physical and mental strength to govern my vast empire. Nicholas is a reasonable and comprehending person, the right man to guide Russia down the right path.*

On the day of his coronation I shall be among the crowd
at the foot of the great stairs of honor of the Kremlin, and
I shall be among the first to shout, "Hurrah!"

A few nights later while dining with his younger brother Grand Duke Nicholas and his wife, Alexandra Feodorovna, Alexander said, "Nicholas, you must prepare yourself to become tsar."

Nicholas wiped his mouth with a napkin. "Whatever do you mean, Your Majesty? After your reign, Constantine is next in line for the throne."

"We have discussed the matter," said Alexander. "Should I abdicate, Constantine will follow suit. He has a morganatic marriage to the Polish Joanna Grudzinska—he cannot produce a legitimate heir. You will inherit the throne. Besides, Constantine is not suited to the task. His harsh conduct in Poland brings no honor to the Romanov name."

"The Poles need an iron hammer over their heads!" said Nicholas. "Constantine does what is needed."

An iron hammer. Is that truly what they need? It seems to be what everyone clamors for, this blasted hammer!

Alexander sighed. "You will be the next tsar. And someday soon." The Tsar saw a minute movement across the table from him. The Grand Duchess Alexandra Feodorovna's eyes widened.

"Ah, my dear sister-in-law!" said Alexander. "Do not worry. I am in fine health. But your husband must prepare for the role of tsar. I shall cheer him from the throngs as you pass by in the imperial coach."

The grand duchess was speechless.

As they left the dining room, Alexandra Feodorovna whispered to her husband, "He speaks as if he will abdicate. And soon."

Nicholas gazed up at the gilded moldings of the ceilings and the magnificent spill of the Jordan Staircase illuminated by hundreds of candles.

"My brother the Tsar renounced the throne even before he was given it," he said. "I wonder what he means to do."

In the first week of November 1824, the Baltic Sea churned with hurricane-force winds. The storm beset St. Petersburg from the southwest, driving the ocean water up the Neva River and causing a flood of catastrophic proportions. The entire city was deluged, drowning more than five hundred people in a little over five hours. Brave souls rowed boats in the tempest, trying to save the desperate in every part of the city.

Alexander and the royal family took refuge in the highest level of the Winter Palace. Below them they saw animal carcasses, bloated human bodies, houses, timbers, and bridges carried swiftly away in the sea that rose inch by inch, foot by foot.

When the waters finally subsided, a cemetery cross carried across the Neva wedged itself directly in front of the Winter Palace.

Alexander looked down at it from the third floor.

"It is a sign," he said to Elizabeth.

Alexander descended the sweeping Jordan Staircase, the most stunning hallmark of the palace, now littered with thick mud and debris. The rose-colored marble was ringed with watermarks and the alabaster statues of Wisdom and Justice laced with filth.

What harbingers are these? How fares the rest of my capital?

The Tsar insisted on inspecting the city immediately to survey the destruction.

What met his senses was the low wail of despair, the sobs and laments of those who had lost their loved ones. All St. Petersburg moaned, the howl permeating even the Tsar's one deaf ear.

He clapped a handkerchief over his nose and mouth, the stench of decay overwhelming him. He remembered that a similar flood had struck the city in 1777—the year of his birth.

Alexander stepped out of his carriage at the beginning of Nevsky Prospekt. His cheeks were wet with tears as he stood and listened to the mourning of St. Petersburg.

The Tsar of all Russia sobbed. The footmen and escorts stood motionless, not knowing what to do.

An old man hobbled by and seeing the Tsar's tears, spoke to him.

"God is punishing us for our sins!"

Alexander looked at the old man and shook his head.

"No, Grandfather. Not for *our* sins. For mine!"

Alexander turned away, his head in his hands.

While Alexander was in good health, the Tsarina Elizabeth was not. She had breathing troubles that perplexed her physicians. As her condition worsened her doctors recommended that the tsarina spend the winter in a warmer climate. Italy was suggested.

Elizabeth remembered wistfully how Adam Czartoryski had loved Italy.

But Alexander insisted that his wife could not travel without him— and he could not leave Russia. There were rumors of a coup. Alexander could not risk traveling beyond the Russian borders.

"No," he said to her doctors. "She must remain with me for the winter."

"Your Majesty," said the senior member of the team. "The tsarina has an acute lung condition. She needs a drier, warmer climate. The weather of St. Petersburg will kill her!"

"Find a locale within Russia. In my vast empire, there must be some place that is suitable."

After considerable consultation, the physicians suggested Crimea.

But the next day, Alexander countered with a much more obscure location, the southern port of Taganrog, close to Crimea but on the Sea of Azov rather than the Black Sea. Taganrog was a three-week journey by coach from St. Petersburg.

"There is nothing in Taganrog, your majesty!" said Doctor Wylie, the chief physician. "You will not have the luxuries—not even the necessities!—that Crimea would offer. Taganrog is a humble port with rough seas. Better to travel a little further to Crimea."

"Taganrog is where the tsarina and I shall reside for the winter. It is quiet and isolated. Make preparations immediately."

That night Alexander spoke with his wife.

"This will be a second honeymoon for us, my love. We shall take simple quarters—maybe a half dozen rooms for your apartment, a few larger rooms for my own. We shall walk the coastline, my dear, and remember our youth."

Elizabeth began to answer but her reply was stifled by a fit of coughing.

"Oh!" she managed to say. "Alexander!"

He held his wife's hand and looked at her tenderly until the spasm of coughing passed.

What a fool I have been all my life! If she were to die I would be lost. And yet, I have not yet told her my plan. What she will think when she hears it!

"Elise, my love. I have thought long and hard about my reign and about Russia herself."

"What, dearest?" she said. "Tell me."

"Russia—Russians crave a strong man. The nation is an anvil, the Tsar is the hammer. They'd rather be under a blunt force than the yielding hand of an enlightened leader."

Elise wrinkled her soft brow.

"I think you are wrong, Alexander."

"Wrong?"

"The Russians may behave as if they crave a hammer because history has given them no choice. But there will always be those who know the difference. And they will always hunger for a government that promotes freedom and never stop searching until they find it."

Alexander frowned.

"Do you think I do wrong by appointing Count Arakcheyev as minister?"

"Yes," said Elise. "Of course I do! He is too much like your father—brutal and militaristic."

"He keeps men in line."

"In line? Is that all that is required of a minister?"

"He crushes opposition," argued Alexander.

"Listen to yourself, Alexander!" said Elizabeth. "Can't you hear? Crush! Might makes right. Arakcheyev is not of the caliber of the fine men who have held similar positions in the past."

"You are thinking of Adam Czartoryski, aren't you?" said Alexander, his eyes intense in the dimming light of dusk.

"*Da*," she said, sighing. "Adam gave good advice whether you liked it or not. Arakcheyev is a sycophant and a tyrant."

"I was persuaded by my advisors he was what Russia needed," said Alexander, walking to the window. He looked out over the Neva, a deep blue in the late summer sun. Young men were fishing in small boats, white seagulls circling their heads, hoping for a taste of the catch.

"Russia needed what? A hammer," said his wife. "To smash dissent?"

"Russians are a hard people to rule," said Alexander. "And at best I am only a silver hammer," said Alexander. "The shape without the strength. Useless against the iron will of Russia's masses, especially the nobility. I fear it is too late for anything but the strong man."

"And you don't have the constitution to play that role," said his wife, taking his hand. "There is too much of a gentle spirit in your heart."

"Exactly," said Alexander. "I am a disaster."

"That compassion you scorn," she said, closing her eyes, "is precisely why I have always loved you, Alexander."

Alexander looked deep into Elizabeth's eyes. Despite her age, they were still a magnificent shade of blue.

How can I tell her? How can I make her understand?

He took a deep breath.

"Elise, my love. Years ago, there was a young soldier—commended for valor, recommended for the St. George Cross, following the battles of Guttstadt and Friedland."

"Bloody engagements," said Elizabeth, drawing a deep breath. "So many lost."

"But this young soldier—perhaps the youngest to ever be honored with the St. George Cross . . . was different," said Alexander. "Only a week before I met him I received a letter from a former cavalry captain living in Sarapul. He wanted the solder sent home. Because . . . that brave soldier was a girl! And that cavalry captain was her father."

"What?" cried Elizabeth. "A girl. Fighting against Napoleon?"

"I awarded her the St. George Cross. And I sent her back to war, back to the bloodiest of all battles—Smolensk and then Borodino."

"Oh! Alexander! How could you do such a thing to a girl, to her family?"

"I did it because she convinced me it was her destiny. She insisted she would have no other life but that of a cavalry soldier. I had the power—of course!—to smash her dreams and send her home safely. But instead I promoted her and sent her to join the Mariupol Hussars."

Elizabeth's hand touched her face with her fingertips.

"And she survived . . . Borodino?"

"She survived," said Alexander, nodding. "She followed her dream and she survived."

"What an extraordinary girl!"

Alexander turned away, looking out the palace windows at the Neva. A sailboat tacked out to sea.

"My darling Elise," he said, still gazing out the window at the sailboat. "I find myself at a similar crossroads. I often think of that girl and her commitment to Russia. To her dream. She took an extraordinary road in her life, one that was impossible for most people to imagine. But nothing could stop her."

He turned away from the window to look at Elizabeth.

"I wish I had that courage."

"Oh, but Alexander, you do!"

"I wish to have the dedication and faith you possess, Elise. I am weary of politics, of war, of duty to Russia."

Chapter 64

Taganrog, Russia, on the Sea of Azov
September 1825

The modest stone house had a glorious view of the sea. Alexander set to work preparing a home where his wife could heal.

Refreshed by the sea breeze, he was inspired not only to supervise the work, but to labor alongside his servants. He took up a spade and began digging.

"The Tsar with a spade in his hand," whispered a peasant. "Could this indeed be our glorious emperor who defeated Napoleon?"

"Shut up and keep digging," muttered his companion. "He could still order your ears lopped off for being lazy. He's a Romanov."

On the day she arrived in Taganrog, Elizabeth alighted from the carriage like a young girl despite the long journey. And from that day on, the Tsar and tsarina seemed healthier and more in love than they had ever been. They walked hand in hand about the gardens and even into the small town. In the evenings, the citizens of Taganrog—mostly Greeks and Tatars—watched their imperial residents from a respectful distance. The tradesmen emerged from their shops and stood along the unpaved road. The butcher wiping ox blood from his hands on his apron. The baker and his wife powdered with flour, sticky dough embedded under their fingernails.

The Tsar and tsarina stood on the shore, looking out to sea. The crowd gasped in delight as two separate silhouettes merged.

"They're in love, those two!" said the baker's wife, rubbing her eye.

"In love," said the butcher. "That's a notion! Tsars don't have time for love."

"Stranger things have happened," replied the baker, kissing his wife's floury cheek.

Chapter 65

Sarapul, Russia
March 1816

My hand was shaking, but I forced my fingers to obey. I wrote the letter, addressed it, and sent it directly to Count Arakcheyev.

I had seen enough war. I had seen enough death. Now I needed to see more life.

I formally resigned from the army.

As I prepared to leave for home, I was summoned to St. Petersburg to report to Count Arakcheyev himself. He had the most terrifying reputation, but he had always treated me with the utmost respect.

"Ah, there you are, Captain Alexandrov. I am glad to see you so fit," said the count. "I trust you have found that I speedily fulfilled any requests on your part?"

"Yes, sir. I thank you for your attention."

"Tsar Alexander has instructed me to see to your welfare. He commends you for your valor. You have served Russia honorably, Captain Alexandrov."

If Emperor Alexander only knew that I never killed anyone in my decade of soldiering.

"The Tsar left something for you as a token of his admiration for your service and a memento of himself."

The count presented me with a finely polished wooden box.

"Open it, please, Captain Alexandrov."

I bowed. My fingers unlocked the catch.

There on the blue plush velvet lay a silver hammer.

What in the world does he mean by this?

My father enveloped me in his arms.

"You've come back to me! My staff in my old age. My Nadya."

Yes, I quit the sword for my father. And for myself. I was tired of death, of killing.

Farewell to my friends, my merry life of the soldier. The end of parades, drills, and mounted formations. Good-bye to the jingle of spurs, the warm smell of excited horses, the smoke and fire of the battlefield.

And good-bye to the screams of the dying and the stench of the dead.

I was home again.

Chapter 66

Yelabuga, Russia
February 1864

I am haunted. My mind is filled with memories of war, memories that terrify me.

I am tired of remembering.

My eyes close. I must have slept, because when they open, a young man stands beside me. He has dark hair and gentle eyes. He studies me with concern.

I stare back at him. His face is so familiar.

"Grandmother," he says.

Who is he talking to? Outside I hear a storm raging. Freezing snow rattles against the windows. No! I cannot let my mind drift away. I must stay right here with this stranger who calls me Grandmother.

"Grandmother, let me get you some more tea." He rings a bell and Maria comes in to fetch the tea tray. The porcelain jingles as she carries the pot to the boiling samovar.

I touch my hand to my face. It is wet with tears and I am shaking. The young man covers my shoulders with a warm blanket my younger sister stitched many years ago.

"I have come to ask your blessing for my marriage," he says.

"Who are you?"

He eyes look deep into my own.

"I am your grandson, Vladimir Chernov."

"Grandson? I have no children. How can I have a grandson?"

"You are Nadezhda Durova Chernova. You were married in the year 1801 to a county clerk. The following year my father, Ivan Chernov, was born."

"What are you telling me? Lies! I am a cavalry soldier, a Hussar, an uhlan!"

"*Da, da*, Grandmama. You were all of this," he says, grasping my hand, stroking it. "But first, before you left for the cavalry, you were a mother—and now you are a grandmother! You left your husband—and your son—to fight Napoleon."

I reach out with my free hand to touch his face.

"I left my own son?"

"You left your husband. Your baby was left with your father and mother. You ran off to the cavalry." He looked away. "To pursue a Cossack. You fell in love, they say."

"Lies! I loved no one but the cavalry. Horses—"

"You have a gift with horses, Grandmama. You have passed on that gift to me."

"Are you good with them?"

"*Da*. I am an animal trainer. A good one."

I touch his cheek. "I am old. There seems to be so much I do not remember. So much I suddenly do not understand."

"Oh, but Grandmama! You do have a remarkable memory. Perhaps your dates, your ages are a bit faulty, but what a tale you have told me!"

My head wobbles the way it does when I'm confused. Wobbles like a baby robin, this frail old head of mine.

"What of Tsar Alexander?" I do not know where that question came from. Or why I do not know the answer. But suddenly I have to know. "Does he still live?"

My grandson exhales slowly, making his cheeks puff out. I sniff his breath like a nervous horse. There is something familiar there. I trust his smell.

"There is a legend, Grandmama. They say he is a mystic, a hermit, and lives still. You know the tale better than I. Try to remember. Tell me. Then I will ask for nothing else but your blessing."

I nod. For my guest—my grandson! I will fight one more battle. I will fight the shadows and I will remember.

Chapter 67

Taganrog, Russia
October 1825

After considerable persuasion, Tsar Alexander granted Count Volkonsky's urgent request that he leave his seaside retreat for a journey to inspect the region of Crimea.

"But why must you leave me?" asked Elizabeth. "We have been so happy together here."

"I must attend to Russia's affairs, Elise," he replied. "It is expected of me. But I shall be back before too long."

The nation was unsettled. There were constant rumors of plots to overthrow the Tsar. Alexander kissed his wife and turned to go.

If I had a son, would he be plotting my assassination? Is this how my father felt before his death?

He touched the cloth sachet tied on a cord around his neck. The little bag that held a scrap of paper his father had written the night before his murder.

Alexander loved Crimea. Feasts were prepared for the Tsar: pilavs studded with meat and carrots, meat-stuffed grape leaves, spicy lamb and eggplant stews, fried turnovers with minced meat and onions.

The Tsar drank the local wines produced from Bordeaux and Champagne vines brought from France and lovingly cultivated on this southern border of Russia. Alexander was delighted with the rich heritage that marked Crimea.

All of these people—many who do not speak Russian—are my children.

He explored far-flung communities on horseback, traveling over nearly impassable roads. His excursions lasted many hours in the volatile maritime climate, where temperatures plunged and storms boiled up without warning. One night in late October he took a shortcut from Balaklava to the Monastery of St. George. A bitter wind came up from the sea. Alexander was wearing only a light uniform. Though shivering, he refused to stop and put on a coat.

When he reached Sevastopol he felt dizzy and asked for hot tea. He refused dinner.

The next morning he woke early and dressed.

"Why do you not rest, Your Majesty?" asked Count Volkonsky.

"I am the father of Russia and I must visit my many children. There are so many places I must visit yet. Only by showing my goodwill and interest will the people know I love them."

"But you are exhausted, Your Majesty. And the weather has turned cruel."

"So be it. I will travel in the barouche."

Tsar Alexander pushed himself on through the day, rushing to visit churches, barracks, hospitals, and fortresses. Late in the afternoon, a courier named Major Maskov from St. Petersburg met his barouche and delivered a packet of dispatches. He was tall and broad shouldered like the tsar, though he sat his horse considerably better.

"Follow our carriage, Major," ordered Alexander. "I will have some replies for you to carry back to St. Petersburg."

The barouche took off scattering dust, the horses pulling the carriage at a gallop. The courier's coach tried to keep up but hit a pothole in the road and overturned. Major Maskov was killed on the spot, his skull split on impact.

The Tsar was distraught at the thought of one more man's blood on his hands.

At the end of the long day, the Tsar was ill with fatigue and nausea. He was haunted by the death of the courier, Major Maskov. He shivered, his teeth chattering, despite sitting by a blazing fire in a small inn.

"I must get home to the tsarina," he insisted.

"First you must rest, Your Majesty," said his doctor, James Wylie. "You are seriously ill."

"You do not understand! I must return to the tsarina," said Alexander.

"But, Your Majesty—" protested the physician.

"On to Taganrog!" ordered the Tsar, lurching upright and heading back out to his carriage.

Driven by the Tsar's fierce insistence, they traveled almost without stopping for two days.

"I must reach home. I must see my wife," he insisted. "Drive on!"

At last, the Tsarina Elizabeth received her husband.

"What is wrong with him?" she asked in panic as he collapsed in her arms.

"His Majesty has bilious gastric fever," Doctor Wylie said. "I could not persuade him to rest."

"But he was so sound, so healthy before he left for Crimea."

"Yes, my tsarina. He took a chill. The illness struck him suddenly. And he had a dreadful shock. A courier was thrown from a coach and died. It seemed to affect the Tsar deeply."

"Elizabeth," whispered the Tsar. "My sweet Elise."

The Tsar refused the medicine Doctor Wylie proposed to put in his drink. Plagued by his fever and a lifetime of fears, he was wary of strange potions, afraid he was being poisoned.

Alexander dreamt that night of this same Doctor Wylie, who had attended his father, Emperor Paul, after his brutal death and had directed a young artist to paint the corpse.

Several days passed and Alexander saw no improvement.

Alexander's skin turned sallow. He passed in and out of consciousness.

Tsarina Elizabeth came to his beside and took his hand.

"My darling, you are gravely ill."

"I think not," he answered. "I'm just weak. Open the sash so I can breathe the sea air."

A servant opened the window. The breeze filled the white curtain like a sail.

"I shall call for a priest," Elizabeth said.

"Am I really so gravely ill?"

"Yes, my darling. You have reached the limits of this world."

Alexander nodded, his eyes meeting hers. "You have always given me good counsel. Give orders. I am ready."

The archpriest of the Cathedral of Taganrog came and performed last rites. Alexander asked all parties to leave his bedchamber while he gave a very long last confession.

Then with his wife, close advisors, and two of his six doctors watching, Alexander Romanov took communion.

At last, he took his wife's hand and kissed it. "I have always relied on you, my dear. Never have I felt a greater pleasure than giving this final confession."

He exchanged a look with his wife.

"It is finished," he said. "Now, physicians. Do your work as you see fit."

The doctors applied thirty-five leeches to the Tsar's body, chiefly behind the ears and on the back of his neck. They applied cold compresses to his head.

His condition improved but only briefly.

He lost consciousness again. Only when the tsarina would speak in his good ear would he respond. He took her hand, pressed it to his heart, and turned toward the icon beside his bed. He quietly prayed.

He fell asleep once more. With strangled groans, he struggled to live.

Only the Tsar's closest confidants stayed in the bedroom. Elizabeth held her husband's hand until his last breath. Her face wet with tears, the tsarina tied up his gaping jaw with her own embroidered handkerchief.

Tsarina Elizabeth was too weak to follow her husband's body back to St. Petersburg. It was December and the weather was frigid. Her health was extremely fragile. Her illness, which had nearly disappeared during her stay in Taganrog, had returned.

She cried as she watched the coach roll away.

She wrote to her mother:

> *All earthly ties are severed. We walked through life together for thirty-two years. Often separated we always found each other in one way or another.*
>
> *Will we ever find each other again in the world beyond?*

The Tsar's coffin was kept closed for the entire trip, though the crowds of his subjects begged to see their great tsar, the man who had defeated Napoleon. Shepherds came down from their hills with their flocks. They prostrated themselves in front of the royal coach. Peasants unhitched the horses and pulled the carriage themselves, their tears freezing on their faces like diamonds.

Chapter 68

Yelabuga, Russia
February 1864

"And that was the end of the great Tsar Alexander?"

Who is asking? Whose voice is that? *My son. Ivan Chernov. The child I had before I ran away with Alcides to join the cavalry. No. That was long ago. This is my grandson. The child of the son I abandoned. How did I get so old?*

I focus on his face. I see it as if in a dream.

Where has my life gone?

The fire crackles, spitting a spark that embeds in the carpet and begins to smolder. A young man jumps up and smothers it with the sole of his boot.

"The end of Tsar Alexander?" I say. I shake my head and the silence stretches out. "So you've heard the legend of Feodor Kuzmich? The hermit who was allegedly Tsar Alexander I, who lived in a hovel in Siberia?"

The young man—my grandson!—shrugs. "I have heard of it. Is it true, Grandmama?"

"True?" I say, shrugging. "What is truth? That I disguised myself as a man for a decade to fight against Napoleon? That I was a daughter and a mother, but also a son and a soldier?"

I press my fingertips to my forehead. I feel deathly old.

"Please tell me."

I hear the clawing of the cat on the wooden door. "Just let my dear cat in. How she insists! I need my friend on my lap to tell you the rest of the tale."

Vladimir opens the door and Babushka runs in and jumps up into my lap. I stroke her fur and she purrs.

"The legend is that Alexander staged his death. He was surrounded by only his most trusted confidants, who kept his secret and arranged his transport from the port. It is said he traveled to Palestine, where he took the name of Feodor Kuzmich and lived for years as a hermit and a monk, practicing his faith in God."

For a moment, I lose my way. I hear the sound of trumpets, the clash of sabers. The thunder of the cannons moving closer.

"Grandmama?"

I will myself to leave those shadows of war.

"They say he returned to Russia and he was flogged in the small town of Kraznoufimsk, Siberia, for not having any identity papers. Neither tsar nor hermit has papers! He was deported into the far reaches of Siberia, where peasants sheltered him. There, his great knowledge of the Scriptures and his holy ways won him renown. They say he cured the sick by the laying on of hands, that a strange perfume emanated from his flesh and beard, that light illuminated his simple hovel without candle or flame."

"But was he really Tsar Alexander?"

I shrugged.

"Feodor Kuzmich was tall, blue eyed, slightly deaf in the left ear. He knew much about St. Petersburg and about the royal family. Impossible things for a simple hermit to know. He spoke several languages fluently.

And the man who would become Tsar Alexander II—Tsar Alexander's nephew—made the long journey from St. Petersburg to Siberia in 1837 to visit the hermit."

I search my memory for more details. I know they are there. How can I remember so much and still, somehow, have forgotten my son. My son!

"When the coffin of Tsar Alexander was opened, years after his death—there was no body resting there. The sepulchre was empty."

"But . . . but what of Elizabeth? Did she follow him to Siberia?"

"I do not think so. Elizabeth was ill for a very long time. She would not have had the strength for that life. Some say that the tsarina took a vow never to speak and entered the convent of the province of Novgorod, where she was known as Vera the Silent."

"And Adam Czartoryski? What became of him?"

"He never stopped fighting for his dream of an independent Polish nation. Let me remember . . . I think Czartoryski led a revolt, but Russia crushed the rebellion and he was sentenced to death. I heard Tsar Nicholas commuted the sentence to exile. He was his brother's best friend, after all."

"Did he ever see the Tsarina Elizabeth again?"

"No. No, I think they never met again. Czartoryski married a Polish noblewoman and moved to Paris. I know nothing more."

I shake my head, trying to clear all this—all these legends—away. Real life is right here beside me.

"What do I know? I am an addled old woman who deserted her son to join the cavalry. Did your grandfather—my . . . husband—ever forgive me?"

"No, Grandmama," he says. "He would never mention your name or allow it to be spoken under his roof." He looks down at the carpet.

I nod silently.

"But I admire you!" my grandson insists. "After Papa died, I had to know who you were. My mysterious grandmother. I asked neighbors. I asked family. Eventually I found my way to Sarapul."

I blink, my eyes begin to tear. I have not heard that town mentioned in so very long. The town where I was raised. The town where I was given Alcides. The town I fled.

My grandson doesn't see that I am crying. He has all the heedlessness of youth. Just as I once did.

"I was so proud to learn that my grandmother fought the great battles against Napoleon. My grandmother! Can you imagine my pride? The friendship you had with Tsar Alexander. Your legend is cherished."

I focus my blurred eyes on Vladimir. He reaches out to stroke Babushka behind her ears. How much he looks like me.

"You weren't ashamed of me?" I ask.

"Ashamed? You are Russia's hero! Would I have made this long trip to see you if I was anything but proud of you, Grandmama?"

"But I left you. No, I mean I left your father. Yes, I remember." And, yes, now I do. I must. "I followed a Cossack. A tall man with green eyes. But a man who kept my secret, just as Tsar Alexander did."

Vladimir lifts his chin. I can see him struggle with his emotions.

"What became of him? That Cossack."

"He died shortly after the great Battle of Leipzig, of the disease they call typhus. Despite all the bloodshed of battle, he died on a straw pallet. I have a letter somewhere," I said. I swallowed hard as if I had a piece of cucumber stuck in my throat.

I knew the letter by heart:

> *Dear Little Alexandrova:*
> *I shall have this letter delivered to the Tsar. General Platov will see that the emperor receives it. Only he knows whether you live or not. To have these words read to you is my last request.*

They say you are dead. I do not believe it. I have looked out over the battlefields and in my heart I see one campfire among the thousands flickering in the night. You must be there. I know it.

I am sorry that you chose to follow me after our night together. To leave your husband! A baby at home. Guilt has chased me ever since, more true than a bullet.

You must forgive me but what could I do? I am a Cossack! To find a girl riding bareback in her thin night-gown in the mountains. Alone.

And was I wrong? I sensed you loved me though you did not say.

Forgive me for what I did to you that night on Startsev Mountain. If you have died on the battlefield I will never forgive myself. Nor will God.

I have heard the battles you have fought—the same as I! Heilsberg, Friedland, Smolensk, Borodino. I have followed your legend and hold you close to my heart even now as I lie dying.

Yet it is not a saber, bullet, or cannonball that now steals my life. I am dying of the disease that has killed so many of our soldiers—and the enemy's too. My body is racked and I can feel my mind slipping away.

An ignoble death is my curse.

May God bless you, Alexandrova, my Nadya Durova. May you and Alcides find your way home safely.

My eternal love and devotion,
Anatoli Denisov

I stretch my stiff neck, looking up at my visitor. Never have I felt so old and so lost.

"Tell me why you are here again."

"To ask for your blessing of my marriage, Grandmama."

Marriage.

"You have my blessing." I rest my hand on the crown of his head as he kneels before me.

We are both silent for a minute. We listen to the whine of the wind as the storm rages outside.

"Do you ever regret anything?" he asks as he settles back into his chair.

"I regret not traveling back to St. Petersburg one last time and thanking the Tsar Alexander for his trust. For keeping his word. For caring for your father and educating him in St. Petersburg."

I suppose he thought I was going to say I regretted leaving my family. But to his credit he only nods, contemplating.

"Was it the Cossack that forced you to leave?" His voice is thick with emotion.

"*Nyet, nyet!*" I say, waving away the words. "People might say that because they don't understand me. Because that is sordid and tasty to foul-mouthed gossips."

I clench my teeth in anger.

"Why must a man be the cause of everything a woman does in her life? I left because I wanted freedom. To ride my horse across the open steppes of Russia, to serve my Tsar. To fight Napoleon. Nothing else. The Cossack was only the spark that started the bonfire within me. But I built that fire stack stick by stick. I fell in love with the cavalry life, not with him."

Vladimir seeks my eyes.

"You are a legend—as much as Tsar Alexander himself."

"Tsar Alexander promised me he would care for my family so that I could fight in the campaign against Napoleon. He gave your father the best education, the best care, as he promised he would. And I see that promise fulfilled by the fine young man that you are. Our great emperor—the Sphinx of Russia, they called him. Inscrutable. Who else could keep such a great secret and give a mother the freedom to serve Russia the same as a man?"

"I shall never forget how good he was to my father." He is on his knees now, beside my chair.

"My son, my son," I murmur, stroking his temples. My mind tells me he is my grandson, not my son—but these are the words I have to speak through him, through my flesh and blood, to the son I left behind. "Promise me never to forget the legacy of Tsar Alexander. For if he had not given me refuge in Russia's cavalry and had he not given me his name, I would have been no more than a terrible mother."

"Neither of the two Alexanders will be forgotten," he promises. "Russia will always remember our heroes!"

He takes my hand in his. I try to smile at his kindness. History and heroes are too easily forgotten. The truth becomes a smudge on the page until it is erased forever.

Where is he, the good tsar who gave me his name?

I look out into the driving snow and feel a strange pain in my heart, as if I have been suddenly separated from a twin.

Epilogue

Merchant Khromov and his daughter attended the body of Feodor Kuzmich. Khromov had given the starets his little cabin outside Tomsk, Siberia, for many years. He had always seen that the mystic had wood for his fire and enough food to keep his old body alive.

"Sonia," he said. "Heat water on the stove. I shall wash the starets and make him ready to meet God."

The young woman poured water from a bucket into the dented pot on the woodstove. She watched as her father knelt silently by the dead man's body and prayed. After he had crossed himself three times and risen to his feet, she touched his shoulder as he wept for the good man, a devoted servant of God.

Khromov drew a deep breath.

"Here. Help me remove his clothes so we can prepare his body for burial."

Sonia bent over the stiff body, reverently untying the starets's shirt.

"Papa!" she said. "Look here!"

She drew back the linen shirt, exposing the dead man's chest. There around his neck was a small cloth bag on a leather cord.

Khromov unknotted the string.

"It's a message of some sort," he murmured. "But it is gibberish."

"Let me see, Papa," said Sonia. "*Da, da.* The only thing I can make out is an *A* and a *P* . . . and numbers. It makes no sense at all."

Khromov looked out the window at the driving snow. "It only made sense to one person, I suspect. And that soul now resides with God."

Author Notes

For the reader who is perplexed at the meaning of the message written in numbered code, so were the Romanovs for more than a century. In 1927, two code breakers working separately came up with this solution to the mystery of the message:

> *Anna Vasilievna [Gargarina], we have discovered an incredible flaw in our son. Count Pahlen informs me of AP's [Alexander Pavlovich's] participation in a conspiracy. We must hide tonight, wherever it is possible.*
> *PAUL*
> *St. Petersburg. March 11, 1801*

Anna Vasilievna Gargarina was Tsar Paul I's mistress who lived in Mikhailovsky Castle with him.

Like Shakespeare's Hamlet, Tsar Alexander was forever haunted by his father's death. While he may not have had anything to do with the actual assassination, he was most probably privy to the plot to force his father's abdication.

Nadezhda Durova was a complex character. She was startlingly brave and unconventional—and she detested the menial role nineteenth-century society forced on women. Her memoir, *The Cavalry Maiden: Journals of a Russian Officer in the Napoleonic Wars,* is a rare insight into the daily life of a Russian cavalry soldier and officer during this era and clearly illustrates her valor.

But there is a striking conflict in stated facts.

The main points of Durova's story, as told in her memoirs, are true. Nadezhda Durova fought in many of the great battles of the Napoleonic Wars. She was in the midst of the fighting at Heilsberg, Guttstadt, Friedland, Borodino, and Smolensk. She received the St. George Cross for her bravery, and from Tsar Alexander I personally. Durova had a special relationship with the Tsar, who essentially "sponsored" her later career, even knowing she was a woman. Tsar Alexander sent Durova money and promoted her to an officer's rank, sending her to serve with the elite Mariupol Hussars. He gave her his name "Alexandrov," son of Alexander—an astonishing honor.

Russia's most notable poet, Alexander Pushkin, encouraged Durova to publish her memoirs, taking the time to edit them himself. Her story was published in Pushkin's literary magazine *Sovremennik,* or *The Contemporary.*

Clearly, Nadezhda Durova was an extraordinary woman.

There was, however, another side of Nadezhda. Her memoirs state she was sixteen years old when she ran away from home to join the cavalry. But official records show she was in fact twenty-three. There were seven years consistently subtracted throughout her memoirs (including for her horse Alcides's age).

In October 1801, desperate to escape her mother's influence, Nadezhda married Vasily Chernov, a judge in Sarapul. The possibility exists that her mother arranged the marriage to tame her rebellious daughter. Nadezhda had a son, Ivan, in 1803.

Nadezhda soon abandoned her husband and returned with her son to her family home in Sarapul. However, she could not abide living with her mother and fled, disguised as a Cossack. It was rumored that she had fallen in love with a Cossack and pursued him, subsequently joining the cavalry.

Despite abandoning her son, Ivan, leaving him with his grandparents, Nadezhda did not forget him. She arranged an excellent education for the boy through her friendship with Tsar Alexander. Alexander saw that Ivan was enrolled in the Imperial Military Orphanage in St. Petersburg. Nadezhda visited him at least once while he was enrolled in the military academy. Ivan was a good student but not in robust health. He remained in the military but not as a soldier, serving instead as a bureaucrat in St. Petersburg.

In my novel, Nadezhda's grandson comes to Yelabuga to ask for her blessing for his marriage. In real life it was her son Ivan who asked her benediction for his pending vows. Her son deeply admired his mother despite the fact she abandoned him as a child.

Beyond her bravery on the battlefield she demonstrated great courage—and took many risks—in other parts of her life. Taming a wild and notoriously aggressive horse with sugar-sprinkled bread is not a simple task! Nadezhda's gift with horses seems to have passed through the generations. Her descendants became famous animal trainers and circus performers of great renown in Russia.

I chose to follow Nadezhda's memoir closely and not divulge the additional information (that even Pushkin did not know) until the end of the novel. This gradual denouement (the inconsistencies in her age, the omission of both her marriage and the birth of her son) reflects how Durova's life story unfolded to the Russian public.

Tsar Alexander I was a deeply elusive character, as indicated by his moniker "Sphinx of Russia." Even before his father's murder, he proclaimed he was unsuited for the role of tsar and repeatedly declared his intention to abdicate. He struggled to fill the role of "strong man" of Russia. His ideals, though repressed, ran more toward democracy, education, and social reform, as espoused by the philosophers of the Enlightenment.

Though egotistical and susceptible to flattery, Alexander was a humanitarian at heart and deeply spiritual. A true Francophile, he grew to hate Napoleon. It was his decision alone to pursue Napoleon into Paris and force the French emperor's abdication.

Tsar Alexander I "conquered" Napoleon Bonaparte.

The legend of Feodor Kuzmich, the starets whom many believed to be Alexander I in disguise, remains pervasive in Russia. The empty sepulchre of the Tsar, the conflicting autopsy reports (the rumor that the courier Major Maskov's body may have been substituted in the imperial coffin transferred back to St. Peterburg), and the mantle of secrecy that swirled around Alexander's remains fed the rumor and speculation. Witnesses say they saw a British yacht in the treacherous Bay of Taganrog pick up a sole passenger dressed in peasant clothes the day of Alexander's death. The vessel then immediately lifted anchor and sailed on to Palestine.

Years later a mysterious starets with a strong resemblance to Alexander I appeared in Siberia.

Thus grew the lore of the hermit tsar.

The fact that two subsequent tsars made the long and arduous journey to visit Kuzmich's grave in a remote post in Siberia attests to the Romanov's family intense interest in the obscure starets.

Both Nadezhda Durova, known during her later cavalry career as Alexander Alexandrov, and Alexander Pavlovich Romanov were fascinating human beings. These two Alexanders were eminently worthy of their places in Russian history.

Acknowledgments

I owe a great deal of gratitude to Nadezhda Durova herself. Her journals, *The Cavalry Maiden: Journals of a Russian Officer in the Napoleonic Wars*, gave me a solid story and a unique opportunity to see into this extraordinary woman's life.

Mary Fleming Zirin made the journals accessible to me as an English speaker. Zirin's translation of Durova's book was indispensible to my story line and character development. Also her extensive research into how Nadezhda Durova's memoirs conflicted with the truth became the skeleton of my novel.

I read many documents and books on Tsar Alexander I. Particularly useful to me were *Alexander I: The Tsar Who Defeated Napoleon*, by Marie-Pierre Rey; *Alexander of Russia: Napoleon's Conqueror*, by Henri Troyat; *Memoirs of Adam Czartoryski and His Correspondence with Alexander I*, by Adam Jerzy Czartoryski; and yes, *War and Peace*, by Leo Tolstoy. Obviously I owe much credit to author Alexis S. Troubetzkoy's *Imperial Legend: The Mysterious Disappearance of Alexander I*. I highly recommend this book for fascinating reading on Tsar Alexander and the legend of Feodor Kuzmich.

I read a stack of books on Napoleon, but these particular tomes gave me a good grounding: *Napoleon: A Life* by Andrew Roberts, and the three-book series *1812*, by Paul Britten Austen: *The March on Moscow, Napoleon in Moscow*, and *The Great Retreat*. Also, *A Military History and Atlas of the Napoleonic Wars*, by Brigadier General Vincent J. Esposito and Colonel John R. Elting, was very useful in writing battle scenes and helping me with the geography of Russia and the rest of Europe.

In Russia

I had a lot of help from my new Russian friends both in St. Petersburg and Moscow. Expert guide Ludmilla Kolesova kept up a jam-packed schedule of museum visits and heritage sites. She crammed in almost all of the sites mentioned in the novel, from St. Petersburg palaces to Tsarkoe Selo and Gatchina.

Alexey Le Porc, art historian and curator, gave my husband and me a private tour of the Hermitage concerning objects mentioned in this book. At Mikhailovsky Castle, Francuzov Vladimir Evgenievich showed us the actual apartments where Tsar Paul, Alexander's father, was murdered.

Tatiana Grigorieva guided us through Moscow and to the battlefield of Borodino, sharing her incredible knowledge of history. At the State History Museum, Matvey Katkov showed us fascinating inventory of the Patriotic Wars, including Napoleon's camp bed and the sleigh he used to escape to Paris. We had a thorough education at the museum of Borodino: uniforms, weapons, maps, and a three-dimensional battlefield replica that lit up the troop movements of both the Russian and French army.

In the United States

Dasha Harrison and Mariana Fisher of Exeter International arranged our extensive research tour in Russia.

Nancy Elisha, my beloved sister, has always encouraged my writing and helped through twenty-seven years of relentless rejection.

The breathtaking Strang Ranch of Carbondale, Colorado, provided a fount of inspiration every day. I conjured up battle scenes from the pages of research books and mapped them in my mind as I rode over the magnificent spread of open fields and rolling hills. Thank you to Bridget Strang and Maree McAteer, who inspire me daily with their horsemanship.

Thank you to Marina Beadleston for her enthusiasm for my writing career. Perhaps my living next door to Romanov descendants years ago subconsciously led me to this subject matter. (At any rate, I know the exact shade of Romanov blue eyes!)

Gratitude to other Roaring Fork Valley residents, especially Sarah Kennedy Flug! Also thanks to Lucia Caretto, Emily and Bel Carpenter, and Sandy MacKay, for their important support in mind and spirit.

Thank you to my great Amazon team: Gabriella Dumpit, Brent Fattore, Tyler Stoops, and Dennelle Catlett, among others. Special appreciation to Danielle Marshall, my acquisitions editor at Lake Union. Thanks for being there right on the spot when we had "snags," no matter the day or time of night.

To Lindsay Guzzardo, former Amazon editor and now screenwriter. I will never forget you.

To my copy editors Katherine Faydash and Sharon Turner Mulvihill. What a vast list of international characters, places, battlefields, dates to check! (Especially as my heroine was notoriously freehanded in her timeline.) I'm deeply grateful for your hard labor on this novel.

To my hardworking proofreader, Leighton Wingate. What a formidable team I have in production!

Melody Guy, my developmental editor, is an incredibly sensitive editor who draws my best work from me. I love working with her. I have been blessed having her guide all five of my published books.

My gratitude to Shasti O'Leary-Soudant for her remarkable cover art.

Gratitude to Jeff Belle. This is my fifth novel published with Amazon! Thanks for your support.

To my foreign rights team at Curtis Brown, especially Betsy Robbins and Sophie Baker, thank you for shopping my book rights around the world.

The team at Gelfman Schneider/ICM Partners has guided my contracts and all matters of business, looking out for me all along the way. And thank you, Cathy Gleason and Victoria Marini.

To my friend and agent Deborah Schneider, who first contacted me in 1993. We've come a long way together.

To my beloved parents, Betty and Fred Lafferty. We all miss you, Mommy. I remember how you always wanted to visit St. Petersburg, how the history of Russia fascinated you. You and Daddy raised all your girls to love books, storytelling, and world travel. We will always love you both.

Finally, my profound gratitude to Andy Stone, my husband, research assistant, and first (and constant!) editor. You are the love of my life. I don't know if I ever could have written all these books without your love, encouragement, and help—especially reading and editing early drafts. I am blessed to have you as my partner.

About the Author

Photo © 2015 Andy Stone

Linda Lafferty was a teacher for nearly three decades, in schools from Madrid, Spain, to Aspen, Colorado. She completed her PhD in bilingual special education and worked in that field; she also taught English as a second language and bilingual American history. Linda is the author of four previous novels—*The Bloodletter's Daughter*, *The Drowning Guard*, *House of Bathory*, and *The Shepherdess of Siena*—all of which have been translated into several languages. *The Drowning Guard* won the Colorado Book Award for Historical Fiction. She lives in Colorado with her husband.